開口就會
美國校園英語
American Campus English

實踐大學應用外語系專任講師
黃 靜 悅 ◎著
Danny O. Neal

五南圖書出版公司 印行

麥克魯漢（Marshall McLuhan）於上世紀六〇年代首度提出了「地球村」的概念，當時他原本用這個新名詞來說明電子媒介對於人類未來之衝擊，實不亞於古騰堡（Johann Gutenberg）印刷術對西方文明的影響；曾幾何時，「地球村」在今天有了新的涵義：天涯若比鄰！

現代科技進步昌明，往昔「五月花」號上的新教徒花了六十幾天，歷經千辛萬苦才橫渡大西洋，今日搭乘超音速飛機只要四個多小時就可完成；網際網路的普及，世界上任何角落所發生的事情對千里以外的地方都會有不可思議的影響，亦即所謂的「蝴蝶效應」；語言文字的互通理解；東方的「博愛」和西方的「charity」使得普天下心懷「人溺己溺」之心的信徒，都能為營造開創一個由愛出發、以和為貴的世界而一起努力！這一切都說明了一個事實：人與人之間不再因距離、時空、障礙和誤解而「老死不相往來」！

當然，在這一片光鮮亮麗的外表下，隱憂依然存在。「全球化」（Globalization）對第三世界的人而言，竟成為新帝國主義和資本主義的同義字！造成這種誤解，甚至於扭曲的主要原因是對不同於自己的文化、風俗、傳統及習慣的一知半解；是不是用法文就顯得比較文明？使用義大利文就會比較熱情？德文，富哲理？英文，有深度？而美語，就「財大氣粗」？是不是有一套介紹書籍，雖不一定包含了所有相關的資訊，但至少對那些想要知道或瞭解異國風物的好奇者，能有所幫助的參考工具書？

放眼今日的自學書刊，林林總總，參差不齊。上

者，艱澀聱牙或孤芳自賞；下者，錯誤百出或言不及意！想要找兼具深度和廣度的語言學習工具書，實屬不易。現有本校應用外語學系黃靜悅和唐凱仁兩位老師，前者留學旅居國外多年，以國人的角度看外國文化；後者則以外國人的立場，以其十數年寄居台灣的經驗，合作撰寫系列叢書，舉凡旅遊、日常生活、社交、校園及商務應用，提供真實情境對話，佐以「實用語句」、「字詞補給站」讓學習者隨查隨用，並穿插「小叮嚀」外加「小祕訣」，提供作者在美生活的點滴、體驗與心得等的第一手資訊。同時，「文化祕笈」及「大補帖」更為同類書刊中之創舉！

學無止境！但唯有輔以正確的學習書籍，才能收「事半功倍」之效。本人對兩位老師的投入與努力，除表示敬意，特此作序說明，並寄望黃唐兩位老師在教學研究之餘，再接再厲，為所有有志向學、自我提昇的學習者，提供更精練、更充實的自學叢書。

前實踐大學 校長

張光正

自序

　　學習外語的動機不外乎外在（instrumental）及內在（intrinsic）兩類：外在動機旨在以語言作為工具，完成工作任務；內在動機則是希望透過外語學習達成自我探索及自我實現的目標。若人們在語言學習上能有所成，則此成就也必然是雙方面的；一方面完成工作任務而得到實質上的利益報償，另一方面則因達成溝通、了解對方文化及想法而得到豐富的感受。

　　現今每個人都是地球公民中的一員，而語言則是自我與世界的連結工具。今日網路科技的發展在彈指間就可以連結到我們想要的網站，人類的學習心與天性因刺激而產生對未知的好奇心及行動力，使我們對於異國語言文化自然產生嚮往；增進對這個世界的了解已不是所謂的個人特色或美德，而是身處現代地球村的每個人都該具備的一種責任與義務！

　　用自己的腳走出去，用自己的眼睛去看、用自己的心靈去感受世界其他國家人們的生活方式，用自己學得的語言當工具，與不同國家的人們交談；或許我們的母語、種族、膚色、性別不同，或許我們的衣著、宗教信仰、喜好以及對事情的看法、做法不同，但人與人之間善意的眼神、微笑、肢體動作、互相尊重、善待他人的同理心，加上適切的語言，對世界和平、國際友邦間相互扶持的共同渴望，使我們深深體會到精彩動人的外語學習旅程其實是自我發現的旅程！只有自己親自走過的旅程、完成過的任務、通過的關卡、遇到的人們、累積的智慧經驗、開拓的視野、體驗過的人生，才是無可替代的真實感受。世界有多大、個人想為自己及世人貢獻

的事有多少，學習外語完成自我實現內在動機的收穫就有多豐富！

今日有機會將自己所學與用腳走世界、用心親感受的經驗交付五南出版社出版叢書，誠摯感謝前實踐大學張光正校長慨為本叢書作序、前鄧景元主編催生本系列書，眾五南伙伴使本書順利完成，及親愛的家人朋友學生們的加油打氣。若讀者大眾能因本系列叢書增進英語文實力，並為自己開啟一道與世界溝通的大門，便是對作者最大的回饋與鼓勵！

願與所有立志於此的讀者共勉之。

作者　黃靜悅　謹誌

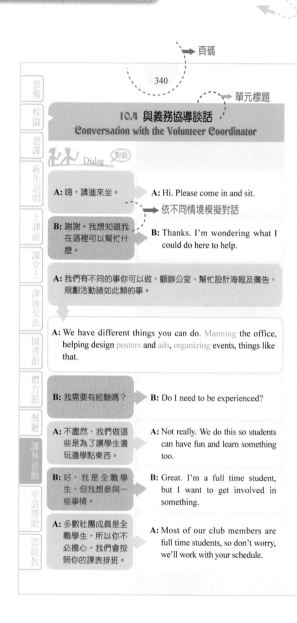

頁碼

340

單元標題

10.4 與義務協導談話
Conversation with the Volunteer Coordinator

Dialog 對話

A: 嗨，請進來坐。

A: Hi. Please come in and sit.

依不同情境模擬對話

B: 謝謝。我想知道我在這裡可以幫忙什麼。

B: Thanks. I'm wondering what I could do here to help.

A: 我們有不同的事你可以做，顧辦公室、幫忙設計海報及廣告、規劃活動諸如此類的事。

A: We have different things you can do. Manning the office, helping design posters and ads, organizing events, things like that.

B: 我需要有經驗嗎？

B: Do I need to be experienced?

A: 不盡然，我們做這些是為了讓學生邊玩邊學點東西。

A: Not really. We do this so students can have fun and learn something too.

B: 好，我是全職學生，但我想參與一些事情。

B: Great. I'm a full time student, but I want to get involved in something.

A: 多數社團成員是全職學生，所以你不必擔心，我們會按照你的課表排班。

A: Most of our club members are full time students, so don't worry, we'll work with your schedule.

預備 校園 選課 新生說明 上課前 課堂上 課後交流 圖書館 體育館 餐廳 課外活動 申請獎助 常助教

B: 我知道了，聽起來很好。 → **B:** I see. Sounds good.

Word Bank 字庫 → 重要單字解釋

man [mæn] v. 守崗位，顧 (辦公室)
poster [`postə] n. 海報
ad [æd] n. 廣告 (=advertisement)
organize [`ɔrgə͵naɪz] v. 規劃

Useful Phrases 實用語句

1. 我想知道我在這裡可以幫忙什麼。
   I'm wondering what I could do here to help.
2. 我需要有經驗嗎？
   Do I need to be experienced?
3. 我們會按照你的課表排班。
   We'll work with your schedule. → 各校園場景常用句子

Tips 小祕訣

   課外活動也包含大學的運動校隊，但是要成為校隊一員要經過一連串嚴格挑選的過程，所以只有來自全國的頂尖選手才有可能成為隊員。然而校內仍有一些運動社團與大學本身正式運動校隊無關，而是基於個人興趣組成的運動隊伍或社團。

→ 快速適應美國校園生活的妙方

預備｜校園｜選課｜新生說明｜上課前｜課堂上｜課後交流｜圖書館｜體育館｜餐廳｜課外活動｜申請獎助｜當助教

特點圖示

◆ 學生保險 Student Insurance

insurance card	保險卡
policy	保單
insurance plan	保險計畫
contract	合約
pre-existing conditions	保險前狀態
health center	健康中心
fees	費用
sign	簽名
brochure	摺頁介紹，小冊子

Notes 小叮嚀

　　美國醫藥費用昂貴，大學強制規定國際學生必須購買保險，在抵達之後應盡快購買保險開始保障自己。大學為學生提供低保費的保單，但並非保費最低就好，國際學生的需要與美國學生有許多不同，因此可以請教校方人員了解保單的內容選擇一個適合的保險，並記得保險要續保不要中斷。出國前也可上網參考美商保險公司針對遊學及留學生需求而設計的「海外留學生綜合保險」。

➤ 在美生活應注意事項

Information Bank 大補帖

◎ 見教授機宜 Preparing Youself to Seek Help from a Professor

很少大學生或研究生在就學時不找教授幫忙，事實上，適時請教教授是必要的，而不是拖到問題變得更嚴重。

1. 為何尋求幫忙？

   如有下列情形，你需要找教授談話：

   (1) 規定或進度需要釐清

   (2) 對作業規定不了解

   (3) 因病導致課程落後

   (4) 考試或作業失敗，不懂課程內容

   (5) 需要主修科目諮詢

   (6) 助教公告輔導時間找不到助教

2. 為何學生逃避教授協助？

   (1) 因為他們困窘、害怕或生性害羞

   (2) 避免與權威者接觸

   (3) 害怕問到笨問題

   (4) 感覺錯過幾堂課失去連結

   (5) 害怕與教授衝突

   (6) 與不同年齡、性別、種族或文化的教授接近而不安

   　　如果你以學生本分依照學業進度學習 (尤其如果是想要進研究所)，一定要把害怕的心態擺一邊，尋求協助。那要怎樣與教授一對一會面呢？

   → 補充快速跟上美國課堂學習的訣竅

目錄

Unit 2 選課及註冊
Choosing Courses and Registration

Unit 3 新生說明會 Orientation

Unit 4 上課前 Before Class

Unit 5 課堂上 In Class

Unit 6 課後交流 After Class

Unit 7 圖書館 The Library

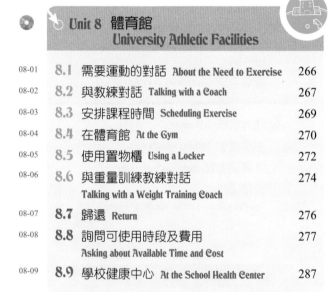

Unit 8 體育館
University Athletic Facilities

Unit 9 學校餐廳及校外餐館
University Food Venues and Restaurants Outside Campus

Unit 10 課外活動
Extracurricular Activities

Unit 11 申請財務獎助及證書
Applying for Financial Aid and Certifications

Unit 12 當助教教課
Leading a Course as a Teaching Assistant

附錄 Appendixes

留學資訊站：
More Information for Studying Abroad

字詞補給站 Language Power

Preparation Unit

預備單元

根據美國外籍學生管理的最新規定，外籍學生可以於開學前 30 天內入境美國。這段時間並不長，必須先做好安頓的準備工作，才能展開遊學或留學生活。一方面要找到合適的住所，熟悉住所附近環境及安全情形，作好交通安排，才能避免經常搬家，有助學習與生活適應；另一方面，也要盡快到銀行開戶、購買學生保險、向外籍學生顧問報到，如果需要自己開車，也要安排考駕照。

預備
校園
選課
新生說明
上課前
課堂上
課後交流
圖書館
體育館
餐廳
課外活動
申請獎助
當助教

0.1 住校
On Campus Housing

住校是許多新生的選擇，在出國前就必須向住宿辦公室 (housing office) 申請，通常需要繳交申請費及押金；如果申請之後不想住，押金會被沒收。在抵美後，如果宿舍仍有空缺也可提出申請入住。

0.1a 宿舍報到 Checking Into the Dormitory

Dialog 對話

A: 哈囉，這是宿舍報到的地方嗎？

A: Hello. Is this where I check in to my dorm room?

B: 是的，歡迎來克倫德，我可以幫你報到。

B: Yes. Welcome to Crandle. I can help you check in.

A: 好，我的名字是辛蒂吳。

A: Great. My name is Cindy Wu.

B: 我可以看一下你的學生證嗎？

B: May I see your student card please?

A: 可以，在這裡。

A: Yes. Here you are.

B: 謝謝，根據我們的登記，你住 328 房。

B: Thanks. According to our registry, you'll be in room 328.

A: 我如何到那裡？

A: How do I get there?

B: 我馬上會帶你過去，但首先我要給你這個。

B: I'll take you there in a minute, but first I need to give you this.

A: 這是什麼？

A: What is it?

B: 這是解釋宿舍規定及告訴你的責任是什麼的手冊。

B: It's a handbook that explains the rules of the dorm and tells you what your responsibilities are.

A: 我懂了。

A: I see.

B: 你也要簽這個表領鑰匙。

B: You also need to sign this form to get your key.

A: 好。

A: Alright.

B: 你在簽這個的時候，我會影印你的證件。

B: While you sign this, I'll make a photocopy of your I.D. card.

A: 好。

A: OK.

預備

校園

選課

新生說明

上課前

課堂上

課後交流

圖書館

體育館

餐廳

課外活動

申請獎助

當助教

Word Bank 字庫

dorm (dormitory) [dɔrm (`dɔrmə,torɪ)] n. 寢室

registry [`rɛdʒɪstrɪ] n. 登記

handbook [`hænd,bʊk] n. 手冊

Useful Phrases 實用語句

1. 這是宿舍報到的地方嗎？

   Is this where I check in to my dorm room?

2. 我有室友嗎？

   Do I have a roommate?

3. 你也是這學校的學生嗎？

   Are you also a student at this university?

4. 這棟宿舍有多少間房間？

   How many dorm rooms are there in this building?

5. 有多少國際學生住在這裡？

   How many international students live in this building?

0.1b 認識室友 Meeting a New Roommate

Dialog 對話

A: 嗨，我是你的室友，辛蒂吳。	A: Hello. I'm your roommate, Cindy Wu.
B: 嗨，辛蒂，我是珊德拉沙利斯，很高興認識你。	B: Hi, Cindy. I'm Sandra Salles. Nice to meet you.
A: 我也很高興認識你。	A: Nice to meet you, too.

B: 我已安頓在房間左側，我希望這樣可以。

B: I've set myself up in the left side of the room. I hope that is OK.

A: 當然，沒問題。

A: Sure. No Problem.

B: 我想這房間對我們兩個夠大。

B: The room is big enough for two of us I think.

A: 是的，我也這麼認為，我們這扇窗戶外有不錯的景觀。

A: Yes. I think so too. We have a nice view out this window.

B: 對，我來幫你整理你的東西。

B: Right. Let me help you with your stuff.

A: 謝謝。

A: Thanks.

Notes 小叮嚀

　　各家大學宿舍設備不同，學費是個因素，但住校費用常偏高，所以許多學生會選擇校外住宿。不論住校內外、室友何國籍、生活方式如何，敦親睦鄰，互相尊重，彼此才能相處愉快。男女宿舍通常有某個程度的區隔，例如男女舍在不同樓層或在不同棟，宿舍可能設有門禁。

預備　校園　選課　新生說明　上課前　課堂上　課後交流　圖書館　體育館　餐廳　課外活動　申請獎助　當助教

預備
校園
選課
新生說明
上課前
課堂上
課後交流
圖書館
體育館
餐廳
課外活動
申請獎助
當助教

0.1c 宿舍導覽 Dorm Orientation

Dialog 1 (對話1)

A: 我帶你去逛一下大樓你才知道每樣東西在哪裡。

A: Let me take you around the building so you know where everything is.

B: 謝謝，那樣很有幫助。

B: Thanks. That would be very helpful.

A: 走吧。

A: Let's go.

B: 你帶路。

B: Lead the way.

A: 直走就是公用洗手間及淋浴間。

A: Down the hall are the shared toilets and showers.

B: 洗衣設備在哪裡？

B: Where are the laundry facilities?

A: 在一樓，我會帶你去，但是先注意，廚房在另一邊盡頭。

A: They are on the first floor. I'll take you there, but first, notice the kitchen is at the other end of the hall.

Dialog 2 (對話2)

A: 我們可以在任何時候煮飯嗎？

A: Are we allowed to cook any time?

B: 可以,但是這地方有時很忙,所以不是隨時都可以用。

B: Yes, but this place gets pretty busy at times, so it's not always available.

A: 我們也有自助餐廳,對嗎?

A: We have a cafeteria too, right?

B: 對,也在一樓,從早上7點營業到晚上9點。

B: That's right. It's also on the first floor, and it's open from 7 a.m. to 9 p.m.

A: 我們要付自助餐的錢嗎?

B: Do we have to pay for the cafeteria food?

B: 不必,已經包含在收費裡了。

B: No. The cost is included in your fees.

A: 好。

A: OK.

B: 有一間娛樂廳,你可以打撞球、桌球、玩紙牌、下西洋棋等,在2樓及4樓還有一間自習室。

B: There is a recreation room where you can play pool, table tennis, cards, chess, etc., and a study lounge is on the second and fourth floors.

A: 自習室設有電腦嗎?

A: Are the study lounges equipped with computers?

預備

校園

選課

新生說明

上課前

課堂上

課後交流

圖書館

體育館

餐廳

課外活動

申請獎助

當助教

B: 沒有，但可以免費無線上網。

B: No, but wireless access is free.

A: 很好。

A: That's good.

Word Bank 字庫

recreation room n. 娛樂廳
pool [pul] n. 撞球
table tennis n. 桌球
chess [tʃɛs] n. 西洋棋
study lounge n. 自習室
wireless access n. 無線上網

Useful Phrases 實用語句

1. 洗衣設備在哪裡？

   Where are the laundry facilities?

2. 我們可以在任何時候煮飯嗎？

   Are we allowed to cook any time?

3. 有自助餐廳嗎？

   Is there a cafeteria?

4. 我們要付自助餐的錢嗎？

   Do we have to pay for the cafeteria food?

5. 自習室設有電腦嗎？

   Are the study lounges equipped with computers?

6. 我們宿舍有無線上網嗎？

   Do we have wireless access in the dorm room?

7. 我要怎麼做才能在寢室上網？

   What do I need to do to have Internet service in the dorm room?

8. 我每個月要付多少網路服務費？

How much do I have to pay for the Internet service per month?

9. 我們寢室有電話嗎？

Do we have a phone in the room?

10. 我們怎麼付電話費？

How do we pay for the phone bills?

11. 有公共清潔用具可以用嗎？

Is there shared cleaning supplies and equipment I can use?

12. 學期結束後，我何時要搬出去？

When do I have to move out after the term finishes?

13. 我還需要知道什麼？

What else should I know?

Notes 小叮嚀

　　如果想要用宿舍廚房，最好避免會造成油煙的料理，否則會弄得警鈴大響，而且油煙及食物味道並不受歡迎。

　　入境隨俗，多數美國人習慣早上洗澡再出門，並視為一種禮貌，晚上如果要參加活動，出門前也會再沖澡保持清爽並提神。因為氣候乾爽，多數人一星期才洗一次衣服，衣服洗烘一起完成，不晾衣。

0.1d 洗衣房 The Laundry

Dialog 對話

A: 這裡是洗衣房。

A: Here is the laundry room.

B: 你怎麼操作機器？

B: How do you operate the machines?

預備

校園

選課

新生說明

上課前

課堂上

課後交流

圖書館

體育館

餐廳

課外活動

申請獎助

當助教

A: 用投幣的，你可以在宿舍辦公室換硬幣。

A: They are coin operated. You can get coins at the dorm office.

B: 你是說在那邊入口的辦公室嗎？

B: Do you mean the office over there at the entrance?

A: 是的。

A: Yes.

0.1e 詢問寢室規則及大眾運輸工具
Asking about Dorm Rules and Public Transportation

Dialog 1 對話1

A: 有舍規嗎？

A: Are there any rules in the dorm?

B: 唔，宿舍裡任何地方都不准抽菸，訪客必須在晚上 11 點前離開。宿舍住宿生沒有指定的車位，但有很多腳踏車停車架。

B: Well. There is no smoking allowed in the dorm anywhere, and visitors have to be out by 11 pm. There are no designated car parking spaces for dorm residents, but there are a lot of bike racks.

A: 那大眾運輸工具呢？

A: What about public transportation?

B: 到公車站大約 2 分鐘路程。

B: It's about a two-minute walk to a bus stop.

Word Bank 字庫

designated [ˋdɛzɪgˏnetɪd] adj. 指定的
dorm residents n. 宿舍住宿生
bike racks n. 腳踏車停車架

Dialog 2 對話2

A: 如果有任何問題，我應該聯絡誰？

A: Whom should I contact if there are any problems?

B: 總辦公室裡有人，打到那裡。

B: The main office always is staffed. Call there.

A: 任何時候嗎？

A: Any time?

B: 每天 24 小時，假日也一樣。

B: 24/7. Even holidays.

A: 謝謝你的幫忙，我很感謝。

A: Thanks for all of your help. I greatly appreciate it.

B: 嘿，我們是室友，這是最基本我該做的事。

B: Hey, we're roommates. It's the least I should do.

A: 我欠你一次。

A: I owe you one.

預備

校園 選課 新生說明 上課前 課堂上 課後交流 圖書館 體育館 餐廳 課外活動 申請獎助 當助教

📖 Useful Phrases 實用語句

1. 有舍規嗎？

   Are there any rules in the dorm?

2. 如果有任何問題，我應該聯絡誰？

   Whom should I contact if there are any problems?

3. 總辦公室裡有人。

   The main office always is staffed.

4. 這是最基本我該做的事。

   It's the least I should do.

5. 我欠你一次。

   I owe you one.

0.2 寄宿家庭
Home Stay

0.2a 到達 Arriving Home Stay

Dialog 對話

A: 哈囉，克雷先生嗎？ → **A:** Hello. Mr. Clay?

B: 是的，你一定是保羅。 → **B:** Yes. You must be Paul.

A: 是的，沒錯。 → **A:** Yes, that's right.

B: 歡迎，請進。 → **B:** Welcome. Come in.

A: 謝謝。

A: Thank you.

B: 我太太現在不在，晚點你會見到她。

B: My wife isn't here right now. You can meet her later.

A: 我很期待。

A: I look forward to it.

B: 讓我幫你把東西提到你房裡，再帶你看看房子。

B: Let me help you take your things to your room. Then I'll show you around the house.

A: 好。

B: OK.

0.2b 家庭規定 House Rules

 Dialog 1 對話I

A: 在我們這裡不用拘束，沒有家規，但我們確實要請你尊重一些事情。

A: We are pretty relaxed about things here. We don't have rules, but we do ask that you respect a few things.

B: 請告訴我。

B: Please tell me.

預備
校園
選課
新生說明
上課前
課堂上
課後交流
圖書館
體育館
餐廳
課外活動
申請獎助
當助教

A: 我們坐在後院談吧。

A: Let's sit in the backyard and talk about it.

B: 聽起來不錯。

B: Sounds nice.

A: 第一，你在外面想待多晚都可以，但是如果你 11 點後回來要輕聲，通常那時我們已經睡了。

A: First, you can stay out as late as you want, but please be very quiet if you come back after 11 p.m. We are usually asleep by then.

B: 我了解，沒問題。

B: I understand. No problem.

A: 我們家裡不許抽菸，但你可以在後院抽。

A: We don't allow smoking in the house, but you can smoke in the backyard.

B: 我不抽菸，但如果我朋友抽，我會告訴他們。

B: I don't smoke, but if my friends do, I'll tell them.

A: 好，謝謝。

A: Fine. Thanks.

📖 Useful Phrases 實用語句

1. 我帶你看看房子。

   I'll show you around the house.

2. 在我們這裡不用拘束。

We are pretty relaxed about things here.

3. 但我們確實要請你尊重一些事情。

But we do ask that you respect a few things.

 Dialog 2 （對話2）

A: 還有，如果你音樂開太大聲，鄰居可能會抱怨，這裡是很安靜的社區。

A: Also, the neighbors might complain if you play music loudly. This is a pretty quiet neighborhood.

B: 是的，我了解，關於那點我會小心。

B: Yes, I see. I'll be careful about that.

A: 請隨意使用我們的洗衣機和烘乾機或在廚房烹飪。

A: Feel free to use our washer and dryer or cook in our kitchen.

B: 好，謝謝。

B: Great. Thank you.

B: 那看電視呢？

B: What about watching TV?

A: 喔，是的，我忘記提到我們會放一臺電視及一具電話在你房間，電視也是有線電視。

A: Oh, yes. I forgot to mention that we are going to put a TV and a phone in your bedroom. The TV will have cable too.

預備 校園 選課 新生說明 上課前 課堂上 課後交流 圖書館 體育館 餐廳 課外活動 申請獎助 當助教

B: 非常感謝，你們真好。

B: Thank you so much. That's very nice of you.

A: 這是我們的榮幸，我們希望你住在這裡很舒適。

A: It's our pleasure. We hope you are comfortable here.

B: 聽起來我會的。

B: It sounds like I will be.

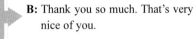

Notes 小叮嚀

注意如果你住在寄宿家庭，要有責任感，要適當的社交，並且主動幫忙家裡的事，你不是住旅館，所以要善待家裡的人。

0.2c 責任分擔：電話帳單
Sharing Responsibilities: the Phone Bill

Dialog 對話

A: 嗨，克雷先生，我要給你電話帳單的費用。

A: Hi, Mr. Clay. I need to give you some money for the phone bill.

B: 謝謝你對那件事有責任感。

B: Thanks for being so responsible about that.

A: 沒什麼，這是我該做的。

A: No problem. It's what I have to do.

預備

校園

選課

新生說明

上課前

課堂上

課後交流

圖書館

體育館

餐廳

課外活動

申請獎助

當助教

B: 我們看帳單，我們可以很簡單地看你要付多少。

B: Let's look at the bill. We can easily see how much you owe.

A: 好。

A: OK.

B: 帳單詳細列出從這裡打出的所有電話，所以我們可以看哪一通是你打的，還有每一通要多少錢。

B: The phone bill itemizes all the calls made from here, so we can see which ones are calls you made and how much each call cost.

A: 好，這樣對我們很方便。

A: Good. That will make it easy for all of us.

0.2d 責任分擔：打掃 Sharing Responsibilities: Cleaning

Dialog 對話

A: 嗨，克雷太太。

A: Hi, Mrs. Clay.

B: 嗨，保羅。

B: Hello, Paul.

A: 我需要打掃我的房間，我可以借吸塵器嗎？

A: I need to clean my room. Can I borrow the vacuum cleaner?

預備

校園

選課

新生說明

上課前

課堂上

課後交流

圖書館

體育館

餐廳

課外活動

申請獎助

當助教

B: 當然可以，在那個衣櫥裡面。

B: Sure. It's in that closet.

A: 謝謝，你要我幫你吸其他的地方嗎？

A: Thanks. Would you like me to help you vacuum any other place?

B: 喔，你願意嗎？我需要幫忙。

B: Oh. Would you? I need some help.

A: 當然，沒問題，你要我吸哪邊？

A: Sure. No problem. Where would you like me to vacuum?

B: 樓上走道和客廳。

B: The hallway upstairs and the living room.

A: 好，我房間一吸塵完畢就會盡快做。

A: OK. I'll do it as soon as I'm done vacuuming my bedroom.

B: 多謝。

B: Thank you very much.

A: 不客氣。

A: Any time.

📖 Useful Phrases 實用語句

1. 我要給你電話帳單的費用。

   I need to give you some money for the phone bill.

2. 這是我該做的。

   It's what I have to do.

3. 帳單詳細列出從這裡打出的所有電話。

The phone bill itemizes all the calls made from here.

4. 你要我幫你吸其他的地方嗎？

Would you like me to help you vacuum any other place?

5. 你需要我順便買什麼東西嗎？

Do you need me to pick up any groceries?

0.3 找校外公寓：回應報紙廣告
Looking for an Apartment off Campus: Responding to Newspaper Ads

找校外住宿，要考慮交通、日常購物便利、環境安全、房東風評等因素，學生預算有限，但還是要有適當的居住品質，才能確保求學品質。簽約多為一年一約，訂契約 (及退租) 時要雙方一起檢視房屋狀況，並充分了解合約內容之權利義務，有必要時可以拍照 (要有日期)，共同檢查，列出清單。租屋需要押金 (deposit)，訂約時繳交第一和最後一個月租金及大約 $200 押金 (有時稱為清潔費或安全費)，房東可收取的押金須遵守該州額度規定，不可多收，可上網查詢 security deposit limits by state 確認你的房租押金限額。

如不續租通常在約滿前 30 天要書面通知房東，通知不續租後不再交房租 (最後一個月房租簽約時已付)，$200 押金在房東扣除必要費用後於約定期限前必須退還。

Dialog 1 　對話1

A: 哈囉，我打電話來問一個我在報上看到的關於一間公寓的廣告。

A: Hello. I'm calling about an ad I saw for an apartment in the newspaper.

預備　校園　選課　新生說明　上課前　課堂上　課後交流　圖書館　體育館　餐廳　課外活動　申請獎助　當助教

預備
校園
選課
新生說明
上課前
課堂上
課後交流
圖書館
體育館
餐廳
課外活動
申請獎助
當助教

B: 是的，你想知道什麼？

B: Yes. What would you like to know?

A: 還有出租嗎？

A: Is it still available?

B: 有。

B: Yes, it is.

A: 房租多少呢？

A: How much is the rent for the place?

B: 月租是 450 元，含水、電、瓦斯。

B: The monthly rent is \$450 and that includes utilities.

A: 其他的費用呢？

A: What about any other additional fees?

B: 一輛車免停車費。

B: Parking for one car is free.

A: 訪客可以在哪裡停車呢？

A: Where can guests park?

B: 事實上在街上也有很多停車位。

B: Actually there is a lot of free parking available on the street too.

A: 押金多少錢呢，還有我們必須預付多少個月？

A: How much is the security deposit, and how many months do we have to pay in advance?

B: 房東要第一和最後一個月租金以及200元安全費用。

B: We require first and last month, and a \$200 security fee.

A: 好,如果房子有任何問題的話,我需要知道跟誰聯絡。

A: OK. And I need to know who to contact if there are any problems with the house.

B: 房東不管事,我們代為管理,所以你可以聯絡我。

B: The landlord is an absentee owner. We manage the property for him, so you can contact me.

Word Bank 字庫

utilities [ju`tɪlətɪz] n. 水、電等公共費用
security fee n. 安全費用

Dialog 2 對話2

A: 我今天可以看房子嗎?

A: Can I see it today?

B: 可以,你要何時過來?

B: Yes. What time would you like to come over?

A: 今天下午3點好嗎?

A: Is three this afternoon good?

B: 好的,可以。

B: Yes, that's fine.

A: 好,我需要地址。

A: Great. I'll need the address.

預備

校園

選課

新生說明

上課前

課堂上

課後交流

圖書館

體育館

餐廳

課外活動

申請獎助

當助教

B: 當然,你準備寫下來了嗎?

B: Certainly. Are you ready to write it down?

A: 是的,請說。

A: Yes. Go ahead.

B: 好,地址是西史塔克街 245 號。

B: OK. The address is 245 W. Stark Street.

A: 知道了,謝謝,我的名字是泰瑞李。

A: Got it. Thanks. My name is Terry Lee.

B: 我是泰德史提拉,今天下午 3 點見。

B: I'm Ted Stiles. I'll see you at 3 today.

A: 對,再見。

A: Right. Bye.

B: 再見。

B: Bye.

Useful Phrases 實用語句

- 房客詢問費用及租約內容
  Tenant asking about payments, fees, and contract details

1. 每月租金多少?

   What is the rent each month?

2. 包含水、電、瓦斯等費用嗎?

   Are utilities included in the price?

3. 有維護 (管理) 費嗎?

   Is there a maintenance fee?

4. 停車要收費嗎？

   Are there any charges for parking?

5. 我何時及如何付房租呢？

   When and how do I pay the rent?

6. 押金多少呢？

   How much is the security deposit?

7. 租約多久呢？

   How long will the lease last?

8. 合約何時到期呢？

   When will the contract expire?

9. 我要看合約影本。

   I'd like to see a copy of the contract.

10. 公寓何時會弄好呢？

    When will the apartment be ready?

11. 我們要搬出去多久以前要預先通知？

    How much advance notice do we need to give before we move out?

○ **房東 [仲介] 回答費用及租約細節 Landlord [Agent] talking about payments, fees, and contract details**

1. 租金是一個月 450 元。

   The rent is $450 a month.

2. 水、電、瓦斯有 [沒有] 包含在內。

   The utilities are (not) included.

3. 合約裡明訂房客要付所有公共服務如水、電、瓦斯等費用。

   The contract states the renter is responsible for all utility payments.

4. 有維護 (管理) 費，每個月 25 元。

   There is a maintenance fee of $25 a month.

5. 停車免費。

   Parking is free.

6. 停車另外收費。

   Parking costs extra.

校園
選課
新生說明
上課前
課堂上
課後交流
圖書館
體育館
餐廳
課外活動
申請獎助
當助教

7. 房租可以用個人支票付給我，或者你可以用自動提款機轉帳到我的帳戶。

The rent can be paid by personal check to me, or you can transfer the money at an ATM to my account.

8. 房租每月一日到期。

The rent is due on the first of the month.

9. 支票開給查爾斯提史密斯先生。

Make out the check to Mr. Charles T. Smith.

10. 合約一年後到期。

The lease expires after one year.

11. 我們將會每年談新合約。

We'll talk about a new lease agreement each year.

12. 下星期房子會弄好。

The house will be ready next week.

13. 如果你要搬走，你要在 30 天前預先通知。

You need to tell thirty days in advance if you plan to move out.

Notes 小叮嚀

　　不住在當地的房東稱為「缺席房東」，也就是不管事的房東，這類房東通常交給公寓經理代管租賃及修繕事宜。租屋是法律行為，房客房東各有權利義務，退租、轉租、中途解約、押金取回等法律問題要好好了解，萬一房東未退還合理扣除後剩餘的押金並給予扣除費用之清單，可以找學校免費律師諮詢。

Language Power 字詞補給站

房屋廣告 Housing Ads

- an apartment with all the amenities 設備齊全舒適的公寓
- comfortably appointed 設備完善的
- controlled gate [access] 門禁
- intercom entry 對講機進入
- fully equipped kitchen 設備完善的廚房
- pet friendly 對寵物友善的
- heated outdoor pool 溫水室外游泳池
- walk-in closet 走入式衣櫥
- short-term lease available 可以簽短期合約
- laundry facilities 洗衣設備
- garbage disposal 垃圾處理
- convenient location 地點方便
- schools nearby 鄰近學校
- safe neighborhood 安全社區
- close to parks 鄰近公園
- shopping nearby 鄰近購物
- parking included 包含停車
- close to public transportation 鄰近大眾運輸
- newly remodeled 新裝潢
- spacious kitchen 寬敞的廚房
- central heating 中央暖氣
- 24 hour security 24小時警衛

預備
校園
選課
新生說明
上課前
課堂上
課後交流
圖書館
體育館
餐廳
課外活動
申請獎助
當助教

預備

校園

選課

新生說明

上課前

課堂上

課後交流

圖書館

體育館

餐廳

課外活動

申請獎助

當助教

0.4 詢問學生保險
Asking about Student Insurance

 Dialog 對話

A: 嗨，我可以幫你嗎？

A: Hi, may I help you?

B: 可以，這是學生保險辦公室嗎？

B: Yes. Is this the Student Insurance Office?

A: 是的。

A: Yes, it is.

B: 我想了解保險保障的範圍，我可以怎麼做？

B: I'd like to know about insurance coverage. What can I do about it?

A: 學校提供低價的健康保險計畫給研究生及大學生。

A: The university offers low cost health insurance plans for graduates and undergrads.

B: 我是國際學生，這樣有差別嗎？

B: I'm an international student. Does that make a difference?

A: 沒有，你可以買像本州生一樣價錢的計畫。

A: No. You can buy a plan for the same price as resident students.

B: 如何付款？

B: How do I pay for it?

A: 一旦你簽約，費用會加到每期開始的學雜費內。

A: Once you are signed up for it, the cost will be added to your tuition and fees charged at the beginning of each session.

B: 費用多少？

B: How much is it?

A: 每學期 175 元。

A: $175 a session.

B: 好，我要考慮一下，你有可以讓我參考的資料嗎？

B: OK. I'd like to think about it. Is there anything you can give me to read about it?

A: 有，讀這個小冊子，它有 (保險) 計畫的資料，你也可以上網看，網址在小冊子的封底。

A: Yes. Read this booklet. It has much information about the plans. You can also read about it online. The website address is on the booklet's back cover.

B: 好，謝謝，你認為我現在還應該知道些什麼嗎？

B: Great, thank you. Is there anything else you think I should know right now?

預備　校園　選課　新生說明　上課前　課堂上　課後交流　圖書館　體育館　餐廳　課外活動　申請獎助　當助教

預備
校園
選課
新生說明
上課前
課堂上
課後交流
圖書館
體育館
餐廳
課外活動
申請獎助
當助教

A: 你可以打電話給我們問更多問題，這是簡介，上面有電話，還有，記住你全都可以上網做，但如果你喜歡，我們這裡很樂意幫你安排。

A: You can call us if you have more questions. Here is a brochure with our number on it. Also remember that you can do this all online, but we are very willing to help you set things up here at the office if you prefer.

B: 謝謝你的幫忙，我很感激。

B: Thanks for your help. I really appreciate it.

A: 沒什麼。

A: No problem.

📖 Useful Phrases 實用語句

1. 我要買保險。

   I need to buy insurance.

2. 保險費用多少？

   What does insurance cost?

3. 我是國際學生，這樣有差別嗎？

   I'm an international student. Does that make a difference?

4. 保障何時開始？

   When does the coverage start?

5. 我如何支付？

   How do I pay for it?

6. 我想了解保險保障的範圍。

   I'd like to know about insurance coverage.

7. 出了國有保障嗎？

   Is it good overseas?

8. 保單保障什麼？

   What does the plan cover?

9. 醫藥費有給付嗎？

   Does it cover the cost of medicine?

10. 我的配偶也有保障嗎？

    Will it cover my spouse too?

11. 我可以去看任何我選的醫師嗎？

    Can I go to any doctor I choose?

12. 你有可以讓我參考的資料嗎？

    Is there anything you can give me to read about it?

13. 你認為我現在還應該知道些什麼？

    Is there anything else you think I should know right now?

Notes 小叮嚀

美國醫藥費用昂貴，大學強制規定國際學生必須購買保
險，在抵達之後應盡快購買保險開始保障自己。大學為學生提
供低保費的保單，但並非保費最低就好，國際學生的需要與美
國學生有許多不同，因此可以請教校方人員了解保單的內容選
擇一個適合的保險，並記得保險要續保不要中斷。出國前也可
上網參考美商保險公司針對遊學及留學生需求而設計的「海外
留學生綜合保險」。

Language Power 字詞補給站

◆ 學生保險 Student Insurance

insurance card	保險卡
policy	保單
insurance plan	保險計畫
contract	合約
pre-existing conditions	保險前狀態
health center	健康中心
fees	費用
sign	簽名
brochure	摺頁介紹，小冊子

預備

booklet	小冊子
deductible	自付額
claim	索賠
terms	條件
effect	生效
limits	限制
coverage	保障
benefits	保險金津貼
compensation, reimbursement	賠償
policyholder	投保人
beneficiary	受益人
premium	保險費
clause	條款
grace period	有效期限後的寬限時間
life insurance	人壽保險
accident insurance	意外險
health insurance	醫療險
travel insurance	旅遊險

0.5 交通
Transportation

如果住在學校附近，通常步行或騎單車就可以，但如果要到附近辦事，可不要輕忽行車看來短短的距離，就算是幾個街區的距離，也可能要走上或騎單車騎上好一陣子。如果住的較遠，除了利用校車、公車、地鐵、電車 (看居住地區及便利性) 等大眾運輸工具，自行開車通常是必要的選擇。

0.5a 公車系統 Public Bus System

 Dialog 對話

A: 嗨，我可以在這裡買一張學生公車卡嗎？

A: Hi. Can I buy a student bus pass here?

31

B: 是的，可以。 → **B:** Yes, you can.

A: 多少錢？ → **A:** How much is it?

B: 學生公車卡四個月 40 元。 → **B:** A student bus pass costs \$40 for four months.

A: 我知道了，如果我買一張能用八個月的卡會比較便宜嗎？ → **A:** I see. Is it cheaper if I buy one good for eight months?

B: 不行，這間大學唯一的選擇是四個月的卡。 → **B:** No. At this university the only option is the four-month pass.

A: 好，但現在是十月中，（四學期制）學期何時開始？ → **A:** OK, but now it's mid October. When does each quarter start?

B: 最後一學期九月開始，但是別擔心，你的費用會按照比例算。 → **B:** The last one started in September, but don't worry, your charge will be prorated.

B: 好，謝謝。 → **B:** Great. Thanks.

Word Bank 字庫

bus pass n. 公車卡
option [`ɑpʃən] n. 選擇
prorated [pro`retɪd] adj. 按比例分配的

0.5b 考駕照 Getting a Driver's License

Dialog 1　對話1

A: 我抽到 20 號。

A: I pulled number 20.

B: 20 號是下一個。

B: Number 20 is next.

A: 嗨，我想要一張駕照。

A: Hi. I want to get a driver's license.

B: 好，你要先填這張表，然後考筆試。

B: OK. You'll need to fill out this form first. Then, take the written test.

A: 我要去哪裡考試？

A: Where do I take the test?

B: 那邊，考試用電腦考。

B: Over there. It's done on a computer.

(稍後 A little later)

A: 這是填好的表，我可以現在考筆試嗎？

A: Here is the filled out form. Can I take the written test now?

B: 可以，請跟我來。

B: Yes. Follow me, please.

Dialog 2 對話2

A: 我已考完筆試。

A: I've finished the written test.

B: 好，我看一下。

B: Alright. I'll check it.

(稍後 A little later)

B: 恭喜！你通過了。

B: Congratulations! You passed.

A: 太好了！我現在可以考路試嗎？

A: Great! Can I take the driving test now?

B: 很快，你要等其中一位考官有空的時候。

B: Soon. You'll have to wait until one of the testers is available.

A: 你想大概要多久呢？

A: How long do you think that will be?

B: 不會太久，我猜10分鐘吧。

B: Not too long. I'd say ten minutes.

A: 我知道了，我坐那裡等。

A: I see. I'll sit over there and wait.

B: 別擔心。考官好的時候，我會告訴你。

B: Don't worry. I'll tell you when the tester is ready.

預備　校園　選課　新生說明　上課前　課堂上　課後交流　圖書館　體育館　餐廳　課外活動　申請獎助　當助教

A: 謝謝。

A: Thanks.

Useful Phrases 實用語句

1. 我要如何申請駕照？

   How do I apply for a driver's license?

2. 請取一個號碼。

   Please take a number.

3. 請先填這張表。

   Fill out this form first.

4. 機動車輛部門在哪裡？

   Where is the DMV?

5. 我要考駕照。

   I want to take a driving test.

6. 我需要一份駕駛手冊。

   I need a copy of the driver's manual.

7. 你們有中文的駕駛手冊嗎？

   Do you have a Chinese language driver's manual?

8. 你們這裡有說中文的人嗎？我需要幫忙。

   Do you have Chinese-speaking people here? I need some help.

9. 你要檢查視力。

   You need to take an eye test.

10. 我何時可以考試？

    What time can I take the test?

11. 你要先考筆試。

    You must take the written test first.

12. 我要考中文版的駕照筆試。

    I'd like to take a driving test in Chinese.

13. 考場在哪裡？

    Where is the testing room?

預備　校園　選課　新生說明　上課前　課堂上　課後交流　圖書館　體育館　餐廳　課外活動　申請獎助　當助教

14. 你通過考試了。

You passed the test.

15. 我們要幫你拍照。

We need to take your picture.

16. 你要成為器官捐贈者嗎？

Do you want to be an organ donor?

17. 這是你的駕照。

Here's your license.

18. 我要考機車駕照。

I want to take the motorcycle test.

Are you interested in buying a used car?

Tips 小祕訣

　　到美國短期居住，可以使用國際駕照，但務必隨身攜帶臺灣駕照備查。國際駕照合法使用期限，各州規定不同，30 天到一年都有，有的以母國駕照期限為準。在美國生活，多數地方出門就要用車，所以拿到駕照是一件很重要的事。如果在美國不開車又需要身分證件，可以到 DMV 申請非駕照身分證(non-driver I.D.)，或稱為州身分證(state I.D.)。

　　申請駕照時，除了填寫所需的資料外，表格會有是否願意器官捐贈的問題。在移民較多的州內，有不同族裔的服務人員為移民服務，也有多種移民語言的駕駛手冊(driver's handbook)及考題可供選擇，最好先拿到該州印製的駕駛手冊(DMV 網路可取得，也有模擬試題)，準備好再考試，因為萬一答錯幾題就得過幾天再繳費重考。考筆試(written test)時間不會很長，有的地區筆試已電腦化，有些仍是紙筆測驗。筆試通過後，有時可以直接繳費路考(road test)，但有些地方必須要預約考試。筆試通過後，DMV 會發給學習駕駛許可(learner permit)，可以在有駕照的旁人陪伴下開車。

　　對開車沒信心的人可以找教練上幾個鐘點熟悉路況，再準備考試。路考時必須自己提供可以正常運作的車輛及該車行照(car registration)，可以選擇用自排或手排車考試；要練習路邊停車，你只有兩次機會把車停好。如果路考失敗，多數州必須要等一星期才能再考，也必須再繳費。考照記得變換車道時，除了打方向燈外，要回頭(一定要過肩)查看後方車輛(已習慣在臺灣開車的人務必注意)，確定盲點處沒有車輛，才可以變換車道。路試通過後，接下來是 DMV 拍照，幾分鐘後就可以拿到駕照了。

Language Power 字詞補給站

◆ 駕照 Driver's License

written test	筆試
driving [road] test	路試
automatic	自排的
manual, stick shift	手排的

DMV (Department of Motor Vehicles)	機動車輛部門 (如臺灣的監理處)
defensive driving	防禦性 [小心] 駕駛
parallel park	路邊停車
front [back] in parking	車頭朝內停車 [倒車入庫]
driver's manual	駕駛手冊
organ donor	器官捐贈者
restrictions (on license)	(駕照) 限制

0.5c 買車 Buying a Car

買車對任何人都是個考驗，尤其購買二手車更是如此。選擇新車或二手車各有不同優缺點，衡量自己經濟能力，選擇經濟省油、性能好的車子，還是要多做功課或找懂車的人幫忙。

Dialog 1 對話1

A: 嗨，我可以為你服務嗎？

A: Hi, may I help you?

B: 我想買一輛二手車，所以先看看。

B: I'm interested in buying a used car, so I'm looking around.

A: 好，你知道你要哪種車款嗎？

A: Great. Do you know what kind of car you want?

B: 我想看不同款的車。

B: I want to look at different ones.

A: 我帶你到停車場看看。

A: Let me show you around the lot.

B: 這部如何？　　　**B:** How about this one?

A: 這是本田雅歌。　　　**A:** This is a Honda Accord.

B: 多少錢？　　　**B:** What is the price?

A: 大約 5,000 元。　　　**A:** Its price is $5,000.

B: 這臺車有 CD 音響嗎？　　　**B:** Does it have a CD player?

A: 有，還有兩個安全氣囊。　　　**A:** Yes. It is also equipped with two air bags.

Notes 小叮嚀

　　不管是買新車 (brand new car) 或是二手車 (used car)，買車時盡量問問題。別急著完成交易，如果售車商服務不夠好，就到下一家去，沒有必要接受不夠優質的服務或不能充分合作的車商。如果想買中古車，最好能找一位信得過的汽車技師跟你去，通常技師會收費 \$30-\$50。除非自己很懂車，否則不冒險購買狀況已經很差的車輛才是保護自己最好的方法。

Dialog 2 對話2

A: 我想試開這部車。　　　**A:** I'd like to take this car for a test drive.

B: 好，沒問題，我只需要看一下一張有效的駕照。

B: Sure. No problem. I just need to see a valid driver's license.

A: 好，這是我的駕照。

A: OK. Here's mine.

B: 好的，我們去兜風一下吧！

B: Great. Let's go for a ride.

Useful Phrases 實用語句

1. 我想買一輛新車。

   I'm interested in buying a new car.

2. 我們去試車。

   Let's go for a test drive.

3. 你們有什麼付款方案？

   What type of financing do you have?

4. 我想看你們的二手車。

   I'd like to look at your used cars.

5. 這輛車跑了多少英里了？

   How many miles does it have?

6. 這輛車多少錢？

   How much is it?

7. 這輛車有什麼配備可以選擇？

   What optional equipment does it have?

8. 這輛車是什麼年份？

   What year is it?

9. 你們有維修紀錄嗎？

   Do you have the maintenance records?

10. 告訴我保固的事。

    Tell me about the guarantee.

預備 校園 選課 新生說明 上課前 課堂上 課後交流 圖書館 體育館 餐廳 課外活動 申請獎助 當助教

11. 我想找個技師來看車。

   I'd like to have a mechanic look at it.

12. 我是個學生，沒辦法付太多錢。

   I'm a student. I can't pay too much.

 Notes 小叮嚀

有時售車員會與你一起試車，將車開出確實完全的試駕，15-20 分鐘的試車並不少見，試車時也必須包含高速試車。如果購買新車，保固時間為 5 年或是 50,000 英里，視哪一個先到期；二手車保固期間就相對短了許多，頂多 1 年，如果是向私人買車，就完全沒有保固的保障。如果必須貸款買車，盡可能自己辦貸款而不要用車行提供的貸款，因為利率會比較高。車商廣告的低利率通常是為促銷某些車款，因此有許多限制。

Let's go for a test drive.

Language Power 字詞補給站

買　車 Buying a Car

- auto dealer 汽車商
- car dealership 汽車代理商
- used car 二手車
- makes and models 車廠及車型
- high [low] mileage 高[低]哩程
- warranty 保固
- maintenance 維修
- body repair shop 車殼修理店
- lube job 換機油
- tune up 調引擎
- deposit 訂金
- auto loan 汽車貸款
- compact 小型車

- car lot (汽車商)停車場
- sales rep. 售車代表
- test drive 試車
- guarantee 保證
- contract 合約
- repair shop 汽車修理店
- disc brakes 碟煞
- oil 機油
- insurance 保險
- alignment 校正
- down payment 頭期款
- sedan 轎車
- hatchback 掀背式汽車

sunroof 天窗
trunk 後車廂
air bags 安全氣囊
mechanic 技師
gas 汽油
hood 車蓋
interior 車輛內部
tires 輪胎
engine 引擎

預備

校園

選課

新生說明

上課前

課堂上

課後交流

圖書館

體育館

餐廳

課外活動

申請獎助

當助教

0.5d 校園停車證 Campus Parking Permit

Dialog 1 對話1

A: 嗨，我需要買一張校園停車證。

A: Hi. I need to buy a parking permit for on campus parking.

B: 你在學校工作嗎？

B: Do you work at the university?

A: 不，但我是這裡的學生。

A: No. I'm a student here though.

B: 抱歉，本校沒有學生停車證。

B: I'm sorry, but there are no student parking permits at this university.

A: 我可以在哪裡停車？

A: Where can I park?

B: 任何付費的停車格內，晚上6點以後停車免費。

B: In any available pay parking space. Parking is free after 6 p.m.

A: 早上幾點開始付費？

A: What time do I have to start paying in the morning?

B: 早上7點。

B: 7 a.m.

A: 有任何收費停車場嗎？

A: Are there any pay parking lots available?

預備

校園

選課

新生說明

上課前

課堂上

課後交流

圖書館

體育館

餐廳

課外活動

申請獎助

當助教

B: 沒有，附近沒有。 → **B:** No. Not close ones anyway.

A: 我要怎麼付停車費？ → **A:** How do I pay for the parking?

B: 有停車計時器，2 小時 25 分錢。 → **B:** The spaces have meters. It cost 25 cents for two hours of parking.

A: 有限制我可以停多久嗎？ → **A:** Is there a limit to how long I can park?

B: 有，5 小時。 → **B:** Yes. Five hours.

A: 謝謝你的資訊。 → **A:** Thanks for the information.

Word Bank 字庫

parking permit n. 校園停車證
pay parking lot n. 收費停車場
meter [`mitɚ] n. (停車) 計時器

Useful Phrases 實用語句

1. 我需要買一張校園停車證。
   I need to buy a parking permit for on campus parking.
2. 我可以在哪裡停車？
   Where can I park?
3. 早上幾點開始付費？
   What time do I have to start paying in the morning?

預備
校園
選課
新生說明
上課前
課堂上
課後交流
圖書館
體育館
餐廳
課外活動
申請獎助
當助教

4. 有任何收費停車場嗎？

   Are there any pay parking lots available?

5. 我要怎麼付停車費？

   How do I pay for the parking?

6. 有限制我可以停多久嗎？

   Is there a limit to how long I can park?

Dialog 2 對話2

A: 嗨，我想知道如何購買校園停車證。

A: Hi. I'd like to find out about purchasing a parking permit for parking on campus.

B: 好。你要買多久？

B: Fine. How long do you want it for?

A: 我不知道，我有什麼選擇？

A: I don't know. What are my options?

B: 你可以買一期或兩期，有了它你就可以在校園找到的任一停車格停車。

B: You may buy a permit that is good for one session or two. With it you can park anywhere around campus where you can find a parking space.

A: 多少錢？

A: What is the cost?

B: 一期 150 元。

B: $150 a session.

A: 那夏天呢？

A: What about summer?

B: 你可以買 50 元的暑期停車證，或你現在買兩期，暑期只需多付 20 元。

B: You can buy a summer time parking permit for \$50, or if you pay for two sessions now, you only have to pay another \$20 for summer.

A: 還有其他的停車選擇嗎？

A: Are there any other parking options?

B: 有，你可以停在被保留的停車格內。

B: Yes. You can park in one of the reserved parking lots.

A: 停車場何時開？

A: What time does the parking lot open?

B: 早上 6 點開，晚上 11 點關。

B: 6 a.m., and it closes at 11 p.m.

A: 那多少錢？

A: What does that cost?

B: 6 個月 125 元，或一年 200 元。

B: \$125 for six months or \$200 a year.

A: 如果我停過夜會怎樣？

A: What happens if I leave it parked overnight?

B: 你的牌照號碼會被記錄，晚上 11 點後會以每小時 2 元向你收費。

B: Your license plate number will be recorded, and you'll be charged \$2 an hour for each hour you leave it parked past 11 p.m.

預備　校園　選課　新生說明　上課前　課堂上　課後交流　圖書館　體育館　餐廳　課外活動　申請獎助　當助教

預備 | 校園 | 選課 | 新生說明 | 上課前 | 課堂上 | 課後交流 | 圖書館 | 體育館 | 餐廳 | 課外活動 | 申請獎助 | 當助教

A: 為何他們要記我的牌照號碼？

A: Why do they record my license number?

B: 如果你沒有準時付款，你會收到郵件通知提醒你。如果你超過一個月付款期限，收費加倍。

B: In case you don't pay on time, you'll receive a notice in the mail reminding you about it. If you go past the one month deadline for paying, then the charge will double.

A: 停車場安全嗎？

A: Is the parking lot secure?

B: 開放時間連續監視，11 點後本地警察及校園警衛偶爾巡邏。

B: It's watched continuously during operating hours. After 11, it is patrolled occasionally by the local police and campus security.

A: 好，我想我知道了，多謝。

A: OK. I think I understand. Thank you very much.

B: 沒什麼，如果你決定要買停車證，你可以來這裡或去學生中心的總櫃臺。

B: No problem. If you decide you want to buy one of the permits, you can come here or go to the Main Desk in the Student Union building.

A: 真多謝。

A: Thanks very much.

Word Bank 字庫

reserved parking lots n. 被保留的 (專屬) 停車格
license plate number n. 牌照號碼
notice [`notɪs] n. 通知
remind [rɪ`maɪnd] v. 提醒
patrol [pə`trol] v. 巡邏

Useful Phrases 實用語句

1. 你可以停在任何地方。
   You can park anywhere.
2. 停車場早上 6 點開。
   The parking lot opens at 6 a.m.
3. 停車場晚上 11 點關。
   The lot closes at 11 p.m.
4. 停車場有監視器。
   The parking lot has security cameras.
5. 停車場照明佳。
   It is well lit.
6. 開放時間有警衛值班。
   It has a security guard on duty during operating hours.
7. 幾個地方有緊急電話。
   There are emergency phones located in several places.
8. 有三個地點。
   There are three locations.
9. 你可以[不可以]停車過夜。
   You can [can't] leave it overnight.
10. 你可以按小時付費。
    You can pay by the hour.

校園 選課 新生說明 上課前 課堂上 課後交流 圖書館 體育館 餐廳 課外活動 申請獎助 當助教

Notes 小叮嚀

　　每個學校停車情況不同，有些有停車場，有些沒有；有些停車免費，但多數學校要收費，停車情形必須向學校行政單位查詢。

Unit 1 Campus Tour

校園巡禮

許多美國大學校園很大，但也有許多校園並不太大，全美校園提供給學生的服務在數量及形式上都差不多，但校園大小對學生的生活形態有決定性的影響。校園小的學校大多在城市內，因交通便利，校規與校園較大的學校之校規未必相同，每個人在選擇學校時，要把許多因素考慮進去。

預備

校園

選課

新生說明

上課前

課堂上

課後交流

圖書館

體育館

餐廳

課外活動

申請獎助

當助教

1.1 校園導覽
Touring the Campus

 Dialog 對話

A:（學生大使）歡迎來到 S.T.U.，我是凱文，我會在這兩小時校園導覽帶大家看看校園各處，在我們開始前，請來這裡拿一份校園地圖。

A: (student ambassador) Welcome to S.T.U. My name is Kevin. I'll show you where everything is in this two hour campus tour. Before we begin, please come over and take a school map here.

B: 你可以指給我看我們在哪裡嗎？

B: Can you point out where we are on the map?

A: 當然可以，我們就在這裡（指地圖），在噴泉前面，這是校園最受歡迎的會面處之一。大家都在地圖上找到了嗎？

A: Sure, we're right here (pointing and showing the map), in front of the fountain. This is one of the most popular meeting points around campus. Has everyone found it on the map?

B: 找到了。

B: Yes.

A: 好的，我們一起逛逛校園吧，我們先去行政大樓。

A: OK. Let's walk around the campus. We'll go to the Administrative Building first.

B: 在哪裡呢？

B: Where is it?

A: 是鐘樓右邊的那棟紅色建築物。

A: It's the red building on the right of the clock tower.

B: 行政大樓提供什麼服務？

B: What services does the Administration Building offer?

A: 行政大樓是可以幫你處理任何事情的地方。

A: The Admin Building is where any business you need to take care of can be done.

B: 譬如說？

B: Like what?

A: 像是繳學費、更改課程、繳學生保險費、或是獲得關於大學校規及規定問題的解答。

A: Like paying tuition, changing classes, paying for student insurance, or getting answers to your questions about university rules and requirements.

B: 我了解了。

B: I see.

預備 | 校園 | 選課 | 新生說明 | 上課前 | 課堂上 | 課後交流 | 圖書館 | 體育館 | 餐廳 | 課外活動 | 申請獎助 | 當助教

Word Bank 字庫

fountain [`fauntn] n. 噴泉
meeting point n. 會面地點
campus [`kæmpəs] n. 校園
tuition [tju`ɪʃən] n. 學費
requirement [rɪ`kwaɪrmənt] n. 規定

Useful Phrases 實用語句

1. 你可以在地圖上指給我看我們在哪裡嗎？
   Can you point out where we are on the map?
2. 行政大樓提供什麼服務？
   What services does the Administration Building offer?

Tips 小祕訣

導覽安排

　　許多大學網站設有簡單的線上校園導覽，透過網路可以在千里外就先看到學校的風貌。為了讓學生 (及家人) 親自了解學校設施，大學都會安排校園導覽，但是參加導覽前必須先上網或在學校登記，單人或團體的導覽通常都可以安排。導覽時間多為兩個小時左右，導覽員會發校園地圖，當然也會回答關於校園的各類問題。

Language Power 字詞補給站

◆ 學院 [大學] 校園 College [University] Campus

professor	教授
university president	大學校長
hall	走廊，廳堂
campus bookstore	校園書店
library	圖書館
dormitory	宿舍
off-campus housing	校外住宿

married student housing	已婚學生住宿
administration(s) office	教務處
admin.[administrative/ administration] building	行政大樓
cashier's office	出納室
student services	學生服務處
international students office	國際學生辦公室
overseas students club	海外學生社團
upper classmates	學長姐
(fellow) classmates	同學
lower classmates	學弟妹
gym	體育館，健身房
stadium	體育館，球場
student body	學生全體
bike path	腳踏車道
Student Union	學生中心
campus health center	校園健康中心
campus security	校園安全
student card	學生證
registration	註冊
add [drop]	加 [退]
waiting list	候補名單
deadline	截止日
credits	學分
audit	旁聽
school symbol	校徽
school mascot	學校吉祥物
school colors	學校顏色 (校隊制服、紀念品的顏色等)

預備
校園
選課
新生說明
上課前
課堂上
課後交流
圖書館
體育館
餐廳
課外活動
申請獎助
當助教

預備
校園
選課
新生說明
上課前
課堂上
課後交流
圖書館
體育館
餐廳
課外活動
申請獎助
當助教

1.2 行政大樓
Administrative Building

Dialog 1 （對話1）

A: 就是這裡。

A: Here it is.

B: 很高。

B: It's tall.

A: 是的，但你要找的多在一樓。

A: Yes, but what you will be looking for will probably always be on the first floor.

B: 你是說大樓多數是大學事務辦公室？

B: You mean most of the building is university business offices?

A: 對，教職員使用大樓的多數地方執行各式各樣的職責，但是一二樓多服務學生。

A: Right. Staff conducting various duties for the university use most of the building, but the first and second floor serves students mostly.

B: 這棟大樓什麼時候開放？

B: When is this building open?

A: 行政大樓正常開放時間是早上9點到下午6點。

A: The Admin Building is open regular business hours, 9 a.m. to 6 p.m.

B: 週末有開嗎？

B: Are they open on the weekend?

A: 只有每學期的前兩週。

A: Only during the first two weeks of each semester.

 Word Bank 字庫

staff [stæf] n. 工作人員
conduct [`kɑndʌkt] v. 處理，指導
duty [`djutɪ] n. 責任

 Useful Phrases 實用語句

1. 這棟大樓什麼時候開放？
   When is this building open?

2. 週末有開嗎？
   Are they open on the weekend?

3. 有晚上工作的行政人員嗎？
   Are there any administrative staff who work in the evening?

Dialog 2 對話2

A: 這裡是主要的服務櫃臺。

A: Here is the main information desk.

B: 所以這是問一般資訊的地方嗎？

B: So this is the place to go for general information?

A: 是的，你可以按照我們的需要問他們去哪裡或怎麼辦事情。

A: Right. You can ask them where to go, or what to do, depending on what we need.

預備 校園 選課 新生說明 上課前 課堂上 課後交流 圖書館 體育館 餐廳 課外活動 申請獎助 當助教

預備
校園
選課
新生說明
上課前
課堂上
課後交流
圖書館
體育館
餐廳
課外活動
申請獎助
當助教

B: 我可以問他們關於校園安全的問題嗎？

B: Can I ask them a question about campus security?

A: 當然可以。

A: Sure.

 Word Bank 字庫

> information desk n. 服務櫃臺
> campus security n. 校園安全

 Useful Phrases 實用語句

1. 這是問一般資訊的地方嗎？

   Is this the place to go for general information?

2. 我可以問他們關於校園安全的問題嗎？

   Can I ask them a question about campus security?

3. 學校在安全區嗎？

   Is this university in a safe area?

4. 你可以告訴我學校附近一些安全 [危險] 的社區嗎？

   Can you tell me some safe [dangerous] neighborhoods near the school?

5. 這裡犯罪嚴重嗎？

   Is crime serious here?

6. 我該怎麼對流浪漢？

   What should I do about the homeless?

7. 如果我晚上下課走幾個街區回家會有危險嗎？

   Is it dangerous if I walk a few blocks home after evening class?

8. 如果我騎單車呢？會好一點嗎？

   What if I ride a bike? Is it better?

預備
校園
選課
新生說明
上課前
課堂上
課後交流
圖書館
體育館
餐廳
課外活動
申請獎助
當助教

1.3 校園安全問答
Getting Answers at the Campus Security Office

 Dialog （對話）

A: 請問我可以問個問題嗎？

A: Excuse me. Can I ask you a question?

B: 當然可以。

B: Certainly.

A: 我聽說有些校園有腳踏車失竊的問題，你可以給我一些建議嗎？

A: I've heard that bike theft is a problem on some campuses. Can you give me some advice?

B: 首先，我建議你向大學校園安全室註冊腳踏車，然後如果被偷，你應當立即聯絡他們，他們的電話在你的學生手冊裡。

B: First, we recommend you register your bike with the university campus security office. Then, if it is stolen, you should immediately contact them. Their phone number is in your student packet.

A: 你是說主要校園資訊小冊子嗎？

A: You mean the main campus information booklet?

預備｜校園｜選課｜新生說明｜上課前｜課堂上｜課後交流｜圖書館｜體育館｜餐廳｜課外活動｜申請獎助｜當助教

B: 是的，所有關於校園事務的電話號碼都在裡面，你最好將你的腳踏車鎖在校園提供的腳踏車架，並且晚上把它們放在室內。

B: Yes. All phone numbers relating to campus business are in there. It's best that you lock your bike securely to the bike racks provided on campus, and keep them inside at night.

A: 校園也有其他東西被竊的問題嗎？

A: Is theft on campus a problem for other types of things too?

B: 多數竊盜因為有機可趁而發生。

B: Most theft occurs because of opportunity.

A: 我了解了，謝謝你的建議。

A: I see. Thanks for the advice.

Word Bank 字庫

theft [θæft] n. 竊盜
advice [əd`vaɪs] n. 建議
register [`rɛdʒɪstə] v. 註冊
contact [`kɑntækt] v. 聯絡
packet [`pækɪt] n. 小包，小捆
rack [ræk] n. 架子

Useful Phrases 實用語句

1. 我聽說有些校園有腳踏車失竊的問題。

   I've heard that bike theft is a problem on some campuses.

2. 你可以給我一些建議嗎？

   Can you give me some advice?

3. 我建議你向大學校園安全室註冊腳踏車。

   We recommend you register your bike with the university campus security office.

4. 你最好將你的腳踏車鎖在校園提供的腳踏車架。

   It's best that you lock your bike securely to the bike racks provided on campus.

5. 校園也有其他東西被竊的問題嗎？

   Is theft on campus a problem for other types of things too?

1.4 校園安全室
Campus Security Office

 Dialog 對話

A: 我想了解校園安全護送服務。

A: I'd like to know about the campus safe escort service.

B: 好的，學校提供免費志願護送，可在你需要陪伴人員的任何時候陪你安全回到宿舍或公寓。

B: Sure. The university provides volunteer escorts for free, any time you need an escort to see you safely make it back to your dorm or apartment.

A: 我必須住學校附近嗎？

A: Do I have to live close to the campus?

B: 只要在校園三個街區內，他們就會護送。

B: As long as it is within three blocks of the campus, they'll escort you.

A: 我如何聯絡他們？

A: How do I contact them?

B: 打卡片上的這個號碼，他們會安排人到你所在之處。

B: Just call the number on this card. They'll arrange to have somebody come to where you are.

A: 誰是護送員？

A: Who are the escorts?

B: 他們都是學校的學生，男女志願生。

B: They are all university students. Men and women volunteer to do this.

A: 我如何辨認他們？

A: How will I know who they are?

B: 他們都佩帶藍色臂章，所以很容易辨識。

B: They all wear blue armbands, so it is easy to identify them.

A: 我還需要知道別的嗎？

A: Is there anything else I should know?

B: 我要告訴你護送員都有背景查核，而且我們有面談，所以我們知道他們是真誠地想要幫助其他人。

B: I'd like to tell you that the escorts have all had background checks, and we interview them so we know they are earnest about wanting to help others.

A: 感謝你所有的幫忙。

A: Thanks for all your help.

 Word Bank 字庫

escort [`ɛskɔrt] n. 護送員；護送
volunteer [ˌvɑlən`tɪr] v. 志願
armband [`ɑrm ˌbænd] n. 臂章
identify [aɪ`dɛntə ˌfaɪ] v. 辨識
earnest [`ɝnɪst] adj. 真誠的

 Useful Phrases 實用語句

1. 我如何聯絡他們？

   How do I contact them?

2. 誰是護送人員？

   Who are the escorts?

3. 他們都是男同學嗎？

   Are they all male students?

4. 有女的護送員嗎？

   Are there female escorts?

5. 我如何辨認他們？

   How will I know who they are?

6. 他們都佩帶藍色臂章，所以很容易辨識。

   They all wear blue armbands, so it is easy to identify them.

預備
校園
選課
新生說明
上課前
課堂上
課後交流
圖書館
體育館
餐廳
課外活動
申請獎助
當助教

7. 我還需要知道別的嗎？

Is there anything else I should know?

1.5 校園安全室：夜間停車
Campus Security Office: Night Parking

Dialog 對話

A: 我想了解晚上在校園停車場停車有多安全。

A: I'd like to know how safe it is to park in the campus parking lot at night.

B: 我們有全天 24 小時保全監視，而且經常監看。

B: We have security cameras on 24 hours a day, and they are constantly monitored.

A: 晚上有守衛值班嗎？

A: Is there a guard on duty at night?

B: 有，兩個人，而且校警及本地警車經常巡邏那裡。

B: Yes. Two of them, and both campus and local police cars cruise the area often.

A: 照明好嗎？

A: Is the area well lit?

B: 很好，但凌晨有些燈會關掉。

B: Yes, it is. However, after midnight some of the lights are turned off.

A: 可以有人陪我去取車嗎？

A: Can I have someone escort me to my car?

B: 可以，校園護送會樂意為你服務，而且守衛也會願意，如果你問他們的話。

B: Yes. The campus escort service will be happy to do that for you, and the security guards will too if you ask them to.

A: 我可以停在那裡多久？

A: How long can I park there?

B: 如果你有學校停車證，無論平日或週末，你想停多久都可以。

B: If you have a university parking permit, you can park there as long as you want any day of the week.

A: 如果我沒有停車證呢？

A: What if I don't have a permit?

B: 那一小時 50 分。

B: Then parking costs 50 cents an hour.

A: 多謝你的幫忙。

A: Thanks very much for your help.

Word Bank 字庫

security camera n. 保全監視
monitor [`mɑnətə] v. 監看
cruise [kruz] v. 巡邏
permit [`pɝmɪt] n. 停車證

Useful Phrases 實用語句

1. 晚上有守衛值班嗎？
   Is there a guard on duty at night?

2. 照明好嗎？
   Is the area well lit?

3. 我可以有人陪我去取車嗎？
   Can I have someone escort me to my car?

4. 我可以停在那裡多久？
   How long can I park there?

5. 如果我沒有停車證呢？
   What if I don't have a permit?

6. 我停車過夜要付多少錢？
   How much will I be charged for overnight parking?

7. 校園停車場何時關閉？
   What time does the campus parking lot close?

8. 週末有開放停車嗎？
   Is the parking lot open on weekends?

9. 校警及本地警車經常巡邏那裡。
   Both campus and local police cars cruise the area often.

10. 但凌晨有些燈會關掉。
    After midnight some of the lights are turned off.

11. 我們有全天 24 小時保全監視。
    We have security cameras on 24 hours a day.

12. 監視器經常被監看。
    The cameras are constantly monitored.

13. 無論平日或週末，你想停多久都可以。

You can park there as long as you want any day of the week.

Notes 小叮嚀

　　美國校園有校警及當地警車巡邏維護校園治安，因為公立學校校園是公共空間，任何人皆可進入，學校若位於市中心，更要擔心入夜後的安全問題。美國是可以合法擁有槍械的國家，大學也多設有校園酒吧，為避免濫用酒精、藥物、持有槍械，甚至不同族裔衝突 (這些情形高中可能比大學常見) 等各種情況，校警或警察巡邏司空見慣。

　　校園在許多角落會有緊急電話箱 (emergency call box 或簡稱 call box)，有緊急事故或需要陪伴護送時可以立刻與校警連線；多數電話放在有黃色底部的藍色盒子內，晚上會亮燈，所以又稱為 blue box 或 blue light box，護送員男女學生都有。

1.6 在註冊室
At the Registrar's Office

Dialog 對話

A: 嗨，我有一個關於退選日期的問題。

A: Hi. I have a question about drop dates.

B: 我可以幫你，你的問題是什麼？

B: I can help you. What is your question?

A: 我可以退選的最後一天是何時？

A: What is the last day I can drop a class?

預備 校園 選課 新生說明 上課前 課堂上 課後交流 圖書館 體育館 餐廳 課外活動 申請獎助 當助教

B: 最後一天可以退選而不被記錄在 (成績) 卡上的日期是 10 月 2 日。

B: The last day you can drop a class without getting a W on your card is October 2nd.

A: 如果我不在乎被記錄呢？

A: What if I don't care about the W?

B: 那你可以等到 11 月 12 日。

B: Then you can wait until November 12th.

A: 真的，那麼晚嗎？

A: Really? That late?

B: 是的，但記住你可以加課的最晚時間是 10 月 5 日。

B: Yes. Remember though that October 5th is the latest you can add a class.

A: 好，謝謝你的幫忙。

A: OK. Thanks a lot for the help.

Word Bank 字庫

Registrar's Office n. 註冊室
drop date n. 退選日期

Useful Phrases 實用語句

1. 最後一天可以退選而不被記錄在 (成績) 卡上的日期是何時？

When is the last day I can drop a class without getting a W on the card?

2. 如果我成績卡上有 W 表示什麼？

   What does it mean if I have a W on my card?

3. 它表示你在早期退選日後退選。

   It means you dropped after the early withdraw date.

4. 它會影響我的平均成績嗎？

   Will it affect my GPA?

5. 加 [退] 選何時截止？

   When is the deadline for adding [dropping] classes?

Notes 小叮嚀

　　成績單上的 W 表示是在拖到早期退選日之後才退選，這時當然任何人都不能加進來了，拖延退選雖然不會影響平均成績 (GPA)，但如果不想要成績單上有任何汙點，就要小心不留紀錄的日期。如果讀的是正式課程，要修的課不僅在開學前就要到學校書店把該教授指定教材準備妥當，開學的第一堂課更是非常重要，課堂大綱、進度、作業、報告、考試日期等都在第一堂就會說清楚，也會有功課要預習，錯過第一週很吃力，越晚加選一堂課就錯過越多，而且萬一適應不良要退選可能已經錯過不留紀錄的日期。

1.7 詢問旁聽
Asking about Auditing

Dialog 對話

A: 我們可以旁聽嗎？　　**A:** Can we audit a class?

預備
校園
選課
新生說明
上課前
課堂上
課後交流
圖書館
體育館
餐廳
課外活動
申請獎助
當助教

B: 可以，但你要填我們提供的表格，並且得到你要旁聽的系的允許。

B: Yes, but you have to fill out the form we provide you and get permission from the department you want to audit the class in.

A: 截止期限是何時？

A: When is that deadline?

B: 跟加選日期一樣。

B: It's the same as the add class deadline.

A: 謝謝。

A: Thank you.

Useful Phrases 實用語句

1. 我們可以旁聽嗎？

   Can we audit a class?

2. 你要填我們提供的表格。

   You have to fill out the form we provide you.

3. 你要得到你要旁聽的系的允許。

   You have to get permission from the department you want to audit the class in.

4. 截止期限是何時？

   When is that deadline?

Language Power 字詞補給站

◆ **課程目錄 Course Catalog**

register   註冊

add [drop]	加 [退]
admin. (administration)	行政
deadline	截止期限
audit	旁聽
apply	申請
application	申請
W (withdraw)	退選
tuition	學費
fees	費用
advising	忠告
academic requirements	學業規定
form	表格
transfer courses	轉修
major	主修
minor	副修
double major	雙主修
required course	必修
elective	選修
core courses	核心課程
credits	學分
transcripts	成績單
schedule	課表
P / N (pass / no pass)	通過 / 不通過 (適用於沒有成績計分的課程)
campus codes	校園代號
credit [non-credit] course	採計 [不採計] 學分課程
GPA (grade point average)	平均成績

Tips 小祕訣

　　關於就讀大學的任何問題，幾乎都可以在學校網站得到解答，註冊組網頁有課程方面的資料，其他行政單位的政策舉凡停車、宿舍、工讀機會等公告都涵蓋其中。如果一開始覺得看不懂需要幫忙，可以到國際學生處尋求解答。

預備

校園

選課

新生說明

上課前

課堂上

課後交流

圖書館

體育館

餐廳

課外活動

申請獎助

當助教

1.8 學生中心大樓
Student Union Building

Dialog 對話

A: 我們應該要到學生中心大樓。

A: We ought to go over to the Student Union building.

B: 好,那裡有什麼?

B: OK. What's there?

A: 學生中心是我們可以吃東西、讀書、與朋友聊天或去許多學生社團的辦公室。

A: The Student Union is where we can find things to eat, study, chat with friends, or go to the offices of many student activities groups.

B: 聽起來是很繁忙的地方。

B: It sounds like a busy place.

A: 是的,但是很大,所以不會感覺太擁擠。

A: Yes, but it's big, so it doesn't feel too crowded.

Useful Phrases 實用語句

1. 那裡有什麼?

   What's there?

2. 是我們可以從事許多學生活動的地方。

   It's a place where we can have many student activities.

1.9 學生證
Student I.D. Card

 Dialog 對話

A: 嗨，各位，我們現在要去圖書館，你有圖書館證了嗎？

A: Hi, everyone, we are now going to the library. Have you got your library card yet?

B: 我還沒有。

B: I don't have mine yet.

A: 你要到學生中心的發卡中心去。

A: You'll need to go to the card office in the Student Union.

B: 好，我需要帶什麼嗎？要照片嗎？

B: OK. What do I need to bring? Any photos?

A: 不用，他們會為你拍照，但是你需要帶一張有照片的證件以及已註冊課程的繳費證明。

A: No, they'll take photos for you, but you'll need a photo I.D. and the proof of payment for your registered classes.

B: 我知道了。

B: I see.

預備

校園

選課

新生說明

上課前

課堂上

課後交流

圖書館

體育館

餐廳

課外活動

申請獎助

當助教

A: 事實上，我們可以用學生證進入圖書館及借書，你的卡片可以為你做很多事，可以用來影印、買書，還可以免費搭乘市區巴士系統。

A: Actually, we can use our student I.D. card to enter or check out books. Your card can do a lot for you. It can be used to pay for copying, buy books, and ride for free on the city bus system too.

B: 真的嗎？它怎麼付款？

B: Really? How can it pay for things?

A: 你可以到校園加值站去加值，就像用扣款卡一樣。

A: You can go to add value stations around the campus and add credit to it. It acts like a debit card.

B: 所以我搭巴士其實要付費。

B: So really I have to pay to ride the bus.

A: 不，學生真的免費。

A: No, that really is free for students.

B: 太棒了！

B: Cool!

 Useful Phrases （實用語句）

1. 它怎麼付款？

   How can it pay for things?

2. 你可以到校園加值站去加值。

   You can go to add values station around the campus and add credit to it.

3. 我每次加值要加多少錢？

   How much do I have to pay for adding value to the card every time?

4. 我可以加值的選擇是什麼？

   What are the options of value that I can add?

5. 它像用扣款卡一樣。

   It acts like a debit card.

6. 它可以在學校付很多東西。

   It can be used to pay for many things at school.

Tips （小祕訣）

　　學生證 (student I.D. card) 與其他身分證明一樣都是在申請時當場拍攝照片 (有些學校也接受學生線上申請及上傳符合規定之照片)。學生證除證明身分外，尚有其他用途，如作為借閱書籍之圖書館卡 (Library Card) 及校園內外書店週邊商店之學生優惠卡 ((on and off campus) Student Discount Card)。卡片加值後可以作為校園扣款卡 (On-Campus Debit Card)、影印卡 (Pay for Print Card) 或免費搭乘不同校園間的接駁巴士 (campus shuttle) 等用途，因為集各種功能於一卡，有些學校又稱為 Key Card。

預備
校園
選課
新生說明
上課前
課堂上
課後交流
圖書館
體育館
餐廳
課外活動
申請獎助
當助教

1.10 申請學生證
Getting a Student Card

 Dialog 對話

A: 嗨,我需要一張學生證。

A: Hi. I need to get a student I.D. card.

B: 好,我們要幫你拍一張照片,你也要填這張小資料表。

B: OK. We'll need to take a photo of you, and you'll need to fill out this little information form.

A: 好,謝謝。

A: OK. Thanks.

B: 你填好以後我們會幫你拍照,然後你的證件 5 分鐘就好了。

B: After you fill out the form, we'll take your picture. Then your card will be ready in about five minutes.

A: 很好,我也可以設定成扣款卡嗎?

A: Great. Can I set it up as a debit card too?

B: 可以,我們這裡也可以為你安排那些事情。

B: Yes. We can arrange all that for you here also.

A: 謝謝。

A: Thanks.

Word Bank 字庫

debit card **n.** 扣款卡

arrange [əˋrendʒ] **v.** 安排

Useful Phrases 實用語句

1. 我也可以設定成扣款卡嗎？

   Can I set it up as a debit card too?

2. 我在校園書店有折扣嗎？

   Do I get a discount at the campus bookstore?

3. 我可以用學生證付影印費嗎？

   Can I use the card to pay for copies?

4. 當我搭校園巴士時我要出示我的學生證嗎？

   Do I need to show my card when I take the campus shuttle?

1.11 大學體育館
University Stadium

Dialog 對話

A: 請靠近且並走這邊。

A: Please stay close and come this way.

B: 我們可以問問題嗎？

B: Can we ask questions?

A: 喔，當然，任何時候都可以。

A: Oh, sure. Any time.

B: 這間體育館可以坐多少人？

B: How many people will this stadium seat?

預備
校園
選課
新生說明
上課前
課堂上
課後交流
圖書館
體育館
餐廳
課外活動
申請獎助
當助教

A: 大概二萬人。

A: About twenty thousand.

B: 我們可以從任何一個門進來嗎？

B: Can we enter from any door?

A: 多數學生從南入口進來，因為它離學生座位區最近。

A: Most students come in from the south entrance because it's closest to the student seating section.

B: 我知道了。

B: I see.

A: 每層南北端都有浴室，東西側有點心吧。

A: Every deck has bathrooms on both North and South ends, and snack bars on both East and West sides.

B: 體育館是何時蓋的？

B: When was the stadium built?

A: 1960 年，在 1982 年更新。

A: In 1960. It was remodeled in 1982.

B: 有售票處嗎？

B: Is there a ticket office?

A: 入口左邊有售票處，入口在體育館的所有方向。

A: There are ticket offices on the left of the entrance gates. The gates are on all sides of the stadium.

B: 我們可以多看看這個地方嗎？

B: Can we see some more of this place?

A: 當然可以，我們逛逛。

A: Sure. Let's look around.

Word Bank 字庫

deck [dɛk] n. 層
student seating section n. 學生座位區
remodel [ri`madl] v. 更新
ticket office n. 售票處

Useful Phrases 實用語句

1. 這個體育館可以坐多少人？
   How many people will this stadium seat?
2. 我們可以從任何一個門進來嗎？
   Can we enter from any door?
3. 體育館是何時蓋的？
   When was the stadium built?
4. 有售票處嗎？
   Is there a ticket office?
5. 我們可以多看看這個地方嗎？
   Can we see some more of this place?

預備
校園
選課
新生說明
上課前
課堂上
課後交流
圖書館
體育館
餐廳
課外活動
申請獎助
當助教

預備
校園
選課
新生說明
上課前
課堂上
課後交流
圖書館
體育館
餐廳
課外活動
申請獎助
當助教

1.12 校園健康服務
Health Services on Campus

在大學健康中心的就醫過程與一般診所相同,通常校園的健康中心有如診所一般。購買學生保險是強制的,有些大學將健康保險包含在學費裡,所以以學生完成註冊繳費,保險就已經啟動;有些大學將保險分開,學生另外購買,外籍學生可以加入外籍學生保險。

 Dialog 對話

A: 嗨,我們想知道怎麼使用校園健康服務。

A: Hi. We would like to know how to access health services.

B: 你可以預約看校園護士,但如果是緊急事故,隨時過來。

B: You can make an appointment to see a staff nurse, but if it's an emergency, come here any time.

A: 有救護車服務嗎?

A: Is there an ambulance service?

B: 沒有,但校園安全人員會用他們的車輛帶你來這裡,如果你被判定必須去不同醫院,那就會叫救護車。

B: No, but campus security personnel can bring you here in one of their vehicles. If it is decided you need to go to a different hospital, then an ambulance would be called.

A: 使用這裡的服務要多少費用?

A: What does it cost to use services here?

B: 學生免費，費用是由學生保險支付。

B: It's free for students. The cost is covered by your student insurance policy.

A: 你是說我們學費內含的保單費用。

A: You mean the policy that is included in our tuition?

B: 是的。

B: Yes.

A: 好，謝謝。

A: Good. Thanks.

Word Bank 字庫

access [`æksɛs] v. 接近，進入
ambulance service n. 救護車服務
vehicle [`viɪkl̩] n. 車輛
student insurance policy n. 學生保險單
tuition [tju`ɪʃən] n. 學費

Useful Phrases 實用語句

1. 我們想知道怎麼使用校園健康服務。

   We would like to know how to access health services.

2. 有救護車服務嗎？

   Is there an ambulance service?

3. 使用這裡的服務要多少費用？

   What does it cost to use services here?

4. 費用是由學生保險支付。

   The cost is covered by your student insurance policy.

Notes 小叮嚀

　　多數校園開放時間到晚上十一點，有些地方甚至更晚，不同校園有不同開放時間的規定，在期中期末考前學生準備考試時，開放時間會長一些。大一點的學校有自己的健康及安全(警局)服務，甚至有自己的消防部，不管是在校園內外，緊急電話號碼要隨身攜帶，並記住 911 是緊急電話。

預備
校園
選課
新生說明
上課前
課堂上
課後交流
圖書館
體育館
餐廳
課外活動
申請獎助
當助教

1.13 學術部門類別
List of University Academic Departments

❧ 自然科學學院 School of Natural Sciences

天文學 Astronomy / 天體物理學 Astrophysics
行為組織學 Behavioral Science
生物學 Biology
化學 Chemistry
地球科學 Earth sciences
物理學 Physics
氣象 Meteorology

❧ 數學及電腦科學學院
School of Mathemetics And Computer Science

數學 Mathematics
電腦科學 Computer Science

❧ 社會科學學院 School of Social Sciences

人類學 Anthropology
考古學 Archeology
傳播學 Communications
經濟學 Economics
民族研究 Ethnic Studies
民族學 Ethnology
歷史 History
地理 Geography

政治學 Political Science
都市計畫 Urban and Regional Planning
語言學 Linguistics
符號學 Semiotics
社會科學 Sociology
心理學 Psychology

人文藝術學院 School of Humanities And Arts

地區研究 (文化研究)Area Studies (Cultural Studies)
藝術 Art
古典學 Classics
舞蹈 Dance
英語文研究 English Studies
電影研究 Film Studies
民俗 Folklore
性別研究 Gender Studies
文學 Literature
音樂 Music
哲學 Philosophy
宗教研究 Religious Studies
戲劇 Theater

應用科學 / 應用藝術學院
School of Applied Sciences / Applied Arts

農業 Agriculture
商業 Business
設計 Design
教育 Education
工程 Engineering
人體工學 Ergonomics
家庭及消費科學 Family and Consumer Science
林業 Forestry
健康科學 Health Sciences
新聞 Journalism
法律 Law

預備
校園
選課
新生說明
上課前
課堂上
課後交流
圖書館
體育館
餐廳
課外活動
申請獎助
當助教

圖書館及資訊科學 Library and Information Science
軍事科學 Military Science
公關事務 Public Affairs
社會工作 Social Work

Notes 小叮嚀

　　各大學可能使用不同的名稱來稱呼同一個學系或學院。例如一所大學的商業學院可以是 Business School 或是 School of Business，經濟系可以是 Department of Economics 或是 The Economics Department。在你就讀前，當然要確認你的學校如何稱呼你就讀的科系。

Language Power 字詞補給站

◆ 學校成員、學位、課程活動
School Members, Degrees, Class Activities

register	註冊
enroll	入學
teacher, instructor	老師
classrooms	教室
textbooks	教科書
admin [administrations] office	教務處
class schedule	課表
lab class	實習課
professor	教授
audit	旁聽
credits	學分
diploma	學位
required [elective] class	必 [選] 修
Bachelor's Degree	大學部學位
B.S.	理學士
B.A.	文學士
undergraduate program	大學課程
graduate program	研究所課程
Master's [Graduate] Degree	碩士學位
M.S.	理學碩士

預備 校園 選課 新生說明 上課前 課堂上 課後交流 圖書館 體育館 餐廳 課外活動 申請獎助 當助教

M.A.	人文碩士
MBA	企管碩士
Doctorate	博士學位
PhD.	博士
lecture	演講
seminar	研討
workshop	研習會
presentation	介紹；報告
speech	演講
oral report	口頭報告
written report	書面報告
placement test	分級測驗
interview	面談
take notes	做筆記
group discussion	小組討論
team [group] project	團體作業

Notes 小叮嚀

　　亞洲學生上大學選科系常是聽從父母師長意見，許多學生可能到大學畢業都不是很了解自己的志向及人生目標，學生年紀幾乎相同，在文化因素及文憑觀念下，學生上課也多半較被動。美國的大學生則不是如此，他們從小就被期待要有自己的看法，要早日獨立不依賴家人，美國大學生可能年紀稍長，在上大學前許多人都有些工作經驗，體會到自己要什麼和為什麼上大學，另一方面也要存錢或自食其力完成學業，他們認為學歷固然是個敲門磚，但是美國也是高度重視能力及競爭力的社會，因此大學生主動求知是典型的美國教室文化。

Unit 2 Choosing Courses and Registration

選課及註冊

美國大學一年分為兩學期 (semester) 或四學期制 (quarter)，兩學期制每學期十五週，四學期制十週為一期，寒暑期課程不分學制通常都較短。大學部 (undergraduate) 及研究所 (graduate school) 排課時間可能包含中午 12 點及晚上。社區學院 (community college) 也有夜間課程，但一般而言，全部上夜間課程完成學業的情形並不多見。

所有課程以英文授課，外籍學生必須具備一定的英文能力才能勝任，所以學校將此列為入學要件；如果是條件式入學，即學校先行允許英文未達要求標準的外籍生入學，但要求他們去上密集英文課程，並重複報考托福或其他標準測驗直到通過標準。除了英文能力之外，當然必須會使用電腦，學校提供各種電腦課程，包含為從沒碰過電腦的人開課，美國大學電腦室 (computer labs) 多為 24 小時開放。

預備　校園　選課　新生說明　上課前　課堂上　課後交流　圖書館　體育館　餐廳　課外活動　申請獎助　當助教

2.1 註冊流程說明
Registration Process

學校採用網路註冊，所有的課程資料都在學校網站上，學生在開放時間內按照指示步驟可以完成線上註冊，註冊時需要學生輸入密碼，有些學校要求學生輸入正確電子郵件地址，有些學校會為學生列出網路註冊資訊 (course registration information)，註冊步驟通常很類似：

註冊課程

在指定的系統開放時間內連結學校網頁 → 學生輸入個人帳號及密碼 (username and password)

搜尋瀏覽課程 (course search) → 進入(login)全校課程網頁

點選欲加退選課程並閱讀說明(course description) → 點選加(add)或退(drop)

確認(confirm)或取消(cancel) ← 點選該科成績選擇 (grade option)：學分(credit)、通過/不通過(pass/fail)、旁聽(audit)

繼續加退選直到完成後按檢視(view) → 確認

進入繳費階段

點選全部課程學分列表 (course list)及學費付款清單(payment due) → 點選是否辦理自動分期付款 (automatic payment plan)，從信用卡或銀行帳號分期扣除，可能要收取設定費 (setup fee)

點選付款方式(支票、信用卡或銀行帳戶扣款) ← 付支票者列印學費單至出納組繳費，信用卡或帳戶扣款繳納者輸入卡號或帳號、線上全期或分期付款

列印信用卡繳費完成收據 ←

有些學校也提供學生紙上註冊流程 (paper-based registration process)—— 在網頁下載列印課程註冊單 (Course Registration Form)，填上課程，繳交註冊組完成註冊，並到出納組完成繳費。

預備
校園
選課
新生說明
上課前
課堂上
課後交流
圖書館
體育館
餐廳
課外活動
申請獎助
當助教

2.2 選課及註冊
Choosing Courses and Registration

Dialog 1 對話1

A: 嗨，我是這裡的新生，我需要註冊課程。

A: Hi, I'm a new student here. I need to register for classes.

B: 你可以線上註冊。

B: You can register online.

A: 聽起來很方便，你可以教我怎麼在網路上選課嗎？

A: That sounds convenient. Can you show me how?

B: 當然可以，很簡單，所有課程都在大學的註冊網頁這裡。只要到註冊頁點看課程清單，直到找到你想要的課程。

B: Sure. It's pretty easy. All the classes are here on the University's registration website. Just go to the registration page and click through the class lists until you find the ones you want.

A: 我也可以讀到課程（資料）嗎？

A: Can I read about the classes too?

B: 可以，關於課程內容、誰教的課程及何時有課。

B: Yes. What it is about, who is teaching the class, and what times it is available.

預備

校園

選課

新生說明

上課前

課堂上

課後交流

圖書館

體育館

餐廳

課外活動

申請獎助

當助教

A: 如果有一門課在我選入前就滿了，它會告訴我嗎？

A: Does it tell me if a class is full before I select it?

B: 會，你也可以把自己排在候補名單。

B: Yes. You can add yourself to a waiting list too.

A: 我選完該怎麼做？

A: What should I do when I finish choosing?

B: 你確定弄好了，要點「送出」鍵。

B: You have to click on the "send" button when you are sure you're ready.

A: 我了解了，謝謝。

A: I see. Thanks.

Word Bank 字庫

register [`rɛdʒɪstə] v. 註冊
available [ə`veləbl] adj. 可使用的
waiting list n. 候補名單

Useful Phrases 實用語句

1. 我可以讀到課程（資料）嗎？

   Can I read about the classes?

2. 你可以教我怎麼在網路上選課嗎？

   Can you show me how I can choose classes on the net?

3. 我選完該怎麼做？

   What should I do when I finish choosing?

4. 我怎麼取得使用者名稱及密碼？

   How do I get the username and password?

5. 點選 MyUC 建立一個新帳戶。

   Click on MyUC and create a user account.

6. 所有課程都在大學的註冊網頁上。

   All the classes are here on the University's registration website.

7. 你可以把自己排在候補名單。

   You can add yourself to a waiting list.

8. 你確定弄好了，要點選「送出」鍵。

   You have to click on the "send" button when you are sure you're ready.

 Dialog 2 對話2

A: 我該修什麼課？

A: Which classes should I take?

B: 你要確定修必修課。

B: You need to be sure to take the required courses.

A: 好，我怎麼知道什麼是必修？

A: OK. How do I know what's required?

B: 你要先看你就讀領域的核心課程，你也該先找你的學業指導教授。

B: You need to look at the core curriculum for your area of study. You should meet with your academic advisor too.

A: 我今天不能用電腦。

A: I don't have access to a computer today.

預備
校園
選課
新生說明
上課前
課堂上
課後交流
圖書館
體育館
餐廳
課外活動
申請獎助
當助教

預備
校園
選課
新生說明
上課前
課堂上
課後交流
圖書館
體育館
餐廳
課外活動
申請獎助
當助教

B: 這裡有一個印出的課程目錄，你可以查。

B: Here is a printed course catalog. You can look in it.

A: 好主意，我可以隨時隨地看。

A: Good idea. I can read it any time, anywhere.

B: 它還有很好的課程說明。

B: It has very good course descriptions too.

Word Bank 字庫

required [rɪˋkwaɪrd] adj. 必修的
core curriculum n. 核心課程
academic advisor n. 學業指導教授
access [ˋæksɛs] n. 進入；存取
catalog [ˋkætəˌlɔg] n. 目錄
course description n. 課程說明

Useful Phrases 實用語句

1. 我該修什麼課？

   Which classes should I take?

2. 我怎麼知道什麼是必修？

   How do I know what's required?

3. 你要先看你就讀領域的核心課程。

   You need to look at the core curriculum for your area of study.

4. 你也該先找你的學業指導教授。

   You should meet with your academic advisor too.

5. 我今天不能用電腦。

   I don't have access to a computer today.

6. 這裡有一個印出的課程目錄。

   Here is a printed course catalog.

7. 我去哪裡註冊課程？

Where do I go to register for classes?

8. 你要到行政大樓。

You must go to the administration building.

9. 你可以線上註冊。

You can register online.

10. 我需要一個課程目錄。

I need a course catalog.

11. 我要到哪裡付課程費用？

Where do I pay for classes?

12. 一個學分多少錢？

How much does a credit cost?

13. 每個課程有幾個學分？

How many credits per class are there?

14. 這堂課在哪幢大樓？

Which Hall [building] is this class in?

15. 這堂課有額外費用嗎？

Are there any additional fees for this class?

16. 這堂實習課要額外付費嗎？

Does this class's lab cost extra?

17. 這堂課也有實習課嗎？

Does this class have a lab class, too?

18. 視聽室在哪裡？

Where is the audio-visual room?

Notes 小叮嚀

　　在選課前必須與學業指導教授談話，確認自己修課選擇獲得認可。在開始網路註冊之前，先了解如何使用註冊系統才不會收到許多錯誤訊息；除了每學期向學業指導教授確定該修哪些課及修課順序配合你的學位外，還要經常(上網)查看你的學位審核(degree audit)，追蹤你的學位進展(track your degree progress)。

　　網路註冊錯誤訊息說明請參考附錄；不要害怕向辦公室的人員尋求幫助，新生對新環境不了解，大家都能體會。

2.3 約見學業指導教授
Making an Appointment with an Academic Advisor

Dialog 對話

A: 我想約見學業指導教授。

A: I'd like to make an appointment to see an academic advisor.

B: 你有系上分配的指導教授嗎？

B: Have you been assigned an advisor from your department yet?

A: 我不確定。

A: I'm not sure.

B: 我先查一下登記名冊，如果你有被指定，你應該先見那位。

B: Let me check the registry first. If you have been assigned one, you should see that person first.

A: 我知道了，謝謝。　　　　**A:** I understand. Thanks.

Word Bank　字庫

academic [ˌækəˋdɛmɪk] adj. 學業的
advisor [ədˋvaɪzɚ] n. 指導教授
registry [ˋrɛdʒɪstrɪ] n. 登記名冊

Useful Phrases　實用語句

1. 我想約見學業指導教授。

   I'd like to make an appointment to see an academic advisor.
2. 你有系上分配的指導教授嗎？

   Have you been assigned an advisor from your department
   yet?

Notes　小叮嚀

　　身為學生，對大學裡的許多事務要有所了解，最切身的如
自己的學業指導教授及外籍學生服務等事項（重要事項學校也
會通知你）。其他如租屋、健康服務、學生保險、社團活動及娛
樂活動、學業輔導協助等，學校也有各類部門可以幫忙。

2.4 與學業指導教授談修課
Talking with an Academic Advisor about Taking Courses

Dialog 1　對話 1

A: 嗨，請進來坐下。　　　　**A:** Hi. Please come in and sit down.

預備 校園 選課 新生說明 上課前 課堂上 課後交流 圖書館 體育館 餐廳 課外活動 申請獎助 當助教

B: 謝謝。

B: Thank you.

A: 我怎麼幫你呢？

A: How can I help you?

B: 我需要一些該修什麼課的建議。

B: I need some advice on which classes I should take.

A: 好，你主修什麼？

A: OK. What is your major?

B: 我主修電腦科學。

B: I'm majoring in computer science.

A: 你是新生嗎？

A: Are you a freshman?

B: 是的，我是。

B: Yes, I am.

A: 好，我們先看你主修的必修課。

A: OK. Let's look at the required courses for your major first.

B: 我也可以選修嗎？

B: Will I be able to take electives, too?

A: 我們要先確定你沒錯過一年只開一次的必修課。

A: We need to make sure that you don't miss taking required courses that are only offered once.

B: 我知道了。　　　**B:** I see.

Word Bank　字庫

major [`medʒɚ] v., n. 主修
elective [ɪ`lɛktɪv] adj. 選修
offer [`ɔfɚ] v. 提供

Useful Phrases　實用語句

1. 我需要一些該修什麼課的建議。

   I need some advice on which classes I should take.

2. 我主修電腦科學。

   I'm majoring in computer science.

3. 我也可以選修嗎？

   Will I be able to take electives, too?

4. 我們要先確定你沒錯過一年只開一次的必修課。

   We need to make sure that you don't miss taking required courses that are only offered once.

I can show you how you can choose classes on the net.

預備
校園
選課
新生說明
上課前
課堂上
課後交流
圖書館
體育館
餐廳
課外活動
申請獎助
當助教

Notes 小叮嚀

通常學生們要把課程表及問題準備好再找指導教授，學校可能只有一位通科指導教授 (general academic advisor) 為所有科系同學輔導如何修課。系上也可能為學生分配指導教授，多數學生會向自己覺得較親近的教授諮詢。美國大學並不像臺灣以開課班級為單位，而是以開課課程等級為主，大學不分配班級導師或教官，而是個人諮詢教師或校警。美國及臺灣學生在某些課程可能擔任 group leader 帶領小組討論，但在課餘美國大學生沒有臺灣大學傳統的全班開週會、班會、選班級幹部幫忙服務全班或學長姐家族這類以班級為主的活動。臺灣大學生多數被視為班級的一員，而美國大學生是一個獨立意志的個人。

美國大學新生會有志願的學長姐 (upper classmate) 提供第一年諮詢，幫助適應校園生活，但所有學生理當主動為自己負責。

Dialog 2 對話2

A: 這些號碼代表什麼？

A: What do these numbers mean?

B: 那些是註冊課程代號。

B: Those are the registration numbers for the classes.

A: 我了解了，每個課程有自己的註冊號碼。

A: I see. Each class has its own registration number.

A: 那這是什麼號碼？

A: Then, what is this number?

預備

選課

新生說明

上課前

課堂上

課後交流

圖書館

體育館

餐廳

課外活動

申請獎助

當助教

B: 101？ → **B:** 101?

A: 是的。 → **A:** Yes.

B: 那號碼表示這課程的級數。 → **B:** That number tells you what level the class is.

A: 你是說 100 號碼是第一年？ → **A:** You mean 100 numbers are first year?

B: 是的，200 是第二年，300 是第三年，400 是第四年。 → **B:** Yes, and 200 is second year, and 300 is third, and 400 is fourth.

A: 我懂了。 → **A:** Got it.

✏️ Word Bank 字庫

registration [ˌrɛdʒɪˋstreʃən] n. 註冊
level [ˋlɛvḷ] n. 級數

📖 Useful Phrases 實用語句

1. 這些號碼代表什麼？

   What do these numbers mean?

2. 每個課程有自己的註冊號碼。

   Each class has its own registration number.

3. 那號碼表示這課程的級數。

   That number tells you what level the class is.

預備
校園
選課
新生說明
上課前
課堂上
課後交流
圖書館
體育館
餐廳
課外活動
申請獎助
當助教

Dialog 3 對話3

A: 這「Lab」是什麼意思？

A: What does this "Lab" mean?

B: 它表示除了上正規課程外，你每週還要出席那個課程的額外課程。

B: It means besides regular class attendance, you also have an extra class you must attend each week for that course.

A: 為什麼？

A: Why?

B: 實習課是讓你親自操作的特別課程。

B: The lab class is a special class where you will do some type of hands on work.

A: 你可以為我舉個例嗎？

A: Can you give me an example?

B: 當然可以，如果你修生物課你會有正規課堂授課，但你也要參加實習課親自操作某些實驗。

B: Sure. If you take a biology class, you'll have regular classroom lectures, but you'll also have to attend a lab where you would actually conduct an experiment on something.

A: 我懂了，實習使學生確實地學習第一手經驗。

A: I see. A lab allows the student to actually get some firsthand experience.

B: 對的。

B: That's right.

Word Bank 字庫

lab [læb] n. 實習課，實驗室
regular [`rɛgjələ] adj. 正規的
attend [ə`tɛnd] v. 參加
hands on work 親自操作
lecture [`lɛktʃə] n. 講課
conduct [`kɑndʌkt] v. 操作
experiment [ɪk`spɛrəmənt] n. 實驗
firsthand [`fɜst͵hænd] adj. 第一手的

Dialog 4 對話4

A: 我今年不要修這門課。

A: I'm not taking this class this year.

B: 你一定要。

B: You have to.

A: 為什麼？

A: Why?

B: 因為是必修。

B: Because it is required.

預備 校園 選課 新生說明 上課前 課堂上 課後交流 圖書館 體育館 餐廳 課外活動 申請獎助 當助教

A: 我知道，但我明年再修。

A: I know, but I'll just take it next year.

B: 如果你今年不修，你明年將不能修必修的第二門課。

B: If you don't take it this year, you won't be able to take the required second class next year.

A: 我了解了，那我下學期修。

A: I see. OK, I'll take it next term.

B: 沒辦法，它只有秋季開課。

B: You can't. It's only offered during Fall term.

A: 喔，我的天哪！

A: My God!!

Useful Phrases 實用語句

1. 這「Lab」是什麼意思？

   What does this "Lab" mean?

2. 你可以為我舉個例嗎？

   Can you give me an example?

3. 實習使學生確實地學習第一手經驗。

   A lab allows the student to actually get some firsthand experience.

4. 這門課只有秋季開課。

   This course is only offered during Fall term.

5. 你可以夏天修那門課。

   You can take that class in the summer.

預備

校園

選課

新生說明

上課前

課堂上

課後交流

圖書館

體育館

餐廳

課外活動

申請獎助

當助教

Tips 小祕訣

　　兩或三位教授可能同時教授相同的課,如果是這樣就要打聽一下教授們的教學風格及個性,選擇適合自己的教授。可以安排與教授見面或向其他修過課的同學請教,當然也要問考試、作業、報告等各種評量的方式及頻率。

Language Power 字詞補給站

◆ 修課 Taking Courses

apply (v.)/application (n.)	申請
tuition	學費
application form	申請表格
class	課程
hands on	親手
attendance	出席
freshman	新生
sophomore	大二
junior	大三
senior	大四
Bachelor's Degree	大學學位
Master's Degree	碩士學位
graduate school	研究所
grad student	研究生
Ph.D.	博士學位
professor	教授
semester	學期
term	(一)期
midterm	期中考
final	期末考
test	測驗
quiz	小考
pop quiz	隨堂考
examination	考試
summer session	暑修

預備 校園 選課 新生說明 上課前 課堂上 課後交流 圖書館 體育館 餐廳 課外活動 申請獎助 當助教

audit	旁聽
audit a course	旁聽一門課
academic advisor	學業指導教授
school's website	學校網址
credit	學分
teaching style	教學風格
teaching method	教學方法

2.5 加退選
Adding and Dropping Classes

Dialog 1 對話1

A: 請問這是註冊組嗎？

A: Excuse me. Is this the registrar's office?

B: 是的，我可以幫你嗎？

B: Yes, it is. May I help you?

A: 我要加退幾門科目。

A: I want to add and drop some classes.

B: 好，你要填這個表，包括科目代號，我也要確定你可以加進其他課程，課可能滿了。

B: Fine. You'll need to fill out this form including the number of the class. I'll also have to check to make sure you can add the other class. The class might be full.

A: 謝謝。

A: Thanks.

預備

校園

選課

新生說明

上課前

課堂上

課後交流

圖書館

體育館

餐廳

課外活動

申請獎助

當助教

Word Bank 字庫

registrar's office n. 註冊組

Useful Phrases 實用語句

1. 這是註冊組嗎？

   Is this the registrar's office?

2. 我要加退幾門科目。

   I want to add and drop some classes.

3. 你要填這個表，包括科目代號。

   You'll need to fill out this form including the number of the class.

Dialog 2 對話2

A: 我填好表了。

A: I've finished filling out the form.

B: 好，我看一下。

B: OK, let me see it.

A: 我什麼時候知道更正完成？

A: When will I know if the changes are accepted?

B: 等幾分鐘，我在電腦裡改一下，電腦會顯示是否一切都沒問題。

B: Wait just a couple of minutes. I'll put the changes into my computer. It will tell us if everything is OK.

A: 好。

A: OK.

預備
校園
選課
新生說明
上課前
課堂上
課後交流
圖書館
體育館
餐廳
課外活動
申請獎助
當助教

B: 退選沒問題，但你要加選的已經滿了，但你可以問教授是否可以讓你加入。

B: Well, dropping this class is no problem, but the class you want to add is full. You can ask the professor if it's OK for you to join, though.

A: 我要怎麼做？

A: How do I do that?

B: 你要和他約時間並且讓他簽這張加選表。

B: You'll have to make an appointment with him and have him sign this add form.

A: 我知道了，我今天就做。

A: I see. I'll do it today.

B: 你最好先打電話給那個系的祕書，看你何時可以和他談，如果他說好，讓他簽名，然後帶表格回來這裡。

B: You'd better call the secretary of that department first to see when you can talk to him. If he says yes, have him sign the form, then bring it back here.

A: 謝謝你的幫忙。

A: Thanks for your help.

Useful Phrases 實用語句

1. 我什麼時候知道更正完成？

   When will I know if the changes are accepted?

2. 電腦會顯示是否一切都沒問題。

   My computer will tell us if everything is OK.

3. 你要加選的已經滿了。

   The class you want to add is full.

4. 你可以問教授是否可以讓你加入。

   You can ask the professor if it's OK for you to join.

5. 你要和他約時間。

   You'll have to make an appointment with him.

6. 讓他簽這張加選表。

   Have him sign this add form.

7. 你最好先打電話給那個系的祕書。

   You'd better call the secretary of that department.

2.6 和教授談加課
Talking with a Professor for Adding a Class

Dialog 對話

A: 哈囉，安德森教授，我是蘇林，我和你有約要和你談話。

A: Hello, Professor Anderson. I'm Sue Lin. I have an appointment to speak with you.

B: 是的，當然，請進來坐下，有什麼問題嗎？

B: Yes, of course. Please come in and sit down. What is your question?

A: 我想加入您的企業倫理課，但是已經滿了。

A: I'd like to join your business ethics class, but it's full.

預備
校園
選課
新生說明
上課前
課堂上
課後交流
圖書館
體育館
餐廳
課外活動
申請獎助
當助教

B: 喔,我知道了,我查一下有多少學生在我加選名單上。(幾秒鐘後)看來我已收兩名了,讓我問你一個問題。

B: Oh. I see. Let me check to see how many students are on my add list. (a few seconds later) It appears that I've accepted two more already. Let me ask you a question.

A: 好。

A: Sure.

B: 你主修企管碩士課程嗎?

B: Are you majoring in the MBA program?

A: 是的。

A: Yes.

B: 好,我最多多收六名學生,如果他們是修那個課程。

B: Good. I accept up to six more students if they are in that program.

A: 對我來說太好了,請簽這張表格。

A: That's great for me. Please sign this form.

B: 沒問題。

B: No problem.

Word Bank 字庫

business ethics n. 企業倫理

 Useful Phrases 實用語句

1. 我要加[退]選。

   I want to add [drop] a class.

2. 這更正將會影響我的學費嗎？

   Will this change affect my tuition?

3. 加[退]選截止日是何時？

   What is the add [drop] deadline?

4. 有候補名單嗎？

   Is there a waiting list?

5. 多少學生可以加入？

   How many students can be in that class?

6. 課滿了嗎？

   Is the class full?

Notes 小叮嚀

現在學校選課多透過網路進行，加退選截止日多在開課後第六或第七週，加退選當然也會影響到學費的多寡。

2.7 打聽了解教授
Checking Out a Professor

 Dialog 1 對話1

A: 哈囉，林區教授，我是傑瑞施。

A: Hello, Professor Linch. I'm Jerry Shi.

B: 請進來坐下。

B: Please come in and sit down.

預備｜校園｜選課｜新生說明｜上課前｜課堂上｜課後交流｜圖書館｜體育館｜餐廳｜課外活動｜申請獎助｜當助教

預備
校園
選課
新生說明
上課前
課堂上
課後交流
圖書館
體育館
餐廳
課外活動
申請獎助
當助教

A: 謝謝。

A: Thank you.

B: 我可以為你做什麼？

B: What can I do for you?

A: 我想問幾個關於化學 101 課的問題。

A: I want to ask a few questions about Chemistry 101.

B: 好。

B: OK.

A: 一般而言，您怎麼上這門課？

A: Generally, how do you teach the class?

B: 我們會用一個標準的課本，它的名字在課程敘述內，而且在(學校)書店可以買到，我也有講義，當然還有每週的講課。

B: We'll use a standard text. It's named in the course description and available at the bookstore. I also have handouts; of course there are weekly lectures.

A: 我們可以在講課時發問嗎？

A: Can we ask questions during the lectures?

B: 可以，但是班級很大，所以很難做到，最好在實習課問。

B: Yes, but the class is large, so it's difficult to do that. It's better to ask questions during lab.

A: 我朋友和我是從外國來的，我們怕您沒時間與我們談話，我們也覺得我們會有許多疑問。

A: My friend and I are from another country. We are afraid you won't have time to talk to us, and we think we'll have many questions.

B: 這門課也有兩位研究生助理，你們也可以在辦公室時間跟他們談話。

B: There are two graduate assistants for this class also. You may talk to them during office hours too.

A: 我知道了，謝謝。

A: I see. Thank you.

 Word Bank 字庫

> text [tɛkst] n. 課本
> handout [`hænd͵aʊt] n. 講義
> graduate assistant n. 研究生助理

 Useful Phrases 實用語句

1. 我想問幾個關於化學 101 課的問題。

   I want to ask a few questions about Chemistry 101.

2. 一般而言，您怎麼上這門課？

   Generally, how do you teach the class?

3. 我們可以在講課時發問嗎？

   Can we ask questions during the lectures?

4. 我們怕您沒時間與我們談話。

   We are afraid you won't have time to talk to us.

5. 我們覺得我們會有許多疑問。

   We think we'll have many questions.

預備
校園
選課
新生說明
上課前
課堂上
課後交流
圖書館
體育館
餐廳
課外活動
申請獎助
當助教

6. 最好在實習課問。

   It's better to ask questions during lab.

7. 你可以找這門課的兩位研究生助理談話。

   You can talk to the graduate assistants for this class.

 Dialog 2 對話2

A: 嗨,我是杰馮,有人告訴我你上學期修卡爾森教授的課,我可以問你關於他教學風格的事嗎?

A: Hi. I'm Jay Feng. Someone told me you had a class with Professor Carlson last term. Could I ask you a couple of questions about his teaching style?

B: 當然可以,請坐。

B: Sure. Please sit down.

A: 謝謝,我想知道他的課堂說話方式。

A: Thanks. I'd like to know about his classroom speaking style.

B: 嗯,他說話很快,但很容易說上話,所以別擔心稍後發問,他很樂意幫助學生。

B: Well, he talks fast. He is easy to talk to, so don't worry about asking questions later. He's really happy to help students.

A: 可以錄他的講課嗎?

A: Is it OK to record his lectures?

B: 可以，我們很多人這樣做。

B: Yes. A lot of us do that.

 Useful Phrases 實用語句

1. 有人告訴我你上學期修卡爾森教授的課。

   Someone told me you had a class with Professor Carlson last term.

2. 我可以問你關於他教學風格的事嗎？

   Could I ask you a couple of questions about his teaching style?

3. 他很容易說上話。

   He is easy to talk to.

4. 別擔心晚點發問

   Don't worry about asking questions later.

5. 他很樂意幫忙學生。

   He's really happy to help students.

6. 可以錄他的講課嗎？

   Is it OK to record his lectures?

 Notes 小叮嚀

許多教授不介意課堂錄音，但是應該要事先徵得同意。

2.8 向學業指導教授諮詢選課：暑修
Asking the Advisor for Choosing Courses: Taking Summer Session

 Dialog 對話

A: 我要雙主修，所以這學期我要修 27 個學分。

A: I want to double major, so I'm going to take 27 credits this semester.

預備　校園　選課　新生說明　上課前　課堂上　課後交流　圖書館　體育館　餐廳　課外活動　申請獎助　當助教

B: 那樣很多。

B: That's a lot.

A: 我想快點完成學業。

A: I want to get done with school fast.

B: 那樣會花費更多。

B: It will cost more money that way.

A: 為什麼？

A: Why?

B: 超過 21 個學分你要付更多。

B: You have to pay more for each credit over 21.

A: 我得了解這大學收多少額外學分費。

A: I'd better find out how much this university charges for extra credits.

B: 你可以用暑修代替。

B: You might want to go to summer sessions instead.

A: 你的意思是指？

A: What do you mean?

B: 在暑期，大學有許多短期課程可以修。

B: In the summer the university has many classes available in a shorter session.

A: 我懂了，我會再考慮課程安排，謝謝。

A: I see. I'll think about my course arrangement again. Thanks.

預備

校園

選課

新生說明

上課前

課堂上

課後交流

圖書館

體育館

餐廳

課外活動

申請獎助

當助教

B: 不客氣。　　　　　**B:** No problem.

Word Bank 字庫

double major **n.** 雙主修
credit [`krɛdɪt] **n.** 學分
charge [tʃɑrdʒ] **v.** 收費
summer session **n.** 暑期班

Useful Phrases 實用語句

1. 我想快點完成學業。

   I want to get done with school fast.

2. 我得了解這大學收多少額外的學分費。

   I'd better find out how much this university charges for extra credits.

3. 超過 21 個學分你要付更多。

   You have to pay more for each credit over 21.

4. 在暑期，大學有許多短期課程可以修。

   In the summer the university has many classes available in a shorter session.

 Tips 小祕訣

多數全職大學生每學期修 12-18 學分課程 (超過 21 學分要多收學費)，研究生一般至少必須修習 9 學分 (有些系所規定不同)，最多不得超過 15 學分。在技術、職業或其他非學術性學校學習的學生，每週上課時間至少 18-22 個小時。大學生支付學費有多種方式，存款、貸款、家庭資助、打工 (全職或兼職) 都很常見，美國大學生通常希望在四年內完成大學學業，但許多人修得快些，也有些人會多上一年。有關大學及研究所總學分數規定，請見 146 頁。

2.9 付學費
Paying for Tuition

Dialog 1 對話1

A: 哈囉，我可以為你效勞嗎？

A: Hello. May I help you?

B: 可以，我要付學費。

B: Yes. I'd like to pay my tuition.

A: 好，你要怎麼付？

A: All right. How would you like to pay?

B: 我可以開支票嗎？

B: Can I write a check?

A: 可以，我們接受本地支票，你也可以就用你的扣款卡。

A: Yes. We accept local checks. You can also just use your debit card.

B: 真的嗎？那很方便，我要那麼做。

B: Really? That's convenient. I'll do that.

A: 好，我加總一下你的學分，再告訴你應付金額。

A: OK. I'll add up your credits and tell you the amount due.

B: 我要現在付所有的學費嗎？

B: Do I have to pay all my tuition now?

預備 校園 選課 新生說明 上課前 課堂上 課後交流 圖書館 體育館 餐廳 課外活動 申請獎助 當助教

A: 不用，你現在先付 1/3，11 月 1 日前 再付 1/3，12 月 5 日前付最後的 1/3。

A: No. You can pay one third now, another third by November 1st, and the last third by December 15th.

Word Bank 字庫

debit card n. 扣款卡
due [dju] adj. 到期的
tuition [tjuˋɪʃən] n. 學費

Dialog 2 對話2

A: 這裡是我付學費的地方嗎？

A: Is this where I pay tuition?

B: 是的，你可以在這裡或者可以上網付。

B: Yes, you can pay here, or you can pay online.

A: 我知道，但我還無法用電腦。

A: I know, but I don't have access to a computer yet.

B: 沒問題，你要付現金還是支票？

B: No problem. Will you pay by cash or check?

A: 我可以用信用卡嗎？

A: May I use a credit card?

B: 可以。

B: Yes, you may.

預備
校園
選課
新生說明
上課前
課堂上
課後交流
圖書館
體育館
餐廳
課外活動
申請獎助
當助教

A: 我是外籍學生，我不確定我要支付的總額是多少。

A: I'm a foreign student. I'm not sure what the total amount I need to pay is.

B: 我可以幫你算。

B: I'll calculate it for you.

A: 你知道其中有任何一課有額外費用嗎？

A: Do you know if any of these classes have extra fees?

B: 我把它們輸入電腦馬上就會知道。

B: We'll know right now as I enter them in the computer.

A: 謝謝。

A: Thanks.

Word Bank 字庫

online [`ɑn͵laɪn] adv. 在網路上
amount [ə`maʊnt] n. 金額
calculate [`kælkjə͵let] v. 計算

Useful Phrases 實用語句

1. 我要現在付所有的學費嗎？
   Do I have to pay all my tuition now?
2. 我是外籍學生，我不確定我需要付的總額是多少。
   I'm a foreign student. I'm not sure what the total amount I need to pay is.
3. 你知道其中有任何一課有額外費用嗎？
   Do you know if any of these classes have extra fees?
4. 有分期付款計畫嗎？
   Is there a payment plan?

5. 分期付款怎麼做？

   How does the payment plan work?

6. 你可以在這裡或者可以上網付。

   You can pay here, or you can pay online.

7. 我們有讓你分期付款的銀行自動扣款計畫。

   We have an automatic bank withdrawal plan that allows you to pay in installments.

8. 有一筆 25 元的設定費。

   There is a charge of $25 for the set-up fee.

Tips 小祕訣

如果就讀公立大學，美籍本州生比外州生便宜，外籍學生學費是最貴的；若就讀私立大學，不管身分如何，學費都一樣昂貴。

每間大學學費收取日期及方式不一，支票和信用卡都可以付學費，許多學校可以直接在網路上完成註冊及繳費，許多學校有分期付款計畫，學生可以分期自行繳費，或是辦理信用卡或帳戶自動扣款分期繳付，但可能有手續費。

Language Power 字詞補給站

◆ 選課 Choosing Courses

open classes	課程招生中
closed classes	課程已滿
service deck	服務櫃臺
Dean's office	院長室
CRN(class registration number)	課程註冊代號
override	推翻
submit	繳交
solution	解決辦法
conflict with	衝突
schedule	課程表
Pre-requisite	先修
student status	學生身分

預備
校園
選課
新生說明
上課前
課堂上
課後交流
圖書館
體育館
餐廳
課外活動
申請獎助
當助教

| petition | 請願書 |
| select | 選（課） |

2.10 改變主修談話
Talking about Changing Majors

Dialog 1 對話1

A: 我想改變我的主修。

A: I'd like to change my major.

B: 我知道了，為什麼？

B: I see. Why?

A: 我是建築系的學生，但我想現在我對藝術更有興趣。

A: I'm an architecture student, but now I believe I'm more interested in fine arts.

B: 你有查過課程了嗎？

B: Have you checked out the program?

A: 有，我也和那個系的一些教授及學生談過話。

A: Yes. I've talked to some of the professors and students in that department too.

B: 你要申請進入那個系，我會給你申請單。

B: You will need to apply for entry into that department. I'll give you the application.

A: 過程要多久？

A: How long will the process take?

B: 一般大約需要兩週左右決定。

B: The decision takes about two weeks on average.

A: 我怎麼知道決定是什麼？

A: How will I know what the decision is?

B: 你可以打電話到要進入的系，但他們應該會電子郵件告知你。

B: You can call the department you want to enter, but they ought to inform you by email.

A: 謝謝，我會確定他們有我的電子郵件地址。

A: Thanks. I'll make sure they have my email address.

Word Bank 字庫

architecture [`ɑrkə͵tɛktʃə] n. 建築
fine arts n. 藝術
application [͵æplə`keʃən] n. 申請

Dialog 2 對話2

A: 我要改變我的主修。

A: I want to change my major.

B: 你要改成什麼？

B: What do you want to change it to?

A: 我現在是建築系的學生，我要改成藝術主修。

A: Now I am an architecture student. I want to become a fine arts major.

B: 你要聯絡藝術系，並查看他們的學業要求。

B: You need to contact the department of Fine Arts and check their academic requirements.

預備 校園 選課 新生說明 上課前 課堂上 課後交流 圖書館 體育館 餐廳 課外活動 申請獎助 當助教

預備
校園
選課
新生說明
上課前
課堂上
課後交流
圖書館
體育館
餐廳
課外活動
申請獎助
當助教

A: 我做了,我也填了申請單,並且被接受了。

A: I did. I also filled out the application. It's been accepted.

B: 我了解了,請給我你的申請變更單。

B: I see. Please give your application for change to me.

A: 在這裡。

A: Here you are.

B: 你要填這個表,取得簽名並且帶回這裡。

B: You'll need to fill out this form, get it signed, and bring it back here.

A: 那之後呢?

A: What will happen after that?

B: 我們會註冊你的主修選項變更。

B: We'll register the change in your choice of major.

A: 我知道了,謝謝你。

A: I see. Thank you.

Useful Phrases 實用語句

1. 我想改變我的主修。

   I'd like to change my major.

2. 現在我對藝術更有興趣。

   I'm more interested in fine arts now.

3. 過程要多久?

   How long will the process take?

4. 我怎麼知道決定是什麼?

   How will I know what the decision is?

5. 我也填了申請單，並且被接受了。

   I also filled out the application. It's been accepted.

6. 那之後呢？

   What will happen after that?

Notes 小叮嚀

> 許多大學使用「改變主修」電子檔，到網站下載即可。
> 改變主修程式如下：
> 1. 聯絡系所確認學術要求及申請程序與期限。
> 2. 完成申請要求。
> 3. 如果核可，到學生服務中心或學系辦公室索取主 [副]
>   修表格。
> 4. 系辦公室可以協助你完成表格、簽名並繳還表格。
>
> 記住每所學校有不同規定，每州有不同的標準，了解任何
> 與學業相關的課程或身分變更、日期、程序。不要假設任何事
> 情，要與學業指導教授保持聯繫，盡快了解及解決任何衝突或
> 疑問之處，並加以確認，同時確定修課順序無誤，可以在規劃
> 時限內順利畢業。

Information Bank 大補帖

◎ 研究生入學條件身分說明 Graduate Student Status

1. 無條件或有條件式入學 Classified or Conditional Admission

研究生可能被允許有附帶條件(Conditionally Classified) 或無附帶條件(Classified or Unclassified Classified)入學。有附帶條件入學(或稱為條件式入學)的研究生被允許入學，條件是必須在某一段時間內或盡可能在時間內(as soon as practical)完成入學前欠缺的條件(deficiency)滿足入學要求(admission requirements)。在滿足條件後，原學生身分將透過「前進到候選」(Advancement to Candidacy)過程，更改為無條件的研究生(正式生)；入學條件在接受入學的文件中明載(stipulated)，有無附帶條件入學都享有相同的學生權益。

2. 正式生 VS 附讀研究生身分

Classified VS Unclassified Graduate Status

某些科系研究生在被接受入學時即被授予(confer)無附帶條件(正式)研究生身分(Classified Graduate Status)，除非他們畢業或解除學

預備
校園
選課
新生說明
上課前
課堂上
課後交流
圖書館
體育館
餐廳
課外活動
申請獎助
當助教

預備

校園

選課

新生說明

上課前

課堂上

課後交流

圖書館

體育館

餐廳

課外活動

申請獎助

當助教

生身分(declassified)。如果學生未註冊(unenrolled)超過兩學期(外籍學生必須每學期註冊維持全職學生身分)，該生學籍身分將自動解除(eliminated)。

附讀研究生(Unclassified Graduate Students)是被允許修習課程的學士後學生(post-baccalaureate students)，附讀研究生欲進入研究所必須通過申請。

拿到學校的入學許可，一定要搞清楚入學條件，Classified, Conditionally Classified, Unclassified 意義完全不同。外籍生如果拿到 Unclassified 入學許可，通常是因為托福或GRE/GMAT分數不夠，必須修習學校規定的語言課程(ESL)並且通過一定標準的研究所考試，修課也會受到限制，或許只能修習大學部課程或研究所入門課，在再次申請通過成為正式生前恐怕已花掉大量時間及金錢！拿到 Conditionally Classified入學許可者，就程序上而言，在滿足修課規定後才算是正式生；也有一些系所規定所有研究生(無論國籍)必須通過嚴格寫作測驗才能修習研究所學術寫作課程，成為正式生，但有些研究所並無此規定。

2.11 外籍研究生學生身分
About International Graduate Student Status

Dialog 對話

A: 哈囉，我可以為你效勞嗎？

A: Hello. May I help you?

B: 可以，我要知道我在學校這邊的研究生學生身分。

B: Yes, I need to know my status as a graduate student here at the university.

A: 好，告訴我你的學生證號碼，我在電腦系統裡找。

A: Ok. Tell me your student I.D. number. I'll find you in our computer system.

預備

校園

選課

新生說明

上課前

課堂上

課後交流

圖書館

體育館

餐廳

課外活動

申請獎助

當助教

B: 我的號碼是 83720566。

B: My number is 83720566.

A: 好,我們的系統說你是有條件(入學的)研究生。

A: OK. Our system says you are Conditionally Classified.

B: 我可以改成正式生嗎?

B: Can I change to Classified?

A: 你必須先符合學校有關條件入學的規定,之後才能改變身分成為正式生。

A: You'll have to satisfy the requirements of the university pertaining to Conditionally Classified students first. After that you can change your status to become a classified graduate student.

B: 我要到哪裡去申請身分改變?

B: Where would I need to go to apply for a change of status?

A: 院長辦公室。

A: The Office of the Dean.

✎ Word Bank 字庫

pertain [pə`ten] v. 相關
conditionally classified adj. 有條件入學的
classified graduate n. 正式研究生

預備 | 校園 | 選課 | 新生說明 | 上課前 | 課堂上 | 課後交流 | 圖書館 | 體育館 | 餐廳 | 課外活動 | 申請獎助 | 當助教

📖 Useful Phrases 實用語句

1. 我想了解我的身分。

   I'd like to know my status.

2. 我要如何改變我的身分？

   How do I change my status?

3. 學校的規定是什麼？

   What are the university's requirements?

4. 我要到哪裡去申請身分改變？

   Where do I apply for a change of status?

5. 身分改變要多久？

   How long will it take to change it?

6. 你有系上規定的影本嗎？

   Do you have a copy of this department's requirements?

7. 我有要求的文件。

   I have the documentation required.

8. 我要申請改變我的外籍研究生身分。

   I want to apply for a change of status as an international graduate student.

2.12 外籍學生英語課程
ESL Program

 Dialog 對話

A: 我想了解學校的英語課程。

A: I'd like to find out some information about the school's ESL program.

B: 你想了解什麼呢？

B: What would you like to know?

A: 我想知道是誰教的。

A: I'd like to know who teaches it.

B: 我們有許多優良老師，如果你想和他們見面也可以。

B: We have several well-qualified teachers. You can meet them if you'd like.

A: 我知道了，謝謝，班級大嗎？

A: I see. Thanks. Are the classes large?

B: 不大，事實上有些才三、四個學生，絕不會超過八個？

B: No. Actually some only have three or four students. There is never more than eight.

A: 每天都有課嗎？

A: Are the classes every day?

B: 有，每堂兩小時。

B: Yes, and each class lasts two hours.

A: 你們有其他英語課程嗎？

A: Do you have other ESL programs?

B: 有，我們也有密集班，每天四小時，週一到週五。

B: Yes. We have an intensive program too. It lasts four hours everyday, Monday through Friday.

✎ Word Bank 字庫

well-qualified [`wɛl`kwɑləˌfaɪd] adj. 資格優良的

intensive [ɪn`tɛnsɪv] adj. 密集的

Useful Phrases 實用語句

1. 我想了解學校的英語課程。

   I'd like to find out some information about the school's ESL program.

2. 我想知道是誰教的。

   I'd like to know who teaches it.

3. 每天都有課嗎？

   Are the classes every day?

4. 班級大嗎？

   Are the classes large?

5. 你們有其他英語課程嗎？

   Do you have other ESL programs?

6. 每堂兩小時。

   Each class lasts two hours.

7. 我們也有密集班。

   We have an intensive program too.

Where would I need to go to apply for a change of status?

Unit 3 Orientation

新生說明會

新生說明會幫助新生了解即將就讀學校的概況，家長也可以參加，多數活動設計讓新生了解校園環境設備以及為學生提供各種服務場所的名稱及位置。

預備

校園

選課

新生說明

上課前

課堂上

課後交流

圖書館

體育館

餐廳

課外活動

申請獎助

當助教

3.1 新生說明會(活動範例)
Sample Freshman Orientation Schedule

(This schedule is subject to change. 行事曆可能會更動)

❧ First Day of Freshman Orientation 首日

8:00-8:40 a.m. Check In at Wilson Hall 報到

Freshmen check into their orientation group. 新生報到

Drop off luggage, get room key, and receive Orientation program materials. Then be directed to the Student Union for the Welcome. 放行李、領鑰匙及新生說明資料，之後到學生中心參加歡迎會

9:00 a.m. Welcome to Orientation 歡迎會

Location: Student Union Center 學生中心

9:30 a.m. Orientation Groups Depart to begin Orientation. 小組帶開，開始新生說明

11:30 p.m. Lunch begins for some student groups. (某些小組)午餐開始

Location: West Wing Dining Hall 西側餐廳

12:45 p.m. Orientation Groups meet to leave dining hall for Pre-Advising sessions. 小組集合帶離餐廳準備開始諮詢暖身時段

1:00-3:00 p.m. Pre-Advising Sessions for Freshmen 新生諮詢暖身時段

Students meet with their academic advisors to get an overview of the class registration process. 學生與指導教授見面了解課程註冊過程

3:15-6:15 p.m. Computer Technology Sessions for all groups. 所有小組共同電腦時段

One hour session for each group on the use of technology includes: NetID, e-mail, VISTA & how to register for classes using the Student Administration System. 每組 1 小時使用學校電腦，包含網路身分、電子郵件、VISTA 及如何使用學生行政系統註冊課程

4:30-6:15 p.m. Dinner. Student groups will be brought to dinner at different times between this time period. 晚餐 (此期間不同小

組不同時段進餐）

5:30-7:30 p.m. Freshmen who need to complete loan counseling will be taken to the Financial Aid Office to do so. 需要完成助學金諮詢的新生會被帶往財務獎助室。

5:30-7:30 p.m. Structured Free Time [Athletics] around Wilson Hall Wilson樓附近半自由[體育]活動

7:45-10:00p.m. Evening Program Vignettes followed by individual group discussions. 夜晚活動及小組討論

10:00-11:30 p.m. Evening activities in & around Wilson Hall 夜晚活動

11:30-12 a.m. Wilson Hall closes for the evening. Good night! 就寢

-Up at 6:00 a.m. tomorrow for Day 2. 六點起床

Second Day 第二天

7:00 a.m. Breakfast 早餐

Student groups will be brought to breakfast between 7:00-7:30 a.m. 學生前往用餐

8:00 a.m. with Professor Ellen Miller 與教授談話

One of our most popular professors at the university talks about the differences between high school and college. 人氣教授談高中與大學的不同

9:00 a.m. Advising [Class] Registration for some groups and attendance at Student Life Sessions for others. 某些小組去諮詢[課程]註冊時段，其他學生去學生生活時段

10:30 a.m. Advising [Class] Registration for some groups 某些小組去諮詢[課程]註冊時段

11:30-12:45 p.m. Lunch 午餐

Student groups will be brought to lunch at different times between this time period. 不同組別不同時段前往用餐

1:00 p.m. Advising [Class] Registration for some groups and attendance at Student Life Sessions for others. 某些小組去諮詢[課程]註冊時段，其他學生去學生生活時段

3:00 p.m. ID Photos and student employment stop 拍攝學生證照片及去學生就業站

4:00 p.m. End of Program at Wilson Hall 結束新生說明會

預備 校園 選課 新生說明 上課前 課堂上 課後交流 圖書館 體育館 餐廳 課外活動 申請獎助 當助教

預備 校園 選課 新生說明 上課前 課堂上 課後交流 圖書館 體育館 餐廳 課外活動 申請獎助 當助教

Dialog 對話

A: 對不起，我得找到新生說明處。

A: Excuse me. I need to find out where orientation is.

B: 你是國際學生嗎？

B: Are you an international student?

A: 是的。

A: Yes, I am.

B: 嗯，一般說明會在寇那廳開始，但國際學生可能晚點要到凱爾廳做進一步說明。

B: Well, general orientation will start at Conner Hall, but international students may want to go to Kyle Hall later in the day for further orientation.

A: 謝謝。

A: Thanks.

Word Bank 字庫

orientation [ˌorɪɛnˋteʃən] n. 新生說明
further [ˋfɝðɚ] adj. 進一步的

Useful Phrases 實用語句

1. 我需要住校的資料。

   I need information about housing on campus.

2. 我需要在外住宿的資料。

   I need to find out about off-campus housing.

3. 我需要一些國際學生社團的資料。

   I need some information about international student groups.

4. 我需要約個時間見格林教授。

   I want to make an appointment to see Professor Green.

5. 我要去校園書店。

   I want to go to the campus bookstore.

6. 讀書小組通常在哪裡碰面？

   Where do the study groups usually meet?

7. 學生中心大廳是最受歡迎的見面場所。

   The Student Union Hall is the most popular place to meet.

8. 我需要一張學生證。

   I need to get a student I.D. card.

 Tips 小祕訣

First year advising 新生諮詢

除了系上的學業指導教授及校內生活輔導諮商單位，許多學校有由志願擔任及受過訓練的高年級生擔任首年輔導員 (The First-Year Advisor) 協助新生學業及個人適應，並且及早發現新生可能經歷的任何問題，通常新生的問題多是課業、室友、新環境和學業上的不確定，輔導員可以連結新生與校方，提供及時輔導。

大學的首年諮商輔導體系不止與校內系上連結，而且與教務及整個學生活動部門一起合作，提供新生包含宿舍生活 (Residence Life)、宿舍服務 (Accommodative Services)、校園安全 (Campus Safety)、首年研討 (First-Year Seminar)、課後輔導 (Tutoring Services)、兄弟會、姐妹會 (Greek Life)、學生發展、諮詢及就業中心 (Student Development, Counseling and the Career Center) 等各方面的輔導。

預備　校園　選課　新生說明　上課前　課堂上　課後交流　圖書館　體育館　餐廳　課外活動　申請獎助　當助教

預備
校園
選課
新生說明
上課前
課堂上
課後交流
圖書館
體育館
餐廳
課外活動
申請獎助
當助教

Notes 小叮嚀

　　因為移民局必須掌控外籍學生 (或稱國際學生) 在美情形，包括是否全時就讀、有無非法工作、有無轉學等等，所以學校有外籍或國際學生顧問 (foreign/international student advisor) 專門處理外國學生身分之事務。入境時要攜帶入學文件及外籍學生顧問姓名、電話備查，抵校就讀，須向校內國際學生辦公室 (international student office) 的外籍學生顧問報到註冊，之後顧問必須向移民局完成學生狀況報告。任何有關就學停留時間、學生身分等問題都必須向國際學生顧問諮詢，出入美國都要向顧問報到並取得其在 I-20 上之簽名。

3.2 課程介紹
Introducing a Program

Dialog 1 對話1

A: 嗨，各位，我是奈爾斯教授，我想為你們介紹科學管理課程。這是概括的管理觀念，以全面組織觀點來看商業功能，課程的精髓在於了解商業策略如何發展以及管理而產生價值，我們會從你們至今已經研讀的個人功能面加以建立。

A: Hi, everyone. I'm Professor Nells. I want to introduce the Management Science Program to you. It's a general management perspective, viewing the whole organization and looking at all business functions. The essence of the course is to understand how business strategies are developed and managed to create value. We will build on the individual functional pieces that each of you has studied to date.

B: 對不起，教授。

B: Professor, excuse me.

A: 是的。

A: Yes.

B: 我們都有不同程度的經驗及背景，這個對大家可行嗎？

B: We all have different levels of experience and backgrounds. Will this work for everyone?

A: 是的，綜合而言，這課程的目標在於建立你已有的策略背景，不論是什麼程度，並且增進你策略性的思考和獲得這門課程如何被配合起來的洞察力。你會有很多在需要策略性思考情況下運用你知識的練習。這種形式的練習是發展你技巧及能力很重要的手段。

A: Yes. In general terms, the objectives of this course are to build on the strategy background you already have, whatever level that might be, and to improve your ability to think strategically, and gain insight on how pieces of this program fit together. You will get a lot of practice applying your knowledge to situations that require strategic thinking. This type of action is an important means of developing your skills and ability.

B: 你可以更仔細地說明這門課的目標嗎？

B: Can you be more specific about the program's objectives?

A: 可以的。你會發展你的策略性思考能力並且獲得如何增進組織表現的見解。你也會了解一個公司各層面如何互動。最後你還會學到如何處理困境及特定的挑戰,並將你在此課程所學的原理運用到真實的商業世界。

A: Yes, I can. You'll develop your ability to think strategically and gain insight into how to improve organizational performance. You'll also gain understanding of how all aspects of a firm interact with each other. Plus you will end up learning how to deal with difficulties and specific challenges, and practice the principles you learn in this program to real world business.

B: 我懂了,謝謝教授把它解釋清楚。

B: I see. Thank you, Professor, for making it clear.

A: 沒什麼,我的榮幸。

A: No problem. My pleasure.

Word Bank 字庫

essence [`ɛsəns] n. 精髓
perspective [pəˋspɛktɪv] n. 觀念
strategy [`strætədʒɪ] n. 策略
to date 至今
objective [əbˋdʒɛktɪv] n. 目標
insight [`ɪn͵saɪt] n. 見解
means [minz] n. 手段
aspect [`æspɛkt] n. 層面
firm [fɜm] n. 公司
interact [͵ɪntəˋækt] v. 互動
principle [`prɪnsəpl] n. 原理

預備 校園 選課 新生說明 上課前 課堂上 課後交流 圖書館 體育館 餐廳 課外活動 申請獎助 當助教

Useful Phrases 實用語句

1. 綜合目標是什麼？
   What are the general goals?

2. 請多解釋點。
   Please explain more.

3. 特定目標是什麼？
   What are the specific goals?

4. 我們會用什麼方法？
   What methods will we use?

 Dialog 2 對話2

A: 你可以告訴我課程註冊何時開始嗎？

A: Can you tell me when class registration will start?

B: 研究生從星期一開始。

B: That will begin on Monday for graduate students.

A: 那大學部呢？

A: What about four year students?

B: 你可以現在上網註冊。

B: You can register online now.

A: 我可以在哪裡用電腦？

A: Where can I get access to a computer?

B: 學生中心有電腦可以供學生使用。

B: There are computers available for students at the Student Union.

預備

校園

選課

新生說明

上課前

課堂上

課後交流

圖書館

體育館

餐廳

課外活動

申請獎助

當助教

Word Bank 字庫

graduate [`grædʒuɪt] n., adj. 研究所 (的)
access [`æksɛs] n. 通道，入口

Useful Phrases 實用語句

1. 你可以告訴我課程註冊何時開始嗎？

   Can you tell me when class registration will start?

2. 你可以現在上網註冊。

   You can register online now.

3. 我可以在哪裡用電腦？

   Where can I get access to a computer?

4. 學生中心有電腦可以供學生使用。

   There are computers available for students at the Student Union.

3.3 詢問修業規定
Asking about Requirements

Dialog 1 對話1

A: 我對我的課程有些問題。

A: I have some questions about my program.

B: 好，請進來坐下。

B: OK. Please come in and sit down.

A: 謝謝，我不確定我必須修的課。

A: Thanks. I'm not sure about the courses I have to take.

B: 告訴我你的主修，我們可以上網看看課程。

B: Tell me what your major is, and we can look at the curriculum online.

A: 好，我主修資訊工程。

A: Sure. I'm a computer science major.

B: 好，我們看看。

B: Great. Let's look.

Word Bank 字庫

curriculum [kəˋrɪkjələm] n. 課程

Useful Phrases 實用語句

1. 我對我的課程有些問題。

   I have some questions about my program.

2. 我不確定我必須修的課。

   I'm not sure about the courses I have to take.

Dialog 2 對話2

A: 我可以明年修這堂課嗎？

A: Can I take this course next year?

B: 可以，但明年你就不能修 200 級的課。

B: Yes, but you won't be able to take the 200 level class next year.

A: 為什麼不可以？

A: Why not?

B: 100 級的課是先修課程。

B: The 100 level class is a prerequisite.

A: 我懂了。

A: I see.

A: 我必須今年修 (這門課)。

A: I must take it this year.

B: 是的，但它兩學期都有開。

B: Yes, however it is offered both terms.

A: 那樣不尋常嗎？

A: Is that unusual?

B: 有時有些課每年只有開一學期。

B: Sometimes classes are only offered for one session each year.

Word Bank 字庫

prerequisite [priˋrɛkwəzɪt] n. 先修
term [tɝm] n. 期

Dialog 3 對話3

A: 我需要多少學分才可以畢業？

A: How many credits will I need to graduate?

B: 你的主修要求你要通過 300 以上級數的 40 個學分，但是全部要 125 學分。

B: Your major requires that you pass 40 credit hours at 300 level or above, but the overall requirement is 125 credits.

A: 我不懂。

A: I don't understand.

B: 學校要求你修到 125 學分才能畢業，其中 40 學分必須是 300 以上級數。而且，這 40 學分全部通過的成績必須至少要 B。

B: The University requires that you obtain a total of 125 credits to graduate from this program. 40 of those credits must be 300 level or above. Also, all of the 40-credit requirement must be passed with at least a grade of B.

A: 我最好仔細看課表。

A: I'd better look closely at the class schedule.

B: 對，知道你要修什麼以及何時必須修是非常重要的。

B: Right. It's very important to know what you have to take, and when you have to take it.

 Word Bank 字庫

require [rɪ`kwaɪr] v. 要求
overall [`ovɚ͵ɔl] adj. 全面的，所有的
obtain [əb`ten] v. 獲得

預備　校園　選課　新生說明　上課前　課堂上　課後交流　圖書館　體育館　餐廳　課外活動　申請獎助　當助教

預備 校園 選課 新生說明 上課前 課堂上 課後交流 圖書館 體育館 餐廳 課外活動 申請獎助 當助教

📖 Useful Phrases 實用語句

1. 100 級的課是先修課程。

   The 100 level class is a prerequisite.

2. 有時有些課每年只開一學期。

   Sometimes classes are only offered for one session each year.

3. 我需要多少學分才可以畢業？

   How many credits will I need to graduate?

3.4 詢問學校及課程規定
Asking about School and Program Policies

 Dialog 對話

A: 對不起，我有個關於課程規定的問題。

A: Excuse me. I have a question about some of the program's policies.

B: 好，我可以試著幫你。

B: Fine. I'll try to help you.

A: 首先，我想知道全部學分要多少才可以畢業。

A: First, I want to know what the total hour requirement is in order to graduate.

B: 這個課程規定你要累積總共 122 學分。

B: This program requires that you accumulate a total of 122 credits.

A: 要全部都是這個系的課程嗎？

A: Must they all come from the program's department?

預備

校園

選課

新生說明

上課前

課堂上

課後交流

圖書館

體育館

餐廳

課外活動

申請獎助

當助教

B: 不必,但 31 學分是核心學分,從系上必修課程得到學分。

B: No, but thirty-one are core requirements. Credits gained from classes taken that are required by the department.

A: 我懂了,還有呢?

A: I see. What else?

B: 18 學分是外語規定,還有 20 學分是從系內選修。

B: Eighteen are foreign language requirements, and twenty are electives chosen within the department.

A: 還有嗎?

A: Is there anything more?

B: 有,其他的是從其他學科修課。

B: Yes. The others are credits that come from classes that are taken in other disciplines.

A: 那數學呢?

A: What about math?

B: 每個人都要修到 300 級。

B: Everyone must take math through the 300 level.

A: 那我每件事都知道了嗎?

A: Is that everything I need to know?

B: 記得你至少要有 40 個高級課程學分。

B: Remember that you must take at least forty upper division courses.

預備
校園
選課
新生說明
上課前
課堂上
課後交流
圖書館
體育館
餐廳
課外活動
申請獎助
當助教

A: 什麼是高級課程？

A: What is an upper division course?

B: 任何 300 或 400 級的課程。

B: Any course that is 300 or 400 level.

A: 我了解了，多謝。

A: I see. Thank you very much.

B: 沒什麼，任何時候都樂意幫忙。

B: No problem. Any time.

Word Bank 字庫

accumulate [ə`kjumjə‚let] v. 累積
core requirements n. 核心學分
elective [ɪ`lɛktɪv] n. 選修
upper division course n. 高級課程

Useful Phrases 實用語句

1. 我有個關於課程規定的問題。

   I have a question about some of the program's policies.

2. 全部學分要多少才可以畢業？

   What is the total hour requirement in order to graduate?

3. 這個課程規定你要累積總共 122 學分。

   This program requires that you accumulate a total of 122 credits.

4. 每個人都要修到 300 級。

   Everyone must take math through the 300 level.

5. 要全部都是這個系的課程嗎？

   Must they all come from the program's department?

6. 那我每件事都知道了嗎？

Is that everything I need to know?

7. 什麼是高級課程？

What is an upper division course?

3.5 人員及設備
Asking about Staff and Facilities

Dialog 1 對話1

A: 哈囉。

A: Hello.

B: 嗨，你可以告訴我哪位人員可以幫我處理付款問題嗎？

B: Hi. Can you tell me which staff person can help me with a payment problem?

A: 當然可以，出納在註冊室。

A: Sure, the cashier's at the registration office.

B: 我可以在哪裡找到他們？

B: Where can I find them?

A: 在巴菲爾德樓，也就是註冊組所在，二樓就是出納組，只要找門上的標示即可。

A: Here at Barfield Hall. This is where the registrar's office is. On the second floor is the cashier's office. Just look for the sign above the door.

預備
校園
選課
新生說明
上課前
課堂上
課後交流
圖書館
體育館
餐廳
課外活動
申請獎助
當助教

B: 謝謝。

B: Thank you.

Dialog 2 (對話2)

A: 有校護嗎？

A: Is there a staff nurse available?

B: 你是這裡的學生嗎？

B: Are you a student here?

A: 是的。

A: Yes.

B: 有值班校護，請問有什麼問題？

B: There are nurses on duty. May I ask what the problem is?

A: 我最近感到暈眩。

A: I've been feeling dizzy lately.

B: 好，我聯絡護士，請坐下並且填這張單子。

B: OK. I'll contact a nurse. Please sit down and fill out this form.

A: 謝謝。

A: Thanks.

B: 護士會很快來看你。

B: A nurse will see you soon.

預備

校園

選課

新生說明

上課前

課堂上

課後交流

圖書館

體育館

餐廳

課外活動

申請獎助

當助教

Useful Phrases　實用語句

1. 哪位人員可以幫我處理付款問題？

   Which staff person can help me with a payment problem?

2. 有校護嗎？

   Is there a staff nurse available?

3. 學校哪裡有法律諮詢？

   Where can I go for some legal advice at school?

3.6 抵免學分
Waiving a Course

Dialog　對話

A: 我想知道我必須做什麼來抵免學分。

A: I'd like to know what I have to do to have a course waived.

B: 我來解釋，你可以申請抵免已有學業成績的課，這只適用非選修的課。

B: Let me explain. You can apply to waive a class that you already have academic achievement for. This can only be done for non-elective courses.

A: 我怎樣證明我合乎標準？

A: How do I prove I met the requirement?

B: 你必須繳交以前修過學分的大學正式成績單。

B: You'll have to submit an official transcript from the university that you achieved the credits from.

預備
校園
選課
新生說明
上課前
課堂上
課後交流
圖書館
體育館
餐廳
課外活動
申請獎助
當助教

A: 我何時開始這程序？

A: When do I need to start this process?

B: 你必須在學年一開始就跟學業指導教授談話。

B: You should speak to your academic advisor at the beginning of the academic year.

Word Bank　字庫

waive [wev] v. 抵免
academic achievement n. 學業成績
submit [səb`mɪt] v. 繳交
official transcript n. 正式成績單
achieve [ə`tʃiv] v. 修得，達到

Useful Phrases　實用語句

1. 我想知道我必須做什麼來抵免學分。

   I'd like to know what I have to do to have a course waived.

2. 我怎樣證明我合乎標準？

   How do I prove I met the requirement?

3. 我何時開始這程序？

   When do I need to start this process?

Information Bank　大補帖

◎ 大學及研究所課程規定

Requirements for Undergraduate and Graduate Programs

以下是美國大學一般規定，研究所有些部分會有差異，但大學部學分規定大多雷同，只有全部學分數量的差異，大學一般需要 130 學分左右才能畢業。

1. 註冊 Registration

　(1) 基本規定 Basic requirements

　　學生要根據行事曆完成註冊繳費過程。

　　學生有責任更新學生系統內的個人住址並通知註冊組地址變更。

使用校園設備或服務如圖書館、學生活動中心 (Student Life Center)、校園供餐 (meal plans)、支票兌現 (check cashing) 等都需要出示學生證,由註冊組負責學生證事宜。

學生研讀學位不可長期休假 (without a substantial break),未能連續四期 (four successive academic terms) 註冊將喪失註冊資格 (the loss of matriculated status)。

研究生是全職學生,必須修習至少 9 學分(某些系所可能有不同規定);經系所同意,論文(thesis work)、實習(internships)、擔任助教(teaching assistantships)等課業活動可以視為額外「相等」學分(additional "equivalent" credit)。

(2) 正式與非正式註冊研究生 Matriculated and Nonmatriculated Students

申請系所被接受後並通過正式註冊程序的研究生 (matriculated students) 可以註冊所屬研究所課程,如欲註冊他系課程,須經他系核可。

非正式註冊生 (nonmatriculated students) 若經系所核可有空缺名額 (on a space-available basis) 可以修習研究所課程,但所修習學分未必可以計入。

正式註冊研究生與非正式註冊研究生都可以研讀大學部課程,但所修習學分未必可以計入。課程較健全的研究所,在教授及系所認可下,或許可以將大學部某些課程計入研究所課程;然而,在最少需要 45 學分的研究所課程內,大學部課程最多計入 9 學分。在最少需要 48 學分的研究所課程內,大學部課程最多計入 12 學分。儘管大學部學分可以被計算,研究生還是要仔細評估掌控大學部修課數量,畢竟研究生絕大多數課程就是研究所課程。

2. 學位規定 Degree Requirements

(1) 學分規定 Credit Requirements

研究所最少學分規定是 45 學分,其中至少 36 學分必須是研究所等級並在學位所屬系所內修得。

(2) 轉學承認學分 Transfer Credits

45 學分內最多 9 學分或 48 學分內最多 12 學分可以計入轉學承認學分,在申請研究生身時就要提出承認學分要求,但學分被承認的科目成績必須在 B(3.0) 以上。轉學被承認之學分不計入學生平均成績 (GPA, Grade Point Average),但計入畢業學位學分。轉學承認學分不計入校內就讀期間之計算,研究生欲

預備 校園 選課 新生說明 上課前 課堂上 課後交流 圖書館 體育館 餐廳 課外活動 申請獎助 當助教

轉換學校就讀並且將原先修得學分轉換到新系所必須獲得先前系所主任或所長核可。

(3) 校內就讀期間規定 Residency Requirements

除獨立研究和轉學承認的學分外，學校規定學生需在校內修習數個學期的課程才能畢業。

(4) 碩士學位候選人資格 Candidacy for an Advanced Degree

研究生必須最遲在授予學位前一期被允許成為正式研究生才有碩士學位候選人資格。

(5) 論文規定 Thesis [Project/Dissertation] Requirements

研究報告、論文 (thesis 碩士論文或 dissertation 博士論文) 或特定的系所要求，包含在總學分 (total credit hour requirement) 內，修習 (及被授予之) 學分數在註冊時就已決定。期末時教授授予 R 成績確認研究生之論文學分。在學位被授予之前，學生的永久成績卡必須有論文被接受之紀錄，學生應該注意 (如下列所示) 系所定出之論文相關重要規定。

(6) 論文工作之延續 Continuation of Thesis [Project/Dissertation]

一旦論文工作開始，就被視為延續性的過程直到所有要求被完成。如果研究生已完成其他學位要求之課程而只剩論文，雖然論文未必計入學分，但該生必須完成論文持續註冊 (包含暑期) 並繳交規定之學費，論文完成之時間長短由系所決定；持續註冊保障學生使用所有學校設備服務之資格。如果因不可抗拒因素 (circumstances beyond student's control) 必須中斷論文工作，在教授或系所同意下可以暫時休假 (take an approved leave of absence)；若未持續註冊或未獲得核可便中斷論文寫作，將可能失去研究生資格。

(7) 彙整經驗 Summary Experience

許多研究所委員會 (Graduate Council) 認為研究生必須具備整合各類所學專業知識及經驗 (integrative experience) 之條件，因此各學系研究所雖性質不同，但如全面會考 (comprehensive examination)、報告 (project)、論文口試 (oral examination for the thesis) 及彙總研討會 (summary conference) 等都是常見的考核方式，旨在幫助學生整合全部所學。

(8) 第二學位的重複學分 Overlapping Credit for Second Degree

除非完成第一學位，否則學生不被許可修讀第二學位，某些特定修習第二學位的研究生在系所委員會 (Graduate Committee) 核可下可以將第一學位內的 9 至 12 學分計入第二學位的研究

課程，但前提是這些課程必須是在五年之內修得且是第二學位的必修課。第二學位修習總學分數不可低於 36 學分，如果重複課程導致低於此學分數，該生必須修習其他系所核可課程代替。

(9) 財務情況 Financial Standing

學生必須完全支付學費，否則學校不授予成績單(transcripts)、學位 (degree) 及推薦 (recommendations)。學校在不需事先知會 (without prior notice) 的情形下保有更動學雜費 (tuition and fees) 的權利。

(10) 碩士學位要求匯整 Summary of Requirements for Master's Degree

在極端情形下，具備相當條件之個別研究生可向院長或系所教授提出書面提案申請 (petition) 要求審核授予碩士資格。如果被核可，簽字核可之副本將由註冊組列入該生永久成績內。

(11) 成績定義 Definition of Grades

成績代表修習課程之成果，學期末成績卡記載代表之意義為

A excellent 優

B good 好

C average 中等

D and F 不符合碩士學位所需課程之成績資格

平均成績 GPA(Grade Point Average) 之計算需將字母轉換成點數：

A: 4 點

B: 3 點

C: 2 點

D: 1 點

F: 不算

GPA= 所有積點加總 ÷ 所有學分數加總

研究所學生所有曾經修習課程都計入平均成績，平均成績至少必須達到 B(3.0) 才能達到畢業要求，研究生欲重修課程必須經由該學院院長核可該生之申請才能重修。

其他評量結果，如下所述，不影響 GPA 之計算。

R (Registered): 顯示學生修習論文，為持續性課程但尚未達到要求。論文完成被接受後，論文標題將顯示在成績卡上，學生須繳付論文學分費，R 可計入研究生校內就讀期限規定。

I (Incomplete): 學生因不可抗拒因素未完成該課程時，教授所

預備

校園

選課

新生說明

上課前

課堂上

課後交流

圖書館

體育館

餐廳

課外活動

申請獎助

當助教

給予之暫時成績,如果註冊組未於第二學期末 (包含暑修) 接到成績更動,該生將得到 F 成績。學生須付全部學費。許多學校規定,如果有兩科及以上未完成的科目不能再註冊其他課程。

W(Withdrawn): 學生超過第六週才退選某課或全部課程。

Z(Audit): 顯示學生旁聽過該課,學生必須填寫完整申請表格經過系所旁聽核可,學生不需考試但須繳交半數學分費,旁聽或正式修課可以互換,但是必須在開課 6 天內完成手續,旁聽不計在校內就讀期間規定,不計入 GPA,也不計入學位要求。

X(Credit by Examination): 如果學生成功通過符合系所目標及課程內容相關之各類校外或機構考試,學生事先在註冊某既定課程時就可以得到 X,研究所最多允許 12 學分授予 X 成績,超過此學分數必須以書面提案之方式由院長核可。

W(Waived): 已經修習之課程或許可以抵免,但總修習學分不得低於 45,可抵免課程僅限於必修課程,抵免課程與修習替代課程是兩回事,勿搞混。

(12) 更改成績 Changing Grades

除非是真正計算或紀錄錯誤,否則成績一經交付,無人有權更改。要更正錯誤,教授必須完成表格經由系所核可,再送到註冊組,其中牽涉到學術行為委員會 (Academic Conduct Committee) 爭議成績進行之決議過程,最後決議 (final appeal) 會被送到學術評議委員會 (Institute Hearing and Appeals Board)。

(13) 留校察看及吊銷 Academic Probation and Suspension

任何學生在修習 12 學分後,若無法達到 GPA 3.0,將被留校察看並且由系所輔導教授討論該生是否繼續攻讀研究所,被留校察看之學生必須在 12 學分內提高累計 GPA (cumulative GPA) 到 3.0,否則研究所課程將被吊銷。萬一研究生因學術表現欠佳失去就讀資格,學生仍可以適當理由及表現向該學院院長申請再度入學 (readmission)。

3. 學生行為標準 Standards for Student Conduct

大學校園旨在提供學生自己負責的學習機會,學生當然必須有高度自治能力,並能鼓勵他人正向行為及防止對教育產生負面價值或行為,學生在高標準的專業學習中自我發展,以期將來貢獻社會。

美國大學組成分子向來融合多族群、背景、生活方式及個人價值的多樣性,然而學生必須遵守學校政策、規定並尊重不同人士保有他

們價值觀念的權利。各大學明訂學生權益責任的手冊說明校規及其所期待的學生行為標準；所有學生不管背景如何、來自何方，應該明白他們現在在在美求學，是大學所在當地、州及聯邦的一分子，身為學生或暫時居民都必須守法，沒有例外。

3.7 逛逛系辦
Wandering around the Department Office

A: 嗨，這是區域研究課程的主要辦公室嗎？

A: Hi. Is this the main office for the Area Studies program?

B: 是的，你是新生嗎？

B: Yes, it is. Are you a new student?

A: 是的。

A: Yes, I am.

B: 我是系上的總祕書，我是瑪麗賽姆斯。

B: I'm the head secretary for the department. My name is Mary Simms.

A: 我是山姆林。

A: I'm Sam Lin.

B: 請進，學生大廳在穿過那個門那裡，你也可以用接待室。

B: Please come in. The student lounge is over there through that door. You can use this reception room as well.

A: 系上這裡有任何學生可以用的電腦嗎？

A: Does the department have any computers students can use here?

預備
校園
選課
新生說明
上課前
課堂上
課後交流
圖書館
體育館
餐廳
課外活動
申請獎助
當助教

B: 有，二樓有一個專供區域研究學生使用的電腦資訊區。

B: Yes. The second floor has a computer resource area just for Area Studies students.

A: 我們何時可使用？

A: When can we use it?

B: 週一至週五早上 8 點到晚上 11 點。

B: It's open from 8 a.m. until 11 p.m., Monday through Friday.

A: 那週末呢？

A: What about weekends?

B: 沒有。週末只有一樓開放，但是一樓有無線上網。

B: No. Only the first floor is open on weekends. However, the first floor has wireless Internet access.

A: 所以我們可以在週末使用。

A: So we can use it during the weekend?

B: 是的，但我要看你的學生證，然後才給你連線密碼。

B: Yes, but I'll need to see your student I.D. card, then I can assign you the access code.

A: 好，我們可以在這裡吃東西嗎？

A: OK. Can we eat in here?

B: 可以，你可以在這裡的任何地方進食，除了電腦室。

B: Certainly. You can have food in here anywhere, except the computer room.

A: 我看到大廳有電視。

A: I see a TV in the lounge.

預備
校園
選課
新生說明
上課前
課堂上
課後交流
圖書館
體育館
餐廳
課外活動
申請獎助
當助教

B: 是的，學生常進來看電影，那裡也有 DVD 放影機。

B: Yes. Students often come in and watch movies on it. There is a DVD player too.

A: 還有什麼我該知道的嗎？

A: Is there anything else I should know?

B: 我來帶你多逛一些，你得知道會議室以及研究生助理辦公室在哪。

B: Let me show you around more. You need to know where the meeting rooms and graduate assistants' offices are.

A: 謝謝你的幫忙。

A: Thanks for all your help.

B: 不客氣。

B: No problem.

Word Bank 字庫

area studies n. 區域研究
head secretary n. 總祕書
student lounge n. 學生大廳
reception room n. 接待室
wireless Internet access n. 無線上網
access code n. 連線密碼
meeting room n. 會議室
graduate assistant n. 研究生助理

Useful Phrases 實用語句

1. 嗨！這是區域研究課程的主要辦公室嗎？

   Hi. Is this the main office for the Area Studies program?

預備

校園

選課

新生說明

上課前

課堂上

課後交流

圖書館

體育館

餐廳

課外活動

申請獎助

當助教

2. 系上這裡有任何學生可以用的電腦嗎？

Does the department have any computers students can use here?

3. 我們可以在這裡吃東西嗎？

Can we eat in here?

4. 還有什麼我該知道的嗎？

Is there anything else I should know?

3.8 會見新同學
Meeting Other Students

Dialog 對話

A: 哈囉，我是山姆林。

A: Hello. I'm Sam Lin.

B: 嗨，很高興認識你，我是安迪丹尼森。

B: Hi. I'm pleased to meet you. I'm Andy Denison.

A: 安迪你從哪裡來？

A: Where are you from, Andy?

B: 我是俄亥俄人，你呢？

B: I'm a native of Ohio. How about you?

A: 我從香港來。

A: I'm from Hong Kong.

B: 酷，你來美國多久了？

B: Cool. How long have you been in America?

A: 只有兩個月。

A: Only two months.

B: 嗯,我來這個州只有三個月。

B: Well, I've only been in this state for three months myself.

A: 你喜歡這裡嗎?

A: Do you like it here?

B: 目前為止還不錯,你覺得這地方如何?

B: So far so good. What do you think of the place?

A: 我覺得不錯。

A: It seems OK to me.

B: 嘿,你知道明晚有系派對嗎?

B: Hey. Do you know there is a department party tomorrow night?

A: 不知道。

A: No.

B: 你該來,只有我們系上的學生,而且我們有機會認識其他學生和一些研究生。

B: You should come. It's just for students in our program, and it will give us a chance to meet other students in the program and meet some of the grad students too.

預備
校園
選課
新生說明
上課前
課堂上
課後交流
圖書館
體育館
餐廳
課外活動
申請獎助
當助教

A: 聽來不錯,在哪裡還有何時呢?

A: Sounds like a good idea. Where and when?

B: 學生中心 320 室,應該會在晚上 7 點左右開始。

B: The Student Center. Room 320. It's supposed to start around seven o'clock in the evening.

A: 我在那裡見你了。

A: I'll see you there.

B: 好。

B: Great.

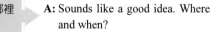

Word Bank 字庫

> department party n. 系派對
> grad [graduate] student n. 研究生
> be supposed to 應該

Useful Phrases 實用語句

1. 嗨,我的名字是珊蒂,你呢?

   Hi, my name is Sandy. What's yours?

2. 我來自臺灣。

   I'm from Taiwan. / I come from Taiwan.

3. 很高興認識你。

   I'm pleased to meet you. / It's nice to meet you.

4. 我主修護理。

   My major is Nursing.

5. 我正在主修物理。

   I'm majoring in Physics.

6. 我剛到這裡,住在學校宿舍。

   I'm new here. I live in the school dormitory.

7. 你在這裡長大嗎？

Did you grow up here?

8. 你熟悉這個城鎮嗎？

Do you know this town well?

9. 我可以問你關於這裡的事嗎？

Is it ok if I ask you about things around here?

Notes 小叮嚀

　　在國外求學、交朋友，最好能主動與人打招呼，與人多互動交流，一回生兩回熟，朋友和同學可以幫助我們融入異地生活。許多當地學生對來自不同文化的人難免怕隔閡或表達錯誤，並不會主動來打招呼或認識，這時我們如果還是被動害羞的話就會感覺孤立沒有朋友，在國外是很痛苦的 (如有教會的同學希望能引領你，可能會主動找你上教會，如果你對教會沒興趣，不妨自己有其他信仰)，當然好的、互相切磋關照的朋友或同學能激發自己學習潛力，豐富學生生活。

預備
校園
選課
新生說明
上課前
課堂上
課後交流
圖書館
體育館
餐廳
課外活動
申請獎助
當助教

Unit 4 Before Class

上課前

在美國就學，學習態度要主動積極，課前預習 (preview)、課後複習 (review)，在課堂上必須適時表達意見，這些都需要足夠的語言能力才能漸入佳境。

上課一定要準時，教授通常會在打上課鐘之前就已進教室準備，鐘響後隨即上課，因此務必提早進教室。準時也是美國人重視的習慣，上課後才進教室的同學，免不了會受到不必要的注目，一旦開始上課當然不可隨意離開教室或使用手機。

預備 校園 選課 新生說明 上課前 課堂上 課後交流 圖書館 體育館 餐廳 課外活動 申請獎助 當助教

4.1 尋找教室
Looking for the Classroom

Dialog 1 對話1

A: 對不起，我想找魏爾曼樓 406 室。

A: Excuse me. I'm trying to find 406, Villman Hall.

B: 喔，你找錯棟了，這裡是喜爾曼樓。

B: Oh. You are in the wrong building. This is Hillman Hall.

A: 了解了，魏爾曼樓在哪裡？

A: I see. Where is Villman Hall?

B: 從這窗戶看出去，在這棟正對面。

B: It's directly across from this building. Look out the window here.

A: 是那棟嗎？

A: Is that it?

B: 是的，現在你知道為什麼迷路了，對吧？

B: Yes. Now you know how you got lost, right?

A: 是啊，那棟看起來就像這棟。

A: Yes. It looks just like this building.

B: 對，除了它們裡面不一樣之外。

B: Right. Except they are different on the inside.

A: 所以這一棟沒有 406 室。

A: So there is no room 406 in this building.

B: 沒錯。

B: That's right.

A: 謝謝你的幫忙。

A: Thanks for your help.

B: 沒什麼。

B: No problem.

Dialog 2 對話2

A: 對不起，406 室在哪裡？

A: Excuse me. Where is room 406?

B: 這裡是 3 樓，所以再往上走一樓。

B: This is the third floor, so go up one more level.

A: 是下一層嗎？

A: It's on the next floor?

B: 是，所以它是 4 開頭。

B: Yes. That's why its number starts with a four.

A: 我懂了，謝謝。

A: I see. Thanks.

預備
校園
選課
新生說明
上課前
課堂上
課後交流
圖書館
體育館
餐廳
課外活動
申請獎助
當助教

B: 沒問題。 → **B:** Sure.

Dialog 3 對話3

A: 對不起，我找不到 406 室。 → **A:** Excuse me. I can't find room 406.

B: 它有點難找，從這走廊往前走再左轉，在右手邊找一條很短的走廊，在那走廊的盡頭你會看到兩扇門，406 在左邊。

B: It's a little hard to find. Go down this hallway, turn left, and look for another very short hallway on your right. At the end of that hallway, you'll see two doors. 406 is the one on the left.

A: 好，走這走廊，找到一條短走廊，繼續走，走到左邊門。 → **A:** OK. Down this hallway, look for a short hallway, go down it, and go to the door on the left.

B: 答對了。 → **B:** You got it.

A: 謝謝。 → **A:** Thanks.

Word Bank 字庫

hall [hɔl] n. 樓，廳
hallway [`hɔl͵we] n. 走廊

Useful Phrases 實用語句

1. 從這走廊往前走再左轉。

   Go down this hallway, turn left.

2. 在右手邊找一條很短的走廊。

   Look for a short hallway on your right.

3. 在那走廊的盡頭你會看到兩扇門。

   At the end of that hallway you'll see two doors.

4. 走到左邊門。

   Go to the door on the left.

4.2 教室變動
Classroom Change

Dialog 1 對話1

A: 就這裡了,234室。

A: Here it is. Room 234.

B: 這裡沒人。

B: There is nobody here.

A: 好奇怪啊。

A: That's strange.

B: 我們看錯課表了嗎?

B: Did we read the schedule incorrectly?

A: 查一下(查課表),不,應該是這裡。

A: Let's check. (looks at the schedule) No. It ought to be here.

預備

校園

選課

新生說明

上課前

課堂上

課後交流

圖書館

體育館

餐廳

課外活動

申請獎助

當助教

B: 也許他們換教室了。

B: Maybe they changed the room.

A: 如果換教室，門上應該有公告。

A: There should be a sign on the door if the room has been changed.

B: 看！他們寫在黑板上。

B: Look. They wrote it on the blackboard instead.

A: 喔，好吧，它寫說這堂課改到334室。

A: Oh. OK. It says this class has been moved to room 334.

B: 那我們要往上走一樓。

B: We need to go up one floor then.

A: 對。

A: Right.

📖 Useful Phrases　實用語句

1. 如果換教室，門上應該有公告。

   There should be a sign on the door if the room has been changed.

2. 我們要往上走一樓。

   We need to go up one floor.

Dialog 2　對話2

A: 看來這堂課被換到別處了。

A: It looks like this class has been moved to someplace else?

B: 是,但是換到哪裡呢?

B: Yes, but where?

A: 我不知道,到處都沒有指示。

A: I don't know. There is no indication anywhere.

B: 我們要打給系辦。

B: We'll have to call the department office.

A: 對,或是教務處。

A: Yes, or academic affairs.

B: 我們也可以上網查。

B: We could check online too.

A: 對,我想這些地方都可以告訴我們這課調到哪了。

A: Yes. I believe any of those places can tell us where the class has been moved to.

Word Bank 字庫

room [classroom] change n. 教室變動

sign [saɪn] n. 公告,指示

indication [ˌɪndə`keʃən] n. 指示

academic affairs n. 教務處

預備 校園 選課 新生說明 上課前 課堂上 課後交流 圖書館 體育館 餐廳 課外活動 申請獎助 當助教

4.3 打電話詢問教室變動
Phoning about a Classroom Change

Dialog 對話

A: 哈囉，教務處，我可以幫你嗎？

A: Hello, Academic Affairs. May I help you?

B: 哈囉，我有一個關於教室變動的問題。

B: Hello. I have a question about a room change.

A: 哪堂課？

A: Which class?

B: 艾克邁教授的全球議題課。

B: Professor Akerman's Global Issues class.

A: 那裡沒有公告告訴學生變動嗎？

A: Isn't there a sign telling students about the change?

B: 沒有。

B: No, there is not.

A: 課號是幾號？

A: What is the number of that class?

B: SS 211。

B: SS 211.

A: 課被調到葛瑞福樓 225 室。

A: It's been moved to Graft Hall, room 225.

B: 好,謝謝,我們要回去將教室變動寫在黑板上嗎?

B: OK. Thank you. Should we go back and write the room change on the board?

A: 不,我會叫人去做。

A: No. I'll call someone to do that.

B: 好。

B: OK.

Word Bank 字庫

global issues n. 全球議題

Useful Phrases 實用語句

1. 我有一個關於教室變動的問題。

   I have a question about a room change.

2. 課被調到葛瑞福樓 225 室。

   It's been moved to Graft Hall, room 225.

3. 我們要回去將教室變動寫在黑板上嗎?

   Should we go back and write the room change on the board?

4.4 在教室內
In the Classroom

早到的時候看看筆記或和同學打招呼,人在國外本來就是少數族裔,有時老美不見得知道如何與你互動,主動與人結交朋友(當然選擇友善溫和的人),即使語言能力尚待加強又何妨,如能獲得友誼並提升語言能力及了解國外生活,何樂不為?找合適的同學加入讀書會,更是求學之路不可或缺的重要活動。

預備
校園
選課
新生說明
上課前
課堂上
課後交流
圖書館
體育館
餐廳
課外活動
申請獎助
當助教

預備
校園
選課
新生說明
上課前
課堂上
課後交流
圖書館
體育館
餐廳
課外活動
申請獎助
當助教

Dialog 對話

A: 這裡有人坐嗎？

A: Is anyone sitting here?

B: 沒有，隨便坐吧。

B: No. Go ahead and use it.

A: 對不起（我不懂）。

A: Excuse me?

B: 喔，我是說請坐。

B: Oh. I mean please sit down.

A: 我懂了，抱歉，我剛沒弄懂。

A: I see. Sorry. I didn't understand.

B: 沒關係，我是傑瑞塔克，你的名字是？

B: No problem. I'm Jerry Tucker. What's your name?

A: 我是吉姆徐。

A: I'm Jim Hsu.

B: 很高興認識你，你以前上過這個教授的課嗎？

B: Nice to meet you. Have you had this professor before?

A: 沒有，你呢？

A: No, I haven't. What about you?

B: 有，我認為他不錯，容易理解而且有耐性。

B: Yes. I think he's not bad. He's easy to understand and patient.

A: 聽起來很好，我可能需要問問題。

A: That sounds good. I may need to ask questions.

B: 喔，沒問題，多數教授喜歡那樣。

B: Oh, no problem. Most of the professors like that.

A: 英語不是我的母語，所以我想這對我很重要。

A: I'm not a native English speaker, so I think it's important for me.

B: 好，如果你有哪裡不懂，你也可以問我。

B: Well, if there is something you don't understand, you can ask me too.

A: 謝謝。

A: Thank you.

B: 很高興幫忙，你應該也要加入讀書會。

B: Glad to help. You should get into one of our student study groups too.

A: 什麼意思？

A: What do you mean?

B: 我是說我們碰面複習一週課程時，你可以加入我們或其他學生。

B: I mean you should join us or other students when we meet to go over the lessons of the week.

A: 你確定我會受到歡迎？

A: Are you sure I'd be welcome?

預備 校園 選課 新生說明 上課前 課堂上 課後交流 圖書館 體育館 餐廳 課外活動 申請獎助 當助教

預備
校園
選課
新生說明
上課前
課堂上
課後交流
圖書館
體育館
餐廳
課外活動
申請獎助
當助教

B: 當然，如果你擔心你的語言能力，別擔心，那不是問題，我們想要與國際學生會面。

B: Of course. If you are worried about your language ability, don't. It's no problem. We want to meet the international students.

A: 那很棒，謝謝你邀請我。

A: That's great. Thanks for inviting me.

B: 這是我的榮幸。

B: My pleasure.

Word Bank 字庫

native English speaker n. 以英語為母語的人
study group n. 讀書會

Useful Phrases 實用語句

1. 這裡有人坐嗎？

   Is anyone sitting here? / Is this seat taken?

2. 你以前上過這個教授的課嗎？

   Have you had this professor before?

3. 我可能需要問問題。

   I may need to ask questions.

4. 多數教授喜歡那樣。

   Most of the professors like that.

5. 英語不是我的母語，所以我想這對我很重要。

   I'm not a native English speaker, so I think it's important for me.

預備

校園

選課

新生說明

上課前

課堂上

課後交流

圖書館

體育館

餐廳

課外活動

申請獎助

當助教

6. 你確定我會受到歡迎？

   Are you sure I'd be welcome?

7. 謝謝你邀請我。

   Thanks for inviting me.

4.5 與同學對話
Chatting with Classmates

除了語言能力外，有些在美國學習的亞洲學生也要克服文化差異及個性問題，亞洲群體社會裡注重謙卑與藏鋒，而美國個人主義的社會講究能力的表現與自信，兩者恰巧背道而馳。因此害羞、內向、安靜、扭捏依賴、話話含在嘴裡的個性在美國求學絕對是行不通的，不了解亞洲文化的人還會以為這樣的人心理有問題。多數會決定出國讀書的同學可能不至於如此，但在國外要克服開口障礙，就要找對象切磋談話，學習美國文化裡大方、侃侃而談的自信，為課堂發言增加磨練的機會，也可了解校園生活及其他事情。

 Dialog 對話

| A: 嗨，傑瑞，最近忙什麼？ | A: Hi, Jerry. What's up? |

| B: 沒什麼，珍，你呢？ | B: Not much, Jane. What about you? |

| A: 我在做傑克森教授的報告。 | A: I'm working on Professor Jackson's paper. |

| B: 做得如何？ | B: How is it going? |

預備 校園 選課 新生說明 **上課前** 課堂上 課後交流 圖書館 體育館 餐廳 課外活動 申請獎助 當助教

A: 我想還好，但某些部分我不確定。

A: OK, I think, but I'm not sure about some parts of it.

B: 我知道你的意思，我寫不出我想要說的。

B: I know what you mean. I have trouble writing what I want to say.

A: 對，寫作很難，你其他課怎麼樣？

A: Yeah, writing is tough. How are your other classes going?

B: 目前為止很好，但我不喜歡統計。

B: Pretty well so far. I don't like statistics though.

A: 我上學期修過，它對我也很難。

A: I took that last term. It's hard for me too.

B: 我想我要去和研究生助理談談。

B: I'll have to go talk to the graduate assistant I think.

A: 應該是個好主意。

A: Probably a good idea.

✎ Word Bank 字庫

tough [tʌf] adj. 很難的
graduate assistant n. 研究生助理
statistics [stə`tɪstɪks] n. 統計

📖 Useful Phrases 實用語句

1. 你其他課怎麼樣？

   How are your other classes going?

2. 我寫不出我想要說的。

  I have trouble writing what I want to say.

3. 我想我要去和研究生助理談談。

  I'll have to go talk to the graduate assistant I think.

Notes 小叮嚀

　　除了了解教材及課外書籍內容之外，美國人強調創新和批判性的見解 (creative and critical thinking/feedback)，而不是重複或抄襲教材、課外書裡的意見，抄襲的報告可是會讓自己被退學的，而且是嚴重的學術紀錄，因此對於老師的要求如有不了解應該要弄懂，對於報告的格式，引用出處的標號、註解、書目錄必要謹慎處理，如果可以在做報告時就先拿給老師過目請教看法，再修正報告會是比較好的作法。

4.6 與同學小聚放鬆
Relaxing Activity with Classmates

Dialog 對話

A: 這週末你要做什麼？

A: What are you doing this weekend?

B: 讀書吧，但我想我週六晚上會去「凱蒂角落」。

B: Studying mostly. But I think I'll go to the Katty Corner on Saturday night.

A: 為何？

A: How come?

B: 他們那晚有一些現場樂團，而且不收娛樂費。

B: They're going to have a couple of live bands that night, and there is no cover charge.

預備
校園
選課
新生說明
上課前
課堂上
課後交流
圖書館
體育館
餐廳
課外活動
申請獎助
當助教

A: 真的嗎？聽來很棒，跟誰去呢？

A: Really? Sounds good. Going with anybody?

B: 貝瑞也會去，我想雪莉也會在。

B: Barry is going, too, and I think Shirley will be there.

A: 我想我不認識雪莉。

A: I don't think I know Shirley.

B: 沒關係，來加入我們，會很好玩。

B: No big deal. Come join us. It'll be fun.

A: 你們何時會在那裡？

A: When are you going to be there?

B: 我不確定，大約9點左右。

B: I'm not sure, but probably around 9:00.

A: 酷，我會去。

A: Cool. I'll be there.

B: 給我你的手機，如果有任何改變，我會打電話給你。

B: Give me your cell number. I'll call you in case anything changes.

A: 我們現在來打給對方，這樣我們可以在電話裡儲存彼此的電話。

A: Let's call each other right now, so we can store each other's numbers in our phones.

B: 好點子。

B: Good idea.

Word Bank 字庫

cell number **n.** 手機
live band **n.** 樂團
cover charge **n.** 娛樂費

Notes 小叮嚀

　　如果美國朋友或同學說「We should get together some time.」，但卻沒下文，別覺得沮喪，在美國文化裡，這並不代表邀請。如果你想跟同學處得較熱絡，倒是可以主動邀請一起聚會，提議或邀約也不代表你要付帳，而是各付各的。

4.7 有關是否與教授談話
About Talking to a Professor or Not

4.7a 與同學討論問題
Talking about problems with a fellow student

Dialog 對話

A: 我錯過四星期的課，因為家裡有緊急事故，我必須飛回家。

A: I missed four weeks of class because I had to fly home suddenly due to a family emergency.

B: 你已跟你的教授們談過嗎？

B: Have you spoken to your professors yet?

A: 沒有，我怕那麼做。

A: No. I'm scared of doing that.

預備
校園
選課
新生說明
上課前
課堂上
課後交流
圖書館
體育館
餐廳
課外活動
申請獎助
當助教

B: 真的嗎？為什麼？

B: Really? Why?

A: 我怕他們會生我的氣，或他們會因為文化差異而不懂造成我缺課的原因。

A: I'm afraid they'll be mad at me, or maybe they won't understand the cultural differences between us that made me miss the classes.

B: 你不應該擔心這些事。

B: You shouldn't worry about those things.

A: 我該怎麼做？

A: What should I do?

B: 打電話預約時間，想好你要怎麼說，從課表了解教授已經上過什麼。

B: Call and make an appointment, plan what you need to say, and find out what the professor had talked about from his or her syllabus.

A: 好建議，我還該做什麼嗎？

A: That's good advice. What else do you think I ought to do?

B: 見面別遲到並且感謝他們的幫忙。

B: Don't be late for the appointment and be sure to thank them for their help.

A: 好，我會做到。

A: OK. I'll do it.

B: 最好（如此），否則你課業會更落後。

B: You'd better. Otherwise you'll fall even further behind in your studies.

✎ Word Bank 字庫

family emergency n. 家庭緊急事故
cultural differences n. 文化差異
advice [əd`vaɪs] n. 建議，忠告
fall behind 落後

📖 Useful Phrases 實用語句

1. 因為家裡有緊急事故，我必須飛回家。

   I had to fly home suddenly due to a family emergency.

2. 我怕他們不懂我們之間的文化差異。

   I'm afraid they won't understand the cultural differences between us.

3. 想好你要怎麼說。

   Plan what you need to say.

4. 從課表了解教授已經上過什麼。

   Find out what the professor had talked about from the syllabus.

5. 你覺得我還該做什麼嗎？

   What else do you think I ought to do?

預備
校園
選課
新生說明
上課前
課堂上
課後交流
圖書館
體育館
餐廳
課外活動
申請獎助
當助教

4.7b 與教授約時間見面
Making an Appointment to See a Professor

Dialog 對話

A: 數學系，我可以為你效勞嗎？

A: Math department. May I help you?

B: 可以，我是南施胡，我想約見雅各教授。

B: Yes. My name is Nancy Hu. I would like to make an appointment to see Professor Jacobs.

A: 我查一下他的行事曆（幾秒鐘後），他明天下午 2 點可以。

A: Let me check his schedule. (after a few seconds) He's available at 2 in the afternoon tomorrow.

B: 星期三嗎？那時我有課，我可以在其他時間見他嗎？

B: Wednesday? I have a class then. Is there another time I can see him?

A: 可以，隔一天 1 點如何？

A: Yes. How about 1 the following day?

B: 可以。

B: That will be fine.

A: 好，請再說一次你的名字。

A: All right. Say your name again, please.

B: 南施胡。

B: Nancy Hu.

預備

校園

選課

新生說明

上課前

課堂上

課後交流

圖書館

體育館

餐廳

課外活動

申請獎助

當助教

A: 你的姓拼法是 Hu 嗎？

A: Is your last name spelled Hu?

B: 是的，正確。

B: Yes, that is correct.

A: 好，我已在他行事曆的星期四 1 點寫上你的名字。

A: OK. I've written your name into his schedule for 1 on Thursday.

B: 多謝。

B: Thank you very much.

A: 不客氣。

A: You're welcome.

Word Bank 字庫

available [ə`veləbl] adj. 有空的

Useful Phrases 實用語句

1. 我想約見雅各教授。

   I would like to make an appointment to see Professor Jacobs.

2. 我可以在其他時間見他嗎？

   Is there another time I can see him?

3. 隔一天 1 點如何？

   How about 1:00 the following day?

4.7c 與教授談缺課
Talking to a Professor about Missing Classes

預備　校園　選課　新生說明　上課前　課堂上　課後交流　圖書館　體育館　餐廳　課外活動　申請獎助　當助教

Dialog 對話

A: 哈囉，雅各教授，我是南施胡。

A: Hello, Professor Jacobs. I'm Nancy Hu.

B: 南施，請進來坐下。

B: Nancy, please come in and sit down.

A: 首先，我要為錯過這麼多課道歉，我因為家人過世而必須突然回家。

A: First, I'd like to apologize for missing so many classes. I had to fly home suddenly because of a death in my family.

B: 我很遺憾聽到這樣，我希望一切沒問題。

B: I'm sorry to hear this. I hope things are OK.

A: 嗯，但是我的學業不妙，我錯過許多堂課。

A: Well, my studies are not OK. I missed many classes.

B: 嗯，我們看看，過去幾週我講解百年戰爭的歐洲。

B: Well, let's see. The last few weeks I've been lecturing about Europe during the time of the 100 years war.

A: 是的，我查過你的課表並且和一些學生談過話，我也買了一些學生服務部門學生記的筆記。

A: Yes. I checked your syllabus and talked to some of the other students. I also bought the notes taken by the student services department.

B: 好，你自己已經趕上來了，很好。

B: Great. You've been catching up on your own. Wonderful!

A: 我有一些關於講課教材及作業的特殊問題。

A: I have some specific questions about the lecture material and the assignment you gave.

B: 請繼續，我很樂意幫你。

B: Please continue. I'm more than glad to help you.

Word Bank 字庫

apologize [ə`pɑlə͵dʒaɪz] v. 道歉
catch up on 趕上
specific [spɪ`sɪfɪk] adj. 特殊的；明確的

Tips 小祕訣

　　準時是美國文化，許多教授雖然沒有規定強制出席，但還是要盡可能每次都準時出席，如果必須缺課，禮貌上要能先知會教授。學生服務中心 (Student Services) 提供學生學業以及娛樂方面的服務，除一般影印服務，有些學校的服務中心還提供某些課的筆記及講義，此外，也出售演唱會門票、舞蹈或校園電影之夜門票，服務中心還有電影光碟、電腦螢幕、撞球桌及其他娛樂設備。

預備
校園
選課
新生說明
上課前
課堂上
課後交流
圖書館
體育館
餐廳
課外活動
申請獎助
當助教

Useful Phrases 實用語句

1. 我要為缺課道歉。

   I'd like to apologize for missing classes.

2. 我的學業不妙，我錯過許多堂課。

   My studies are not OK. I missed many classes.

3. 我有一些關於講課教材的特殊問題。

   I have some specific questions about the lecture material.

4. 我有一些關於作業的特殊問題。

   I have some specific questions about the assignment you gave.

Information Bank 大補帖

見教授機宜 Preparing Youself to Seek Help from a Professor

　　很少有大學生或研究生在就學時不找教授幫忙，事實上，適時請教教授是必要的，而不是拖到問題變得更嚴重。

1. 為何尋求幫忙？

　　如有下列情形，你需要找教授談話：

   (1) 規定或進度需要釐清

   (2) 對作業規定不了解

   (3) 因病導致課程落後

   (4) 考試或作業失敗，不懂課程內容

   (5) 需要主修科目諮詢

   (6) 助教公告輔導時間找不到助教

2. 為何學生逃避教授協助？

   (1) 因為他們困窘、害怕或生性害羞

   (2) 避免與權威者接觸

   (3) 害怕問到笨問題

   (4) 感覺錯過幾堂課失去連結

   (5) 害怕與教授衝突

   (6) 與不同年齡、性別、種族或文化的教授接近而不安

　　如果你以學生本分依照學業進度學習 (尤其如果是想要進研究所)，一定要把害怕的心態擺一邊，尋求協助。那要怎樣與教授一對一會面呢？

3. 禮貌地與教授接觸

(1) 聯繫

決定適合的聯繫方式，查詢課程表中教授所指示最佳聯繫方式，先問自己這件事是否要緊，如果是的話，打電話或在辦公室時間去找他可能是最合邏輯的步驟。否則，你可以試試電子郵件，等個幾天查看回覆 (記住教書雖是教授的職業，但不要期待教授會在晚上、週末或假日回覆郵件)。

(2) 計畫

查詢課程表中教授的辦公室時間及規定，再提出你的要求，如果教授要求你某時來，盡可能按照他 [她] 方便的時間見面 (例如：辦公室時間)。不要要求教授另外挪時間配合你，因為除了上課外，他們仍有許多繁重的任務 (例如：許多系務、校務會議和研究與學術服務)。

(3) 詢問

詢問是了解你教授偏好的最佳方式，可以這麼說：「 史密斯教授，我需要幾分鐘請您幫我了解一個關於 _____ 的問題，現在是否方便呢，或是我們可以安排更方便的時間？ 」(Professor Smith, I need a few minutes of your time so that you can help me with a question [problem] I'm having with _____. Is this a good time, or can we set up something that is more convenient for you?) 要簡短直指重點。

4. 準備見面

見面前思緒整理妥當 (及所有的教材)，準備好讓自己可以敘述及回答，準備與教授有好的互動，到達會面時要有自信。

(1) 問題

如果你對見教授感到緊張，事先準備一張清單，要有效率並且試著在一次見面完成所有事情，而不是重複來回問更多問題。

(2) 教材

如果有關於課程的特殊問題，帶著你的課程筆記及課表，才會有詳細的資料。如果你需要參考教科書，要事先將頁數標示出來以便快速查詢。

(3) 筆記

來時要準備好記筆記，紙筆兼備，筆記會幫你記錄並記得教授對問題的回答，當然也避免了下次在課堂問出相同的問題。

5. 會面時

(1) 準時

要準時，準時意謂尊重教授的時間，勿早到或晚到，多數教授時間壓力很大，如果你必須再次見教授，確認你遵守以上的建議。

(2) 稱謂

除非教授有交代，否則要稱呼教授適當的 稱謂 (Professor, Doctor)。

(3) 致謝

永遠感謝教授與你見面及他的時間，並明確說出你對他幫忙說明部分的感謝，如此才能保持將來會面之門敞開。

Talking to a Professor:

Unit 5 In Class

課堂上

美國的學校是個開放的學習環境，強調引導下的創造性，要求學生展現積極主動求知的精神。上課氣氛通常是輕鬆的，師生彼此尊重，雖然課程不同，教授也會有不同的參與規定，事先預習、課後複習等學生本分務必做到，課堂上教授期待並鼓勵學生在適當時間經常主動舉手發表自己的意見或提出問題，當然言之有物、融會貫通，甚至更進一步挑戰既定觀念提出獨立思辯、批判的看法就更難能可貴。

5.1 詢問課程規定
Asking about Class Requirements

學生必須了解課程規定，除了教授當面說明，通常學校課程目錄會有資料，網路上也會解答許多問題。國際學生可能要直接問教授有關課程規定的問題，當然要查教授辦公室時間並預約和教授見面，先準備好有關課程規定問題再去問教授。

Dialog 對話

A: 哈囉，安德生教授。

A: Hello, Professor Anderson.

B: 嗨，請進來坐下。

B: Hi. Come in and sit down.

A: 謝謝。

A: Thank you.

B: 我怎麼幫你呢？

B: How may I help you?

A: 我想問關於設計230的規定。

A: I want to ask about your requirements for Design 230.

B: 當然，首先有出席的規定，每一期我只允許學生缺課三次。

B: Sure. First, there are attendance requirements. I only allow students to miss three classes per term.

A: 如果因為緊急事件而缺席更多次呢？

A: What if a student must miss more because of an emergency?

B: 那要交給我有關於造成缺席事件由醫生或其他相關權威簽名的正式文件。

B: Then an official document signed by a doctor, or some other authority relevant to the event that caused the absence, must be presented to me.

A: 我了解了。

A: I see.

B: 至於作業，你要做一份素描日誌，並且每四週交一次，還有期中及期末筆試。

B: As for assignments, there is a sketch journal that you must keep and hand in every four weeks, and there is a written Midterm and Final examination.

A: 有小考嗎？

A: Are there any quizzes?

B: 沒有，這門課也沒有報告。

B: No. There are no papers for this class either.

A: 有其他加分機會嗎？

A: Are there any extra credit opportunities?

B: 有，那些想加分的人可以為我大一新生的課程做一份符合我要求的口頭報告。

B: Yes. Giving a PowerPoint presentation to my freshman class that meets my requirements is available for those that want extra credit.

A: 謝謝。

A: Thank you.

Word Bank 字庫

attendance [ə`tɛndəns] n. 出席
official document n. 正式文件
authority [ə`θɔrətɪ] n. 權威
relevant [`rɛləvənt] adj. 相關的
sketch journal n. 素描日誌

Useful Phrases 實用語句

1. 我想問關於設計 230 的規定。

   I want to ask about your requirements for Design 230.

2. 如果因為緊急事件而缺席更多堂呢？

   What if a student must miss more because of an emergency?

3. 有小考嗎？

   Are there any quizzes?

4. 有其他加分機會嗎？

   Are there any extra credit opportunities?

5. 有出席的規定。

   There are attendance requirements.

預備 | 校園 | 選課 | 新生說明 | 上課前 | 課堂上 | 課後交流 | 圖書館 | 體育館 | 餐廳 | 課外活動 | 申請獎助 | 當助教

6. 醫生簽名的正式文件要交給我。

An official document signed by a doctor must be presented to me.

7. 你要做一分素描日誌。

There is a sketch journal that you must keep.

8. 你每四週要交一次素描日誌。

You must hand in the journal every four weeks.

Notes 小叮嚀

　　教授對於學生稱呼他們名字通常很隨性，但是在一開始一定要按照禮貌及學術規矩稱他們＿＿＿＿＿教授，通常他們過一陣子可能會告訴你可以稱呼你可以稱呼他們名字就好，當然不同教授有不同脾氣或喜好，所以一開始就要按照規矩才不會冒犯任何人。中文裡習慣使用的「老師」或英文版的 Teacher (name)，在美國並不適用。Teacher 是職業名稱，並非稱謂。稱呼大學教師是 Dr. / Prof. (last name)，在高中或語言學校老師的稱謂是 Mr. / Ms. (last name)。

5.2 詢問作業規定
Asking about Assignment Requirements

Dialog 1 對話1

A: 瓊斯教授，我可以問幾個關於課程的問題嗎？

A: Professor Jones, may I ask a few questions about the class?

B: 當然可以。

B: Yes, of course.

A: 我不確定我了解學期報告規定。

A: I'm not sure I understand the term paper requirement.

預備｜校園｜選課｜新生說明｜上課前｜課堂上｜課後交流｜圖書館｜體育館｜餐廳｜課外活動｜申請獎助｜當助教

B: 好，我來解釋，規定是你寫一個約 10 到 15 頁長的報告。

B: OK. Let me explain. The requirement is that you write a paper between ten to fifteen pages in length.

A: 我如何知道我寫的是你要的？

A: How do I know that I'm writing what you want?

B: 你真正寫之前要提出大綱。

B: Before you start actually writing the paper, you need to bring in an outline.

A: 我要拿給你看嗎？

A: Should I show the outline to you?

B: 那最好，如果因為某些原因找不到我，你也可以向我的研究生助理尋求幫忙及指導。

B: That would be the best. If you can't find me for some reason, you can also seek help and guidance from my graduate assistant.

A: 謝謝。

A: Thank you.

✎ Word Bank 字庫

outline [`aʊt͵laɪn] n. 大綱
guidance [`gaɪdəns] n. 指導

Useful Phrases 實用語句

1. 我不確定我了解學期報告規定。
   I'm not sure I understand the term paper requirement.
2. 我如何知道我寫的是你要的？
   How do I know that I'm writing what you want?
3. 我要拿給你看嗎？
   Should I show the outline to you?
4. 你真正寫之前要先提出大綱。
   Before you start actually writing the paper, you need to bring in an outline.

Dialog 2 對話2

A: 請問你是保森教授的研究生助理嗎？

A: Excuse me. Are you Professor Paulson's graduate assistant?

B: 是的，我是。

B: Yes, I am.

A: 我是蘇馬，我有個關於課程的問題。

A: I'm Sue Ma. I have a question about the class.

B: 我是馬克辛姆斯，你有什麼疑問？

B: My name is Mark Simms. What question do you have?

A: 我想知道保森教授的課我們該買什麼書？

A: I'm wondering what books we are supposed to buy for Professor Paulson's class.

B: 你上哪門課？

B: Which class are you in?

預備 校園 選課 新生說明 上課前 課堂上 課後交流 圖書館 體育館 餐廳 課外活動 申請獎助 當助教

A: 資訊工程 312。

A: Computer Science 312.

B: 好，沒問題，我這裡有閱讀書單。

B: OK. No problem. I have the reading list right here.

A: 喔，好。

A: Oh, good.

Dialog 3 對話3

A: 這些書是必買，而且大學書店有（指書單給學生看），你也會注意到推薦的閱讀書單，那些書也可以在大學書店買到，但大學圖書館也有。

A: These books are required and available at the University Bookstore (shows student the list). You'll notice a recommended reading list too. Those books can be purchased at the University Bookstore also, but they are also available at the University library.

B: 他們在圖書館很難找到嗎？

B: Are they difficult to find at the library?

A: 不會，只要告訴圖書館員你在找保森教授閱讀書單的書，那些書會在保留書區特別為修此門課的學生保留。

A: No. Just tell the librarian that you are looking for a book on Professor Paulson's reading list. Those books will be on reserve especially for students taking this class.

預備

校園

選課

新生說明

上課前

課堂上

課後交流

圖書館

體育館

餐廳

課外活動

申請獎助

當助教

B: 我可以借出帶回家讀嗎？

B: Can I check them out and take them home to read?

A: 不行，你必須在圖書館那裡閱讀，因為其他學生也需要借得到，你可以每次借兩小時。

A: No. You have to read them there in the library because other students need access to them too. You can check them out for two hours at a time.

B: 好，我知道了，謝謝你的幫忙。

B: OK. I understand. Thank you for your help.

Word Bank 字庫

reserve [rɪˋzɝv] v., n. 保留
access [ˋæksɛs] n. 路徑；取得

Useful Phrases 實用語句

1. 我想知道保森教授的課我們該買什麼書。

   I'm wondering what books we are supposed to buy for Professor Paulson's class.

2. 我這裡有閱讀書單。

   I have the reading list right here.

3. 這些書是必買的。

   These books are required.

4. 也有推薦的閱讀書單。

   There's a recommended reading list too.

5. 這些書大學書店有。

   These books are available at the university bookstore.

預備 校園 選課 新生說明 上課前 課堂上 課後交流 圖書館 體育館 餐廳 課外活動 申請獎助 當助教

6. 那些書會在保留書區。

   Those books will be on reserve.

7. 我可以借出帶回家讀嗎？

   Can I check them out and take them home to read?

Tips 小祕訣

　　要解決教科書又多又昂貴的頭痛問題，最好是買二手書 (used book)，因為數量有限，必須在知道書單後趁早購買，網路也有機會找到你要的二手書。

5.3 給分標準
Grade Criteria

Dialog 對話

A: 哈囉，古柏教授，我可以和你談話嗎？

A: Hello, Professor Cooper. May I talk to you now?

B: 可以，我現在是辦公時間，進來吧。

B: Yes. I have office hours now, come on in.

A: 我想了解你的評分規定。

A: I'd like to know about your grading policy.

B: 它登在這門課的網路大綱上，但我現在很樂意告訴你。

B: It's in the syllabus online for this class, but I'll be glad to tell you now.

A: 抱歉，我沒想到上網查看。

A: Sorry. I didn't think about checking it online.

B: 沒關係，我給分按照出席 20%，小考 15%，期中考 25% 及期末考 40%。

B: That's OK. I figure grades based on attendance for 20%, quizzes for 15%, Midterm for 25%, and the Final for 40%.

A: 期末考是課堂考試嗎？

A: Is the Final an in-class exam?

B: 是的，但期中考不是，是有三天時間完成的寫作作業。

B: Yes, it is, but the Midterm isn't. It's a writing assignment that you have three days to complete.

A: 我知道了，感謝你的時間。

A: I see. Thank you for your time.

 Useful Phrases 實用語句

1. 我想了解你的評分規定。

   I'd like to know about your grading policy.

2. 期末考是課堂考試嗎？

   Is the Final an in-class exam?

3. 我們有多少小考？

   How many quizzes do we have?

4. 有隨堂考嗎？

   Are there pop quizzes?

5. 小考會在一週前宣布嗎？

   Will you announce the quizzes a week before?

6. 報告占多少？

   How much does the presentation count?

7. 每個要求的分數比例是多少？

   What is the percentage of the grade for each requirement?

Notes 小叮嚀

　　每門課的評分按教授個人規定而不同，現在教授都把課程說明及進度大綱、評分方式、作業說明等注意事項放在網站上，供學生選課及隨時查詢，第一堂課教授會說明課程大綱和規定，學生其實在開學前選課就可以查詢規定。教授時間寶貴，最好先查詢該了解的，只問關於規定或課程不明白的部分。

　　除了課堂的測驗評量，上課表現及其他評量如報告、展示都相當重要，教師得以了解學生學習情形；有些教授不一定會自己講課，而是讓學生發言再給評論，如果未事先預習課程內容進而說出自己心得是無法上課的，即使教授自己講課，未預習恐怕也無法聽懂。典型亞洲文化裡被動、沒意見、從不舉手發言的學生，不改變自己的話，很難在美國校園生存；在課前預習時可以先整理問題寫下來，唸熟問題，專心聽課時如果教授沒提到再發問。

5.4 考試規定
Examination Rules and Policies

 Dialog 對話

A: 好的，各位，請注意聽我解釋這次考試的程序，你會有 1.5 小時完成考試，你只能用 2 號鉛筆，不能用原子筆，考試時不准交談，不准帶筆記、書本或字典，請在第一頁右上角簽名。有問題嗎？

A: Alright, everyone, please listen carefully as I explain the procedure for taking this examination. You will have one and a half hours to complete the exam. You may only use a number two pencil. No pens. You are not allowed to talk or communicate with anyone during the test. Also, no notes, books, or dictionaries are allowed. Be sure to sign your name at the top, right corner of the first page. Are there any questions?

B: 我們可以有超過一支的鉛筆及削筆器嗎？

B: Can we have more than one pencil and a sharpener?

A: 可以，有其他問題嗎？

A: Yes. Other questions?

B: 考完了可以離開嗎？

B: Can we leave when we are finished?

A: 可以，將考卷交給我之後就可以離開。但是，不要再回來教室。

A: Yes. Give the exam paper to me. Then, you may leave. Do not come back into the room however.

預備
校園
選課
新生說明
上課前
課堂上
課後交流
圖書館
體育館
餐廳
課外活動
申請獎助
當助教

198

B: 考試時可以去洗手間嗎？

B: Can we go to the toilet during the exam?

A: 考試時任何時間離開教室，就不可以回來。

A: If you leave the examination room any time while the exam is being taken, you cannot return.

 Useful Phrases　實用語句

1. 我們可以有超過一支的鉛筆及削筆器嗎？

   Can we have more than one pencil and a sharpener?

2. 考完了可以離開嗎？

   Can we leave when we are finished?

3. 考試時可以去洗手間嗎？

   Can we go to the toilet during the exam?

 Notes　小叮嚀

　　如果是申論 (essay) 寫作考試，學生必須自己事先準備考試專用的藍色封面筆記本 (bluebook) 做為答案卷。與上課及讀書會發言一樣，考試答題不能死讀書或背多分，而是吸收資訊後用自己的話表達出來。

5.5 課堂發問
Asking Questions in Class

 Dialog　對話

A: 對不起，布朗教授，我有一個問題。

A: Excuse me, Professor Brown. I have a question.

B: 好。

B: OK.

A: 我不確定您的意思，您可以再解釋一次嗎？

A: I'm not sure what you mean. Can you explain it once more?

B: 你哪個部分不了解？

B: Which part do you not understand?

A: 你提的最後一個部分我有點困惑。

A: The last part you mentioned is a little confusing to me.

B: 好，我試著說清楚些。

B: OK. Let me try to make it clearer.

 Useful Phrases 實用語句

1. 對不起。

   Excuse me.

2. 我可以問一個問題嗎？

   May I ask a question?

3. 我有一個問題。

   I have a question.

4. 布朗教授，我想問一些事。

   Professor Brown. I'd like to ask something.

5. 對不起，請您再解釋一次。

   Sorry. Would you explain that again?

6. 我不確定您的意思，您可以多解釋些 [再解釋一次] 嗎？

   I'm not sure what you mean. Can you explain more [again]?

7. 您可以再說一遍嗎？

   Would you please say that again?

預備　校園　選課　新生說明　上課前　**課堂上**　課後交流　圖書館　體育館　餐廳　課外活動　申請獎助　當助教

預備

校園

選課

新生說明

上課前

課堂上

課後交流

圖書館

體育館

餐廳

課外活動

申請獎助

當助教

Notes 小叮嚀

　　如果有聽不懂的地方，可以請教授再說一遍，但不要與同學交頭接耳，這樣是很不禮貌的。如果需要課堂錄音，一定要先徵得教授同意，並在不干擾他人情形下錄音。盡量做筆記而不要依賴錄音，只用錄音補強而不是逐步重聽錄音，否則會很耗時間。

　　課堂舉手發問可以引起老師注意，但是要注意適當的發問時機，如果老師專心闡述重點，最好等到教授說完或講述完某個段落再發問，教授會比較輕鬆些來回應你的問題。多數教授會在某些時間停下來讓學生問問題，當然這就是發問的好時機，許多人在課後發問，雖然這樣也可以，但是因為教授通常必須趕赴別的任務，可能會沒有時間和你談。

　　初期上課若不習慣課堂發言，可以與教授約時間私下表達自己還在適應，並與教授交換課程內容之意見，讓教授了解你並非不認真，並且趕快加入讀書會，加強自己的實力，及早在課堂舉手發言。

5.6 課堂上表達看法
Expressing an Opinion in Class

Dialog 對話

A: 泰德教授，我想指出某些事。

A: Professor Todd. I'd like to point out something.

B: 當然，請便。

B: Sure. Go ahead.

A: 我們今天看到的這個了解系統的方法並無科學證明。

A: This approach to understanding the system we are looking at today isn't scientifically proven.

B: 沒錯，雖然某些元素不斷經過實驗複製。

B: True, though certain elements have been consistently replicated in labs.

A: 我了解，但如果不能經科學重複顯示，那我們就不能宣稱這是事實。

A: I understand, but if it can't be scientifically shown time and again, then we can't really claim it is true.

B: 是的，我了解你的論點，但是現今它是我們有的最精確的解釋。

B: Yes, I see your point, but at this time it is the most accurate explanation we have.

Word Bank 字庫

approach [ə`protʃ] n. 方法
scientifically proven 經科學證明的
element [`ɛləmənt] n. 元素
accurate [`ækjərɪt] adj. 精確的
time and again 重複的

Useful Phrases 實用語句

1. 安德魯斯教授，對不起，我不認為一直是這樣。

   Professor Andrews. Excuse me. I don't think it is that way all the time.

2. 我想表達一個觀點。

   I'd like to make a point.

3. 我有不同看法。

   I have a different view.

5. 我的了解有所不同。

   I have a different understanding.

6. 那關於…又如何呢？

   But what about…?

預備 校園 選課 新生說明 上課前 課堂上 課後交流 圖書館 體育館 餐廳 課外活動 申請獎助 當助教

7. …不也有可能嗎？

   Isn't it also possible that…?

8. 我了解你的意思但是…

   I see what you mean, but…

9. 我聽到其他人說…

   I've heard others say…

10. 抱歉，但我有點搞混，我曾聽說 [讀到]…

    Sorry, but I'm a little confused. I've heard [read]…

Tips 小祕訣

　　如果在課堂或是在教授的辦公室，要表達關於某事自己的意見，要先有準備。教授習慣於被學生挑戰論點，學生被要求要有自己的論點並且禮貌地表達出來，當然在表達時不可有任何人身攻擊的意見。

5.7 口頭報告範例
Sample Oral Report (Physical Therapy)

通常在開學第一次上課，學生拿到課程大綱 (或在網路上印下大綱) 就知道要做哪些報告。在某些情形下，有些教授可能要求學生口頭報告課堂上的主題，或是學生自己選擇教授認可的主題，學生可能有一週或多一點的時間準備，報告通常是在課堂裡對著其他同學及教授報告，以下是一篇口頭報告範例。

Today I would like to talk to you about the field of Physical Therapy. My name is Sharon Tsai, and this area is very familiar to me, as I have worked part time in this field for two years here in Albany, while a student at this school. This report is mainly about physical therapy patients with minor to severe bone, joint, injuries, looking for an alternative to surgery. I will give you some background in the field and some current information. I also will give you an idea of the treatments involved, along with some benefits and disadvantages of each. I hope that after this report, you will have enough information to decide if any of these therapies is the right course of treatment for you.

So what are these therapies? In the field of medical care the use of physical agents such as heat and massage, coupled with exercise, are used to treat certain physical disabilities. The objectives are the relief of pain caused by surgery or from other medical problems. Also, the improvement of muscle strength and mobility, and improvement of basic functions, like standing or walking. The field is rather new, entering into the medical world in the early twentieth century. The American Physical Therapy Association, monitors therapists and their practice, and says that there are close to 70,000 physical therapists in the United States, and the profession is growing fast. Demand far exceeds supply.

People want to know what treatment they can get when they see a therapist. At the first visit, you will usually have an initial evaluation. The therapist may ask about the patient's medical background and how the illness or injury occurred. The therapist will also ask how long you have had the problem. The physical therapist will perform tests to figure out your condition. After the therapist completes the assessment, he or she develops a treatment plan, and then begin. The physical therapist can use many techniques in connection with equipment to treat you. Common techniques are; use of heat, massage, and bone adjustment. There are many other treatments your therapist might use specifically for your condition.

Although there is a lot to say about this profession, this report is only meant to give introductory information on Physical Therapy. If you want to learn more there are many informative websites, and books in the University's career center and library. Thank you for your attention.

5.8 口頭報告致勝祕訣
Tips: How to Deliver an Oral Report Successfully

🔖 掌握主題，充分了解主題內容。

🔖 撰寫口頭報告稿子時，記住觀眾是用聽的不是用讀的，兩者當然不同。一開始練習就可以查覺你寫的稿是否不順或太正式。

🔖 就自己被允許的時間及課堂情形，衡量是否需要準備開場白，可以問問題、引用相關統計數字、名言(或稍加改變)、生活小事、觀察或經驗等引導聽眾進入主題。

預備
校園
選課
新生說明
上課前
課堂上
課後交流
圖書館
體育館
餐廳
課外活動
申請獎助
當助教

🔖 大聲練習報告。如果可以,錄下自己練習的影帶或請同學試聽,修正自己的表現。

🔖 報告當天要先進食,但不要喝汽水,因為碳酸飲料會讓你口乾舌燥。

🔖 適當多層次的衣著,你不知道室溫到時是否會變得較冷或較熱,所以要準備好以免因發抖或燥熱影響表現。不要在報告當天嘗試新髮型或穿著,這樣會使你更緊張。

🔖 早點到達教室,讓自己有時間做好氣定神閒的準備。

🔖 自然腹式呼吸(切忌肺部深呼吸,會造成心跳加速的反效果),一旦上臺,用一點時間整理思緒並放輕鬆。不要擔心給自己一點時間稍作停頓,看一下稿子,這樣做會讓你有機會緩和下來。如果你照這樣子做對了,將會看起來非常專業。

🔖 準備水(自己用慣的加蓋水杯),如果你開始報告但是聲音發抖,暫停一下。清一下喉嚨,喝些水。

🔖 與觀眾眼神接觸是最好的互動,如果沒法做到,可將焦點集中在教室後面,這樣對某些講者有緩和作用,或許感覺有點奇怪,但看起來並不奇怪。

🔖 如果有麥克風,要使用,有些人把麥克風當成唯一聽眾,專注點在麥克風上,反而效果不錯,當然最好還是要看著觀眾。

🔖 掌握臺風,想像自己是電視上的專業人士,如此可以增加信心。

🔖 如果有人提問,有心理準備可能會有回答 "I don't know." 的時候,不要害怕說你不知道,你可以說:「這是很棒的問題,我會去找答案」。

🔖 準備措辭巧妙的結尾。避免尷尬時刻,不要退後喃喃說出:"Well, I guess that's all."。

Unit 6 After Class

課後交流

除了課前預習，上課記筆記是學生非常重要的課業活動，教授期待學生記筆記，學生也必須做筆記並整理筆記，然而上課、聽課、記筆記吸收資訊的成果有限，課後與同學交換意見、討論課程內容、討論筆記、組讀書會一起腦力激盪，才是課業學習真正事半功倍的好辦法。

預備
校園
選課
新生說明
上課前
課堂上
課後交流
圖書館
體育館
餐廳
課外活動
申請獎助
當助教

6.1 借筆記
Borrowing a Classmate's Notes

Dialog 對話

A: 嘿，約翰。

A: Hey, John.

B: 嗨，珊蒂。怎麼了？

B: Hi, Sandy. What's up?

A: 我可以跟你借昨天的筆記嗎？

A: Could I borrow your notes from yesterday?

B: 我現在需要它們，但我們可以去影印機影印一份。

B: I need them now, but we can go to the copy machine and make a copy.

A: 好，謝謝。

A: OK. Thanks.

6.2 還筆記
Returning Notes

Dialog 對話

A: 喔，影印機壞了。

A: Uh oh. The copying machine is out of order.

B: 運氣真背。

B: Bad luck.

A: 你現在需要我的筆記嗎？

A: Do you need my notes now?

B: 我原本希望可以在今晚讀書會時用到它們。

B: I was hoping to use them tonight in my study group.

A: 你們何時碰面？

A: What time do you meet?

B: 大約晚上 7 點。

B: Around seven in the evening.

A: 好，我晚一點可以把筆記給你。

A: Great. I can easily give them to you a little later.

B: 好的，謝謝。我該在哪裡跟你碰面？

B: OK. Thanks. Where should I meet you?

A: 你的讀書會在哪裡碰面？

A: Where does your study group meet?

B: 我們約在凱德曼館二樓大廳。

B: We meet in the lounge at Cadman Hall on the second floor.

A: 我 6 點 30 分會在那附近。

A: That's close to where I'll be around 6:30.

預備 校園 選課 新生說明 上課前 課堂上 課後交流 圖書館 體育館 餐廳 課外活動 申請獎助 當助教

| 預備 | 校園 | 選課 | 新生說明 | 上課前 | 課堂上 | 課後交流 | 圖書館 | 體育館 | 餐廳 | 課外活動 | 申請獎助 | 當助教 |

B: 我那時候也會在那裡。

B: I'll be there at that time too.

A: 太好了，那時候我會在那裡跟你碰面把筆記給你。

A: Perfect. I'll meet you there and give them to you then.

B: 好，我明天會把筆記還你。

B: Fine. I'll give them back to you tomorrow.

A: 好。

A: Sounds good.

Useful Phrases 實用語句

1. 運氣真背。

   Bad luck.

2. 我明天會把筆記還你。

   I'll give them back to you tomorrow.

Notes 小叮嚀

　　有些課程有團體作業，按照教授指定，學生必須分享閱讀心得、分享筆記並且一起做報告。如果不是團體作業，有些學生可能願意和較熟同學交換和分享筆記，但有些人可能認為借筆記是很敏感的事，更別提影印筆記或手機拍照，除非因為你有事缺席並事先請人幫忙，才有可能。很難說哪一種是比較典型的美國想法，但是不管哪一種，學生認真做的筆記都不希望被濫用，如果能共同討論求進步並且相對分享付出，應該是運用筆記求學問最好的方法。

　　學校處理這類事情也各有差異，有些著名教授認為講義或筆記是智慧財產，茲事體大，有些教授則不會介意。現在有些學校授權校內影印店提供不同課程的筆記或講義販售服務，通常可以在學生中心及圖書館購買，也有些學校在獲得教授同意下直接將講義免費放上網路。對借閱課程筆記或講義如果有疑問，最好向教授請教。

Information Bank 大補帖

◎ 記筆記 Taking Notes

1. 記筆記的好處：
   (1) 使你更集中注意聽課並測試自己是否理解授課內容
   (2) 當你在複習筆記時，使你了解教材的重點
   (3) 自己的筆記使你更容易記得教材內容

2. 重點在哪裡？
   教授通常會暗示什麼要記下來，有些經常的暗示是：
   (1) 寫在黑板上的資料
   (2) 重複
   (3) 強調 (音調、手勢、解說及舉例)
   (4) 字彙訊息
       例如：對於…有兩種看法 "There are **two points of view** on... "
       　　　第三個理由是… "The **third** reason is... "
       　　　結論…" In **conclusion**... "
   (5) 課後總結內容
   (6) 課前暖身內容

3. 記筆記技巧：

每個人都有自己的記筆記方法，但學習如何有效率記筆記可以幫你精進課業並養成記住重要資訊的讀書習慣。通常學生以為他們聽懂了課程，因此就記住了內容，這是大錯特錯的想法，一定要記筆記！當你記筆記時，你會發展出一套篩選資訊的技巧，將重點記下，非重點捨去。只有透過練習及經常檢閱筆記，才能熟悉運用、安排重點，精進課業。以下是一些記筆記技巧：

(1) 寫筆記前先思考一下，不要為記筆記而記筆記，而是為以後讀筆記的真正價值而作筆記。

(2) 讓自己的筆記簡短扼要，盡量用單字及片語而不要用一個句子，注意牛肉在哪裡，不要寫下每個字。跳過敘述及全面解釋，筆記簡明扼要，才能精確快速抓住重點。

(3) 統一記號及簡寫，用大綱縮排方式來顯示重要性，為以後添加註解留足夠空白。

(4) 用自己的話記筆記，但不要改變意義。公式、定義、特定用語要確實記錄，引用作者的語句要直接而正確。

(5) 不要擔心錯過一點。教授若講到旁枝末節，通常是回到前面去補充資料。如果錯過某個部分，先寫下重點字，留些空白，晚點查到資料後再補上。

(6) 筆記要記在同一本筆記內且有順序，註記日期及頁數。

(7) 筆記要留足夠空白，將來好整理，邊緣處可以寫重點標題或本頁內容結論。

(8) 記筆記不久後就要整理筆記，添加或把不清楚的地方弄清楚，以免記憶很快遺忘，妥善安排時間整理筆記是精進課業很重要的一步。

(9) 經常閱讀筆記才能牢記內容。

6.3 下課及課後討論課堂心得
Discussing Class Feedback during a Break and after Class

Dialog 1　對話 1

A: 傑瑞，我可以問你一些關於上課的事嗎？

A: Jerry. Can I ask you something about the class?

B: 當然可以，什麼事呢？

B: Sure. What is it?

A: 瓊斯教授說我們實驗沒做好，是嗎？

A: Professor Jones said that we aren't doing well on lab experiments, right?

B: 是的，他確實說過。

B: Yes, he did say that.

A: 我不懂，我交出去的每個實驗報告都得到好成績。

A: I don't understand. I've gotten a high score on every one of the lab reports I've handed in.

B: 他說一般而言全班不是做得很好，有些人一點問題都沒有，聽起來你是其中之一。

B: He means generally speaking the class is not doing well. Some students are having no problem at all. It sounds like you are one of them.

A: 喔，我懂了。

A: Oh. I see.

Word Bank 字庫

experiment [ɪkˋspɛrəmənt] n. 實驗
lab report n. 實驗報告

Dialog 2 對話2

A: 你的課如何？

A: How are your classes going?

B: 我想還可以。

B: OK, I think.

A: 你準備好下週的報告了嗎？

A: Are you ready for next week's presentation?

B: 還沒完全準備好，但越來越接近（完成），你呢？

B: Not completely, but I'm getting closer. How about you?

A: 我需要投入更多準備工作，我還沒組織好。

A: I need to put more work into it. I don't have it organized well yet.

B: 也許我們應該一起練習。

B: Maybe we should get together and practice.

A: 好主意。

A: Good idea.

Word Bank 字庫

presentation [ˌprɛzənˋteʃən] n. （上臺）報告
organize [ˋɔrgəˌnaɪz] v. 組織

Useful Phrases 實用語句

1. 你準備好下週的報告了嗎？

   Are you ready for next week's presentation?

左側邊欄：預備　校園　選課　新生說明　上課前　課堂上　課後交流　圖書館　體育館　餐廳　課外活動　申請獎助　當助教

213

2. 我需要投入更多準備工作。

   I need to put more work into it.

3. 我還沒組織好。

   I don't have it organized well yet.

4. 我越來越接近 (完成準備)。

   I'm getting closer.

6.4 團體作業
Group Work or Project

Dialog 對話

A: 我們需要組織這個課程報告。

A: We need to organize this class project.

B: 是的，我想我們最好分配工作。

B: Yes. I think we'd better divide the work.

A: 好，我來收集一些我們要報告主題的資料。

A: OK. I'll gather some information on the topic we have to report on.

B: 我會開始整理簡報。

B: I'll start putting together the PowerPoint presentation part.

A: 你需要圖片。

A: You'll need pictures.

B: 我可以下載一些我的照片。

B: I can download some of my photos.

預備
校園
選課
新生說明
上課前
課堂上
課後交流
圖書館
體育館
餐廳
課外活動
申請獎助
當助教

A: 我們何時要再碰面？

A: When should we meet again?

B: 週三 6 點。

B: Wednesday at six.

A: 哪裡？

A: Where?

B: 到我那裡。

B: Come over to my place.

A: 沒問題，我會給你看我找到什麼。

A: No problem. I'll show you what I've found then.

B: 好，我們那時也要開始規劃分配閱讀。

B: Good. We'll need to divide up the reading then too.

A: 是的，我會準備一張我們報告需要集中焦點的問題清單。

A: Yes. I'll prepare a list of questions that we need to focus on for the report.

B: 好主意，這樣我們不會浪費時間做同樣的事情。

B: Good idea. That way we won't be wasting time by doing the same thing.

Word Bank 字庫

divide [dəˋvaɪd] v. 分配
gather [ˋgæðɚ] v. 收集

Useful Phrases 實用語句

1. 我們需要組織這個課程報告。

   We need to organize this class project.

2. 我們最好分配工作。

   We'd better divide the work.

3. 我來收集一些我們要報告主題的資料。

   I'll gather some information on the topic we have to report on.

4. 我會開始整理簡報。

   I'll start putting together the PowerPoint presentation part.

5. 我們那時也要開始規劃分配閱讀。

   We'll need to divide up the reading then too.

6. 我會準備一張我們報告需要集中焦點的問題清單。

   I'll prepare a list of questions that we need to focus on for the report.

6.5 上實驗課
Attending a Lab Class

Dialog 1 對話 1

A: 我們每週要用同一個地方。

A: We have to use this same space every week.

B: 好，我們今天要做什麼？

B: OK. What do we have to do today?

A: 我還不知道，凱爾教授還沒來。

A: I don't know yet. Professor Kyle isn't here yet.

預備 校園 選課 新生說明 上課前 課堂上 課後交流 圖書館 體育館 餐廳 課外活動 申請獎助 當助教

B: 我們今天要完成實驗作業嗎？

B: Do we have to finish the lab assignment today?

A: 是的，而且我們也要交出結果。

A: Yes. And we have to hand in the results too.

B: 看來我們需要的設備都有了。

B: It looks like all the equipment we'll need is provided.

A: 是的，我們除了報告書外，不需帶其他東西。

A: Yes. We don't need to bring anything but our report-writing book.

B: 好。

B: Good.

Dialog 2 對話2

A: 對不起，凱爾教授，有件事我不確定。

A: Excuse me, Professor Kyle. I'm not sure about something.

B: 好，我來幫你。

B: OK. Let me help you.

A: 我們應該要現在做程序裡的這個步驟，還是晚一點再做？

A: Are we supposed to do this step in the procedure now or later?

B: 你要等到下一步之後。

B: You should wait until after the next step.

A: 我們要等多久才做下一步？

A: How long will it be before we do the next step?

B: 要有耐心，要幾分鐘，確認記下每個步驟要多久時間來完成的筆記。

B: Be patient. It will be a few minutes. Be sure to keep notes about how much time is needed for the completion of each step.

A: 謝謝。

A: Thank you.

Word Bank 字庫

equipment [ɪ`kwɪpmənt] n. 設備
procedure [prə`sidʒɚ] n. 程序
patient [`peʃənt] adj. 有耐性的
completion [kəm`pliʃən] n. 完成

Useful Phrases 實用語句

1. 我們今天要完成實驗作業嗎？

   Do we have to finish the lab assignment today?

2. 我們需要的設備都有了。

   All the equipment we'll need is provided.

3. 我們應該要現在做程序裡的這個步驟，還是晚一點再做？

   Are we supposed to do this step in the procedure now or later?

4. 我們要等多久才做下一步？

   How long will it be before we do the next step?

5. 你要等到下一步之後。

   You should wait until after the next step.

6. 確認也記下時間。

   Be sure to keep notes about time too.

預備
校園
選課
新生說明
上課前
課堂上
課後交流
圖書館
體育館
餐廳
課外活動
申請獎助
當助教

6.6 課外教學
A Fieldtrip

Dialog 1　對話 1

A: 有一部要載我們去海邊的箱型車。

A: There's the van that's taking us to the coast.

B: 我對這課外教學真得很興奮。

B: I'm really excited about this field-trip.

A: 我也是，可以離開一天真好。

A: Me too. It will be great to get away for a day.

B: 有多少人要去？

B: How many are going?

A: 大約 30 個學生及 2 位老師，加上他們的助教。

A: About thirty students and two teachers, plus their assistants.

B: 到那裡要多久？

B: How long will it take to get there?

A: 大約 4 小時車程。

A: It's about a four-hour drive.

B: 希望我們有時間可以休息。

B: I hope we stop sometimes.

A: 會的，我們確定會停下來吃午餐。

A: We will. We'll stop for lunch for sure.

B: 你有工作單嗎？

B: Do you have your task list?

A: 有，上面有一些我們要做的有趣的事情。

A: Yes. It has some interesting things we have to do.

B: 對，總而言之應該很好玩。

B: I agree. All in all it should be fun.

Dialog 2 對話2

A: 我們在這地點時，一定要小心不要打擾到野生生物或接觸到任何器具及設備。

A: While we are at this site, we must be careful not to disturb the wild creatures or touch any instruments or equipment you see.

B: 為什麼，韓斯教授？

B: Why, Professor Hanes?

預備

校園

選課

新生說明

上課前

課堂上

課後交流

圖書館

體育館

餐廳

課外活動

申請獎助

當助教

A: 許多研究人員在這個地區工作,不要干擾現存情況很重要,這關係著實驗是否能進行成功。

A: Many researchers are working in this area. It is important not to disturb conditions that exist here that are vital to the success of conducting their experiments.

B: 我們可以拍照嗎?

B: Can we take photos?

A: 不要用閃光燈,會嚇到野生動物。

A: Don't use flash. It will frighten the wild life.

B: 我知道了,我們要多安靜?

B: I see. How quiet should we be?

A: 你可以照正常聲調說話,但是絕對不要大喊或尖叫。

A: You can speak in a normal tone, but definitely don't shout or scream.

B: 好,我們會替這裡的環境著想。

B: OK. We'll be considerate of the environment here.

A: 很好,謝謝。

A: Great. Thanks.

Word Bank 字庫

wild creatures n. 野生生物
instrument [`Instrəmənt] n. 器具
vital [`vaɪtḷ] adj. 重要的
conduct [`kɑndʌkt] v. 操作
considerate [kən`sɪdərɪt] adj. 體諒的

Useful Phrases 實用語句

1. 我們可以拍照嗎？

   Can we take photos?

2. 我們要多安靜？

   How quiet should we be?

3. 我們會替這裡的環境著想。

   We'll be considerate of the environment here.

6.7 組讀書會
Forming a Study Group

Dialog 1 對話 1

A: 嗨，傑瑞，我可以和你說一下話嗎？

A: Hi, Jerry. Can I talk to you a minute?

B: 當然可以，你要談什麼？

B: Sure. What do you want to talk about?

A: 我想組一個讀書會，我想你會是很好的會員。

A: I want to form a study group. I think you would be a good group member.

預備
校園
選課
新生說明
上課前
課堂上
課後交流
圖書館
體育館
餐廳
課外活動
申請獎助
當助教

B: 我知道了，你打算何時見面？

B: I see. When do you plan to meet?

A: 星期三晚上，大多數人那時有空。

A: Wednesday nights. Most people have time then.

B: 我們要在哪見面？

B: Where should we meet?

A: 布萊利館。

A: At Bradley Hall.

B: 聽起來很好，我考慮看看，明天打電話給你。

B: It sounds good. I'll think about it and call you tomorrow.

A: 好，謝謝。

A: Great. Thanks.

Useful Phrases 實用語句

1. 我想組一個讀書會，我想你會是很好的會員。

   I want to form a study group. I think you would be a good group member.

2. 你打算何時會面？

   When do you plan to meet?

3. 我們要在哪見面？

   Where should we meet?

4. 我考慮看看，明天打電話給你。

   I'll think about it and call you tomorrow.

Dialog 2 對話2

A: 我準備好一份這週讀書會之夜的議程。

A: I have an agenda ready for this week's study group night.

B: 好,我們得按照進度,所以我們跟緊點。

B: Good. We need to stay on schedule, so let's follow it closely.

A: 對,應該沒問題,因為現在輪到你帶領小組。

A: Right. That should be no problem because it is your turn to lead the group.

B: 好,我會確認討論按照議程進行。

B: OK. I'll make sure things happen according to the agenda.

Word Bank 字庫

agenda [ə`dʒɛndə] n. 議程
turn [tɜn] n. 輪流

Useful Phrases 實用語句

1. 我們得按照進度。

   We need to stay on schedule.

2. 我們跟緊點。

   Let's follow it closely.

3. 現在輪到你帶領小組。

   It is your turn to lead the group.

4. 我會確認討論按照議程進行。

   I'll make sure things happen according to the agenda.

預備
校園
選課
新生說明
上課前
課堂上
課後交流
圖書館
體育館
餐廳
課外活動
申請獎助
當助教

Information Bank 大補帖

讀書會 Study Group

1. 如何組讀書會 How to Form a Study Group

讀書會可說是最有效率精進學業的方式，以下是一些如何組讀書會的祕訣：

(1) 找你認為筆記做得好且認真學習的同學組讀書會，問他們是否要吃個午餐或喝個咖啡討論組讀書會細節，此時所有人不需答應任何事情。

(2) 在黑板寫下你的留言，請有興趣的同學聯絡你或在課堂傳閱登錄名單。

(3) 限制組員數目為 5-6 人，太大的讀書會很難進行，先試過一次會議，如果進行順利，就規劃本學期每週至少會面一次。

2. 讀書會如何進行 How to Conduct a Study Group

(1) 每次會面前要預先計畫議程並決定會面時間多久。

(2) 輪流擔任主席，每週選出下週主席領導討論及遵守進度，主席不是為小組幹活，而是要促進讀書會該有的效率。

(3) 每次討論結束前留 5-10 分鐘腦力激盪可能的測驗題目，下一次會面時一起討論這些題目，提出解答，並在筆記、講義或教材內標出答案在哪裡可以找到。選出該週小組祕書記下答案並註明答案出處，影印給組員。

(4) 比較上課筆記看是否所有組員都記下重要筆記且可以補充任何遺漏部分，記下大家都沒弄懂的那些項目，派一位志願代表替小組與教授談話，該組員回來報告給其他組員了解。如果還是無法搞清楚，自己就要去找教授談話，為自己的課業負責任。

(5) 組員每週為小組準備閱讀所有教材，最好是最近已經上過課的內容而不是下週即將要上課的部分，你的讀書會小組是組員個人的複習過程。

(6) 如果你的教材每章節後面有列出問題，每週將問題分配給組員並且請每位組員為其他組員解釋其負責部分，在任一組員為大家解釋時，其他成員需幫忙將解答釐清並且更正任何錯誤訊息。

(7) 每次結束時為下週會面分配工作。

6.8 主持讀書會
Hosting a Study Group

Dialog 1　對話1

A: 嗨，傑瑞。

A: Hi, Jerry.

B: 嗨，曼蒂。每個人都到了嗎？

B: Hi, Mandy. Is everybody here yet?

A: 幾乎，鮑伯還沒來。

A: Almost. Bob is not here yet.

B: 你們開始了嗎？

B: Have you started yet?

A: 還沒，我們很快會開始，有飲料可以喝，也有咖啡。

A: No. We'll start soon though. There are drinks available. Coffee too.

B: 我看到大家帶點心。

B: I see people brought snacks.

A: 對，我們想今晚討論時大家會餓。

A: Yes. We figured we'd get hungry during tonight's session.

B: 沒錯，我們會在這裡好一陣子，我為大家帶了一些三明治。

B: No doubt. We'll be here a long time. I brought some sandwiches for everyone.

A: 很好，謝謝，我們坐這邊，坐下吧。

A: Great. Thanks. We're sitting at this table. Have a seat.

 Dialog 2　對話2

A: 好，各位，我們可以開始了。

A: Alright, everyone, we are ready to start.

B: 我會發我做的筆記給大家。

B: I'll distribute the notes I made for everyone.

A: 好，我們今晚需要看兩個案子，關於契約法。我們需要為它們的答案作準備，萬一明天被點到的話。

A: OK. We need to look at two cases tonight. They are about Contract Law. We'll need to be ready to answer questions about them if called on in class tomorrow.

B: 先看這個叫做哈爾蒙對提特樂鋼鐵的案子，我們必須先釐清原告的委屈以及先前的判例來支持原告的案子。

B: Look at this case first. It's titled Harmon vs Titler Steel. We must sort out what the grievances of the plaintiff are, and what legal precedence there is to support the plaintiff's case.

A: 對，我們也要決定哪個辯論方法最能用來減弱原告的案子。

A: Right. We also need to determine which method of argument would be the most useful for diminishing the plaintiff's case.

A: 我來讀案子，然後我們分成二人一組建立論點。

A: I'll read the case. Then we'll break into pairs and construct our arguments.

B: 稍後，我們比較並辯論我們的論點。

B: Later, we'll compare and argue our points.

A: 有問題嗎？沒有，那好，我們開始工作。

A: Any questions? No? OK then. Let's get to work.

B: 記住，如果任何時候你要點心，在那邊。

B: Remember. There is food and refreshments over there any time you want them.

Word Bank 字庫

distribute [dɪ`strɪbjʊt] v. 分配
sort out 釐清
grievance [`grivəns] n. 委屈
plaintiff [`plentɪf] n. 原告
legal precedence n. 先前的判例
argument [`ɑrgjəmənt] n. 辯論
diminish [də`mɪnɪʃ] v. 減弱
construct [kən`strʌkt] v. 建立
compare [kəm`pɛr] v. 比較
refreshments [rɪ`frɛʃmənts] n. 點心

📖 Useful Phrases 實用語句

1. 我會發我做的筆記給大家。

   I'll distribute the notes I made for everyone.

2. 我們今晚需要看兩個案子。

   We need to look at two cases tonight.

3. 我們需要為它們的答案作準備。

   We'll need to be ready to answer questions about them.

4. 我們必須釐清原因。

   We must sort out the reasons.

5. 我們也要決定哪個方法最有用。

   We also need to determine which method would be the most useful.

6. 我來讀案子。

   I'll read the case.

7. 然後我們分成二人一組。

   Then we'll break into pairs.

8. 我們要建立論點。

   We'll need to construct our arguments.

9. 我們比較並辯論我們的論點。

   We'll compare and argue our points.

6.9 分配工作
Arranging Share of Work in a Study Group

 Dialog 對話

A: 好，我們最好快點結束，已經很晚了。

A: OK. We'd better stop soon. It's getting pretty late.

B: 我們要分配下次讀書會的工作。

B: We need to divide up work for the next study session.

A: 對，我準備了這週工作的問題，誰要志願做下週的？

A: Right. I prepped questions for this week's work. Who is willing to do it for next week?

B: 我會做一些，我們下週有更多事要做，其他人可以做另外的部分。

B: I'll do some of it. We have much more to do next week. Someone else can do another section.

A: 我同意，一個人分量太多，我們得分配。

A: I agree. There is too much for one person. We'll have to divide it up.

 Useful Phrases 實用語句

1. 找重要的引語。

   Look for important quotes.

2. 分配工作量。

   Divide [Share] the work load.

3. 準備問題。

   Prepare questions.

4. 讀下一段 [節]。

   Read the following passages.

5. 考前複習。

   Review before the test.

6. 對答案。

   Check our answers.

 Language Power 字詞補給站

◆ 讀書會分配工作 Study Group: Share of Work

preview	預習
prep (preparation)	準備
host	主持
bring some snacks	帶一些點心
read ahead	讀下去

預備
校園
選課
新生說明
上課前
課堂上
課後交流
圖書館
體育館
餐廳
課外活動
申請獎助
當助教

research	研究
find out	找出
debate	辯論
counterpoint	相對 [相反] 的論點
list	列出
record	紀錄
plan	計畫
layout	版面
reserve	保留
divide up, share	分配

Tips 小祕訣

讀書會的事前準備、事後複習、討論及磨練思考的訓練是增加課堂發言、學習表達、增強自信，促使自己提升整體課業表現的好機會。

Maybe we should get together and practice.

Good idea.

Unit 7 The Library

圖書館

大學是高等教育場所,提供環境、設備、知識及挑戰,在大學研讀使人更具備知識,在所選擇的專門領域裡更具競爭優勢。大學圖書館設備良好,書籍、參考用書、雜誌、報紙、電腦網路服務,所有你需要找資料的工具一應俱全,圖書館員及助理們可以回答你的問題。通常圖書館開放時間為早上9點到晚上10點,但期中及期末考前會開得較晚。

圖書館

7.1 借書
Checking Out a Book

Dialog 1 對話1

A: 嗨，我可以幫你嗎？

A: Hi. May I help you?

B: 可以，我想知道如何借出書籍。

B: Yes. I'd like to know how to check out a book.

A: 好，讓我看你的學生證及你要的書。

A: Sure. Just let me see your student I.D. card and the book you want.

B: 在這裡。

B: Here they are.

A: 好的。

A: Good.

Dialog 2 對話2

A: 嗨，我想借這本書。

A: Hi. I want to check out this book.

B: 你有學生證嗎？

B: Do you have your student card?

A: 有。

A: Yes, I do.

B: 好，我看一下，然後我會幫你借出。

B: OK. Let me see it, and then I'll sign the book out to you.

A: 我可以借多久？

A: How long can I keep it?

B: 兩個星期。

B: Two weeks.

A: 好，我也預借了一本書。

A: Great. I also reserved a book.

B: 你有收到通知說書在這裡了嗎？

B: Did you receive a notice saying it's here now?

A: 沒有，我只是想問問看。

A: No. I just thought I'd ask.

B: 書名是什麼？我看一下是不是在這裡。

B: What is the book's title? I'll see if it's here now.

A: 書名是「回奔」。

A: The title is Running Back.

B: 沒有，還沒進來，但已經逾期了，我會聯絡借出的人。

B: No. It's not in yet. It's overdue though. I'll contact the person that has it.

A: 這倒提醒我，借書逾期罰款多少錢？

A: That reminds me. What is the fine for overdue books?

預備 校園 選課 新生說明 上課前 課堂上 課後交流 圖書館 體育館 餐廳 課外活動 申請獎助 當助教

B: 每天 50 分錢。 ➤ **B:** Fifty cents a day.

Useful Phrases 實用語句

○ **學生 / 圖書館使用人 Student/Library User**

1. 我想知道如何借出書籍。

   I'd like to know how to check out a book.

2. 我想借這本書。

   I want to check out this book.

3. 我想預借一本書。

   I want to reserve a book.

4. 我有一本逾期的書。

   I have an overdue book.

5. 你有一本叫做「回奔」的書嗎？

   Do you have a book called Running Back?

6. 期刊區在哪裡？

   Where is the periodical section?

7. 我想知道參考書區在哪裡？

   I want to know where the reference section is.

8. 請幫我找這本書。

   Please help me locate this book.

9. 這裡有個人的自修區嗎？

   Are there any private study rooms here?

10. 視聽室在哪裡？

    Where is the audio-visual room?

11. 這裡有影印機嗎？

    Is there a copy machine here?

12. 我需要用網路。

    I need Internet access.

◎ 圖書館員 Librarian

1. 我需要看你的圖書館證或學生證。

   I need to see your library or student card.

2. 我會替你保留那本書。

   I'll reserve the book for you.

3. 請在此簽名。

   Please sign here.

4. 你可以保有兩個星期。

   You can have it for two weeks.

5. 你可以展延借閱期限。

   You may extend the lending period.

6. 期刊區在那邊。

   The periodical section is over there.

7. 我會告訴你那區在哪裡。

   I'll show you where that section is.

8. 你要的書還回來時我會通知你。

   I'll notify you when the book you want is returned.

Language Power 字詞補給站

◆ 圖書館 Library

check out	借出
return	還書
copy machine	影印機
copy card	影印卡
on reserve	保留，備用
on the shelves	架上
overdue	逾期
fine	罰金
late fee	逾期罰金
Head Librarian	圖書館館長
operating hours	開放時間
reading room	閱覽室

預備 校園 選課 新生說明 上課前 課堂上 課後交流 圖書館 體育館 餐廳 課外活動 申請獎助 當助教

預備 校園 選課 新生說明 上課前 課堂上 課後交流 圖書館 體育館 餐廳 課外活動 申請獎助 當助教

7.2 詢問借閱規則
Asking about Rules for Checking Out Books

 Dialog 對話

A: 嗨，我可以問你一個問題嗎？

A: Hi. Can I ask you a question?

B: 可以，什麼問題呢？

B: Yes. What is your question?

A: 我可以保留借出的書多久？

A: How long can I keep a book I check out?

B: 一般藏書可以借2個星期。

B: A book from the general collection can be kept two weeks.

A: 我知道了，所有書都這樣嗎？

A: I see. Is that true of all the books?

B: 不，保留區內的藏書只可借出2天。

B: No. Books that are in reserve can only be checked out for two days.

A: 還有其他的例外我該知道嗎？

A: Are there other exceptions I should know about?

B: 期刊及參考書不能外借。

B: Periodicals and reference books cannot be checked out.

A: 我要如何使用呢？ → **A:** How can I use them?

B: 你必須在圖書館內使用。 → **B:** You must use them in the library.

A: 我需要辦借出嗎？ → **A:** Do I have to check them out?

B: 不用，你只要從架上取下，但只能在館內使用。 → **B:** No. You just take them off the shelf, but you can only use them in the library.

A: 我了解了，謝謝。 → **A:** I see. Thank you.

Word Bank 字庫

> general collection n. 一般藏書
> in reserve 保留的
> exception [ɪk`sɛpʃən] n. 例外
> periodical [ˌpɪrɪ`ɑdɪkl] n. 期刊
> reference book n. 參考書

Useful Phrases 實用語句

1. 我可以保留借出的書多久？

   How long can I keep a book I check out?

2. 所有書都是這樣嗎？

   Is that true of all the books?

3. 還有其他的例外我該知道嗎？

   Are there other exceptions I should know about?

預備｜校園｜選課｜新生說明｜上課前｜課堂上｜課後交流｜圖書館｜體育館｜餐廳｜課外活動｜申請獎助｜當助教

預備
校園
選課
新生說明
上課前
課堂上
課後交流
圖書館
體育館
餐廳
課外活動
申請獎助
當助教

4. 我要如何使用呢？

How can I use them?

5. 我需要辦理借出嗎？

Do I have to check them out?

6. 我需要把書放回架子上嗎？

Do I need to put the books I read back to the shelf?

7. 我該把書留在桌上嗎？

Should I just leave the books on the table?

7.3 還書
Returning a Book

Dialog 對話

A: 不好意思，我要在哪裡還書？

A: Excuse me. Where do I return this book?

B: 你可以放在總櫃臺這裡。

B: You can leave it here at the main desk.

A: 可以在圖書館關門後還書嗎？

A: Is it possible to return books after the library is closed?

B: 可以，在左邊大門外面有一個還書箱。

B: Yes. There is a drop box outside the main doors on the left side.

A: 謝謝。

A: Thank you.

預備

校園

選課

新生說明

上課前

課堂上

課後交流

圖書館

體育館

餐廳

課外活動

申請獎助

當助教

Word Bank 字庫

main desk n. 總櫃臺

drop box n. 還書箱

Useful Phrases 實用語句

1. 我要在哪裡還書？

   Where do I return this book?

2. 可以在圖書館關門後還書嗎？

   Is it possible to return books after the library is closed?

7.4 續借
Renewing a Checked Out Book

Dialog 對話

A: 我想續借這本書。	**A:** I would like to renew this book.
B: 我先看看是否有別人要借。	**B:** First let me see if anyone else has asked for it.
A: 好的。	**A:** All right.
B: 好，沒問題。沒人要借，我需要你的證件。	**B:** OK. No problem. No one has requested it. I'll need your ID card.
A: 在這裡。	**A:** Here you are.

左側邊欄（由上而下）：預備　校園　選課　新生說明　上課前　課堂上　課後交流　**圖書館**　體育館　餐廳　課外活動　申請獎助　當助教

B: 好，我會將你的借書時間延長 2 週。

B: Alright. I'll renew your borrowing period for two more weeks.

A: 謝謝。

A: Thanks.

Word Bank 字庫

renew [rɪ`nju] v. 續借；更新
request [rɪ`kwɛst] v. 要求
borrowing period n. 借書期間

Useful Phrases 實用語句

1. 我想續借這本書。

   I would like to renew this book.

2. 沒人要借。

   No one has requested it.

7.5 逾期罰金
Late Fee

Dialog 對話

A: 我有一本書逾期了。

A: I have a book that is overdue.

B: 我看一下電腦過期多久。

B: Let me look on the computer to see how late it is.

A: 好。

A: OK.

B: 電腦顯示過期 2 天，罰金加起來是 1 元。

B: It says here that it is two days overdue. That will add up to a $1.00 fine.

A: 我要怎麼付？

A: How do I pay the fine?

B: 你可以在總櫃臺付。

B: You can do it here at the main counter.

A: 我可以晚點付嗎？

A: Can I pay it later?

B: 可以，但是記得圖書館會有紀錄。

B: Yes, but remember that the library keeps a record.

A: 我最遲可以什麼時候付？

A: What's the latest I can pay?

B: 你必須在正式畢業前付清所有罰金。

B: You will have to pay all fines before you can officially graduate.

A: 我知道了，謝謝你。

A: I understand. Thank you.

🖊 Word Bank 字庫

overdue [`ovɚ`dju] adj. 過期的
main counter n. 總櫃臺

預備

校園

選課

新生說明

上課前

課堂上

課後交流

圖書館

體育館

餐廳

課外活動

申請獎助

當助教

📖 Useful Phrases 實用語句

1. 我要怎麼付罰金？
   How do I pay the fine?
2. 我可以晚點付嗎？
   Can I pay it later?
3. 我最遲可以什麼時候付？
   What's the latest I can pay?
4. 圖書館會有紀錄。
   The library keeps a record.

7.6 微縮膠片
Microfilm

🏃 Dialog 對話

A: 對不起，我需要找微縮膠片。

A: Excuse me. I need to find an article in the microfilm section.

B: 好，你知道出版品的名稱或印製年份嗎？

B: OK. Do you know the publication, title or year it was printed?

A: 我知道出版品及日期。

A: I know what publication and the date.

B: 好，我給你看膠片檔及閱讀器。

B: Good. Let me show you the film files and the viewers.

A: 謝謝。

A: Thank you.

B: 我也會示範如何裝膠片，如果你有任何問題讓我知道。

B: I'll show you how to load the film too. Let me know if you need any other help.

A: 我想知道可以看多久？

A: I'd like to know how long I can look at the film.

B: 這裡沒有時間限制，但我們這區下午6點關閉。

B: There is no time regulation here. We close this section at 6 p.m. however.

A: 我知道了，多謝。

A: I see. Thank you very much.

✎ Word Bank 字庫

microfilm [`maɪkrə,fɪlm] n. 微縮膠片
publication [,pʌblɪ`keʃən] n. 出版品
film file n. 膠片檔
viewer [`vjuə] n. 閱讀器
time regulation n. 時間規定
section [`sɛkʃən] n. 區

📖 Useful Phrases 實用語句

1. 我需要找微縮膠片。

   I need to find an article in the microfilm section.

2. 我知道出版品及日期。

   I know what publication and the date.

3. 我想知道膠片我可以看多久？

   I'd like to know how long I can look at the film.

4. 我給你看膠片檔及閱讀器。

   Let me show you the film files and the viewers.

預備　校園　選課　新生說明　上課前　課堂上　課後交流　圖書館　體育館　餐廳　課外活動　申請獎助　當助教

5. 我也會示範如何裝膠片。

   I'll show you how to load the film too.

7.7 期刊區
Periodicals Section

Dialog 對話

A: 嗨,我需要找一本過期的「明星生涯」雜誌。

A: Hi. I need to find a past copy of Stars Career magazine.

B: 新一期的雜誌及報紙在那邊的架子上,舊一點的在書架上。

B: New editions of magazines and newspapers are on the racks over there. Older editions are on the shelves.

A: 最快找到的方法是什麼?

A: What is the easiest way to find it?

B: 每本都按字母及日期順序,所以就找 S 區。

B: Everything is in alphabetical order and by date, so just look in the S section.

A: 好,我知道了,謝謝。

A: OK. I see. Thanks.

B: 不客氣。

B: No problem.

預備

校園

選課

新生說明

上課前

課堂上

課後交流

圖書館

體育館

餐廳

課外活動

申請獎助

當助教

Word Bank 字庫

past copy 過期的…(印刷品)

edition [ɪˋdɪʃən] n. 期

shelves [ʃɛlvz] n. 書架

rack [ræk] n. 架子

in alphabetical order 按字母順序

Useful Phrases 實用語句

1. 我需要找一本過期的雜誌。

   I need to find a past copy of a magazine.

2. 最快找到的方法是什麼？

   What is the easiest way to find it?

3. 每本都按字母及日期順序。

   Everything is in alphabetical order and by date.

7.8 影印
Photocopying

Dialog 對話

A: 對不起，我可以在哪裡影印？

A: Excuse me. Where can I make some photocopies?

B: 影印機在影印室。

B: The photocopy machines are in the copying room.

A: 我要怎麼付影印費？

A: How do I pay for the copies?

預備
校園
選課
新生說明
上課前
課堂上
課後交流
圖書館
體育館
餐廳
課外活動
申請獎助
當助教

B: 你可以用學生證，如果它是儲值型的。

B: You can use your student card if it is an account type.

A: 我可以在這裡付嗎？

A: Can I pay here?

B: 可以。

B: Yes.

A: 我要付現金嗎？

A: Do I have to pay cash?

B: 要，我們只接受現金。

B: Yes. We only accept cash for payment.

A: 我了解了。我可以買影印卡嗎？

A: I see. Is it possible to buy a copy card?

B: 可以，你可以在圖書館總櫃臺購買。

B: Yes. You can buy them at the library's main desk.

A: 謝謝。

A: Thank you.

Word Bank 字庫

photocopy [`fotə‚kɑpɪ] v., n. 影印 (本)
an account type n. 儲值型

預備

校園

選課

新生說明

上課前

課堂上

課後交流

圖書館

體育館

餐廳

課外活動

申請獎助

當助教

Useful Phrases 實用語句

1. 我要怎麼付影印費？

   How do I pay for the copies?

2. 我可以買影印卡嗎？

   Is it possible to buy a copy card?

3. 你可以用學生證，如果它是儲值型的。

   You can use your student card if it is an account type.

4. 我們只接受現金。

   We only accept cash for payment.

5. 你可以在圖書館總櫃臺購買。

   You can buy them at the library's main desk.

Notes 小叮嚀

影印及手機拍照應有法律思量，不侵犯他人權益。

7.9 購買影印卡
Buying a Copy Card

Dialog 對話

A: 哈囉，我可以幫你嗎？

A: Hello. May I help you?

B: 可以，我想購買影印卡。

B: Yes. I want to buy a copy card.

A: 要多少金額的呢？

A: What amount?

B: 價錢範圍是多少？

B: What is the price range?

A: 最少是 5 美元。

A: The least you can spend is \$5.

B: 好，我要買 10 美元。

B: OK. I'd like to buy \$10 worth.

A: 好，我拿給你。

A: Sure. I'll get it for you.

B: 謝謝。

B: Thank you.

Useful Phrases 實用語句

1. 我想要購買影印卡。

   I want to buy a copy card.

2. 要多少金額的呢？

   What amount?

3. 價錢範圍是多少？

   What is the price range?

7.10 了解大學圖書館規則
Understanding University Library Rules

上圖書館對學生來說是家常便飯,除了就讀學校的圖書館之外,學生也可能用到校外其他圖書館,雖說每個圖書館有自己的規則及開放時間,但多數美國大學圖書館有一些通則。這些規則是為大學教職員及學生從大學資源設備獲得最大利益而設。

7.10a 會員 Membership

☙ 學生會員 Student Membership

Current students enrolled at the University are entitled to student membership.

大學註冊學生享有學生會員身分。

☙ 區域會員 Regional Membership

Regional Membership is available to staff employed by and students enrolled at partner colleges of the University.

受雇或註冊於大學合作院校之教職員及學生。

☙ 參考會員 Reference Membership

Other persons may be granted Reference Membership, decided by the Librarian. This membership shall be limited to the material within the library.

在圖書館員判定下,未註冊者或可成為參考會員,但會員資格行使僅限圖書館館藏。

☙ 會員資格 Eligibility for Membership

Applicants are required to provide evidence of their eligibility for membership.

申請人必須提供會員資格憑證。

☙ 會員必須 Members shall

Retain membership cards for the duration of their membership; notify the Librarian of any changes of address. Follow the following rules and obligations.

資格期間持有會員卡,通知圖書館員任何地址更改,遵守以下規則及義務。

預備 校園 選課 新生說明 上課前 課堂上 課後交流 圖書館 體育館 餐廳 課外活動 申請獎助 當助教

7.10b 借閱 Borrowing

🔖 圖書館證 Membership Cards

No items or services will be given without a valid card being shown. Cards are not transferable and the person to whom any card is issued will be held responsible for any items taken by the use of the card unless the loss of the card is reported to the Librarian. Any loss must be reported immediately.

需要有效的圖書館證才可以享有服務，證件不可轉讓，證件持有人除向圖書館員舉報遺失證件外，必須為該卡所造成的損失負責；任何損失必須立即報告。

🔖 借閱限制 Loan Allowances

Members can borrow up to the limit allowed within their category of membership but limits may be placed on the number of items loaned for some categories of materials.

會員可以依其身分借到他們被允許的最大數量，但須受特定項目允許借出的限制。

🔖 借閱期限 Period of Loan

All books must be returned on or before the date due or earlier if the member is notified that an item is required by another reader.

所有書籍必須在到期日當日或之前歸還 (如果會員被通知有另外讀者要求借閱)。

🔖 特殊條件 Special Conditions

The Librarian can use his/her discretion, impose special conditions governing the use or loan of any item.

圖書館員判定借閱使用的特殊條件。

🔖 逾期項目 Overdue Items

The operation of the University Library depends on all members co-operating in the prompt return of items.

大學圖書館的運作有賴大家迅速歸還所借項目。

The date and/or time of return will be shown on each item issued.

每項歸還日期及 / 或時間要註記。

Fines start immediately the item falls overdue and are on the basis of day (or part thereof) or hour (or part thereof) as appropriate to the loan category.

罰金在逾期後立即開始計算，罰金需按天數 (或部分) 或時數 (或部分) 計算，視借閱項目而定。

The scale of fines shall be displayed in all libraries and on the library's website. Fines and penalties levied may be reduced or waived by the Librarian.

罰金計算方式在圖書館網站上公告，圖書館員可以裁定減少或免除罰金。

No further loans will be made to members having items overdue or fines not paid.

會員有逾期或未付罰金不能再借閱其他項目。

授權同意及著作權限制

License Agreements and Copyright Restrictions

Information resources, software applications and recordings are subject to license agreements and copyright restrictions. Users must ensure they comply by following advisory notices provided. Access to certain electronic and/or digital services may be restricted to certain categories of membership due to license constraints.

資訊來源、軟體運用及影音視訊受授權及著作權限制。使用者必須確實遵守警語，電子及 / 或數位服務因授權限制可能僅限特定會員。

7.10c 館際借閱 Inter-library Loans

Books and other materials may be borrowed from other libraries for use by members of the University Library.

會員可以向其他圖書館借閱書籍及其他資料。

7.10d 影印 Photocopying

Members using photocopying facilities are bound by the terms of current copyright laws.

會員使用影印機必須受當時著作權法律條款規範。

預備
校園
選課
新生說明
上課前
課堂上
課後交流
圖書館
體育館
餐廳
課外活動
申請獎助
當助教

7.10e 損害或遺失書籍資料賠償
Damage to or Loss of Books and Materials

Any damage to or loss of books or materials from the Libraries shall be charged for at the current replacement value or repair cost. The decision whether to repair or replace the item will be decided by the Librarian.

圖書館之任何損害或遺失書籍要以當時重置市價或修補費用計費,須修補或重置由圖書館員裁定。

Any overdue item not returned after the sending of a final overdue reminder will be considered lost. The Librarian shall assess the cost of replacing the item and the member shall be charged accordingly.

任何逾期不還項目於寄出最後逾期通知後認定為遺失,圖書館員估算重置損失依此向該會員收費。

7.10f 安全 Security

All Library materials shall be issued before removal from the Library.

所有圖書資料要經過借出手續才能從圖書館帶出。

All members shall allow members of the Library staff to examine any items which they are taking with them when leaving the Library.

會員應允許圖書館職員檢查任何他們要帶離圖書館的項目。

7.10g 舉止行為 Conduct

The Libraries of the University are provided for the benefit of everyone. Any person considered to be acting in a way not proper will be excluded from use of the facilities.

大學圖書館是為每位會員利益而設,任何人有不恰當之行為將被免除使用此設備之資格。

Silence must be maintained in areas designated as "quiet" areas, and noise should be kept to reasonable levels.

規劃為安靜之區域要保持安靜,噪音都要在合理範圍內。

Food and drink, with the exception of bottled water, may not be consumed in the Libraries.

除了瓶裝水，不可以在圖書館內飲食。

Members should remove all belongings from tables whenever they leave the Library. The University shall not be responsible for the security of any personal property left within the Library.

會員應該帶走所有桌上屬於他們的物品，圖書館對任何留在館內的物品概不負責。

All animals are prohibited from Library buildings with the exception of guide dogs for the blind.

除導盲犬外，圖書館禁止任何動物入內。

Library users are not permitted to make or take telephone calls within the library. Mobile phones shall be switched to silent mode at all times.

圖書館內不可撥打或接聽電話，手機務必切到靜音模式。

7.10h 緊急關閉 Emergency Closure

In the event of an emergency requiring closure of the Library, everyone must leave immediately.

遇緊急情況需要關閉圖書館，會員必須立即離開。

7.10i 取消圖書館證 Withdrawal of Library Rights

Anyone failing to follow these rules may have their Library privileges withdrawn by the member of the Library Staff on duty. Persistent violators will be reported to the Librarian who will discuss the matter with the appropriate Dean of Faculty. Disciplinary action may follow.

任何人不遵守這些規則可能遭遇值班圖書館職員取消圖書館資格，屢犯將提報圖書館員，他/她將與適當之院長討論採取可能的進一步紀律處分。

Language Power 字詞補給站

◆ 圖書館規則 Library Rules

entitle	享有
grant	授予
discretion	謹慎
eligibility	資格
notify	通知
obligations	義務
valid	有效的
transferable	可轉讓的
prompt return	迅速歸還
impose	加諸於
waive	免除；放棄
copyright restrictions	著作權限制
advisory notice	警語
license constraints	授權限制
restricted	受限制的
bound by the terms of current copyright	受著作權法條款規範
repair or replace	修補或重置
final overdue reminder	最後逾期通知
assess	估算
removal	帶出；移動
benefit	利益
excluded	被免除
exception	例外
belongings	(屬於某人的)物品
prohibited	禁止
guide dogs	導盲犬
silent mode	靜音模式
privileges withdrawn	取消資格[特權]
persistent violators	屢犯
further disciplinary action	進一步紀律處分

7.11 校園網路
Campus Internet

7.11a 連線校園網路：設定帳號 Hooking Up to the Internet on Campus: Set up an Internet Account

Dialog 對話

A: 哈囉，學生服務中心，我可以為你效勞嗎？

A: Hello. Student Services Office. May I help you?

B: 嗨，我打電話來是因為我不知道如何設定網路帳號。

B: Hi. I'm calling because I don't know how to set up an Internet account on campus.

A: 你是本校的學生嗎？

A: Are you a student of this university?

B: 是的。

B: Yes, I am.

A: 你的電腦有無線網路功能嗎？

A: Does your computer have wireless capability?

B: 有。

B: Yes.

A: 到學校首頁點選「網路設定」圖樣。

A: Then just go to the University Home Page and click on the "Internet Setup" icon.

預備 校園 選課 新生說明 上課前 課堂上 課後交流 圖書館 體育館 餐廳 課外活動 申請獎助 當助教

B: 我要付費嗎？

B: Will I have to pay anything?

A: 不必，你已經付費，有上網服務的權利。

A: No. Your fees have already paid for your privilege to hook up to online service.

B: 我需要證件嗎？

B: Will I need I.D.?

A: 要，只要你的學生證號碼。你點選設定圖樣後，你會被導引輸入學生證號碼，之後你會被要求設定名稱及密碼，確定你寫下來，然後電腦會問你一些個人資料，如果你需要的話，你也會被導引到設定學校電子郵件，只要幾分鐘來完成設定。

A: Yes, only your student I.D. number. After you click on the icon, you will be directed to key in your student number. Then you'll be asked to set up your username and password. Make sure you write them down. Then, the computer will ask you some personal information. You'll also be directed to set up a school email account, if you need one. It only takes a few minutes to finish the setup.

B: 多謝，有關安全使用公共電腦我要知道什麼嗎？

B: OK, thank you very much. What do I need to know about using a public computer safely?

A: 如果你用公共電腦，當你完成時，要確認點選「登出」，這樣才沒有人能竊取你的資料。

A: If you use a public computer, be sure to click on "exit" when you finish so that no one can steal your information.

B: 再次感謝，我會記得。

B: Thanks again. I'll remember that.

Useful Phrases 實用語句

1. 我不知道如何設定網路帳號。

   I don't know how to set up an Internet account on campus.

2. 你的電腦有無線網路功能嗎？

   Does your computer have wireless capability?

3. 到學校首頁點選「網路設定」圖樣。

   Go to the University Home Page and click on the "Internet Setup" icon.

4. 有關安全使用公共電腦我要知道什麼嗎？

   What do I need to know about using a public computer safely?

7.11b 帳號出問題
Running into a Problem with the Account

Dialog 1 對話1

A: 嗨，我打來是因為我無法上網。

A: Hi. I'm calling because I can't get online.

預備　校園　選課　新生說明　上課前　課堂上　課後交流　圖書館　體育館　餐廳　課外活動　申請獎助　當助教

B: 你有上網過嗎？

B: Have you been online before?

A: 沒有，我正打算設定。

A: No. I'm trying to get set up.

B: 確認你的使用者名稱，大家常常在輸入使用者名稱時犯錯。

B: Check your username. Most of the time people make the mistake of entering their username incorrectly.

A: 還有其他常見的錯誤嗎？

A: Are there any other common mistakes made?

B: 有，確定你的學生證號碼輸入正確。

B: Yes. Make sure you enter your student I.D. number correctly.

A: 好，我會確認我輸入了什麼，謝謝。

A: Alright. I'll check what I entered. Thank you.

Useful Phrases 實用語句

1. 我無法上網。

   I can't get online.

2. 我正打算設定。

   I'm trying to get set up.

3. 確認你的使用者名稱。

   Check your username.

4. 確定你的學生證號碼輸入正確。

   Make sure you enter your student I.D. number correctly.

5. 還有其他常見的錯誤嗎？

   Are there any other common mistakes?

Dialog 2 （對話2）

A: 我打電話來是因為我忘了密碼，你可以幫我嗎？

A: I'm calling because I forgot my password. Can you help me?

B: 你只要點選「查詢密碼」鍵就行。

B: You simply click on the button that says "searching password."

A: 好，然後呢？

A: OK. Then what?

B: 你有看到電腦要你輸入使用者名稱嗎？

B: Do you see where the computer asks you to put in the username?

A: 有。

A: Yes.

B: 好，自動回覆系統會馬上寄密碼到你的電子郵件。

B: Alright, the automatic reply will send the password to your email right away.

A: 好，多謝。

A: OK. Thank you very much.

7.11c 電腦設備故障
Having a Problem with the Computer Facilities

Dialog （對話）

A: 對不起，我無法讓這部電腦運作。

A: Excuse me. I can't get this computer to function.

預備　校園　選課　新生說明　上課前　課堂上　課後交流　圖書館　體育館　餐廳　課外活動　申請獎助　當助教

預備 校園 選課 新生說明 上課前 課堂上 課後交流 圖書館 體育館 餐廳 課外活動 申請獎助 當助教

B: 讓我試試。

B: Let me try it.

A: 我一直在試著找線上圖書館內的資料。

A: I've been trying to search for something in the online library.

B: 好像是軟體有問題，我必須找工程師看一下。

B: There seems to be a software problem. I'll have to get a technician to look at it.

A: 我要等嗎？

A: Do I have to wait?

B: 不必，我找另一臺電腦給你用。

B: No. I'll find another computer for you to use.

A: 好，謝謝。

A: Great. Thanks.

B: 不客氣，請在這裡等一下。

B: No problem. Please wait here a minute.

A: 好。

A: Sure.

Useful Phrases 實用語句

1. 我要設定一個帳號。

   I want to set up an Internet account.

2. 我的帳號有問題。

   I'm having trouble with my account.

3. 我如何設定帳號？

   How do I set up my account?

4. 我忘了密碼。

   I forgot my password.

5. 我使用網路要另外付費嗎？

   Do I have to pay extra for Internet access?

6. 我無法連線。

   I can't get online.

7. 現在有電腦可以用嗎？

   Are there any computers available to use right now?

8. 這部電腦壞了。

   This computer is not working.

9. 我需要幫忙使用這臺電腦。

   I need help using this computer.

10. 我不懂如何用這系統。

    I don't understand how to use this system.

11. 我可以在中心使用電腦多久？

    How long can I use the computers in the center?

Tips 小祕訣

　　只要確認電腦有連線設備，任何想用校園網路 (包含無線網路) 的學生都可以向學校提出申請，校園網路服務已包含在學費內，不需再付費。要使用校園網路，首先要到學校網站內打開設定頁，輸入學生證號碼，取得使用者名稱及密碼，即可使用，當然你也需要一個電子郵件帳號收發郵件。

　　校園網路及資料庫隨時提供校園資料或公告，學生從加退選、查詢圖書、查詢本身修課狀況到社團活動、留言板等等都需要透過校園網路。如果使用上有任何問題，可以打電話給校園電腦助理獲得線上指導，或把電腦送過去請他們查看設定。

預備 校園 選課 新生說明 上課前 課堂上 課後交流 圖書館 體育館 餐廳 課外活動 申請獎助 當助教

Language Power 字詞補給站

電腦與網路
Computer and the Internet

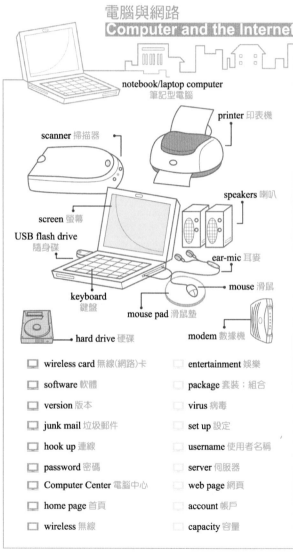

notebook/laptop computer 筆記型電腦

printer 印表機

scanner 掃描器

speakers 喇叭

screen 螢幕

USB flash drive 隨身碟

ear-mic 耳麥

keyboard 鍵盤

mouse 滑鼠

mouse pad 滑鼠墊

hard drive 硬碟

modem 數據機

- ☐ wireless card 無線(網路)卡
- ☐ software 軟體
- ☐ version 版本
- ☐ junk mail 垃圾郵件
- ☐ hook up 連線
- ☐ password 密碼
- ☐ Computer Center 電腦中心
- ☐ home page 首頁
- ☐ wireless 無線

- ☐ entertainment 娛樂
- ☐ package 套裝；組合
- ☐ virus 病毒
- ☐ set up 設定
- ☐ username 使用者名稱
- ☐ server 伺服器
- ☐ web page 網頁
- ☐ account 帳戶
- ☐ capacity 容量

預備 校園 選課 新生說明 上課前 課堂上 課後交流 圖書館 體育館 餐廳 課外活動 申請獎助 當助教

7.12 在學校書店
At the Campus Bookstore

Dialog 對話

A: 嗨，歷史區在哪裡？

A: Hi. Where is the history section?

B: 你要一般歷史或是歷史教科書區？

B: Do you want the general history section or the history textbook section?

A: 歷史教科書。

A: History textbooks.

B: 走到樓上區域，所有教科書都在那上面。

B: Go to the section upstairs. All the textbooks are up there.

A: 謝謝。

A: Thanks.

B: 你準備要買時，確定出示你的學生證。

B: When you are ready to buy, be sure to present your student I.D. card.

A: 我現在還沒有學生證。

A: I don't have mine yet.

B: 你有你已付學費的任何證明嗎？

B: Do you have any proof that you paid tuition?

預備 校園 選課 新生說明 上課前 課堂上 課後交流 圖書館 體育館 餐廳 課外活動 申請獎助 當助教

A: 有，我有收據。

A: Yes, I have a receipt.

B: 出示給出納人員，你可以打八折。

B: Present that to the cashier; you'll get a 20% discount.

A: 謝謝你告訴我。

A: Thank you for telling me.

Word Bank 字庫

textbook [`tɛkst͵bʊk] n. 教科書
section [`sɛkʃən] n. 部門；區域
present [prɪ`zɛnt] v. 出示

Useful Phrases 實用語句

1. 你有你已付學費的任何證明嗎？

   Do you have any proof that you paid tuition?

2. 把收據出示給出納人員。

   Present the receipt to the cashier.

Notes 小叮嚀

　　學生證可以讓你在校園或附近不同種類的商店，如電影院、書店、餐飲店等，享受八或九折的折扣。

Unit 8 University Athletic Facilities

體育館

註冊美國大學的學生通常享有免費使用運動器材的權力，但置物櫃及其他服務可能需要一些費用。設備一般包含游泳池、舉重室、有氧運動器具、籃球場、網球場、跑步區、置物櫃及淋浴間，足球場及棒球場要視校園大小而定。特別的活動或比賽通常需要一點費用。運動設備在白天開放給一般學生，但有部分區域會保留給各式校隊，多數大學的運動設備足夠學生使用。

預備
校園
選課
新生說明
上課前
課堂上
課後交流
圖書館
體育館
餐廳
課外活動
申請獎助
當助教

8.1 需要運動的對話
About the Need to Exercise

Dialog 對話

A: 我越來越胖。

A: I'm getting fat.

B: 你不胖,但是你要練體格。

B: You're not fat, but you need to get into shape.

A: 對,但什麼運動呢?

A: Yes, but what exercise?

B: 校園提供許多選擇,網球、有氧運動、舉重、游泳及其他。

B: The university offers many options, tennis, aerobics, weight lifting, swimming, and others.

A: 我想我應該選一樣來加強。

A: I guess I should pick one to concentrate on.

B: 是的,你也要吃得對。

B: Yes. You have to eat right too.

Word Bank 字庫

option [`ɑpʃən] n. 選擇
aerobics [ɛ`robɪks] n. 有氧運動
weight lifting n. 舉重
concentrate [`kɑnsən͵tret] v. 集中,加強

Useful Phrases 實用語句

1. 我要塑身 [練體格]。

   I need to get into shape.

2. 我應該選一樣加強。

   I should pick one to concentrate on.

3. 你要吃得對。

   You have to eat right.

Notes 小叮嚀

　　許多人都聽過新鮮人 15 磅 (freshman 15) 這個說法,為什麼會變胖呢?一個人在 (國) 外,飲食不知節制或常攝取高熱量食品當然是主因,美國食物分量不少,不好好注意就吃下許多起司、奶油及過甜的食品,晚上讀書吃宵夜也是幫兇;另外,因為壓力、想家、沮喪、焦慮、天氣寒冷也會造成飲食過度 (overeating),運動不夠或運動後狂吃當然也是變胖的原因。運動除了健身外,也是歐美人士避免昂貴醫藥費的重要生活方式。

8.2 與教練對話
Talking with a Coach

Dialog 對話

A: 哈囉,我想要問一些關於運動的問題。

A: Hello. I'd like to ask a few questions about exercising.

B: 我很樂意回答你的問題。

B: I'd be happy to answer your questions.

A: 我想控制我的體重並保持身材,我該怎麼做?

A: I want to control my weight and stay fit. What should I do?

預備
校園
選課
新生說明
上課前
課堂上
課後交流
圖書館
體育館
餐廳
課外活動
申請獎助
當助教

B: 我們這裡有很多課程及設備可以選擇。

B: We have many programs and facilities available here to choose from.

A: 我不習慣運動，如何有好的開始呢？

A: I'm not used to exercising. What is a good way to start?

B: 你可以試試一週三次有氧課並做一些舉重。

B: You should try an aerobics class three times a week, and do some weight lifting too.

A: 我知道了，我該聯絡誰更多詢問關於課程表及協助的資訊？

A: I see. Who should I contact for more information about scheduling and help?

B: 聯絡校園運動部門。

B: Contact the university's Sports and Athletic Department.

A: 好，謝謝。

A: OK. Thank you.

Word Bank 字庫

fit [fɪt] adj. 合適的
facilities [fə`sɪlətɪz] n. 設備

Useful Phrases 實用語句

1. 我想控制我的體重並保持身材。

   I want to control my weight and stay fit.

2. 我不習慣運動。

   I'm not used to exercising.

3. 如何有好的開始呢？

   What is a good way to start?

預備

校園

選課

新生說明

上課前

課堂上

課後交流

圖書館

體育館

餐廳

課外活動

申請獎助

當助教

4. 我該聯絡誰詢問更多資訊？

   Who should I contact for more information?

8.3 安排課程時間
Scheduling Exercise

 Dialog （對話）

A: 嗨，我可以為你服務嗎？

A: Hi. Can I help you?

B: 可以，我需要知道有氧舞蹈課何時開始，以及什麼時候我可以用運動大樓的其他設備。

B: Yes. I need to know when aerobics classes start, and when I can use other facilities at the sports complex.

A: 我們的課程表在網站上，但你也可以拿這張課程表。

A: Our schedule is on the net, but you can take this schedule sheet also.

B: 好，謝謝。

B: Good. Thanks.

 Word Bank （字庫）

sports complex n. 運動大樓

Useful Phrases （實用語句）

1. 有氧舞蹈課何時開始？

   When do aerobics classes start?

預備
校園
選課
新生說明
上課前
課堂上
課後交流
圖書館
體育館
餐廳
課外活動
申請獎助
當助教

2. 我什麼時候可以用運動大樓的其他設備？

When can I use other facilities at the sports complex?

8.4 在體育館
At the Gym

 Dialog （對話）

A: 哈囉，這是體育館的正門嗎？

A: Hello. Is this the main entrance to the gym?

B: 是的，你是這裡的學生嗎？

B: Yes. Are you a student here?

A: 是的。

A: Yes.

B: 你要將學生證留在總櫃臺。

B: You'll need to leave your student card here at the main desk.

A: 好，在這裡。置物間在哪邊？

A: OK. Here you are. Which way is the locker room?

B: 男生在走廊盡頭那邊。

B: Men go down the hall that way.

A: 我需要帶自己的毛巾嗎？

A: Do I need to bring my own towel?

B: 不用，有供應。使用後放在毛巾簍內就可以。

B: No. They are provided. Just make sure you leave it in the towel bin after you use it.

A: 這是我第一次來，有任何我該知道的特別規定嗎？

A: This is the first time I've been here. Are there any special rules I should know?

B: 這裡是我們要大家遵守的規定清單。

B: Here is a list of the rules we ask everyone to follow.

A: 謝謝。

A: Thanks.

B: 如果你有任何問題，問任何一位學生義工或一般值班職員。

B: If you have any questions or problems, ask any of the student volunteer staff or regular staff on duty.

A: 我怎麼知道他們是誰？

A: How will I know who they are?

B: 他們穿著藍黃襯衫。

B: They are the people wearing the blue and yellow shirts.

Word Bank 字庫

towel bin n. 毛巾簍
student volunteer staff n. 學生義工
staff on duty 值班職員

Useful Phrases 實用語句

1. 置物間在哪邊？

   Which way is the locker room?

右側邊欄：預備 校園 選課 新生說明 上課前 課堂上 課後交流 圖書館 體育館 餐廳 課外活動 申請獎助 當助教

預備

校園

選課

新生說明

上課前

課堂上

課後交流

圖書館

體育館

餐廳

課外活動

申請獎助

當助教

2. 我需要帶自己的毛巾嗎？

   Do I need to bring my own towel?

3. 有任何我需要知道的特別規定嗎？

   Are there any special rules I should know?

4. 我怎麼知道他們是誰？

   How will I know who they are?

8.5 使用置物櫃
Using a Locker

Dialog 對話

A: 對不起，我忘了問置物櫃。

A: Sorry. I forgot to ask about a locker.

B: 任何一個空的置物櫃你都可以用。

B: You can use any one that is empty.

A: 可以上鎖嗎？

A: Will it lock?

B: 可以，你可以自己帶鎖或用這裡的。

B: Yes. You need to bring your own lock or get one here.

A: 我需要一個鎖。

A: I need one.

B: 好，在這裡簽名，你回來拿學生證時歸還就可以了。

B: OK. Just sign here and return it when you come back to get your student card.

A: 謝謝。 **A:** Thank you.

Word Bank 字庫

locker [`lakə] n. 置物櫃

Useful Phrases 實用語句

1. 可以上鎖嗎？

   Will it lock?

2. 我需要一個鎖。

   I need a lock.

Information Bank 大補帖

◎ 美國運動設備通則

Typical Rules Common at Athletic Facilities in the USA

＊ Wear appropriate clothing for exercising 穿著適當衣服

＊ Use spill-proof beverage containers 使用防倒飲料容器

＊ Use appropriate entry and exit doors 使用適當出入口

＊ Store clothing and valuables in lockers 衣物及貴重物品放置物櫃

＊ Wear closed-toed shoes in the weight areas 在舉重區穿包鞋

＊ Wear non-marking soled shoes on all hardwood floors 硬木板上穿不會刮花的鞋子

＊ Clean your perspiration off the aerobic and resistive equipment 清除有氧及阻力設備上的汗水

＊ Use the court benches and shelves to store equipment and bags 使用場邊長凳或架子放設備或背包

＊ No eating, spitting, or fighting 勿飲食、吐痰或打鬥

＊ No hanging from the basketball rims 不可吊籃球框

＊ No using abusive language or harassing others 勿辱罵或騷擾他人

8.6 與重量訓練教練對話
Talking with a Weight Training Coach

 Dialog 對話

A: 對不起，我需要一些如何適當舉重的指導。

A: Excuse me. I need some instruction on how to properly lift weights.

B: 我來幫你。

B: I'll help you.

A: 謝謝。

A: Thank you.

B: 最主要是你需要確定開始之前已經做過伸展運動，並且在剛開始健身時不要舉太重。還有，當你舉很重時一定要有督導員在場。

B: Mostly you need to be sure you stretch before you start, and don't lift too much weight in the beginning of your work out. Also, always have a spotter present when you lift heavy weights.

A: 我需要重複舉重幾次？

A: How many times should I repeat a lift?

B: 我建議你從較輕的重量開始，並做三組十次舉重。

B: I suggest you start at a lower weight, and do three sets of ten lifts.

預備 校園 選課 新生說明 上課前 課堂上 課後交流 圖書館 體育館 餐廳 課外活動 申請獎助 當助教

A: 有人可以幫我擬一個舉重課程嗎？

A: Can someone help me develop a lifting program?

B: 可以，我可以為你做，我們來幫你設定，好嗎？

B: Yes. I'll do that for you. Let's get you set up now, OK?

A: 當然好囉，謝謝。

A: Sure. Thanks.

Word Bank 字庫

> instruction [ɪn`strʌkʃən] n. 指 [教] 導
> stretch [strɛtʃ] v. 伸展
> work out 健身
> spotter [`spɑtɚ] n. 督導員 [人]
> lift [lɪft] v. 舉 (起)

Useful Phrases 實用語句

1. 開始前先做伸展運動。

   Stretch before you start.

2. 剛開始時不要舉太重。

   Don't lift too much weight in the beginning.

3. 當你舉很重時一定要有督導員在場。

   Always have a spotter present when you lift heavy weights.

4. 我需要重複舉重幾次？

   How many times should I repeat a lift?

5. 有人可以幫我擬一個舉重課程嗎？

   Can someone help me develop a lifting program?

8.7 歸還
Return

 Dialog 對話

A: 這是我借的鎖。

A: Here is the lock I borrowed.

B: 好,這是你的學生證。

B: OK. Here is your student card.

A: 謝謝,體育館幾點開門及關門?

A: Thanks. What time does the gym open and close?

B: 週一到週六早上 8 點到晚上 11 點,週日早上 10 點開下午 5 點關。

B: The gym is open from 8 a.m. to 11 p.m. Monday through Saturday. On Sunday it opens at 10 a.m. and closes at 5 p.m.

A: 我知道了,那假日呢?

A: I see. What about holidays?

B: 主要假日休館。

B: It's closed on major holidays.

A: 學期中間的休假開放嗎?

A: Is it open during breaks between sessions?

B: 有。

B: Yes, it is.

Useful Phrases 實用語句

1. 這是我借的鎖。

   Here is the lock I borrowed.

2. 體育館幾點開門及關門？

   What time does the gym open and close?

3. 學期中間的休假開放嗎？

   Is it open during breaks between sessions?

8.8 詢問可使用時段及費用
Asking about Available Time and Cost

8.8a 在游泳池 At the Swimming Pool

Dialog 1 對話1

A: 你可以告訴我更衣室及淋浴間在哪裡嗎？

A: Can you tell me where the changing room and showers are?

B: 當然可以，從走廊直走，在你的左手邊。

B: Sure. They are both down the hall on your left.

A: 也有置物櫃嗎？

A: Are there lockers too?

B: 有，但你會需要一個鎖。

B: Yes. You'll need a lock though.

A: 好，那毛巾呢？

A: OK. What about a towel?

預備
校園
選課
新生說明
上課前
課堂上
課後交流
圖書館
體育館
餐廳
課外活動
申請獎助
當助教

預備 校園 選課 新生說明 上課前 課堂上 課後交流 圖書館 體育館 餐廳 課外活動 申請獎助 當助教

B: 你可以花 50 分租一條。

B: You can rent one for 50 cents.

A: 我需要泳帽嗎？

A: Do I need a swimming cap?

B: 不用，但你進泳池前要先沖澡。

B: No, but you must take a shower before entering the pool.

A: 我知道了，謝謝。

A: I see. Thank you.

Word Bank 字庫

changing room n. 更衣室
shower [ˋʃaʊɚ] n. 淋浴(處)
towel [ˋtaʊəl] n. 毛巾
swimming cap n. 泳帽

Useful Phrases 實用語句

1. 你可以告訴我更衣室及淋浴間在哪裡嗎？

   Can you tell me where the changing room and showers are?

2. 也有置物櫃嗎？

   Are there lockers too?

3. 那毛巾呢？

   What about a towel?

4. 我需要泳帽嗎？

   Do I need a swimming cap?

Dialog 2 　對話2

A: 對不起，使用游泳池有特別規定嗎？

A: Excuse me. Are there any special rules for using the pool?

B: 你要有真的泳衣，不可穿剪短的衣褲，飲食也禁止。

B: You need to have a real swimsuit. No cutoffs are allowed. Food and beverages are also prohibited.

Word Bank　字庫

cutoffs [`kʌt͵ɔfs] n. 剪短的衣褲
beverage [`bɛvərɪdʒ] n. 飲料
prohibit [pro`hɪbɪt] v. 禁止

Useful Phrases　實用語句

1. 使用游泳池有特別規定嗎？

   Are there any special rules for using the pool?

2. 不准穿著剪短的衣褲。

   No cutoffs are allowed.

3. 飲食也禁止。

   Food and beverages are also prohibited.

Dialog 3 　對話3

A: 可以潛水嗎？

A: Is diving OK?

B: 如果有救生員在值班就可以。

B: If the lifeguards are on duty, it's OK.

預備
校園
選課
新生說明
上課前
課堂上
課後交流
圖書館
體育館
餐廳
課外活動
申請獎助
當助教

A: 他們何時值班？ → **A:** When are they on duty?

B: 他們整天都在。 → **B:** They are on duty all day.

A: 有淺水區嗎？ → **A:** Is there a lap pool?

B: 有，在運動大樓的南端。 → **B:** Yes. It's on the south end of the sports complex.

Word Bank 字庫

diving [`daɪvɪŋ] n. 潛水
lifeguard [`laɪf͵gɑrd] n. 救生員
on duty 值班
lap pool n. 淺水區

Useful Phrases 實用語句

1. 可以潛水嗎？
   Is diving OK?
2. 他們何時值班？
   When are they on duty?
3. 有淺水區嗎？
   Is there a lap pool?

8.8b 保齡球課 Bowling Class

預備
校園
選課
新生說明
上課前
課堂上
課後交流
圖書館
體育館
餐廳
課外活動
申請獎助
當助教

Dialog 1　對話1

A: 好，各位，我們來拿適合的鞋子及保齡球。

A: OK, everybody. Let's get shoes and bowling balls that fit.

B: 我們怎麼取鞋？

B: How do we get the shoes?

A: 去櫃臺找助理幫忙。

A: Go to the counter and ask the assistant for help.

B: 那球呢？

B: How about the ball?

A: 去那裡試試架上的那些球。

A: Go over there and try out those on that rack.

B: 我使用它們需要付費嗎？

B: Do I have to pay for using them?

A: 球不必，但鞋子要2元。

A: Not for the ball, but you do have to pay $2 for the shoes.

B: 好，謝謝。

B: OK. Thanks.

Word Bank 字庫

> bowling balls n. 保齡球
> assistant [ə`sɪstənt] n. 助理

Dialog 2 對話2

A: 我需要一雙保齡球鞋。

A: I need a pair of bowling shoes.

B: 好,告訴我你的尺寸。

B: OK. Tell me your size.

A: 9 號。

A: 9.

B: 試一下這雙。

B: Try these on.

A: 好,(一秒後)好像太緊。

A: OK. (a second later) They seem too tight.

B: 這裡有一雙 9 號半。

B: Here is a pair of nine and a half.

A: 這雙好一點,很合腳。

A: These are better. They fit fine.

B: 好,將你的普通鞋留在這裡並且付 2元。

B: Good. Leave your regular shoes here and pay $2.

A: 鞋在這裡，還有 2 元。

A: Here you are. And here's $2.

B: 好，祝你玩的開心。

B: OK. Have fun.

 Word Bank 字庫

> bowling shoes n. 保齡球鞋
> regular shoes n. 普通鞋

Useful Phrases 實用語句

1. 我們怎麼取鞋？
   How do we get the shoes?
2. 我使用它們需要付費嗎？
   Do I have to pay for using them?
3. 鞋子好像太緊。
   They seem too tight.
4. 鞋子很合腳。
   The shoes fit fine.

Dialog 3 對話3

A: 這顆球適合我的手，其他的不是太鬆就是太緊。

A: This ball fits my hand well. The others are either too loose, or too tight.

B: 我的問題是大多數都太寬或太窄。

B: My problem is that most were too wide or narrow for my hand.

A: 我們現在準備好了，到球道去吧。

A: We're ready now. Let's go to the lanes.

B: 好，我們打球吧。 **B:** OK. Let's bowl.

Useful Phrases 實用語句

1. 這顆球適合我的手。

   This ball fits my hand well.

2. 其他的不是太鬆就是太緊。

   The others are either too loose or too tight.

3. 到球道去吧。

   Let's go to the lanes.

4. 我們去打球吧。

   Let's bowl.

This ball fits my hand well.

STRIKE

Language Power 字詞補給站

保齡球 Bowling

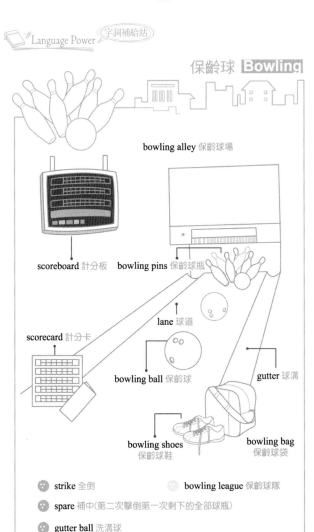

bowling alley 保齡球場

scoreboard 計分板　bowling pins 保齡球瓶

lane 球道

scorecard 計分卡

bowling ball 保齡球

gutter 球溝

bowling shoes
保齡球鞋

bowling bag
保齡球袋

strike 全倒　　　　　bowling league 保齡球隊

spare 補中(第二次擊倒第一次剩下的全部球瓶)

gutter ball 洗溝球

預備　校園　選課　新生說明　上課前　課堂上　課後交流　圖書館　體育館　餐廳　課外活動　申請獎助　當助教

8.8c 有氧舞蹈 Aerobics

Dialog 對話

A: 這是有氧舞蹈課嗎？

A: Is this where the aerobics class is?

B: 是的，30 分鐘後開始。

B: Yes. It will start in thirty minutes.

A: 有多少人上課呢？

A: How many people are in the class?

B: 通常 30 人左右。

B: About thirty usually.

A: 我可以在後面嗎？我是新來的。

A: Can I be in the back? I'm new to the class.

B: 可以，但你要確定可以清楚地看到老師示範。早點到，先來先贏。

B: OK, but make sure you can see the teacher's demo clearly. Come early. It's first come first serve.

A: 我可以穿這雙球鞋嗎？

A: Can I wear these sneakers?

B: 可以，球鞋、慢跑鞋、舞鞋都可以。

B: Sure. Sneakers, running shoes, and dance shoes are all OK.

A: 很好，謝謝。 **A:** Great. Thanks.

Word Bank 字庫

demo (demonstration) [ˋdɛmo] n. 示範 (教學)
sneakers [ˋsnikɚz] n. 球鞋
running shoes n. 慢跑鞋
dance shoes n. 舞鞋

Useful Phrases 實用語句

1. 這是有氧舞蹈課嗎？

   Is this where the aerobics class is?

2. 有多少人上課呢？

   How many people are in the class?

3. 我可以在後面嗎？我是新來的。

   Can I be in the back? I'm new to the class.

4. 先來先贏。

   It's first come first serve.

5. 我可以穿這雙球鞋嗎？

   Can I wear these sneakers?

8.9 學校健康中心
At the School Health Center

Dialog 1 對話1

A: 嗨，我可以幫你嗎？ **A:** Hi, may I help you?

預備
校園
選課
新生說明
上課前
課堂上
課後交流
圖書館
體育館
餐廳
課外活動
申請獎助
當助教

B: 可以，我打籃球受傷了，是我的手腕。

B: Yes. I just got hurt playing basketball. It's my wrist.

A: 坐在這裡，我會找人來看。

A: Sit down here. I'll get someone to look at it.

B: 謝謝。

B: Thanks.

Dialog 2 〈對話2〉

A: 哈囉，我是克瑞夫醫生，我聽說你受傷了。

A: Hello. I'm Doctor Craft. I hear you got hurt.

B: 是的，我與其他人打籃球，我跌倒，現在手腕很痛。

B: Yes. I was playing basketball with some other guys. I fell and now my wrist really hurts.

A: 好，我們看一下，你的手可以動嗎？

A: OK. Let's have a look at it. Can you move it?

B: 只能動一點點，真的很痛。

B: Just a little. It really hurts.

A: 好，可能是嚴重扭傷了，我們最好照一下 X 光確定。

A: OK. It's probably a bad sprain, but we'd better take X-rays and make sure.

B: 我要去哪裡照？

B: Where do I have to go for that?

A: 這裡，我來準備。 → **A:** We can do it here. I'll get things ready.

B: 會很久嗎？ → **B:** Will it take long?

A: 不會，只要幾分鐘。 → **A:** No. Only a couple of minutes.

B: 如果斷了呢？ → **B:** What if it is broken?

A: 我們先看 X 光，如果斷了，我們大概得上石膏。 → **A:** Let's see what the X-rays say first. If it is broken, we'll probably have to put a cast on it.

B: 我知道了。 → **B:** I see.

Word Bank 字庫

wrist [rɪst] n. 手腕
sprain [spren] n. 扭傷
X-rays [`ɛks͵re] n. X 光
cast [kæst] n. 石膏；模造物

Useful Phrases 實用語句

1. 我跌倒，現在手腕很痛。
   I fell and now my wrist really hurts.
2. 真的很痛。
   It really hurts.

預備
校園
選課
新生說明
上課前
課堂上
課後交流
圖書館
體育館
餐廳
課外活動
申請獎助
當助教

3. 可能是嚴重扭傷了。

It's probably a bad sprain.

4. 我要去哪裡照 X 光？

Where do I have to go for taking X-rays?

5. 會很久嗎？

Will it take long?

6. 如果斷了呢？

What if it is broken?

If it is broken, we'll probably have to put a cast on it.

It's broken.

Unit 9 University Food Venues and Restaurants Outide Campus
學校餐廳及校外餐館

美國大學有自己的餐廳、熟食區及點心區，住宿同學所付的租金內已包含學校供應的餐食 (meal plan)；在校內餐廳點餐與校外餐廳無異。

預備
校園
選課
新生說明
上課前
課堂上
課後交流
圖書館
體育館
餐廳
課外活動
申請獎助
當助教

9.1 在自助餐廳
At a Cafeteria

Dialog 對話

A: 對不起，我沒來過，我該怎麼做？

A: Excuse me. I've never been here before. What should I do?

B: 很簡單，只要拿盤子自己取用。

B: It's easy. Just pick up a plate and serve yourself.

A: 餐具在哪裡？

A: Where are the utensils?

B: 盤子旁邊。

B: Next to the plates.

A: 我可以拿第二輪嗎？

A: Can I have seconds?

B: 可以，你可以拿所有你想要的，自己來。

B: Yes. You can have all you want. Help yourself.

A: 謝謝。

A: Thanks.

預備

校園

選課

新生說明

上課前

課堂上

課後交流

圖書館

體育館

餐廳

課外活動

申請獎助

當助教

Word Bank 字庫

plate [plet] n. 盤子
serve [sɜv] v. 服務
utensil [ju`tɛnsl] n. 餐具
second [`sɛkənd] n. 第二輪

Useful Phrases 實用語句

1. 餐具在哪裡？

   Where are the utensils?

2. 只要拿盤子自己取用。

   Just pick up a plate and serve yourself.

3. 我可以拿第二輪嗎？

   Can I have seconds?

9.2 在大學餐廳
At a University Restaurant

Dialog 對話

A: 我們坐那裡。

A: Let's sit over there.

B: 好。

B: OK.

A: 我們得到櫃臺去點菜。

A: We have to go to the counter to order.

B: 好，你先去，我來顧位子。

B: OK. You go first and I'll keep the table.

預備
校園
選課
新生說明
上課前
課堂上
課後交流
圖書館
體育館
餐廳
課外活動
申請獎助
當助教

A: 告訴我你要什麼，我幫你點。

A: Tell me what you want and I'll order for you too.

B: 太好了，謝謝。

B: Great. Thanks.

9.3 在點心吧點餐
Ordering at a Snack Bar

Dialog 對話

A: 你要點什麼？

A: What would you like?

B: 我要兩份鮪魚三明治、兩份薯條、一杯可樂和一杯咖啡。

B: I want two tuna sandwiches, two orders of French fries, a coke and a coffee.

A: 你三明治要加熱嗎？

A: Do you want the sandwiches warmed up?

B: 要，謝謝。

B: Yes, please.

A: 可樂要多大杯？

A: Which size coke?

B: 中杯。

B: Medium.

A: 你的咖啡要奶精跟糖嗎？

A: Do you want cream and sugar for the coffee?

B: 只要奶精。

B: Just cream.

A: 好，總共 8.75 元。

A: OK. That will be $8.75.

B: 在這裡（給 10 元紙鈔）。

B: Here you are. (hands the cashier a $10 bill)

A: 找你 1.25 元。

A: $1.25 is your change.

B: 謝謝。

B: Thanks.

A: 你點的東西幾分鐘就會好。

A: Your order will be ready in a few minutes.

B: 好的。

B: OK.

✏ Word Bank 字庫

tuna sandwich **n.** 鮪魚三明治
French fries **n.** 薯條

預備　校園　選課　新生說明　上課前　課堂上　課後交流　圖書館　體育館　餐廳　課外活動　申請獎助　當助教

預備 校園 選課 新生說明 上課前 課堂上 課後交流 圖書館 體育館 餐廳 課外活動 申請獎助 當助教

📖 Useful Phrases 實用語句

1. 你三明治要加熱嗎？

   Do you want the sandwiches warmed up?

2. 你的咖啡要奶精跟糖嗎？

   Do you want cream and sugar for the coffee?

Language Power 字詞補給站

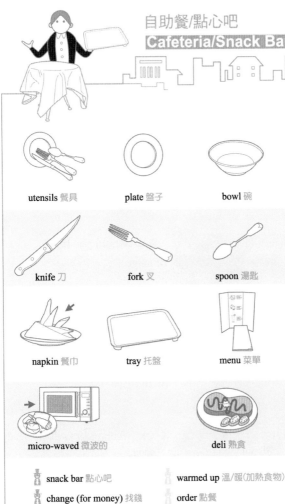

自助餐/點心吧
Cafeteria/Snack Bar

utensils 餐具

plate 盤子

bowl 碗

knife 刀

fork 叉

spoon 湯匙

napkin 餐巾

tray 托盤

menu 菜單

micro-waved 微波的

deli 熟食

snack bar 點心吧

change (for money) 找錢

cafeteria 自助餐

warmed up 溫/暖(加熱食物)

order 點餐

seconds (for food)
第二輪 (取用食物)

預備

校園

選課

新生說明

上課前

課堂上

課後交流

圖書館

體育館

餐廳

課外活動

申請獎助

當助教

預備
校園
選課
新生說明
上課前
課堂上
課後交流
圖書館
體育館
餐廳
課外活動
申請獎助
當助教

9.4 速食
Fast Food

Dialog 1 （對話1）

A: 我可以為你服務嗎？

A: May I help you?

B: 我要一份漢堡、薯條及一杯可樂。

B: I want a hamburger, fries and a coke.

A: 你漢堡要什麼大小呢？

A: Which size (of) hamburger do you want?

B: 大的。

B: Large.

A: 內用還是帶走？

A: Is this for here or to go?

B: 帶走。

B: To go.

A: 好的，你的餐點馬上就好。

A: OK. Your order will be ready soon.

Word Bank （字庫）

hamburger [`hæmbɜgɚ] n. 漢堡
fries (French fries) [fraɪz] n. 薯條

Dialog 2 對話2

A: 不好意思，我可以多要些紙巾嗎？

A: Excuse me. May I have more napkins?

B: 它們在調味料那邊。

B: They are over there with the condiments.

A: 那多要點番茄醬呢？

A: What about some more ketchup?

B: 也在那邊。

B: It's over there, too.

Word Bank 字庫

condiment [`kɑndəmənt] n. 調味料

ketchup [`kɛtʃəp] n. 番茄醬

Useful Phrases 實用語句

1. 我要再點些薯條。

   I want to order more fries.

2. 我要再點一個漢堡。

   I want to order another burger.

3. 我要的是套餐，不是單點漢堡。

   I'd like a meal, not just a hamburger.

4. 請不要放洋蔥。

   No onions, please.

5. 你們有什麼口味的冰淇淋？

   Which flavors of ice cream do you have?

Language Power 字詞補給站

Fast Food Menu (速食菜單)

Meals 餐點

- Hamburger / Cheeseburger / Bacon Cheeseburger (in quarter pound and half pound sizes) 漢堡 / 起司漢堡 / 培根起司漢堡 (1/4 磅及 1/2 磅)
- Chicken Burger 雞肉漢堡
- Fish Burger 魚堡
- Vegetarian Burger 素食漢堡
- French Fries 薯條
- Tatar Tots 薯餅
- Fried Chicken 炸雞
- Chicken Nuggets 炸雞塊
- Hot Dogs 熱狗

Salads 沙拉

- Chicken Salad 雞肉沙拉
- Caesar Salad 凱撒沙拉
- Garden Salad 田園沙拉
- Salad Dressing 沙拉醬 (Thousand Island 千島醬, Italian 義大利醬, oil and vinegar 油醋醬)

Breakfast 早餐

- Croissant Sandwiches 可頌三明治
- Pancakes with Sausage 鬆餅加香腸

Soups 湯

- Corn Soup 玉米濃湯

Beverages 飲料

- Cola 可樂
- Fanta 芬達
- Sprite 雪碧
- Orange juice 柳橙汁
- Ice Tea 冰紅茶
- Coffee 咖啡
- Hot Chocolate 熱巧克力
- Milkshakes 奶昔 (vanilla, chocolate, strawberry 香草、巧克力、草莓)

Desserts 甜點

- Banana Split 香蕉船
- Pie 派

9.5 遇到朋友
Bumping into a Friend

Dialog 對話

A: 嗨，卡爾，好久不見，你在這裡做什麼？

A: Hi, Carl. Long time no see. What are you doing here?

B: 我想吃些點心，今天讀了整天書。

B: I'm getting some snacks. I've been studying all day.

A: 你最近怎麼樣啊？

A: How are things going?

B: 還不錯。我參加滑雪社。

B: Not bad. I joined the skiing club.

A: 聽起來很好玩。

A: That sounds like fun.

B: 我們歡迎更多人參加。

B: We welcome more people to join.

A: 我會考慮，我們吃點東西放鬆一下。

A: I'll consider it. Let's get something to eat and relax for a while.

B: 我們可以去校園之井喝啤酒跟吃些點心。

B: We can go over to the Campus Well and get a beer and some snacks.

預備　校園　選課　新生說明　上課前　課堂上　課後交流　圖書館　體育館　餐廳　課外活動　申請獎助　當助教

A: 好主意，我們可以打電話找其他人來加入我們。

A: Good idea. We can call some others to come join us.

B: 好。

B: Right.

Word Bank 字庫

bump into 偶遇

skiing club n. 滑雪社

Useful Phrases 實用語句

1. 我們吃點東西放鬆一下。

   Let's get something to eat and relax for a while.

2. 我們可以打電話找其他人來加入我們。

   We can call some others to come join us.

Tips 小祕訣

校園內學生中心會有咖啡廳及自助餐廳 (cafeteria) 提供餐飲。校園內其他場所可能會有點心吧 (snack bars)、餐廳或是校園酒吧 (campus pub) (但要進入者必須年滿 21 歲)。

9.6 到校外餐廳
Going to a Restaurant outside Campus

學生常喜歡到校園附近餐廳用餐，在紐約這樣的大城市就有非常多的選擇。以下是一些典型的對話，包含食物名稱及其他校園內外、附近或較遠的餐廳都派得上用場的飲食資訊。

9.6a 選擇餐廳 Choosing a Restaurant

 Dialog 1 對話1

A: 你知道有什麼好餐廳嗎？

A: Do you know of any good restaurants?

B: 直走有一家不錯。

B: There is a good one down the street.

A: 叫什麼名字呢？

A: What is its name?

B: 我不記得，但是它的義大利菜很棒。

B: I don't remember, but it has great Italian food.

Word Bank 字庫

restaurant [`rɛstərənt] n. 餐廳
Italian [ɪ`tæljən] adj. 義大利的

Useful Phrases 實用語句

1. 我們先看菜單吧。

   Let's look at the menu first.

2. 我可以看菜單嗎？

   May I see the menu?

3. 我想預訂明天的位子。

   I want to make a reservation for tomorrow.

4. 這裡有吸煙區嗎？

   Is there a smoking section here?

5. 我們要等多久呢？

   How long will we have to wait?

預備 校園 選課 新生說明 上課前 課堂上 課後交流 圖書館 體育館 餐廳 課外活動 申請獎助 當助教

預備
校園
選課
新生說明
上課前
課堂上
課後交流
圖書館
體育館
餐廳
課外活動
申請獎助
當助教

6. 我們會晚點回來。

We'll come back later.

Dialog 2 對話2

A: 你們這裡有中國菜嗎？

A: Do you serve Chinese food here?

B: 有，我們有西式及中式菜肴。

B: Yes, we have both Western and Chinese dishes.

A: 我可以先看菜單嗎？

A: May I see the menu first?

B: 當然，請等一下。

B: Sure, just a minute.

Word Bank 字庫

western [`wɛstən] adj. 西方的
dish [dɪʃ] n. 菜肴

Useful Phrases 實用語句

1. 請再多給我們一分鐘。

Please give us another minute.

2. 我的叉子掉了，請再給我一支。

I dropped my fork. I need another one, please.

3. 你們有筷子嗎？

Do you have chopsticks?

4. 我想看甜點單。

I'd like to see the dessert menu.

5. 我需要一根吸管，謝謝。

I need a straw, please.

Language Power 字詞補給站

餐　廳　**Restaurant**

utensils 餐具

knife 刀子

fork 叉子

spoon 湯匙

straw 吸管

napkin 紙巾

high chair
（幼兒用）的高椅

plate 盤子

cup 杯子

saucer 碟子

glass 玻璃杯

coaster
（杯、瓶用的）小墊子

steak knife 牛排刀

butter knife 奶油刀

dish 一道菜

salad dressing 沙拉醬

tablecloth 桌布

place mat
（桌面位子上的）墊子

餐　廳 **Restaurant** ②

ashtray 煙灰缸　　　bar 吧檯　　　bar stool 吧檯椅

bartender 酒保　　　wine list 酒單　　　check 帳單

jukebox 點唱機

9.6b 餐廳訂位 Make a Reservation at a Restaurant

Dialog 對話

A: 哈囉，豐月餐廳。

A: Hello. Harvest Moon restaurant.

B: 哈囉，我要預訂今晚的位子。

B: Hello. I'd like to make a reservation for tonight.

A: 好，你們有幾位？

A: Very well. How many will be in your party?

B: 七位。

B: There will be seven of us.

A: 何時會到呢？

A: And what time will you arrive?

B: 大約七點。

B: Around seven.

A: 您的名字是？

A: What is your name, sir?

B: 安迪李。

B: It's Andy Lee.

A: 您的手機號碼是？

A: And your cell phone number?

B: 408-939-2768。

B: It's 408-939-2768.

A: 好的，我們期待見到你們。

A: All right. We look forward to seeing you.

左側直排標籤：預備 校園 選課 新生說明 上課前 課堂上 課後交流 圖書館 體育館 餐廳 課外活動 申請獎助 當助教

Word Bank 字庫

party [`pɑrtɪ] n. 一夥人
look forward to 期待

Useful Phrases 實用語句

1. 你們今晚有位子嗎？

   Do you have any tables available for tonight?

2. 我想訂位。

   I'd like to make a reservation.

3. 今晚有現場演奏嗎？

   Is there live music tonight?

4. 今晚要收娛樂費嗎？

   Is there a cover charge for tonight?

Tips 小祕訣

　　cover charge 通常是在有表演的餐廳或夜店對每人在餐點服務之外多收取的費用，可以稱為「表演費、節目費或娛樂費」。如果在夜店只有飲料或點心的服務，並無太多餐點可供應時，此收費可能包含了免費附贈的飲料及小點心。

9.6c 餐廳內——帶位 Getting Seated

Dialog 1 對話1

A: 歡迎光臨，幾位呢？

A: Welcome. How many?

B: 兩位，謝謝。

B: Table for two , please.

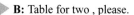

A: 吸煙還是不吸煙呢？ ➤ A: Smoking or non-smoking?

B: 不吸煙。 ➤ B: Non-smoking.

A: 您要靠窗嗎？ ➤ A: Would you like a window seat?

B: 好，謝謝。 ➤ B: Yes, please.

📖 Useful Phrases （實用語句）

1. 我想要坐外面陽臺。

   We'd like to sit out on the terrace.

2. 我們想要在外面平臺用餐。

   We'd like to eat out on the deck, please.

3. 我們要先去吧臺。

   We'll go to the bar first.

🔊 Notes （小叮嚀）

　　到餐廳用餐要等帶位，不要自行入內。餐廳禁菸已漸成趨勢，許多地區的餐廳全面禁菸 (smoke free)。西方文化把喝湯擺第一，且習慣點菜前先點杯冷飲或咖啡。

🏃 Dialog 2 （對話2）

A: 您這裡坐得舒適嗎？ ➤ A: Are you comfortable?

B: 舒服，這裡很好。 ▶ **B:** Yes, this is nice.

A: 菜單在這裡。 ▶ **A:** Here are your menus.

B: 謝謝。 ▶ **B:** Thank you.

A: 您要先點個飲料嗎？ ▶ **A:** Would you like to order a drink first?

B: 我要點瑪格麗塔。 ▶ **B:** I'd like a Margarita.

Word Bank 字庫

comfortable [`kʌmfətəb]] adj. 舒適的
menu [`mɛnju] n. 菜單
Margarita [ˌmɑrgə`ritə] n. 瑪格麗塔（一種墨西哥雞尾酒）

Useful Phrases 實用語句

1. 我們可以先看飲料單嗎？
   May we see your drink list?
2. 我們想先喝飲料。
   We'd like our drinks first.
3. 我們想要邊用晚餐邊喝飲料。
   We want our drinks with our dinner.
4. 我們要晚點喝飲料。
   We'll have drinks later.
5. 我們今晚不想喝飲料 [雞尾酒]。
   We don't want any drinks [cocktails] tonight.

Language Power 字詞補給站

食物及餐廳
Food and Restaurants

waiter 服務生　　waitress 女服務生　　terrace 陽台

menu 菜單　　juice 果汁　　tea 茶

coffee 咖啡　　appetizers 開胃菜　　entree 主菜

dessert 甜點　　sauce 醬汁　　steak 牛排

fish fillet 魚排　　cocktail 雞尾酒　　chowder 濃湯

soup 湯　　salad 沙拉　　salad dressing 沙拉醬

預備　校園　選課　新生說明　上課前　課堂上　課後交流　圖書館　體育館　餐廳　課外活動　申請獎助　當助教

預備
校園
選課
新生說明
上課前
課堂上
課後交流
圖書館
體育館
餐廳
課外活動
申請獎助
當助教

312

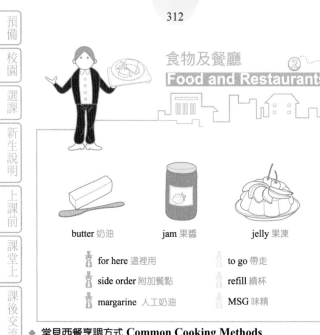

butter 奶油　　jam 果醬　　jelly 果凍

for here 這裡用　　　　to go 帶走

side order 附加餐點　　refill 續杯

margarine 人工奶油　　MSG 味精

◆ 常見西餐烹調方式 Common Cooking Methods

baked	烤
broiled	燒烤
fried	油煎、炸
deep fried	油炸
boiled	煮
steamed	蒸
sautéed	於少許熱油中嫩煎的（尤指肉或魚）

9.6d 點餐 Ordering Meals (and Drinks)

Dialog 1 對話1

A: 這裡是您的飲料，您準備點餐了嗎？

A: Here are your drinks. Are you ready to order?

B: 今日特餐是什麼呢？

B: What is today's special?

A: 雞肉袋餅加摩雷醬汁。

A: Chicken Fajitas, with mole sauce.

B: 包含哪些附餐呢？

B: What else is included?

A: 這套餐包含湯或沙拉及一杯飲料。

A: The meal includes soup or salad and a drink.

Word Bank 字庫

fajita [fə`hitə] n. (墨西哥)袋餅(內有生菜、番茄、紅蘿蔔絲、洋蔥絲、起司及肉條)

mole sauce n. 摩雷醬汁(一種墨西哥沾醬，由豆子、巧克力、薑、香辛料做成)

soup [sup] n. 湯

salad [`sæləd] n. 沙拉

Useful Phrases 實用語句

1. 您準備點餐了嗎？

   Are you ready to order?

2. 今日特餐是什麼呢？

   What is today's special?

3. 你推薦我們什麼呢？

   What do you recommend we try?

4. 本店特餐是什麼呢？

   What is the house special?

5. 這裡什麼較受歡迎呢？

   What's popular here?

6. 你們有兩人份的套餐嗎？

   Do you have set meals for two?

Dialog 2 對話2

A: 我要點牛排。

A: I would like to order steak.

B: 你要幾分熟？

B: How do you want it cooked?

A: 五分熟。

A: I'd like it medium rare.

B: 你要牛排醬嗎？

B: Do you want steak sauce?

A: 要。

A: Yes, I do.

B: 你要馬鈴薯泥還是烤馬鈴薯？

B: Do you want mashed or baked potato with that?

A: 烤的。

A: Baked.

Dialog 3 對話3

A: 我要菜單上的六號餐，但不要太辣。

A: I want number 6 on the menu, but not very spicy.

預備
校園
選課
新生說明
上課前
課堂上
課後交流
圖書館
體育館
餐廳
課外活動
申請獎助
當助教

B: 好的,要不要來個開胃菜? → **B:** Certainly. Would you like an appetizer?

A: 好,我點(炸)烏賊。 → **A:** Yes. I'll have the calamari.

B: 很好,要喝什麼嗎? → **B:** Very well. Anything to drink?

A: 你們有啤酒嗎? → **A:** Do you have beer?

B: 有的,我們有精選微釀(啤酒)。 → **B:** Yes, we have a selection of micro brews.

A: 你們有啤酒單嗎? → **A:** Do you have a list of your beers?

B: 有,我去拿給你。 → **B:** Yes, I'll get it for you.

Word Bank 字庫

spicy [`spaɪsɪ] adj. 辣的
calamari [`kælə‚mɛrɪ] n. 烏賊(通常是炸的)
selection [sə`lɛkʃən] n. 選擇
micro brew n. 小規模酒廠釀製的酒
list [lɪst] n. 清單;目錄

預備
校園
選課
新生說明
上課前
課堂上
課後交流
圖書館
體育館
餐廳
課外活動
申請獎助
當助教

Useful Phrases 實用語句

1. 你們有供應雞尾酒嗎？

   Do you serve cocktails?

2. 我可以看一下飲料單嗎？

   May I see the drink list?

3. 請描述這啤酒。

   Please describe this beer.

4. 我想要再一杯 (指你的飲料)。

   I'd like another one of these.

Language Power 字詞補給站

◆ 煎牛排的說法 Frying the Steak as You Wish

I'd like my steak medium rare, please.	我想要我的牛排三分熟
Medium rare, please.	三分熟。
Medium, please.	五分熟。
Medium well, please.	七分熟。
Well-done, please.	全熟。
Please make sure the steak is cooked just right, not overcooked or under-cooked.	請確認牛排煎得剛剛好，不要太老或太生。

Notes 小叮嚀

　　基本餐桌禮儀不可忽略，喝湯勿低頭就碗，吃麵包要先撕成小片。用餐時有刺或骨頭，千萬不要直接從嘴裡吐在盤子上，要用叉子接著，放到盤子旁邊，不可放在餐桌上，也不可以打嗝，這些都是失禮的。萬一打嗝，要道歉說「Excuse me.」再加上解釋「I ate too much.」，在人前打哈欠、伸懶腰、打噴嚏這些動作都要表示抱歉及解釋，要擤鼻涕、剔牙或女士補妝要去洗手間才不會失禮。別人道歉時可以說「沒關係」(It's OK.)、「上帝保佑你」(God bless you.) 或「保重」(Take care.)。

9.6e 點酒 Ordering Wine

Dialog 對話

A: 服務生,我們要一瓶酒。

A: Waiter. We would like a bottle of wine.

B: 好的,你要什麼酒?

B: Certainly, what would you like?

A: 你有任何推薦嗎?

A: Do you have any recommendations?

B: 我們有一種不錯的本店酒,一紅一白。

B: We have a good house wine. A red and a white.

A: 我們試試白酒,還有請給兩個冰酒杯。

A: We'll try the white. Two chilled glasses, too, please.

B: 馬上來,女士。

B: Right away, ma'am.

Word Bank 字庫

recommendation [ˌrɛkəmɛn`deʃən] n. 推薦
chilled [tʃɪld] adj. (冰) 冷的

Tips 小祕訣

葡萄酒分紅酒 (red wine)、白酒 (white wine)、甜 (sweet) 及不甜 (dry) 等種類。

9.6f 滿意服務 Service Satisfaction

預備
校園
選課
新生說明
上課前
課堂上
課後交流
圖書館
體育館
餐廳
課外活動
申請獎助
當助教

Dialog 1 對話1

A: 您喜歡您的餐點嗎？

A: Are you enjoying your meal?

B: 是的，不錯。

B: Yes, it's good.

A: 要來份甜點嗎？

A: How about dessert?

B: 不了，謝謝，我飽了。

B: No thanks. I'm full.

Dialog 2 對話2

A: 您喜歡您的餐點嗎？

A: Are you enjoying your meal?

B: 是的，不錯。可以幫我加水嗎？

B: Yes, it's good. Can I have more water, please?

A: 當然可以。

A: Yes, of course.

B: 我還需要一條餐巾。

B: I need another napkin also.

A: 我會拿一條來，你還需要什麼嗎？

A: I'll get you one. Do you want anything else?

B: 我決定要再來個甜點。

B: I've decided I want a dessert, too.

A: 那我也拿甜點單給你看。

A: Let me bring the dessert menu to you also.

 Word Bank 字庫

meal [mil] n. 餐點
napkin [`næpkɪn] n. 餐巾
dessert [dɪ`zɜt] n. 甜點

 Useful Phrases 實用語句

1. 服務生，我打翻了我的飲料。
   Waiter, I spilled my drink.
2. 你可以收走這個嗎？
   Would you take this, please?
3. 請加點水。
   More water, please.
4. 請多點沾醬。
   More dipping sauce, please.

 Dialog 3 對話3

A: 這是免費招待的脆餅及莎莎醬。

A: Here is your complimentary chips and salsa.

預備
校園
選課
新生說明
上課前
課堂上
課後交流
圖書館
體育館
餐廳
課外活動
申請獎助
當助教

B: 謝謝，我可以多要點水嗎？

B: Thank you. Can I have more water?

A: 當然可以，我馬上過來。

A: Sure. I'll be right back.

Word Bank 字庫

complimentary [ˌkɑmpləˋmɛntərɪ] adj. 免費的

chips [tʃɪps] n. 脆餅

salsa [ˋsɑlsə] n. 莎莎醬

Useful Phrases 實用語句

1. 請多給點脆餅。
   More chips, please.
2. 我們要一份點心帶走。
   We want a dessert to go.
3. 我們的帳單，謝謝。
   Our bill, please.

We have apple, strawberry, peach, blueberry, lemon and chocolate cream.

Language Power 字詞補給站

醬 料 **Sauces**

salt 鹽巴		pepper 胡椒	
ketchup 番茄醬		sugar 糖	
steak sauce 牛排醬		mustard 芥茉醬	
sweet and sour sauce 甜酸醬		barbecue sauce 烤肉醬	
salsa 莎莎醬		guacamole 酪梨醬	

9.6g 點甜點 Ordering Desserts

Dialog 對話

A: 你們有什麼派呢？

A: What kind of pie do you have?

B: 我們有蘋果、草莓、水蜜桃、藍莓、檸檬及巧克力醬。

B: We have apple, strawberry, peach, blueberry, lemon and chocolate cream.

A: 我要一片藍莓派。

A: I'd like a piece of blueberry pie.

B: 你要加冰淇淋嗎？

B: Do you want it à la mode?

預備
校園
選課
新生說明
上課前
課堂上
課後交流
圖書館
體育館
餐廳
課外活動
申請獎助
當助教

預備
校園
選課
新生說明
上課前
課堂上
課後交流
圖書館
體育館
餐廳
課外活動
申請獎助
當助教

322

A: 要。

A: Yes.

Word Bank 字庫

strawberry [`strɔ͵bɛrɪ] n. 草莓
peach [pitʃ] n. 水蜜桃
blueberry [`blu͵bɛrɪ] n. 藍莓
à la mode [͵ɑlə`mod] adj. 加冰淇淋的

9.6h 買單 Paying the Bill

Dialog 1 對話1

A: 我們要付帳，謝謝。

A: We would like the bill, please.

B: 我去拿給你。

B: I'll get it for you.

（帳單來了 bill arrives）

A: 你想我們該留多少小費呢？帳單是 30.50 元。

A: How much do you think we should leave a tip? Our bill is $30.50.

B: 不用，你看，已經有 10% 的服務費了。

B: No. Look. There is already a 10% service charge.

A: 好，那就不必給小費了。

A: OK, then we don't need to tip.

Word Bank 字庫

bill [bɪl] n. 帳單
tip [tɪp] n. 小費

Useful Phrases 實用語句

1. 這裡收服務費嗎？
   Is there a service charge here?
2. 服務費是多少呢？
   How much is the service charge?
3. （這是小費，）謝謝。（給小費時其實說謝謝就可以了）
   (Here's your tip.) Thank you.
4. 我們來分攤小費。
   Let's split the tip.

Dialog 2 對話2

A: 我們得走了，帳單在哪裡呢？

A: We need to go. Where is the bill?

B: 服務生放在桌子這裡。

B: The waiter left it here on the table.

A: 我們看一下，總共 54 元，我們應該留 10% 小費。

A: Let's see. It comes to $54. We should leave a 10% tip.

B: 我認為服務生的服務特別好，我們應該多給點小費。

B: I think the waiter's service was especially good. I think we ought to tip more.

A: 好，我留 15%，那是多少錢呢？

A: OK, I'll leave 15%. How much is that?

預備
校園
選課
新生說明
上課前
課堂上
課後交流
圖書館
體育館
餐廳
課外活動
申請獎助
當助教

B: 大約 8 元。

B: About eight dollars.

A: 我有 5 元紙鈔，你有 1 元的紙鈔嗎？

A: I've got a five dollar bill. Do you have any ones?

B: 有，這裡有 3 元。

B: Yes, here is three bucks.

A: 好，我們搞定了。

A: Good. We got it covered.

Notes 小叮嚀

　　與朋友、同學一起用餐，一般都是各付各的。在一般的美國餐廳用餐，小費約為消費額的 10-15%，若是在較高級優質服務的餐廳用餐，則為 15-20% 的小費。如果帳單已包含 10% 的服務費 (service charge)，就不必再給小費。服務生必須靠小費補貼過低的薪資，因此小費這部分最好不要刷卡而是給現金，只要將小費留在桌上就可以，但記得不要給過於零碎的小費。有些服務生因為希望拿到較好的小費而頻獻殷勤，不必因此受影響，按自己感受給小費就好。若是餐廳為吃到飽的自助式 buffet，有提供少許服務如倒咖啡、收盤子等就酌量給小費。至於機場、學校等自己拿餐盤點餐結帳的自助式 cafeteria 及速食店，因為服務都是自己來，就不必給小費了。

9.6i 幸運餅 Fortune Cookies

Dialog 對話

A: 看，我們的餐點有幸運餅。

A: Hey, look. We got fortune cookies with our meal.

B: 真的耶！我們打開吧。

B: Really! Let's open them.

A: 這真是在西方的中國餐館可愛的傳統。

A: This is a cute Chinese restaurant custom here in the West.

B: 是啊，我想也是。

B: Yes, I think so, too.

A: 你的幸運餅寫什麼？

A: What does your cookie's fortune say?

Word Bank 字庫

fortune cookies n. 幸運餅
cute [kjut] adj. 可愛的
custom [`kʌstəm] n. 傳統；習俗

預備　校園　選課　新生說明　上課前　課堂上　課後交流　圖書館　體育館　餐廳　課外活動　申請獎助　當助教

預備
校園
選課
新生說明
上課前
課堂上
課後交流
圖書館
體育館
餐廳
課外活動
申請獎助
當助教

326

Notes 小叮嚀

　　除了華人聚集的大城市，海外的中國餐館多數已加入當地人的口味，因此感覺不中不西。這類中國餐廳的菜肴通常都是酸甜 (sweet and sour) 口味，在國外的白米飯也幾乎都是乾硬的泰國米。如果帶老外同學到中國餐館用餐，可以告訴餐廳不要放味精 (MSG)，許多老外對味精過敏。在美國的中國餐館用餐後要結帳時，服務生會送來幸運餅，內有處事格言或運勢預測，後又加入樂透明牌，這是海外的中國餐館吸引顧客的手法。另一個特點是海外的中國餐館皆在戶外懸掛紅燈籠。

9.6j 打包剩餘食物 Taking Extra Food Home

Dialog 對話

A: 我們想把剩餘的食物打包回家。

A: We'd like to take the leftover food home.

B: 好的，先生。

B: Yes, Sir.

A: 可以多要一些醬料嗎？

A: Is it possible to get some extra sauce?

B: 稍等一下，我去問。

B: Just a moment, I'll go ask.

Word Bank 字庫

leftover [`lɛft͵ovɚ] n. 剩菜
extra [`ɛkstrə] adj. 多餘的

📖 Useful Phrases 實用語句

1. 我想另外點餐帶走。

   I'd like to place an extra order to go.

2. 請把這些用盒子裝起來。

   Please box these up.

Tips 小祕訣

　　將多餘食物帶回家，也可以問可否給一個 bag 或 doggy bag，意指剩菜是要給小狗吃的。如果要外帶的話直接說食物 加 to go 就 可 以。 例 如：「A chicken salad to go.」「A cheeseburger to go. 」「A coffee to go. 」。

I'd like to take the leftover food home.

OK~~

9.6k 傳統餐廳菜單範例
Traditional Restaurant Sample Menu

Traditional Restaurant Sample Menu
(傳統餐廳菜單範例)

Appetizers 開胃菜
- Potato skins with cheese 馬鈴薯皮加起司
- Buffalo wings 炸雞翅加特製醬料
- Calamari (炸)烏賊
- Deep fried mushrooms 炸香菇
- French Fries 炸薯條
- Onion Rings 洋蔥圈
- Chips and salsa 脆片與莎莎沾醬

Breakfast 早餐
- *Breakfast Meat Lovers Special* 愛肉者早餐特餐
  sausage, bacon and ham, with hash browns, eggs and toast 香腸、培根和火腿加油炸刨絲馬鈴薯塊、蛋及土司
- *Breakfast Fajitas* 早餐袋餅
  Mexican fajitas prepared with potatoes and grated cheese 墨西哥袋餅加馬鈴薯及刨絲起司
- *Pancake Stacks* 鬆餅層
  one, two, or three pancakes with real butter, syrup and bacon or sausage 一片、兩片或三片鬆餅加奶油、楓糖漿、培根或香腸
- *Eggs* 蛋
  two halves English muffin topped with poached eggs, sauce and served with hash browns 對半分開之英式馬芬(杯形鬆餅)，上加白煮蛋、醬汁及油炸刨絲馬鈴薯塊
- *Vegetarian Breakfast* 素食者早餐
  grilled vegetables, fresh fruit and yogurt served with whole wheat toast and orange juice 烤蔬果、新鮮水果及優格，配全麥土司及柳橙汁

Traditional Restaurant Sample Menu
（傳統餐廳菜單範例）

- *French Toast 法國土司*

  three pieces served with syrup and butter 三片法國土司加上楓糖漿及奶油

Lunch Selections 午餐

- *House Burger/House Cheese Burger/House Bacon Cheese Burger* 本店漢堡 / 本店起司漢堡 / 本店培根起司漢堡

  special burgers served with French fries, and a drink 特別漢堡加炸薯條及飲料

- *Garden Burger 蔬菜漢堡*

  a burger made of fresh vegetables and a meatless burger patty 由新鮮蔬菜加無肉之漢堡餡做成

- *Club Sandwich 總匯三明治*

  smoked chicken, bacon, lettuce and tomatoes in a sandwich sliced into four sections served with potato chips 三明治由燻雞、培根、生菜、番茄做成，切成四份，外加薯條

- *Meat or vegetable lasagna 肉或蔬菜千層麵*

  a choice of Italian style lasagna served hot with garlic bread 熱騰騰的義大利千層麵加大蒜麵包

- *Hot Turkey Sandwich 熱火雞三明治*

  a hot turkey sandwich topped with gravy and served with a salad and fries 熱火雞三明治加上肉汁，外加沙拉及薯條

- *Fish and Chips 魚及薯條*

  deep fried fish and fries served with a special sauce 炸魚及薯條加上特別醬料

預備
校園
選課
新生說明
上課前
課堂上
課後交流
圖書館
體育館
餐廳
課外活動
申請獎助
當助教

Traditional Restaurant Sample Menu
(傳統餐廳菜單範例)

Soups 湯
- Vegetable soup 蔬菜湯
- Corn soup 玉米濃湯
- Clam chowder 文蛤巧達濃湯 (以蛤肉、馬鈴薯等煮成之濃湯)
- Minestrone 義大利濃湯 (以豆類煮成)

Salads 沙拉
- *Green Garden Salad* 青菜沙拉
  fresh picked vegetables, sliced, with your choice of dressing 鮮採蔬菜切片加上任你挑選之沙拉醬
- *Chicken Salad* 雞肉沙拉
  fried chicken strips over mixed greens, bacon pieces, ham and dressing 炸雞肉條加什錦蔬菜、培根碎片、火腿及沙拉醬
- *Mexican Salad* 墨西哥沙拉
  lettuce, tomato, salsa, taco chips, olives, and beef with a special dressing 生菜、番茄、莎莎醬、玉米片、橄欖及牛肉與特別的沙拉醬汁

Dinner Selections 晚餐
- *Stir Fry Chicken* 炒雞肉
  grilled chicken, oriental vegetables, served with a sauce 烤雞、亞洲蔬菜配醬汁
- *Salmon* 鮭魚
  a thick slice of fresh salmon served with a baked potato, salad, and dinner rolls 厚片新鮮鮭魚配烤馬鈴薯、沙拉及麵包捲

Traditional Restaurant Sample Menu
(傳統餐廳菜單範例)

- *T-Bone Steak 丁骨牛排*
  a thick slice of steak served with a baked potato, vegetables, and a salad 厚片牛排配烤馬鈴薯、蔬菜及沙拉
- *Sirloin Steak 沙朗牛排*
  same as above, but a sirloin 同上，但用沙朗牛排
- *Pork Loin Steak 豬排 (腰肉)*
  same as above, but a pork loin 同上，但用豬排 (腰肉)

Drinks 飲料

- coffee / tea (tea bags) / milk / fruit juices, including tomato juice
  咖啡 / 茶 (茶包) / 牛奶 / 果汁，包括番茄汁
- soft drinks—Coca Cola or Pepsi /Sprite / Root Beer / ginger ale/ ice tea / other flavors
  汽水類—可口可樂或百事可樂 / 雪碧 / 露比 (沙士) / 薑汁汽水 / 冰紅茶 / 其他口味
- beer and wine (in many, but not all restaurants)
  啤酒及酒(多數餐廳供應)
- cocktails (in many, but not all restaurants)
  雞尾酒(多數餐廳供應)

Desserts 點心

- ice cream (vanilla, chocolate, strawberry)
  冰淇淋 (香草、巧克力、草莓)
- apple pie, banana pie, chocolate pie, lemon pie, pie à la mode 蘋果派、香蕉派、巧克力派、檸檬派、冰淇淋派
- cheesecake, blueberry cake
  起司蛋糕、藍莓蛋糕

預備 校園 選課 新生說明 上課前 課堂上 課後交流 圖書館 體育館 餐廳 課外活動 申請獎助 當助教

預備
校園
選課
新生說明．上課前
課堂上
課後交流
圖書館
體育館
餐廳
課外活動
申請獎助
當助教

Unit 10 Extracurricular Activities

課外活動

大學提供許多參加課外活動的機會，藝術、舞蹈、攝影、表演及各類運動 (如獨木舟、健行) 等諸多社團，許多社團可以免費參加。

10.1 談論活動
Talking about Activities

Dialog 對話

A: 我們應該加入社團。

A: We should join a club.

B: 哪一個？

B: Which one?

A: 我不知道。

A: I don't know.

B: 他們都有辦公室，我們可以獲得一些資訊。

B: They all have offices. We can get some information.

A: 是的，我們也可以去他們的會員募集活動會議。

A: Yes. We can go to their membership drive meetings too.

Word Bank 字庫

membership drive meetings n. 會員募集活動會議

Tips 小祕訣

　　美國大學裡的希臘系統 (the Greek system) 是眾所皆知的，也就是兄弟會 (Fraternities) 或姊妹會 (Sororities)。因此兩字源自拉丁文，且兄弟會或姊妹會除少數特例之外，都以二到三個希臘字母命名，兄弟會及姊妹會通稱為希臘系統，會員為「希臘人」(the Greeks)。青年學子聚在一起為共同目標努力（如社交、領導能力、社區服務、專業學習及榮譽等）並做一輩子像兄弟姊妹般情誼的朋友，會員必須經過面試並通過入會過程。雖然這些社團立意良善，但美國各地大學的兄弟會卻經常傳出酗酒鬧事，有些大學已對兄弟會開出禁酒令。

10.2 詢問訓練課程
Asking about a Training Session

Dialog 對話

A: 哈囉，我想了解明天在學生中心的訓練課程。

A: Hello. I want to find out about tomorrow's training session at the Student Center.

B: 哪一個？

B: Which one?

A: 關於嘻哈舞。

A: The one about hip hop dancing.

B: 好。

B: OK.

A: 我需要登記嗎？

A: Do I need to sign up for it?

預備
校園
選課
新生說明
上課前
課堂上
課後交流
圖書館
體育館
餐廳
課外活動
申請獎助
當助教

B: 要,因為有名額限制,所以要現在登記。

B: Yes. There is a limit, so you ought to sign up now.

A: 好,要費用嗎?

A: All right. Is there a fee?

B: 要,4元。

B: Yes. It's $4.

A: 我要付給誰?

A: Who do I pay?

B: 你可以在這裡付。

B: You can pay here.

A: 我可以用我的學生卡嗎?

A: Can I pay using my Student Card?

B: 可以,沒問題。

B: Sure. No problem.

Useful Phrases 實用語句

1. 我需要登記嗎?

   Do I need to sign up for it?

2. 有名額限制。

   There is a limit.

3. 要費用嗎?

   Is there a fee?

4. 我要付給誰?

   Who do I pay?

5. 我可以用我的學生卡嗎？

   Can I pay using my Student Card?

10.3 在社團辦公室
At a Club Office

Dialog 對話

A: 嗨，我想獲得你們社團的資訊。

A: Hi. I'd like to get some information about your club's activities.

B: 我們有小冊子可以參考，我也可以回答你的問題。

B: We have this brochure you can read, and I can answer your questions too.

A: 我想了解費用。

A: I'm wondering about cost.

B: 我們一年收 10 元會費來付房租。

B: We have a $10 a year membership fee to help pay for rent.

A: 有其他費用嗎？

A: Are there any other fees?

B: 如果你要參加我們特別的活動才要。

B: Only if you want to join one of our special events.

A: 那要多少費用？

A: What do those cost?

B: 不一定，但通常 10 到 15 元。

B: It varies, but usually it's around $10 to $15.

A: 社團聚會是何時？

A: When are the club meetings?

B: 我們一個月聚會 2 次，在第一、三週的週二晚上 7 點左右。

B: We meet twice a month on the first and third Tuesdays around 7 p.m.

A: 好，謝謝你的資訊。

A: OK. Thanks for the information.

B: 不客氣。

B: No problem.

(稍後 Later)

A: 嗨，我之前來過，我還有一些問題。

A: Hi. I was here earlier. I have a few more questions.

B: 好的，你想知道什麼呢？

B: Sure. What would you like to know?

A: 我可以在這辦公室做些什麼嗎？

A: Is there anything I can do here in the office?

B: 是的，我們社團內有許多事你可以幫忙。

B: Yes. We have many things you can help out with in the club.

A: 我想這是比較好認識人的方式。

A: I think it would be a better way to meet people.

B: 你是對的，讓我介紹你認識我們的義務協導。

B: You're right. Let me introduce you to our volunteer coordinator.

A: 謝謝。

A: Thanks.

Word Bank 字庫

brochure [bro`ʃʊr] n. 小冊子
membership fee n. 會費
volunteer coordinator n. 義務協導

Useful Phrases 實用語句

1. 我想了解費用。

   I'm wondering about cost.

2. 有其他費用嗎？

   Are there any other fees?

3. 社團聚會是何時？

   When are the club meetings?

4. 我可以在這辦公室做些什麼嗎？

   Is there anything I can do here in the office?

5. 我們社團內有許多事你可以幫忙。

   We have many things you can help out with in the club.

預備
校園
選課
新生說明
上課前
課堂上
課後交流
圖書館
體育館
餐廳
課外活動
申請獎助
當助教

10.4 與義務協導談話
Conversation with the Volunteer Coordinator

 Dialog 對話

A: 嗨,請進來坐。

A: Hi. Please come in and sit.

B: 謝謝。我想知道我在這裡可以幫忙什麼。

B: Thanks. I'm wondering what I could do here to help.

A: 我們有不同的事你可以做,顧辦公室、幫忙設計海報及廣告、規劃活動諸如此類的事。

A: We have different things you can do. Manning the office, helping design posters and ads, organizing events, things like that.

B: 我需要有經驗嗎?

B: Do I need to be experienced?

A: 不盡然,我們做這些是為了讓學生邊玩邊學點東西。

A: Not really. We do this so students can have fun and learn something too.

B: 好,我是全職學生,但我想參與一些事情。

B: Great. I'm a full time student, but I want to get involved in something.

A: 多數社團成員是全職學生,所以你不必擔心,我們會按照你的課表排班。

A: Most of our club members are full time students, so don't worry, we'll work with your schedule.

B: 我知道了，聽起來很好。

B: I see. Sounds good.

Word Bank 字庫

man [mæn] v. 守崗位，顧 (辦公室)
poster [`postə] n. 海報
ad [æd] n. 廣告 (=advertisement)
organize [`ɔrgə͵naɪz] v. 規劃

Useful Phrases 實用語句

1. 我想知道我在這裡可以幫忙什麼。

   I'm wondering what I could do here to help.

2. 我需要有經驗嗎？

   Do I need to be experienced?

3. 我們會按照你的課表排班。

   We'll work with your schedule.

Tips 小祕訣

　　課外活動也包含大學的運動校隊，但是要成為校隊一員要經過一連串嚴格挑選的過程，所以只有來自全國的頂尖選手才有可能成為隊員。然而校內仍有一些運動社團與大學本身正式運動校隊無關，而是基於個人興趣組成的運動隊伍或社團。

預備
校園
選課
新生說明
上課前
課堂上
課後交流
圖書館
體育館
餐廳
課外活動
申請獎助
當助教

預備
校園
選課
新生說明
上課前
課堂上
課後交流
圖書館
體育館
餐廳
課外活動
申請獎助
當助教

342

10.5 社團會議
Club Meeting

Dialog　對話

A: 好，我們開始會議，我們有一位新成員要介紹。這是傑瑞馬，歡迎。

A: OK. Let's start the meeting. We have a new member I need to introduce. This is Jerry Ma. Welcome.

B: 嗨，大家好。

B: Hi, everyone.

A: 傑瑞會在週三下午來辦公室幫忙，還有週五也是。你有話要說嗎，傑瑞？

A: Jerry is going to help out in the office on Wednesday afternoons, and Fridays too. Is there anything you'd like to say, Jerry?

B: 我只想向大家問好，同時我期待跟大家認識並且一起做事。

B: I just want to say hello and that I look forward to meeting and working with all of you.

A: 好，再次謝謝你成為我們社團的一員。

A: Great. Thanks again for becoming a part of our club.

Useful Phrases　實用語句

1. 我期待跟大家認識並且一起做事。

   I look forward to meeting and working with all of you.

2. 我想參與我喜歡的事物。

I'd like to get involved in something I like.

3. 有機會學習社團活動很棒。

It's great to have the chance to learn about club activities.

10.5a 年度活動 The Year's Activities

Dialog 對話

A: 嗨,卡洛,你在看什麼?

A: Hi, Carol. What are you looking at?

B: 嗨,山姆,我在看年度活動的清單。

B: Hi, Sam. I'm looking at this year's list of activities.

A: 這些都在校內嗎?

A: Are all of these at the university?

B: 是的,有好多活動啊。

B: Yes. There are a lot.

A: 對啊,你要參加任何活動嗎?

A: I agree. Are you going to get involved in any?

B: 我想是的,你呢?

B: I think so. How about you?

A: 我不知道,我可以嗎?

A: I don't know. Can I?

B: 當然，所有這些活動都需要義工。

B: Sure. All of these events and activities will need volunteers.

A: 我最好再看一下清單。

A: I'd better take a closer look at that list.

B: 這裡，拿一張。

B: Here. Take one.

A: 謝謝。

A: Thanks.

Word Bank 字庫

involve [ɪnˋvɑlv] v. 參與
volunteer [ˌvɑlənˋtɪr] n. 義 [志] 工

Useful Phrases 實用語句

1. 我在看年度活動的清單。

   I'm looking at this year's list of activities.

2. 你要參加任何活動嗎？

   Are you going to get involved in any?

3. 所有這些活動都需要義工。

   All of these events and activities will need volunteers.

預備 校園 選課 新生說明 上課前 課堂上 課後交流 圖書館 體育館 餐廳 課外活動 申請獎助 當助教

10.5b 準備活動 Preparing for an Activity

Dialog 對話

A: 這個活動我們有許多工作要做。

A: We have a lot of work to do for this event.

B: 我知道，我們要分組並完成邀請。

B: I know. We need to divide up the work and get the invitations made.

A: 我今天最好多找一些人來幫忙。

A: I'd better get more people down here to help today.

B: 我同意，人這麼少，我們無法完成所有事情。

B: I agree. We can't do all this with so few people.

A: 我來開始打電話給一些其他社團成員。

A: I'll start calling some of the other club members.

B: 好，我會開始將邀請函放入信封內。

B: OK. I'll start putting the invitations in envelopes.

A: 打完電話後，我會在信封上寫地址。

A: After I call people, I'll start addressing the envelopes.

B: 好，聽來很棒。

B: OK. Sounds good.

預備 校園 選課 新生說明 上課前 課堂上 課後交流 圖書館 體育館 餐廳 課外活動 申請獎助 當助教

Word Bank 字庫

invitation [ˌɪnvəˋteʃən] n. 邀請
address [əˋdrɛs] v. 寫地址
envelope [ˋɛnvəˌlop] n. 信封

Useful Phrases 實用語句

1. 我們要分組並完成邀請。

   We need to divide up the work and get the invitations made.

2. 我今天最好多找些人過來這裡幫忙。

   I'd better get more people down here to help today.

3. 我來開始打電話給一些其他社團成員。

   I'll start calling some of the other club members.

4. 我會開始將邀請函放入信封內。

   I'll start putting the invitations in envelopes.

5. 我會在信封上寫地址。

   I'll start addressing the envelopes.

10.5c 海報 Posters

Dialog 對話

A: 我需要跟你談一下
海報。

A: I need to talk to you about the poster.

B: 好，你要告訴我什麼？

B: Sure. What do you want to tell me?

A: 我覺得我們原本的背景顏色並不好。

A: I think our original background color is bad.

B: 真的嗎？為什麼？

B: Really? Why?

A: 看我這邊的電腦螢幕，我有一個模型。

A: Look here on my computer screen. I have a mock-up.

B: 我懂你的意思，背景顏色無法突顯出影像。

B: I see what you mean. The background color doesn't let the images stand out.

A: 對，我想我們最好更改一下。

A: Right. I think we'd better change it.

B: 好，看來我們選的字型不錯。

B: OK. It looks like the font we chose is good.

A: 是的，字型可以，但我認為字體要大一點。

A: Yes, that is fine. Although the words need to be larger, I think.

B: 我想也是，你想大家會很容易看到時間及日期嗎？

B: I guess so. Do you think people will easily notice the time and date?

A: 我不確定。我可以把它移到這裡，這樣會比較明顯。

A: I'm not sure. I can move it to here. It will be more noticeable.

B: 是的，看起來好多了。

B: Yes. That looks better.

預備
校園
選課
新生說明
上課前
課堂上
課後交流
圖書館
體育館
餐廳
課外活動
申請獎助
當助教

Word Bank 字庫

mock-up [`mɑk͵ʌp] n. 模型

stand out 突出

font [fɑnt] n. 字型，字體

noticeable [`notɪsəbḷ] adj. 明顯的

Useful Phrases 實用語句

1. 看我這邊的電腦螢幕，我有一個模型。

   Look here on my computer screen. I have a mock-up.

2. 背景顏色無法突顯出影像。

   The background color doesn't let the images stand out.

3. 看來我們選的字型不錯。

   It looks like the font we chose is good.

4. 我認為字要大一點。

   The words need to be larger, I think.

5. 你想大家會很容易看到時間及日期嗎？

   Do you think people will easily notice the time and date?

6. 我可以把它移到這裡，這樣會比較明顯。

   I can move it to here. It will be more noticeable.

10.5d 安排活動 Arranging a Meeting

Dialog 對話

A: 嗨，傑瑞，我們週五要跟大家會面。	**A:** Hi, Jerry. We need to have everyone meet on Friday.
B: 要嗎？為什麼？	**B:** We do? Why?

A: 我們的演講貴賓比預定日期早兩天到。

A: Our guest speaker is coming two days earlier than we expected.

B: 我知道了，我們有些事情要改及組織會不一樣。

B: I see. We'll need to get things changed and organized differently.

A: 對，我們也需要有人帶她走走看看。

A: Right. We'll need someone to show her around too.

B: 好，無論如何，我們何時何地要開會？

B: OK. Anyway, when and where shall we have the meeting?

A: 我們要先在學生活動中心保留一間會議室。

A: We'll have to try to reserve a meeting room in the Student Activity Center.

Word Bank 字庫

guest speaker n. 演講貴賓
reserve [rɪˋzɝv] v. 保留
meeting room n. 會議室

Useful Phrases 實用語句

1. 我們週五要跟大家會面。
   We need to have everyone meet on Friday.

2. 我們有一些事情要改及組織會不一樣。
   We'll need to get things changed and organized differently.

3. 我們需要有人帶演講者去走走看看。
   We'll need someone to show the speaker around.

4. 我們何時何地要開會？
   When and where shall we have the meeting?

預備

校園

選課

新生說明

上課前

課堂上

課後交流

圖書館

體育館

餐廳

課外活動

申請獎助

當助教

5. 我們要先保留一間會議室。

We'll have to try to reserve a meeting room.

10.6 社團會議後
After the Club Meeting

Dialog 對話

A: 傑瑞,我們要去「壞蛋」,你要去嗎?

A: Jerry. We're all going to Scoundrels. Want to come?

B: 「壞蛋」是什麼?

B: What is Scoundrels?

A: 一間本地酒吧,也有好吃的東西,是個消磨時間的好地方。

A: A local bar. They have good food too, and it's a cool place to hang out.

B: 聽起來很棒,我也會去。

B: It sounds good. I'll go too.

A: 很好,你會有機會跟社團裡更多的人聊聊。

A: Great. You'll have a chance to talk to more people in the club.

B: 酷,不管怎樣,我很餓。

B: Cool. I'm pretty hungry anyway.

A: 我也是。

A: Me too.

Word Bank 字庫

hang out 消磨時間

Useful Phrases 實用語句

1. 它是個消磨時間的好地方。

   It's a cool place to hang out.

2. 你會有機會遇見更多的人。

   You'll have a chance to meet people.

Tips 小祕訣

　　除社團外，學生可以參加學生會組織。每個校園學生會組織可能有所不同，一般而言，學生會會長、副會長、評議員、財政長等幹部由學生選出，且只有學生可以投票及參選，過程如同一般選舉。

Language Power 字詞補給站

◆ 社團 Student Clubs

club	社團
association	協會
members	會員
membership	會員身分
fees	費用
meetings	會議
agenda	議程
activities	活動
outings	出外（郊遊）
extracurricular	課外的
athletic teams	運動隊伍
student government	學生會
Senate	學生代表
President	會長
Vice-president	副會長

representative	代表
elections	選舉

Information Bank 大補帖

◎ 美國校園常見的社團及協會 a List of Common Clubs and Associations on American Campuses

學校社團不勝枚舉，端看學生興趣，以下是一些美國校園常見的社團及協會：

🐾 Alternative Dispute Resolution Advocates 爭議解決替代方案 (非司法途徑) 促進社

🐾 American Advertising Federation Ad Club 美國廣告聯盟廣告社

🐾 American Institute of Architecture Students 美國建築系學生會

🐾 American Marketing Association 美國市場行銷協會

🐾 American Sign Language Association 美國手語社

🐾 Art Club 藝術社

🐾 Art History Association 藝術歷史協會

🐾 Arts & Administration Student Forum 藝術及行政學生論壇

🐾 Asian/Pacific American Students Club 亞太美國學生

🐾 Associated Students for Historic Preservation 史跡保護學生會

🐾 Association of Anthropology Students 人類學學生會

🐾 Association of School Psychology Students 心理學院學生會

🐾 Athletic Department 運動社

🐾 African Students Association 非裔學生會

🐾 Black Law Students Association 非裔法律系學生會

🐾 Black Student Union 非裔學生會

🐾 Black Women of Achievement 非裔成就女士社

🐾 Center for the Advancement of Sustainable Living 簡約生活促進中心

🐾 Chess Club 棋社

🐾 Chinese Student Association 中籍學生會

🐾 Chinese Students and Scholars Association 中籍學生及學者協會

🐾 College Democrats 大學民主黨員

🐾 College Republicans 大學共和黨員

🐾 Collegiate Music Educators 大學音樂教育社

🐾 Computer club 電腦社

- Dance Club 舞蹈社
- Ecological Design 生態設計
- Educational Leadership Organization 教育領導社
- Environmental Policymakers and Planners 環境政策制定及規劃
- European Student Association 歐洲學生會
- Geology Club 地質學社
- Hong Kong Student Association 香港學生會
- International Honor Society 國際榮譽社
- International Business and Economics Club 國際商業及經濟社
- International Law Students Association 國際法律系學生會
- International Students Association 國際學生會
- Jewish Student Union 猶太學生會
- Korean Student Association 韓國學生會
- Mathematics Club 數學社
- Martial Arts Club 武術社
- Men's Center 男士中心
- Minority Law Students Association 少數族裔法律系學生會
- Mortar Board 方帽社
- Music Club 音樂社
- Multicultural Center 多元文化中心
- Muslim Student Association 穆斯林學生會
- National Association of Black Journalists 非裔記者國際協會
- Native American Students Association 美國原住民學生會
- Old Ballroom Dance Club 老式社交舞社團
- Pan Hellenic Council 泛希臘協會
- Philosophy Club 哲學社
- Public Relations Student Society of America 美國公關學生社
- Society of Professional Journals 專業記者社
- Student Association for Architecture 建築系學生會
- Student Bar Association 學生法律協會
- Student Cooperative Association 學生合作會
- Student Senate 學生評議會
- Taiwan Student Association 臺灣學生會
- The Pacific Islands Club 太平洋島嶼社
- Toastmasters 演講協會

預備
校園
選課
新生說明
上課前
課堂上
課後交流
圖書館
體育館
餐廳
課外活動
申請獎助
當助教

🐚 United States Student Association 美國學生會

🐚 United Nations Club 聯合國社

🐚 Veterans Student Association 退伍軍人學生會

Tips 小祕訣

　　學生會 (Student Government) 為全體學生之權益而產生的組織，是學生發聲表達意見的溝通管道，提供校方政策制定及推行之重要參考，學生會議題包含校內所有關於學生需求與權益，如學生住宿、法律服務、課程需求及其他方面的事務。

10.7 有關學生會的談論
Talking about Student Government

Dialog 對話

A: 我對一門課很不滿。

A: I have a complaint about a class.

B: 怎麼了？

B: What's wrong?

A: 我真的認為器材不夠全部學生使用。

A: I really think there is not enough equipment for all of the students.

B: 你應該聯絡學生會課務組。

B: You should contact the Student Office of Academic Affairs.

A: 為什麼？

A: Why?

B: 那是學生會的一個分部，處理學生所關心的課程事務。

B: It's a branch of student government that deals with student concerns about their classes.

A: 我了解了。

A: I see.

10.8 與學生會會員談話
Talking to a Member of Student Government

Dialog （對話）

A: 哈囉，這是學生會課務組嗎？

A: Hello. Is this the Student Office of Academic Affairs?

B: 是的，請進。

B: Yes, it is. Come on in.

A: 謝謝，我被告知你們可以幫我處理我對一門課的不滿。

A: Thanks. I've been told that you can help me with a complaint I have about a class.

B: 要看你的抱怨是什麼。

B: It depends on the type of complaint you have.

A: 是關於我修的化學課，註冊學生缺乏可用器材。

A: It is about the lack of equipment available to students enrolled in a chemistry class I'm in.

B: 我知道了，我相信我們可以幫你。

B: I see. Yes. I believe we can help you.

A: 很好。

A: Great.

B: 多告訴我一點，你擔心的是什麼。

B: Tell me more about what concerns you.

A: 最主要的是我們很多人無法做必要的實驗，因為實驗室器材不夠。

A: Mostly, a lot of us cannot do our required lab work because there is not enough equipment in the lab.

B: 讓我把這個寫下來，然後我會告訴你我們會怎麼做。

B: Let me write this down, and then I'll tell you what we'll do.

Word Bank 字庫

complaint [kəm`plent] n. 不滿
concern [kən`sɜn] n., v. 關心
Student Office of Academic Affairs n. 學生會課務組
enroll [ɪn`rol] v. 註冊

Useful Phrases 實用語句

1. 我對一門課很不滿。

   I have a complaint about a class.

2. 器材不夠全部學生使用。

   There is not enough equipment for all of the students.

3. 多告訴我一點，你擔心的是什麼。

   Tell me more about what concerns you.

預備 校園 選課 新生說明 上課前 課堂上 課後交流 圖書館 體育館 餐廳 課外活動 申請獎助 當助教

10.9 大學校慶
University Anniversary

美國的大學並非每年過校慶，通常只有在創校 100 或 150 週年這種大日子才會慶祝。

 Dialog 1 對話1

A: 這週因為學校校慶所以有很多活動。

A: There are a lot of activities this week because of the University's Anniversary.

B: 真的嗎？什麼活動？

B: Really? What are they?

A: 有許多演講來賓在這裡談學校及它的歷史。

A: There are many guest speakers here to talk about the University and its past.

B: 可能滿有趣的。

B: That might be interesting.

A: 週三晚有舞會及現場樂團表演。

A: There is going to be a dance and live band on Wednesday night.

B: 在哪裡？

B: Where?

A: 在籃球場。

A: In the basketball stadium.

預備
校園
選課
新生說明
上課前
課堂上
課後交流
圖書館
體育館
餐廳
課外活動
申請獎助
當助教

B: 進場要多少錢？ ▶ **B:** What does it cost to enter?

A: 註冊學生免費。 ▶ **A:** It's free for registered students.

B: 我們去吧！ ▶ **B:** Let's go to that!

✎ Word Bank 字庫

anniversary [ˌænəˈvɜsərɪ] n. 週年紀念日
live band n. 現場樂團
basketball stadium n. 籃球場

📖 Useful Phrases 實用語句

1. 進場要多少錢？
   What does it cost to enter?
2. 註冊學生免費。
   It's free for registered students.

Dialog 2 對話2

A: 你要去藝術學院聽校長演講嗎？ ▶ **A:** Are you going to the University President's speech at the Arts School?

B: 什麼時候？ ▶ **B:** When is it?

A: 2 點 30 分在達克大會堂。 ▶ **A:** 2:30 at Dack Hall.

B: 你要去嗎？

B: Are you going?

A: 要。

A: Yes.

B: 為什麼？

B: Why?

A: 演講後有一個招待茶會。

A: After the speech there will be a reception.

B: 我知道了，會有很多免費的食物及飲料。

B: I see. There will be a lot of free food and drinks.

A: 對。

A: Right.

Word Bank 字庫

reception [rɪˋsɛpʃən] n. 招待茶會

Dialog 3 對話3

A: 我們可以去看攝影比賽。

A: We can go to see the photography competition.

B: 我聽說只有學生可以參賽。

B: I hear only students can enter it.

預備 校園 選課 新生說明 上課前 課堂上 課後交流 圖書館 體育館 餐廳 課外活動 申請獎助 當助教

A: 對，但比賽很激烈。

A: That's right, but the competition is fierce.

B: 為什麼？

B: Why?

A: 學生以他們的能力為榮，所以贏得比賽是很大的榮耀。

A: The students are proud of their ability, so winning is a great honor.

B: 我懂了，要錢嗎？

B: I see. Does it cost anything?

A: 不必，幾乎所有校慶期間的節目對學生及大眾都是免費。

A: No. Almost all the events during the anniversary are free for students and the public.

Word Bank 字庫

photography competition n. 攝影比賽
enter [`ɛntɚ] v. 參賽
fierce [fɪrs] adj. 激烈的
event [ɪ`vɛnt] n. 節目，活動

Useful Phrases 實用語句

1. 比賽很激烈。

   The competition is fierce.

2. 學生以他們的能力為榮。

   The students are proud of their ability.

3. 贏得比賽是很大的榮耀。

   Winning is a great honor.

10.10 到教授家聚會
Gathering at a Professor's Home

Dialog 1 對話1

A: 哈囉，強森教授。

A: Hello, Professor Johnson.

B: 哈囉，歡迎，請進來。

B: Hello. Welcome. Please come in.

A: 謝謝。

A: Thank you.

B: 所有人都在另一個房間，但我想先向你介紹我太太。

B: Everybody is in the other room, but first I want to introduce my wife to you.

A: 好的，很好。

A: OK. Great!

B: 瑪格麗特，這是艾立克蘇。

B: Margaret. This is Eric Su.

A: 我很高興認識你，強森太太。

A: I'm pleased to meet you Mrs. Johnson.

C: 我也很高興認識你，艾立克。

C: I'm pleased to meet you too, Eric.

預備
校園
選課
新生說明
上課前
課堂上
課後交流
圖書館
體育館
餐廳
課外活動
申請獎助
當助教

Useful Phrases 實用語句

1. 我想先向你介紹我太太。

   I want to introduce my wife to you.

2. 我很高興認識你。

   I'm pleased to meet you. (初次見面較正式)

   I'm happy to meet you. (初次見面較不正式)

Dialog 2 對話2

A: 嗨，大家好。

A: Hi, everybody.

B: 嗨，艾立克。你好嗎？

B: Hi, Eric. How is it going?

A: 不錯，大家在做什麼呢？

A: Not bad. What's happening?

B: 我們只是在聊天及吃點東西，都很隨意。

B: We're just chatting and having some food. It's all very informal.

A: 很好。

A: That's cool.

B: 教授在告訴我們他以前的故事，就好玩。

B: The professor has been telling us stories about his past. It's all just for fun.

A: 我可以喝點東西嗎？

A: Can I get something to drink?

B: 當然，食物及飲料都在那邊的桌上，自己來。

B: Sure. Food and drinks are on the table over there. Help yourself.

A: 謝謝。

A: Thanks.

✏️ **Word Bank** 字庫

chat [tʃæt] v. 聊天
informal [ɪn`fɔrml] adj. 非正式的，隨意的

📖 **Useful Phrases** 實用語句

1. 你好嗎？
   How is it going?
2. 大家在做什麼呢？
   What's happening?
3. 我們在聊天及吃點東西。
   We're just chatting and having some food.
4. 都很隨意。
   It's all very informal.

🏃 **Dialog 3** 對話3

A: 你們有帶禮物給教授嗎？

A: Did you bring a gift to give to the professor?

B: 沒有，沒有人帶，我們被告知不需要帶。

B: No. Nobody did. We were told it isn't necessary.

A: 好，我也沒有帶。

A: Good. I didn't bring one either.

預備　校園　選課　新生說明　上課前　課堂上　課後交流　圖書館　體育館　餐廳　課外活動　申請獎助　當助教

預備
校園
選課
新生說明
上課前
課堂上
課後交流
圖書館
體育館
餐廳
課外活動
申請獎助
當助教

B: 你有參觀這房子嗎？

B: Did you tour the house?

A: 沒有，可以嗎？

A: No. Is it OK?

B: 可以，至少樓下是開放給我們的。

B: Yes. At least the downstairs is open to us.

A: 你已經參觀了嗎？

A: Did you look around already?

B: 是的，他們收集了許多有趣的東西。

B: Yes. They have collected many interesting things.

A: 我最好看看。

A: I'd better have a look.

Useful Phrases 實用語句

1. 你有帶禮物給教授嗎？

   Did you bring a gift to give to the professor?

2. 我們被告知不需要帶。

   We were told it isn't necessary.

3. 你有參觀這房子嗎？

   Did you tour the house?

4. 樓下是開放給我們的。

   The downstairs is open to us.

5. 你已經參觀了嗎？

   Did you look around already?

Tips 小祕訣

如果你被邀請去教授家，放輕鬆並自然應對，因為教授希望你和其他被邀請的學生一樣了解教授跟其他普通人一樣生活，並希望你自在、輕鬆享受這段時光。雖說這是輕鬆聚會，還是要記得注意禮貌，你不被期望要帶禮物。有時教授可能安排大家帶一道菜肴 (potluck)，這時應該要帶些食物分享。

Dialog 4 對話4

A: 強森教授，謝謝你邀請我來。

A: Thanks for having me over, Professor Johnson.

B: 我樂意之至，希望你玩的開心。

B: My pleasure. I hope you had fun.

A: 我有，我真的喜歡在這裡並且認識您太太。

A: I did. I really enjoyed being here and meeting your wife.

B: 週五在課堂上見。

B: I'll see you in class Friday.

A: 當然囉，再見。

A: For sure. Bye.

B: 再見。

B: See you.

Useful Phrases 實用語句

1. 我真的喜歡在這裡並且認識您太太。

   I really enjoyed being here and meeting your wife.

預備

校園

選課

新生說明

上課前

課堂上

課後交流

圖書館

體育館

餐廳

課外活動

申請獎助

當助教

2. 謝謝你邀請我過來。

Thanks for having me over.

10.11 學生受獎場合
Student Awards Events

10.11a 較不正式場合：學生社團獎
Less Formal Occasion: Student Club Awards

 Dialog 對話

A: 大家注意，我要宣布今年最有影響力的會員，得獎的是王金！金，請過來。

A: Your attention, everyone. I want to make an announcement. This year's award for "Most Influential Member" goes to Kim Wang! Kim, come here please.

B: 謝謝大家，這完全是個驚喜，我真的很榮幸，再次感謝你們。

B: Thank you, everybody. This a total surprise. I'm really honored. Thanks again.

A: 金，你還有什麼話要說嗎？

A: Kim, is there anything else you'd like to say?

B: 我真的要謝謝每個幫過我的人，沒有他們我不可能辦到。

B: I really need to thank everyone that helped me. I couldn't have succeeded without them.

A: 好。恭喜你，金！　　　**A:** OK. Congratulations, Kim!

Word Bank 字庫

announcement [ə`naʊnsmənt] n. 宣布
award [ə`wɔrd] n. 獎
Most Influential Member n. 最有影響力的會員

Useful Phrases 實用語句

1. 我要宣布一件事。
   I want to make an announcement.

2. 這完全是個驚喜。
   This a total surprise.

3. 我真的很榮幸。
   I'm really honored.

4. 我真的要謝謝每個幫過我的人。
   I really need to thank everyone that helped me.

5. 沒有他們我不可能辦到。
   I couldn't have succeeded without them.

6. 你還有什麼話要說嗎？
   Is there anything else you'd like to say?

10.11b 頒獎 (較正式) Award Giving (More Formal)

 Dialog 對話

A: 各位女士先生，我很榮幸頒發今年的翰林亞頓優秀傑出學生研究獎學金，瑞秋王小姐！(她在掌聲中上臺)

A: Ladies and Gentlemen. I'm honored to present this year's recipient of the Hamlin-Alton Scholarship Award for excellence in student research. Miss Rachael Wong . (She would then come to the podium as people applaud)

B: 謝謝大家，我非常高興被選中為今年的受獎人，我必須要感謝大家在我研究期間給我的支持及肯定，我也要謝謝我的家人，特別是我的母親及父親這幾年來給我的愛及支持。

B: Thank you, everyone. I'm very pleased to be chosen as this year's recipient. I must thank everyone for the support and recognition I have received while doing my research here at the university. I also want to thank my family, especially my mother and father for all their love and support over these years.

Word Bank 字庫

present [prɪ`zɛnt] v. 頒發
recipient [rɪ`sɪpɪənt] n. 受獎人
recognition [ˌrɛkəg`nɪʃən] n. 肯定

預備　校園　選課　新生說明　上課前　課堂上　課後交流　圖書館　體育館　餐廳　課外活動　申請獎助　當助教

預備

校園

選課

新生說明

上課前

課堂上

課後交流

圖書館

體育館

餐廳

課外活動

申請獎助

當助教

📖 Useful Phrases 實用語句

1. 我很榮幸頒發這個獎。

   I'm honored to present this award.

2. 我非常高興被選中。

   I'm very pleased to be chosen.

📢 Notes 小叮嚀

　　正式場合要展現出正式氣氛及禮儀，參加者要穿著端莊，舉止有禮，合宜行為是當天的準則。

10.11c 祝賀 Giving Congratulations

Dialog 1 對話1

A: 嗨，傑瑞。

A: Hi, Jerry.

B: 嗨，麥斯。你認識金嗎？

B: Hi, Max. Do you know Kim?

A: 認識，我幾個月前跟她一起工作。

A: Yes, I worked with her a couple of months ago.

B: 她得獎了，真是太棒了。

B: It's great that she won the award.

A: 是的。

A: Yes, it is.

預備
校園
選課
新生說明
上課前
課堂上
課後交流
圖書館
體育館
餐廳
課外活動
申請獎助
當助教

B: 我們過去恭喜她。

B: Let's go over and congratulate her.

A: 好主意。

A: Good idea.

 Useful Phrases 實用語句

1. 太棒了,她得獎了。

   It's great that she won the award.

2. 我們過去恭喜她。

   Let's go over and congratulate her.

 Dialog 2 對話2

A: 嗨,金,恭喜你得獎!

A: Hi, Kim. Congratulations for winning the award!

B: 謝謝,我不認為我該得。

B: Thanks. I don't think I deserve it.

A: 當然是你應得的,你很努力。

A: Sure you do. You work hard.

B: 謝謝,活動結束後我要去慶祝,一起來吧。

B: Thanks. I'm going to celebrate after the event. Join me.

A: 沒問題。

A: No problem.

Word Bank 字庫

deserve [dɪ`zɝv] v. 值得

Useful Phrases 實用語句

○ 恭喜 Congratulatory phrases

1. 恭喜你的成功。

   Congratulations to your success.

2. 恭喜你得獎！

   Congratulations for winning the award!

3. 做得好！

   To a job well done!

4. 做得好！我真替你高興。

   Great job! I'm very happy for you.

5. 恭喜！我想他們確實作對了決定。

   Congratulations! I think they certainly made the right choice.

6. 你應得的，恭喜！

   You really deserve it. Congratulations!

7. 當然是你應得的，你很努力。

   Sure you do. You work hard.

○ 舉杯祝賀 Toasting

1. 做得好！（敬工作成就！）

   To a job well done.

2. 恭喜你的成功。

   Congratulations to your success.

3. 乾杯！

   Cheers!

3. 敬你及你的成就。

   To you and your success.

4. 敬今年的傑出得主。

   To this year's outstanding winner.

預備
校園
選課
新生說明
上課前
課堂上
課後交流
圖書館
體育館
餐廳
課外活動
申請獎助
當助教

○ **同伴祝賀 Peer students to the award recipient**

1. 恭喜！

   Congratulations !

2. 做得好！

   Good work!

3. 做得好！

   Way to go!

4. 太棒了，恭喜！

   This is so great. Congratulations!

5. 可以碰你嗎？（開玩笑，因得獎者像神一般榮耀）

   Can I touch you? (said in jest)

6. 我可以看（你的）獎嗎？

   Can I see the award?

○ **回應 Responses**

1. 謝謝。

   Thank you.

2. 謝謝大家。

   Thank you, everyone.

3. 非常感謝。

   Thank you so much.

4. 我很榮幸。

   I'm honored.

5. 我配不上這個（獎）。

   I don't deserve this.

6. 我不認為我該得。

   I don't think I deserve it.

7. 我不知道要說什麼，我很幸運。

   I don't know what to say. I'm very fortunate.

8. 這是很大的榮耀。

   This is a great honor.

○ **得獎人對教授 Award winner to a professor**

1. 謝謝你，教授。

   Thank you, Professor.

2. 為這個榮耀，謝謝你。

   Thank you for this honor.

3. 我很榮幸。

   I'm honored.

4. 我配不上這個。(謙虛地說)

   I don't deserve this. (said humbly)

Tips 小祕訣

> 頒獎儀式 (Awards Ceremony) 可以是正式及非正式場合，
> 要依照校園內對獎項的層級而定。一般而言，學生社團頒獎是
> 非正式的，但教職員多是正式的。

10.12 教授受獎場合
Faculty Awards Event

10.12a 頒獎 (正式) Award Giving (formal)

Dialog 對話

A: 各位先生女士，我非常榮幸頒發今年的克拉森畢爾斯研究獎給
安東畢凱特教授，讓我們熱烈歡迎他。

A: Ladies and Gentlemen. It's my honor to present this year's
winner of the Clarkson-Beals Research Award to Professor
Anton B. Kitt. Let's all give him a warm welcome.

B: 謝謝各位，謝謝。讓我先感謝校內生物研究系的教職員們，他們在我研究期間給我全力支援，當然我必須感謝我的太太，內麗，她忍受我的缺席及超過任何人該忍耐的脾氣。

B: Thank you, everyone. Thank you. Let me start by thanking the staff of the Department of Bio Research here at the University. They have been extremely supportive throughout the period of time of my research. I of course must thank my wife, Nelly. She has put up with my absence and temper far more than anyone should ever have to.

Word Bank 字庫

supportive [sə`pɔrtɪv] adj. 支持的；贊助的
temper [`tɛmpɚ] n. 脾氣

Useful Phrases 實用語句

1. 我非常榮幸頒發 (獎名) 給 (受獎人)。

   It's my honor to present (name of award) to (person).

2. 讓我們熱烈歡迎他。

   Let's all give him a warm welcome.

10.12b 祝賀 Giving Congratulations

Dialog 對話

A: 恭喜，凱特教授！我為你感到開心。

A: Congratulations, Professor Kitt! I'm very happy for you.

B: 謝謝你，班。

B: Thank you, Ben.

預備 校園 選課 新生說明 上課前 課堂上 課後交流 圖書館 體育館 餐廳 課外活動 申請獎助 當助教

A: 我很開心學校選了你。

A: I'm really happy the school chose you.

B: 非常感謝你,希望你留下來開慶祝會。

B: Thank you very much. I hope you'll stay for the reception.

A: 當然。

A: Yes, of course.

B: 太好了,待會見。

B: Great. See you there.

Useful Phrases 實用語句

1. 我很開心學校選了你。

   I'm really happy the school chose you.

2. 希望你留下來開慶祝會。

   I hope you'll stay for the reception.

10.13 慶祝派對
Celebration Parties

大學慶祝活動有幾個原因——學生社團慶祝、學系頒獎或其他原因慶祝，最大的慶祝當然是畢業典禮。畢業典禮既是儀式也是慶祝，學生至少都會參加畢業典禮。

10.13a 畢業典禮 Graduation

Dialog 1　對話1

A: 你準備好參加畢業典禮了嗎？

A: Are you ready for the graduation ceremony?

B: 還沒。

B: No.

A: 為什麼？

A: Why not?

B: 我沒有學士帽和學士服。

B: I don't have my mortar board and robe.

A: 為什麼？

A: Why not?

B: 我不知道去哪裡拿。

B: I don't know where to pick them up yet.

A: 真的嗎？學校在書店發放。

A: Really? This university distributes them at the bookstore.

B: 喔，我不知道。

B: Oh, I didn't know that.

Word Bank 字庫

mortar board n. 學士帽

robe [rob] n. 學士服

Dialog 2 對話2

A: 我們的區在哪裡？

A: Where is our section?

B: 在那邊，所有化學系的學生坐在那區。

B: Over there. All the Chem. Students sit in that section.

A: 今天的演講來賓是誰？

A: Who will be the guest speaker today?

B: 巴瑞特路卡，「旅行袋」的創辦人及執行長。

B: Barry Tellooka. He is the founder and C.E.O. of Travel Bag.

A: 你是說旅行供貨連鎖。

A: You mean the travel supplies franchise?

B: 是的。

B: Yes.

預備／校園／選課／新生說明／上課前／課堂上／課後交流／圖書館／體育館／餐廳／課外活動／申請獎助／當助教

A: 我想聽他演講應該很有趣。

A: I think he will be interesting to listen to.

B: 我想也是。

B: I think so too.

A: 嘿，在宣布我們畢業之後，別忘了將你的帽穗移到左邊。

A: Hey. Don't forget to move your tassel to the left side of your cap after it's been announced that we've graduated.

Word Bank 字庫

guest speaker n. 演講來賓
founder [`faʊndɚ] n. 創辦人
C.E.O. n. 執行長
franchise [`fræntʃaɪz] n. 連鎖
tassel [`tæsl] n. 帽穗；流蘇

Useful Phrases 實用語句

1. 我們的區在哪裡？

   Where is our section?

2. 今天的演講來賓是誰？

   Who will be the guest speaker today?

3. 聽他演講應該很有趣。

   He will be interesting to listen to.

4. 別忘了將你的帽穗移到左邊。

   Don't forget to move your tassel to the left side.

 Dialog 3 對話3

A: 恭喜你，莎莉！

A: Congratulations, Sally!

預備

校園

選課

新生說明

上課前

課堂上

課後交流

圖書館

體育館

餐廳

課外活動

申請獎助

當助教

B: 謝謝，吉姆。也恭喜你。

B: Thanks, Jim. Same to you.

A: 你要去參加今晚的派對嗎？

A: Are you going to the party to-night?

B: 要，我希望每個人都去。

B: Yes. Everyone is, I hope.

A: 是的，我想每個人都會去那裡。

A: Yes. I think everyone will be there.

 Dialog 4 （對話4）

A: 乾杯！

A: Cheers!

B: 乾杯！

B: Cheers!

A: 這是個很棒的派對。

A: This is a great party.

B: 是的，我很高興我終於畢業了。

B: Yes, it is. I'm so glad I've finally graduated.

A: 我也是。

A: Me too.

B: 接下來你要做什麼？

B: What are you going to do next?

A: 我想旅行一下吧，你呢？

A: Travel a little I think. What about you?

B: 我不知道，但現在我要去參加派對！

B: I don't know, but right now I'm going to party!

A: 對！

A: Yeah!

Useful Phrases　實用語句

1. 畢業典禮是什麼時候？

   When is graduation?

2. 戴上你的帽子並穿上長袍。

   Put on your cap and gown.

3. 恭喜！

   Congratulations!

4. 我們去參加畢業後派對吧。

   Let's go to the after ceremony party.

5. 乾杯！

   Cheers!

10.13b 系慶祝派對 Department Celebration Party

Dialog　對話

A: 嗨，泰瑞莎！

A: Hi, Teresa.

B: 哈囉，吉姆，一切如何？

B: Hello, Tim. How is it going?

A: 很好，那邊有食物及飲料。

A: Great. There is food and drink over there.

B: 好，我很餓。

B: Great. I'm starving.

A: 你有帶禮物來嗎？

A: Did you bring a gift?

B: 有，在這裡，我要怎麼做？

B: Yes. Here it is. What should I do with it?

A: 跟其他的一起放在那邊的桌上。

A: Put it over there on that table with the others.

B: 好，我聽說我們派對要做一些搞笑的活動。

B: OK. I hear we're going to do some goofy activities at this party.

A: 是的，他們有一些蠢活動給我們做。

A: Yes. They have some silly activities for us to do.

B: 音樂呢？

B: How about music?

A: 很多，但什麼都可以，你有帶一些來放嗎？

A: Plenty, but anything is OK. Did you bring something to play?

預備
校園
選課
新生說明
上課前
課堂上
課後交流
圖書館
體育館
餐廳
課外活動
申請獎助
當助教

B: 有，我有一片好笑的 CD。

B: Yes. I have a funny music CD.

A: 好，我們晚點可以放。

A: Great. We can play it later.

B: 我聽說我們也會看電影。

B: I hear we're going to watch a movie too?

A: 如果你要的話，有人帶了洛基恐怖秀。

A: If you want to. Somebody brought Rocky Horror Picture Show.

B: 聽起來我們會玩得很開心。

B: Sounds like we'll have a lot of fun.

A: 沒錯。

A: No doubt about it.

Word Bank 字庫

goofy [`gufɪ] adj. 呆的

Useful Phrases 實用語句

1. 我很餓。

   I'm starving.

2. 你有帶禮物來嗎？

   Did you bring a gift?

3. 你有帶一些音樂來放嗎？

   Did you bring some music to play?

4. 沒錯。

   No doubt about it.

Unit 11 Applying for Financial Aid and Certifications

申請財務獎助及證書

美國教育非常昂貴，依各校收費不同，大學部的學雜費、食宿費用每年至少 $15,000- $40,000，研究所甚至更貴，外籍學生光是學費就比美籍學生要貴出許多，學校每年更新學費公告，且學費仍不斷上漲，除了美籍本國生、加拿大籍及墨西哥籍的學生外，美國對其他外籍學生的就學資金援助 (financial aid) 相當有限。大多數的公共或私人獎學金限制申請人身分必須是美國公民，因此除非有專門為外籍生而設某些獎學金的情況 (稀少且多所限制) 或你能證明確實是該校系所需的優秀人才，外籍學生獲得美國獎助金的情況相當少見。

11.1 在美就學的費用
Financial Cost of Attending Schools in America

美國大學理事會(The College Board)在每年出版的*美國外籍學生指南*(*The International Student Handbook of US Colleges*)內公告大學費用、入學考試及其他有用資訊,當你在計算某所美國大學每年的教育費用時,在公告的學費及食宿費用上多加$6,000。當你準備預算時,要將下列費用計算在內:

- 申請費每所平均 $50 - $100。
- 每次入學考試至少 $150,每個學生至少考兩個考試,在考試上至少要花費 $500。
- 依各學科及學校不同,學費每學年 (9個月) 約 $5,000 - $40,000。
- 每年書籍及補充教材大約需花費 $500 - $1,000。
- 赴美花費看地點,交通從 $500 - $2,000 都有可能,美國境內為 $300 - $700。
- 食宿 (room and board) 每年為 $3,000 - $7,500,另加 $1,000 - $2,000 因寒暑假宿舍關閉必須多出的額外花費。
- 校外住宿每月租金為 $300 - $600,但學校附近可能讓租金更昂貴。若不常在餐廳用餐,餐費每年約 $2,500。
- 服裝費每年約 $500 或更多。
- 健康保險費每年每人約 $300 - $500,每家庭約 $2,000 - $3,500。
- 其他個人花費估算每年約 $2,000。

如果帶家人同行,每年花費大約要增加15%或每人多$5,000。如果你要買車,每年會多出$4,000。如果你打算暑期旅遊,每天的預算約為$50-$75。如果你暑修,多加你所算出每學年費用的一半。通貨膨漲會使每年費用增加5%,別忘記多抓10%的外匯兌換波動成本。各校每年依其政策及物價景氣通膨等因素調整學費,但學費向來只漲不跌,近年調漲幅度驚人,即使美國本州生也已不堪負荷(外州生學費為本地生三倍),何況學費為本地生至少三倍以上的外籍生。經濟不景氣時,美國大學尤其需要從外籍生所支付高額學費中籌措財源,選擇學校時務必參照各校最新公告,選擇位於大都會(如紐約、洛杉磯、舊金山、芝加哥等)或私立大學(研究所)就讀者,留學費用必然較非大都會區或公立大學要昂貴許多。因為外籍生學費超高又難獲補助,所以每所學校在外籍生提出入學申請時,都要求附上足夠的財產證明,證明在沒有金援的情形下,外籍生還可以靠自己的財力就讀,不致彈盡糧絕,半途而廢。

11.2 外籍學生獎學金來源
Sources of Financial Aid for International Students

因為教育補助是如此有限，想申請的人必須想辦法嘗試每個機會，若有意到他國留學，可以向駐我國的大使館或辦事處詢問或到該網站搜尋獎學金資料。記住你應該查詢免費的獎學金資料庫，有一些搜尋獎學金的服務會要求你繳交一些費用，再幫你搜尋符合你條件的獎學金資料庫，這極有可能是詐騙手段，即使不是，其結果絕大多數是花了錢卻找到限美國人申請的獎學金，因此需要花錢才能申請的服務就不必嘗試了。

11.2a 國際教育財務支援資料庫
International Education Financial Aid (IEFA)

☑ http://www.iefa.com 是為外籍學生列出獎學金的網站，其設立宗旨在促進美國籍學生及世界其他國際學生到國外留學，其網站列出許多外籍學生可以申請的獎學金。

11.2b 國際組織的援助 Aid from International Organizations

極少數外籍學生可以拿到國際援助，這些援助多數要求外籍生在赴美前就要在母國申請。如果你已在美，可能就喪失申請資格。有些國際組織提供研究生到美就讀，這些包含聯合國 (the United Nations)、美洲國家組織 (the Organization of American States OAS)、美國中東教育訓練中心 (AMIDEAST)、國際海洋組織 (the International Maritime Organization)、國際電訊聯盟 (the International Telecommunications Union)、紅十字社團 (the League of Red Cross Societies)、索羅斯基金會 (the Soros Foundation)、世界衛生組織 (the World Health Organization) 及世界基督教會聯合會 (the World Council of Churches)，這些獎學金競爭非常激烈。

11.2c 來自美國政府的援助 Aid from the US Government

除非政策需要或履行協定外，美國政府向來不提供外國學生獎助學金，民間機構亦同。美國政府可能援助某些特定國家的學生，要知道

預備

校園

選課

新生說明

上課前

課堂上

課後交流

圖書館

體育館

餐廳

課外活動

申請獎助

當助教

美國是否提供援助給自己國家或提供哪些獎助，可以查詢下列網站：

1. 美國大使館 (或駐台辦事處 AIT) ☑ http://www.ait.org.tw/zh/
2. 隸屬美國國務院之美國國際開發總署 (Agency for International Development, AID) ☑ http://www.usaid.gov/
3. 同樣隸屬美國國務院 (the US Department of State) 之教育與文化事務局 (Bureau of Eucational and Cultural Affairs, ECA)
   ☑ http://exchanges.state.gov/ 網站已有中文 (簡體)

該網站提供在美就學及獎學金資訊 (如 Fulbright 及 the Hubert H. Humphrey Fellowship Program)，但是援助計畫如 the Pell Grant、貸款如 Stafford and PLUS loans 及工讀計畫 work-study programs 並不提供給外籍學生。

尋求其他獎助可洽詢 ECA 支援世界各地超過 450 個地點的 EducationUSA。台灣的對口點為美國教育基金會 (American International Education Foundation, AIEF) 或學術交流基金會。如果人已在美，可洽詢學校之國際學生顧問。

美國教育諮詢 EducationUSA

☑ http://educationusa.state.gov/ 網站已有中文 (正體)

美國教育基金會 ☑ http://www.aief.org.tw
學術交流基金會 ☑ http://www.fulbright.org.tw/

11.2d 來自美國教育機構的援助
Aid from US Educational Institution

提供給外籍大學部學生的經濟援助機會很少，獎助有限。近年有些學校為吸引新生或更多樣的國際生，提供大一新生 (國際生) 獎學金，申請者須自各大學系所網站搜尋，也可查詢外國學生獎學金 eduPASS 網站 ☑ http://www.edupass.org，或查看教育部公告之外國政府、學校或民間機構補助之各類留學獎學金資訊。外籍研究生相對有較多機會，但獎金仍是很有限。有些美國學校有直接的學生交換計畫，這類計畫通常包含對外籍學生的財務援助，這類資訊要詢問就讀的大學。

想要赴美就讀研究所或博士 (或博士後課程) 的外籍學生可以直接寫信給想就讀學校的財務支援室 (Financial Aid Office) 詢問該校對外籍學生是否有學費援助之事宜。大多數美國大學以提供助教及研究助理工作的方式給予研究生財務援助，這些工作是以優良的學業表現而非財務困窘的程度決定是否獲得助教工作及財務支援，此外學校可能

會要求外籍研究生通過 TSE (Test of Spoken English) 才能勝任助教工作。

就讀語言學校是不可能獲得財務援助的，外籍研究生至少要有托福 213（即舊制 550）以上的成績才可能有一絲機會申請獎助金，在其他條件相當之下，獎學金當然都是由高分者獲得。已經註冊的外籍學生可以詢問國際學生顧問 (International Student Advisor)、財務援助室 (Financial Aid Office) 及就業輔導室 (Career Planning & Placement Office)，學校圖書館可能也有相關資訊。

11.2e 美國私人援助
Aid from Private US Organizations and Sponsors

外籍學生很難從私人管道（如基金會及個人贊助等）獲得財務援助。比較可行的辦法是多留意美國出版的族裔報紙，有些財務援助資訊只能在外語報紙獲得。如果沒有任何資訊可以打電話給報社編輯，確認是否有被任何社團或個人贊助的機會。

即使獲知有慷慨的贊助人，接受贊助在美就讀的機會也少於萬分之一。美國贊助人與國際贊助人一樣慷慨，但由於尋求贊助的外籍學生數量龐大及在美就讀費用昂貴，要獲得援助相當不易，尋求國內贊助人可能機會大一些。

11.2f 美國傅爾布萊特 (Fulbright) 獎學金

每年授予全世界約 4,700 位外籍研究生獎學金，申請者都要通過研究所入學考試 (TOEFL and GRE or GMAT)，此外獲獎者必須以交換學生簽證 J-1 身分赴美，有關 Fulbright 獎學金及其他提供國際學生獎學金的網站資訊可查詢：

傅爾布萊特基金會（學術交流基金會網站）
☑ http://www.fulbright.org.tw

EducationUSA ☑ https://educationusa.state.gov/

學術交流基金會美國教育資訊中心 US Education Information Center
☑ http://www.educationusa.tw

美國教育基金會 (AIEF)　☑ http://www.aief.org.tw

11.2g 來自自己國家政府及私人的援助
Aid from Your Home Country

在美國讀書最好的金援是來自自己國家，自己國家的政府可能對留學生有經濟援助(通常要求須在學業完成後返國服務)，許多教育部及外交文化部會有這類資料，但是許多獎學金或經濟援助需要獲得自己政府的提名才能取得，競爭激烈。此外國內私人企業、基金會及宗教團體也有提供海外就學獎學金，但基於創辦理由，常限定就讀國家及就讀學校系所。下列網站可供參考：

　　教育部全球資訊網 ▪ http://www.edu.tw
　　　　教育部獎學金：1. 公費獎學金 2. 教育部與世界百大合作設置獎學金甄選 3.（一般生及弱勢生）留學獎學金甄試 4. 教育部「學海」計畫：補助大學生出國研修或實習。
　　科技部(科教發展及國際合作司)菁英專案留學獎學金及國際交流方案補助 ▪ https://www.most.gov.tw

11.2h 外籍生自己及家庭的援助
Assistance from Yourself and Your Family

統計顯示 2/3 的外籍學生是自己籌措或由家庭提供就學費用，絕大部分的外籍大學部學生和半數的外籍研究生完全靠自己及家庭的財務支援在美就讀，少於 1/10 的外籍大學部學生獲得學校經濟支援，獲得自己國家政府支援及獲得私人企業支援者僅 1/20，從美國獲得財務支援的學生不到 1/5。綜合以上所提，外籍生最有可能獲得的經濟支援是自己或家人親戚。

允許外籍學生入學，除在文化及教育上可為大學帶來不同刺激外，國外大學也需要外籍學生支付較高學費來平衡大學財務，學生之生活必要支出還可活絡當地經濟。

11.2i 留學貸款 Getting Loans for Studying Abroad

留學貸款依個人條件不同，可申請到的貸款金額、利率及還款條件也不同。一般而言，可分成信貸及擔保貸款，要求提供保證人的信貸或有財務擔保貸款可貸得較高金額，約為免保證人信貸的兩倍。貸款其實是透支未來的作法，貸款越多將來還款也較吃力，償還期數越長也表示所付利息成本越多，因此要仔細評估自己在求學期間的財務支出及順利取得

學位後償還貸款的金額及期限。以下是留學貸款相關網站：
教育部補助留學生就學貸款—承貸銀行 ☑ http://www/edu.tw

1. 臺灣銀行
2. 合作金庫商業銀行
3. 臺灣土地銀行
4. 兆豐國際商業銀行
5. 玉山商業銀行
6. 中國信託商業銀行
7. 台北富邦商業銀行
8. 其他經教育部核可之銀行。

11.3 詢問財務支援
Asking about Financial Aid

Dialog 1 （對話1）

A: 哈囉，這是獎助學金辦公室嗎？

A: Hello. Is this the Financial Aid Office?

B: 是的，我可以幫你嗎？

B: Yes, it is. May I help you?

A: 可以，我想要了解一個給外籍學生的獎學金資訊。

A: Yes. I want to get more information about a scholarship available to foreign students.

B: 是從這大學可以獲得的嗎？

B: Is it available from this university?

A: 是的，叫做太平洋環東獎學金。

A: Yes, it is. It's called the Pac Rim East Scholarship.

B: 好，你要知道什麼？

B: OK. What do you need to know?

預備 校園 選課 新生說明 上課前 課堂上 課後交流 圖書館 體育館 餐廳 課外活動 申請獎助 當助教

A: 事實上我想申請，所以我想了解怎麼辦理。

A: Actually I want to apply for it, so I need to find out how.

B: 我知道了，我會給你表格。

B: I see. I'll give you the form.

A: 謝謝。

A: Thank you.

 Word Bank 字庫

financial aid n. 獎助學金
Pac (Pacific) Rim 環太平洋

 Useful Phrases 實用語句

1. 這是獎助學金辦公室嗎？

   Is this the Financial Aid Office?

2. 我想要了解一個給外籍學生的獎學金資訊。

   I want to get more information about a scholarship available to foreign students.

3. 是從這大學可以獲得的嗎？

   Is it available from this university?

 Dialog 2 對話2

A: 關於這獎學金，我有一些問題。

A: I have some questions about this scholarship.

B: 好。

B: OK.

A: 截止日期是何時？

A: When is the deadline?

B: 2 月 15 日，如果你要（申請）9 月的獎學金。

B: It's February 15th if you want it for the following September.

A: 我懂了，我要把表格給誰？

A: I understand. Who do I give the form to?

B: 填好後把表格帶回這裡。

B: Bring it back here when it's ready.

A: 好，謝謝。

A: OK. Thanks.

 Useful Phrases 實用語句

1. 截止日期是何時？

   When is the deadline?

2. 我要把表格給誰？

   Who do I give the form to?

3. 要求是什麼？

   What are the requirements?

4. 我要填哪份表格？

   Which form do I need to fill out?

5. 論文要多長？

   How long should the essay be?

6. 可以請你再解釋一次這個嗎？

   Can you explain this again please?

7. 我對這部分有疑問。

   I have a question about this part.

預備
校園
選課
新生說明
上課前
課堂上
課後交流
圖書館
體育館
餐廳
課外活動
申請獎助
當助教

8. 我要影印幾份？

How many copies should I make?

11.4 工讀
Work-Study

學校在外籍學生申請就讀時，都會要求提供財力證明 (financial status) 來證明自己不須打工便足以應付學雜費及生活開銷，外籍學生也必須註冊為全職學生，因此要靠打工支付學雜費及開銷的念頭是不被學校允許的。

外籍學生除非是因為接受獎助學金而必須在校外承擔某項工作，才無須移民局批准可在校外打工，或是在就讀超過一年並且突然遭遇嚴重經濟困難，在通過種種條件考核下 (成績優良且校內工讀時數不夠等等)，經過外籍學生顧問 (foreign student advisor) 向移民局申請工作許可證 (work permit)，才可能被允許校外打工 (off-campus work)，畢竟美國大學收外籍學生重要因素之一是要靠外籍學生支付較高學費平衡學校財務，而不是反倒賠上美國人的工作機會。

但小量校內打工是被允許的，按照美國對外籍學生打工的規定，拿 F1 及 J1 簽證的學生在正常學期期間每週校內工最多 20 小時，不需向外籍學生顧問報備。持 F1 簽證的學生可以在校內餐廳、圖書館等處打工，但機會不多且多半是勞力工作，時薪是微薄的美國最低工資 (因州而異)。J1 學生按照規定，校內工作需與所學課業相符，如擔任助教等。

假期期間外籍學生如向外籍學生顧問報備且經過申請向移民局取得工作許可證，可以打工，但每週工作上限 40 小時。遠赴重洋至國外就讀不易，若違法打工可能失去學生資格，不可不慎。移民法常有修正，有關工作實習等規定，要與外籍學生顧問確認。

11.4a 詢問工讀工作 Asking about Work-Study

Dialog 1 對話1

A: 嗨，我想申請一個工讀職位。

A: Hi. I would like to apply for a work-study position.

B: 你知道哪一個工作嗎？

B: Do you know which job you want?

A: 對不起，我對工讀服務知道不多。

A: Sorry. I don't know much about this program.

B: 我知道了，首先你要先找一兩個你要的工作來申請。

B: I see. First you need to find one or two jobs you want to apply for.

A: 我要去哪裡找？

A: Where do I look?

B: 我們都列在網站上了，你可以在我們那邊的電腦上找。

B: We have them all listed online. You can check them out on one of our computers over there.

A: 好。

A: OK.

Useful Phrases 實用語句

1. 我想申請一個工讀職位。

   I would like to apply for a work-study position.

2. 我對這工讀服務知道不多。

   I don't know much about this program.

預備
校園
選課
新生說明
上課前
課堂上
課後交流
圖書館
體育館
餐廳
課外活動
申請獎助
當助教

Dialog 2　對話2

A: 我找到一個我喜歡的工作。

A: I found a job I'm interested in.

B: 好，告訴我哪一個。

B: Do you know which job you want?

A: 這一個，實驗室助理。

A: This one. Lab Assistant.

B: 我知道了，你需要聯絡這些人來安排面談。

B: I see. You will need to contact these people and set up an appointment to talk to them.

A: 我可以打電話給他們嗎？

A: Is it OK for me to call them?

B: 可以，他們期待有興趣申請的學生與他們聯絡。

B: Yes. They expect interested student applicants to make contact with them.

A: 這裡列出的薪水正確嗎？

A: Is the pay listed here correct?

B: 正確。

B: Yes.

A: 我每週可以工作幾小時？

A: How many hours a week can I work?

B: 不超過 20 小時。　**B:** No more than twenty.

A: 這工作說明未列出工作時間表。　**A:** The job description doesn't tell the schedule.

B: 多數工讀的工作都有彈性時間符合學生需求。　**B:** Most of the work-study jobs have flexible hours to fit student needs.

A: 好的，我懂了，謝謝。　**A:** OK. I understand. Thanks.

 Word Bank 字庫

> lab assistant n. 實驗室助理
> applicant [ˋæpləkənt] n. 申請人
> flexible hours n. 彈性時間

 Useful Phrases 實用語句

1. 我可以打電話給他們嗎？
   Is it OK for me to call them?

2. 這裡列出的薪水正確嗎？
   Is the pay listed here correct?

3. 我每週可以工作幾小時？
   How many hours a week can I work?

4. 他們期待申請人與他們聯絡。
   They expect applicants to make contact with them.

5. 工讀都有彈性時間。
   Work-study jobs have flexible hours.

6. 多數工作符合學生需求。
   Most jobs fit student needs.

預備
校園
選課
新生說明
上課前
課堂上
課後交流
圖書館
體育館
餐廳
課外活動
申請獎助
當助教

7. 我要去哪裡？

Where should I go?

8. 我需要履歷表嗎？

Do I need a resume?

9. 班表如何？

What is the schedule?

11.4b 工讀面談 Work-Study Interview

Dialog 對話

A: 哈囉，我是鮑伯涂。

A: Hello. I'm Bob Tu.

B: 嗨，我是琳達凱，請坐。

B: Hi. I'm Linda Kay. Please sit down.

A: 謝謝。

A: Thanks.

B: 學生活動中心打電話給我，他們告訴我你對實驗助理的工作有興趣。

B: The Student Work Center called me. They told me you are interested in the Lab Assistant job.

A: 是的。

A: Yes, I am.

預備

校園

選課

新生說明

上課前

課堂上

課後交流

圖書館

體育館

餐廳

課外活動

申請獎助

當助教

B: 你有經驗嗎？

B: Do you have any experience?

A: 有，我高中時就當過實驗助理。

A: Yes, I do. I was a lab assistant in High School.

B: 很好，你在那裡當了多久助理？

B: Great. How long were you an assistant there?

A: 一年。

A: One year.

B: 你為什麼對當這裡的助理感興趣？

B: Why are you interested in being an assistant here?

A: 我喜歡這類的工作，很適合我，而且我覺得很有趣。

A: I like this type of work. It is suitable for me, and I think it is quite interesting.

B: 你何時可以開始？

B: When can you start?

A: 隨時。

A: Any time.

B: 好，下週一如何？

B: OK. How about this coming Monday?

A: 我週一早上有課到中午。

A: I have classes on Monday morning until noon.

B: 沒問題,你可以從下午1點或1點30分開始。

B: No problem. You can start at 1 p.m. or 1:30 p.m..

A: 1點可以,我要帶什麼東西來嗎?

A: 1:00 is fine. Do I need to bring anything?

B: 不用,實驗室有你要的所有東西。

B: No. The lab will provide everything you need.

A: 好,那每週其他的時間呢?

A: Great. What about the rest of the week?

B: 好,我們坐下來把你全部的工作表排好。

B: Right. Let's sit down and make a full schedule for you.

A: 好。

A: OK.

📖 Useful Phrases 實用語句

1. 你有經驗嗎?

   Do you have any experience?

2. 你在那裡當了多久助理?

   How long were you an assistant there?

3. 你為什麼對當這裡的助理感興趣?

   Why are you interested in being an assistant here?

4. 你何時可以開始?

   When can you start?

5. 我要帶任何東西嗎?

   Do I need to bring anything?

預備
校園
選課
新生說明
上課前
課堂上
課後交流
圖書館
體育館
餐廳
課外活動
申請獎助
當助教

6. 那每週其他的時間呢？

   What about the rest of the week?

7. 薪資多少？

   How much is the pay?

8. 我何時領薪水？

   When do I get paid?

9. 我何時開始？

   When do I start?

10. 我有經驗。

    I have experience.

11. 我是這個系的學生。

    I'm a student in this department.

12. 我主修電腦科學。

    I'm a computer science major.

13. 我對這工作有興趣，因為它跟我的主修有關。

    I'm interested in this job because it's related to my major.

14. 我擅長計畫及組織。

    I'm very good at planning and organizing.

15. 我要向誰報到？

    Who do I report to?

11.4c 詢問成為研究生助理
Asking about Being a Graduate Assistant

Dialog 對話

| A: 哈囉，強森教授。 | A: Hello, Professor Johnson. |

| B: 嗨，約翰，我可以為你做什麼？ | B: Hi, John. What can I do for you? |

預備
校園
選課
新生說明
上課前
課堂上
課後交流
圖書館
體育館
餐廳
課外活動
申請獎助
當助教

A: 我想請問您關於成為研究生助理的事。

A: I'd like to ask you about being a Graduate Assistant.

B: 我了解了，請坐。

B: I see. Please sit down.

A: 謝謝，您可以告訴我有哪些責任嗎？

A: Thanks. Can you tell me what the responsibilities are?

B: 可以，你要幫我備課以及批改大學生作業。

B: Yes. You will need to help me with class preparation and correction of undergrad assignments.

A: 我每週需要幫您多少小時？

A: How many hours a week would I need to assist you?

B: 很難說，不一定。有些星期會比其他時間更忙。

B: It's hard to say. It will vary. Some weeks are much busier than others.

A: 助理還有其他責任嗎？

A: What other duties does an assistant have?

B: 研究生助理要值辦公室時間以及作示範教學。

B: Graduate Assistants have to keep office hours and give demonstrations too.

A: 我需要任何專門技術嗎？

A: Do I need any technical skills?

B: 你要會用錄影設備及簡報。

B: You'll need to be able to use video equipment and PowerPoint.

A: 好，我知道了，沒問題。我要如何正式申請？

A: OK. I see. No problem. How do I formally apply?

B: 你需要我的核可，之後你要簽一份我們系上提供的職缺合約。

B: You'll need my approval, and then you'll need to sign the contract provided by our department for the position.

A: 我何時會知道我是否獲得這份工作？

A: When can I know if I can have the job?

B: 另外兩位學生已表示過要成為我的研究生助理，我週五前會決定。

B: Two other students have asked to be my Grad Assistant. I'll decide by Friday.

A: 好，謝謝您考慮我。

A: Great. Thank you for considering me.

Word Bank 字庫

Grad(uate) Assistant n. 研究生助理
undergrad(uate) [ˋʌndəˌgræd] adj., n. 大學部的 (學生)
vary [ˋvɛrɪ] v. 變化
office hours n. 辦公室時間
demonstration [ˌdɛmənˋstreʃən] n. 示範
approval [əˋpruvl] n. 核可

Useful Phrases 實用語句

1. 我想請問您關於成為研究生助理的事。

   I'd like to ask you about being a Graduate Assistant.

2. 您可以告訴我有哪些責任嗎？

   Can you tell me what the responsibilities are?

預備　校園　選課　新生說明　上課前　課堂上　課後交流　圖書館　體育館　餐廳　課外活動　申請獎助　當助教

預備
校園
選課
新生說明
上課前
課堂上
課後交流
圖書館
體育館
餐廳
課外活動
申請獎助
當助教

3. 我每週需要幫您多少小時？

   How many hours a week would I need to assist you?

4. 助理還有其他責任嗎？

   What other duties does an assistant have?

5. 我需要任何專門技術嗎？

   Do I need any technical skills?

6. 我要如何正式申請？

   How do I formally apply?

7. 我何時會知道我是否獲得這份工作？

   When can I know if I can have the job?

Tips 小祕訣

要成為研究生助理 (graduate assistant)— 研究助理 (research assistant) 或教學助教 (teaching assistant)，雖各校及各州的規定不一，但當助理工讀的好處包含學費減免 (tuition reduction)、醫療及牙齒補助 (medical and dental plans) 和一些病假 (sick leave)，合約上會詳細說明。

學生要了解申請實習、證照、模組、訓練及其他各就學階段所需的申請手續與資格，才不致耽誤修課時限，申請證書需要填 petition 書面申請。

11.5 申請證書
Applying for a Certificate

Dialog 對話

A: 嗨，我有一個關於最近參加工作坊的問題。

A: Hi. I have a question about a recent workshop I attended.

B: 是什麼問題？

B: What is your question?

A: 我想要獲得一張證書證明我已成功地完成工作坊提供的訓練。

A: I want to get a certificate stating I successfully completed the training the workshop provided.

B: 我了解了，是什麼工作坊？

B: I see. What workshop was it?

A: 是關於組織溝通。

A: It was about Organizational Communication.

B: 是何時舉辦的？

B: When was it held?

A: 上個月11月11日，在戈登大會堂。

A: Last month on November 11th, at Gordon Hall.

B: 好，我會查查一下，確定你可以被核發證書。

B: OK. I'll check to make sure you are approved for a certificate.

A: 我何時會知道是否被核可？

A: When will I know if it is approved?

B: 明天早上10點之後打電話來。

B: Call tomorrow after 10 a.m.

A: 好，謝謝。

A: Great. Thanks.

Word Bank 字庫

certificate [səˋtɪfəkɪt] n. 證照
workshop [ˋwɝk͵ʃɑp] n. 工作坊
approve [əˋpruv] v. 核可

Useful Phrases 實用語句

1. 我想要獲得一張證書。
   I want to get a certificate.
2. 我何時會知道是否被核可？
   When will I know if it is approved?

11.6 實習
Internships

11.6a 詢問實習 Asking about Internships

實習可分為兩種：課程實習和畢業實習。根據美國移民局「外國學生交換學者資訊追蹤系統」(SEVIS) 中有關美國外籍學生實習的最新規定，學生通常在開始就學一年後，可以開始從事與就讀課程有關的課程實習 (仍在就讀英語課程者除外)，期限一般不超過一年 (主修 STEM 學生例外，見 11.8 說明)，但外籍學生要做實習工作必須符合美國政府的規範。

學生若在學業完成後要畢業實習必須在畢業前 90-120 天前就要申請，獲得移民局批准後自完成學業起有一年的工作期。就學的每一階段只有一次實習機會，如果同階段已做過課程實習用掉實習機會，就不可以再申請畢業實習。

美國外籍學生實習的管理規則因反恐而更趨嚴格，任何有關外籍學生的規定必須時常注意，可以上 SEVIS 網站 ✔ http://www.ice.gov/sevis/students/index.htm 或教育部駐外文教處網站查詢 (見附錄 5)。

Dialog 1 對話1

A: 嗨，我可以為你效勞嗎？

A: Hi. May I help you?

B: 可以，我想要了解一下實習。

B: Yes. I want to find out about an internship.

A: 哪一個？

A: Which one?

B: 就是沙克教授的計畫。

B: It's the one for Professor Sack's project.

A: 我知道了，請等一下。

A: I see. Just a minute.

B: 好。

B: Sure.

A: 這是申請單，你填好後交回這辦公室。

A: Here is the application. You need to fill it out and return it to this office.

B: 截止日期是什麼時候？

B: When is the deadline?

A: 下星期二。

A: Tuesday of next week.

預備
校園
選課
新生說明
上課前
課堂上
課後交流
圖書館
體育館
餐廳
課外活動
申請獎助
當助教

Word Bank 字庫

internship [ˋɪntɝnˏʃɪp] n. 實習
application [ˏæpləˋkeʃən] n. 申請
deadline [ˋdɛdˏlaɪn] n. 截止期限

Useful Phrases 實用語句

1. 我想要了解一下實習。

   I want to find out about an internship.

2. 截止日期是什麼時候？

   When is the deadline?

Dialog 2 對話2

A: 我可以問幾個問題嗎？

A: Can I ask some more questions?

B: 當然可以。

B: Yes, certainly.

A: 這是有薪資的實習，或是只有學分？

A: Is this a paid internship, or is it only for credit?

B: 這是有薪資也有學分的實習。

B: This is a paid internship with credit.

A: 有任何學費抵免嗎？

A: Is there any tuition waiver?

B: 這個沒有。

B: Not with this one.

A: 值多少學分？

A: How many credits is it worth?

B: 每學期 5 學分。

B: Five per session.

A: 我要付多少費用？

A: Are there any fees that I have to pay?

B: 不必，被選上的學生不必付費。

B: No. There are no additional costs or fees charged to the student selected.

A: 何時開始實習？

A: When does the internship start?

B: 下學期。

B: Next session.

A: 謝謝。

A: Thank you.

✏ Word Bank 字庫

session [`sɛʃən] n. 學期
tuition waiver n. 學費抵免
paid internship n. 有薪資的實習
for credit only 只有學分

📖 Useful Phrases 實用語句

1. 何時開始實習？

   When does the internship start?

預備
校園
選課
新生說明
上課前
課堂上
課後交流
圖書館
體育館
餐廳
課外活動
申請獎助
當助教

2. 這是有薪資的實習嗎？

   Is this a paid internship?

3. 實習期間多久？

   How long does it last?

4. 包含多少學分？

   How many credits does it include?

5. 有任何費用嗎？

   Are there any fees?

6. 有哪些種類的實習？

   What kinds of internships are offered?

7. 我想做研究。

   I want to do research.

8. 我想和教授一起工作。

   I want to work with professors.

9. 我想多學一些物理治療。

   I want to learn more about physical therapy.

10. 我要找誰談？

    Who do I talk to?

11. 有面談嗎？

    Is there an interview?

11.6b 與教授談實習
Talking with a Professor about Internships

Dialog 對話

A: 哈囉，湯普森教授，我想詢問下年度的實習。

A: Hello, Professor Thompson. I'd like to ask about next year's internships.

B: 好。

B: All right.

A: 有什麼選擇？

A: What are the choices?

B: 我們明年有幾個職缺開放給實習生。你有興趣做什麼？

B: We have several positions open for interns next year. What are you interested in doing?

A: 我想與研究人員一起工作多學點經驗。

A: I'd like to get more experience working with researchers.

B: 好，有兩個研究助理的職缺。

B: Fine. There are a couple of positions available as a research assistant.

A: 我該怎麼申請呢？

A: What do I have to do to apply?

B: 我們要讓找實習生的人知道你有興趣，你必須要與其中一人或兩人面談。

B: We'll need to let the persons looking for interns know you are interested. You'll have to interview with one or both.

A: 我要準備什麼東西嗎？

A: Should I prepare anything?

B: 只要準備告訴他們為什麼你感興趣。

B: Just be ready to tell them about why you are interested in the position.

A: 我也想知道我可以獲得幾個學分。

A: I'm also wondering how many credits I can get.

預備
校園
選課
新生說明
上課前
課堂上
課後交流
圖書館
體育館
餐廳
課外活動
申請獎助
當助教

B: 實習持續一整年，你每學期可得到 6 個學分。

B: The internship lasts all of the academic year, and you'll get six credits each session.

A: 我如何被評量？

A: How will I be evaluated?

B: 你去實習服務的人會定期提供你表現的書面報告，在實驗結束時你也要寫報告交給你的指導者。

B: The person you are working for will provide periodical written reports on your performance, and you'll need to write a report of your own to hand into your advisor at the end of the internship.

A: 我何時可以面談這實習職缺呢？

A: When can I interview for the position?

B: 我今天幫你登記，明天前會讓你知道。

B: I'll set it up for you today, and then I'll let you know by tomorrow.

A: 好，多謝。

A: Great. Thanks a lot.

✎ Word Bank 字庫

positions available 有空缺
intern [`ɪntɜn] n. 實習生
interview [`ɪntɚ͵vju] v. 面談 [試]
evaluate [ɪ`vælju͵et] v. 評量

Useful Phrases 實用語句

1. 我想詢問下年度的實習。

   I'd like to ask about next year's internships.

2. 有什麼選擇？

   What are the choices?

3. 我想與研究人員一起工作多學點經驗。

   I'd like to get more experience working with researchers.

4. 我該怎麼申請呢？

   What do I have to do to apply?

5. 我要準備什麼東西嗎？

   Should I prepare anything?

6. 我也想知道我可以獲得幾個學分。

   I'm also wondering how many credits I can get.

7. 我如何被評量？

   How will I be evaluated?

8. 我何時可以進行實習職缺面談？

   When can I interview for the position?

Notes 小叮嚀

　　有給付薪資的工讀或實習因為有報稅問題，所以需要申請社會安全號碼 (Social Security Number, SSN)。原本 SSN 是用來追查報稅資料及社會福利的工具，但因為卡片上除了 9 個數字及名字、簽名外沒有任何其他個人資料，所以也成為最被廣泛使用的身分證明工具。每個人一生只有一個 SSN，其遺失補發次數都有限制，如果取得 SSN，務必要小心使用。

預備 校園 選課 新生說明 上課前 課堂上 課後交流 圖書館 體育館 餐廳 課外活動 申請獎助 當助教

11.7 社會安全號碼及卡
Social Security Number (SSN) and Card

Dialog 對話

A: 哈囉，這是社會安全局辦公室嗎？

A: Hello. Is this the Social Security Office?

B: 是的，我可以為你服務嗎？

B: Yes, it is. May I help you?

A: 我是國際學生，我需要了解如何取得社會安全卡。

A: I'm an international student, and I need to find out about getting a Social Security Card.

B: 你需要提供資料，特別是你需要國土安全部文件說你可以在美國這裡有工作。

B: You'll need to provide information. Especially you'll have to have documents from the Office of Homeland Security saying it is OK for you to have a job here in the United States.

A: 我要如何開始呢？

A: How do I start?

B: 你必須填一張社會安全卡申請表 (SS-5 表)，並且給我們看由核發機關證明你的居留身分、年齡及身分的正本或影本證明。

B: You must complete an application for a Social Security Card (Form SS-5); and show us original documents or copies certified by the issuing agency proving your immigration status, age and identity.

A: 什麼文件可以證明我的身分？

A: What documents qualify for proving my status?

B: 你不是公民，所以社會安全局會要求看你現在的居留身分文件，可以接受的文件包括 I-551、I-94 表格及你未過期的護照。

B: You are not a citizen, so Social Security will ask to see your current U.S. immigration documents. Acceptable documents include your Form I-551, I-94 and your unexpired passport.

A: 之後我要做什麼？

A: What do I do after that?

B: 然後將完整的文件拿到或寄到當地社會安全局辦公室。

B: Then, take or mail your completed documents to your local Social Security Office.

A: 有哪裡可以讓我讀到關於這個的更多資料嗎？

A: Is there someplace I can read more about all of this?

預備
校園
選課
新生說明
上課前
課堂上
課後交流
圖書館
體育館
餐廳
課外活動
申請獎助
當助教

B: 有，拿著這個手冊並注意背面的網站，那網站提供所有你該知道有關工作或不工作社會安全號碼的申請步驟。

B: Yes. Take this handbook and also notice the web address on the back of it. That website will provide everything you need to know about work or non-work Social Security Card application procedures.

A: 要多少錢呢？

A: How much does it cost?

B: 不用錢，是免費的。

B: There is no charge. It's free.

A: 我知道了，真是個好消息，多謝你的幫忙。

A: I see. That's good news. Thank you very much for all of your help.

B: 我的榮幸，記住如果你還有問題，可以打電話也可以來這裡。

B: My pleasure. Remember that you can call and come here too if you have more questions or problems.

A: 好，謝謝。

A: Great. Thanks.

B: 還有，我們一收到你所有的申請資料並且與核發單位確認你的文件，就會寄出你的號碼及卡片。

B: By the way, we will mail your number and card as soon as we have all of your information and have verified your documents with the issuing offices.

A: 好，多謝。

A: OK. Thank you very much.

✎ Word Bank 字庫

the Office of Homeland Security n. 國土安全部
certify [`sɜtə,faɪ] v. 證明
issuing agency n. 核發機關
immigration status n. 居留身分

📖 Useful Phrases 實用語句

1. 我要申請社會安全卡。

   I want to apply for a Social Security Card.

2. 我要提供什麼文件？

   What documents do I need to provide?

3. 要多久？

   How long will it take?

4. 要多少錢？

   What does it cost?

5. 我要先做什麼？

   What do I need to do first?

6. 我需要有人來幫我。

   I'd like someone to assist me.

預備
校園
選課
新生說明
上課前
課堂上
課後交流
圖書館
體育館
餐廳
課外活動
申請獎助
當助教

7. 我有許多問題。

   I have a lot of questions.

8. 我不懂所有的要求。

   I don't understand all the requirements.

9. 你可以幫我這個嗎？

   Can you please help me with this?

10. 這是我的居留身分。

    This shows my immigration status.

11. 這可以證明我的身分。

    This will prove my identification.

Hello, I'd like to ask about next year's internships.

Fine. There are a couple of positions available as a research assistant.

Notes 小叮嚀

　　社會安全號碼 (Social Security number, SSN) 是美國聯邦政府發給個人的一組九位數號碼，作為追蹤個人稅賦資料，但實際上已成為個人身分及信用的識別。因為反恐政策使然及為了使公民及非公民的權利關係獲得最好的結果，社會安全福利號碼的政策幾經修訂，「社會安全卡」官網 ☑ http://www.ssa.gov/ 現已具備各種語言版本，包含正體中文。SSN 卡分成三種：

(1) 美國公民及合法永久居留者

(2) 外國人合法受雇者

(3) 合法居留但不得受雇者。

　　外國學生需要社會安全卡才能完成銀行開戶、申請信用卡、辦駕照、買車、租車、辦手機等各種需求，除非被允許在校園內外工作，否則僅能申請「NOT VALID FOR EMPLOYMENT」「不允許工作」的社會安全卡，申請時須提交 I-20 證明。被允許在校園內外工作或實習的外籍學生 (見 11.4) 申請 SSN 時，必須提供學校或雇主發出的工作證明。

預備
校園
選課
新生說明
上課前
課堂上
課後交流
圖書館
體育館
餐廳
課外活動
申請獎助
當助教

418

11.8 申請選擇性畢業實習
Asking about Optional Practical Training (OPT)

Dialog （對話）

A: 哈囉，我可以跟負責選擇性畢業實習的人說話嗎？

A: Hello. Can I speak to someone about Optional Practical Training?

B: 可以，我可以幫你，我是 OPT 的主任。

B: Yes, I can help you. I'm the OPT Director.

A: 好，我何時可以申請？

A: Great. When can I apply?

B: 你必須在完成所有課程至少 90 天前申請。

B: You have to apply at least 90 days before you complete all of your course work.

A: 我要到六月課程才會結束。

A: I won't finish until June.

B: 很好，六月離現在約有 120 天。

B: That's fine. June is about 120 days from now.

A: 我如何知道我的實習期限是多久？

A: How do I know how long my OPT period is?

B: 如果你通過，你會收到一張實習卡，上面註明開始及結束日期。

B: If you are approved, you'll receive an OPT Card with a specific starting and ending date on it.

A: 誰決定日期？

A: Who sets the dates?

B: 你，你要決定何時開始，OPT 期限一年，到期日會顯示。

B: You. You have to choose the starting date. The OPT period ends one year later, which the expiration date will show.

A: 我了解了。

A: I see.

B: 你要確定開始日期不可以遲於完成課業後 60 天。

B: You must also make sure that the starting date is no later than 60 days after you finish your program.

A: 好。

A: OK.

預備
校園
選課
新生說明
上課前
課堂上
課後交流
圖書館
體育館
餐廳
課外活動
申請獎助
當助教

Word Bank 字庫

OPT(Optional Practical Training) n. 選擇性畢業實習

OPT Director n. 畢業實習的主任

apply [əˋplaɪ] v. 申請

course work n. 課程

approved [əˋpruvd] adj. 被核可的

OPT Card n. 實習卡

starting date n. 開始日期

ending date n. 結束日期

OPT period n. 實習期限

expiration date n. 到期日

program [ˋprogræm] n. 課程

Useful Phrases 實用語句

1. 我想了解畢業實習。

   I'd like to know about OPT.

2. 我首先該怎麼做？

   What should I do first?

3. 我可以去哪裡申請？

   Where can I apply?

4. 我何時可以申請？

   When can I apply?

5. 我可以工作多久？

   How long can I work?

6. 我何時會收到我的卡片？

   When will I receive my card?

7. 到期日是何時？

   What's the expiration date?

8. 我的開始日是何時？

   When is my starting date?

9. 何時是我的結束日？

   When is my ending date?

　　外籍學生實習 (Practical Training) 可分為就學中的課程實習 (Curricular Practical Training, CPT) 或畢業後實習 (Optional Practical Training, OPT)，實習工作需與所學專業相關。學生完成學業後無論科系，皆可選擇實習，期限為 12 個月。

　　自 2008 年起，美國給予持有 F1 簽證，主修數理科技工程 STEM (science, technology, engineering, mathematics) 的外籍畢業生，申請延長實習 17 個月 (STEM extension)，共 29 個月的實習，不料 17 個月期限引起諸多公司機構之不滿控告，訴訟於 2014 年獲勝。自 2016 年 5 月起，持有 F1 簽證的 STEM 外籍畢業生，改為可申請延長實習 24 個月，共 36 個月的實習。

　　無論 CPT 或 OPT，美國對於外籍生申請實習之資格、申請時間、工作性質、時數、何時開始及結束等細節，均詳加規範。美國移民海關事務執法部門 (U.S. Immigrantion and Customes Enforcement, USICE ☑ https://www.ice.gov/sevis/practical-training) 可能因應局勢而調整政策，有意申請實習之外籍生應留意其最新規定。

11.9 申請畢業
Applying for Graduation

Dialog 對話

A: 嗨，我可以為你做什麼？

A: Hi. What can I do for you?

B: 我想申請畢業。

B: I'd like to register for graduation.

預備
校園
選課
新生說明
上課前
課堂上
課後交流
圖書館
體育館
餐廳
課外活動
申請獎助
當助教

A: 好，恭喜！

A: OK. Congratulations!

B: 謝謝，我需要做什麼嗎？

B: Thank you. What do I need to do?

A: 很簡單，你要為你的學士學位填這張申請表，順便一提，你也可以上網填寫。

A: It is pretty simple. You'll need to fill out this application form for your bachelor degree diploma, which, by the way, you can do online.

B: 多少費用？

B: What is the fee?

A: 30 元，你可以在這裡付。

A: $30. You can pay it here.

B: 我要今天付嗎？

B: Do I have to pay it today?

A: 你要在交回表格時付款。

A: You'll need to pay it when you turn in the form.

B: 如果我在網站上填呢？

B: What if I do it online?

A: 你可以用信用卡付或從學生卡扣。

A: You can pay by credit card or have it deducted from your student card account.

B: 我知道了，何時截止？

B: I see. When is the deadline?

A: 你必須在畢業那年的三月底前登記。

A: You need to register by the end of March of the year you are graduating.

B: 好。

B: OK.

A: 還有你如果有未結清的費用，你就不能畢業。

A: Also remember that if you have not paid any fees, you will not be allowed to graduate.

B: 什麼費用？

B: What fees?

A: 譬如說，你有圖書館逾期罰金或學校裡任何服務的未付款。

A: For example, you have late fees at the library, or unpaid bills for services provided by the university.

B: 我懂了，謝謝。

B: I understand now. Thanks.

A: 我的榮幸，如果有任何問題可回來或打電話來詢問。

A: My pleasure. Come ask, or call if you have any other questions.

B: 再次謝謝你。

B: Thanks again.

預備　校園　選課　新生說明　上課前　課堂上　課後交流　圖書館　體育館　餐廳　課外活動　申請獎助　當助教

Word Bank 字庫

bachelor degree [diploma] n. 學士學位 [文憑]
deduct [dɪ`dʌkt] v. 扣除
register [`rɛdʒɪstɚ] v. 登記
late fees n. 逾期罰金
unpaid bills n. 未付款

Useful Phrases 實用語句

1. 我要今天付嗎？

   Do I have to pay it today?

2. 如果我在網路上填呢？

   What if I do it online?

3. 何時截止？

   When is the deadline?

4. 什麼費用？

   What fees?

5. 我何時會收到證書？

   When will I get the diploma?

6. 我要如何拿到證書呢？

   How will I receive the diploma?

Hi. What can I do for you?

I'd like to register for graduation.

Unit 12 Leading a Course as a Teaching Assistant
當助教教課

外籍學生要在美國大學當助教是個大挑戰，但美國大學接受外籍學生，而美國學生也知道他們有時會當助教，因此也會願意支援外籍助教，教授除了會要求助教批改大學生的作業、報告、考試之外，研究生助理偶爾也要授課，某些情形下研究生可能要上整學期的課，多數的教授會給予協助。助教必須完成教授交辦的事項並向教授報告，平時也要有辦公室時間 (office hours) 讓學生問問題。如果你具備恰當的溝通能力並為課程做好準備，不妨用較輕鬆的態度面對。美國大學生對國際事務、教育交流未必熟悉，外籍助教可別輕視自己在教育及文化的角色與定位，還有雙方教學相長對彼此可能產生的影響力。

預備 校園 選課 新生說明 上課前 課堂上 課後交流 圖書館 體育館 餐廳 課外活動 申請獎助 當助教

12.1 上一堂課
Leading One Class

 Dialog 1　對話 1

A: 嗨，各位，今天由我上課，大家都知道我是阿諾教授的研究生助理，如果你不知道，我是崔維斯楊，今天我要講複習本的內容，我們將從 22 頁練習 2A 開始。在我們開始前，我想問一下有沒有人有問題。

A: Hi, everyone. I'm teaching the class today. You all know I'm Professor Arnold's Graduate Assistant. If you don't know, my name is Travis Young. Today I'll cover material from the review book. We'll start with exercise 2A on page 22. Before we start, I want to ask if any of you have a question.

B: 我有。

B: I do.

A: 好，什麼問題？

A: Yes. What is it?

B: 今天我們有平時第三節的小考嗎？

B: Are we going to do the regular third hour quiz today?

A: 沒有，阿諾教授告訴我這週跳過。

A: No, we won't. Professor Arnold told me to skip it for this week.

B: 我們會拿到上週的考試卷嗎？

B: Will we get our papers back from last week's test?

A: 會，在我這裡，我會在第一節下課把它們發下去。

A: Yes. I have them here. I'll give them back at the first break.

Notes 小叮嚀

你要請教授解釋課程的細節，完整了解你需要知道的所有規定，才能做一個有效率的教學助理。

Dialog 2 對話2

A: 好的，各位，我們開始吧，今天由我上課，因為史坦頓教授這週要去參加一個研討會。我們先複習上次教的。

A: OK, everybody. Let's start. I'm leading the class today because Professor Stanton must attend a conference this week. First, let's go over what was taught last time.

B: 對不起。

B: Excuse me.

A: 是的。

A: Yes.

B: 我們今天要記筆記嗎？

B: Will we need to take notes today?

A: 是的，要記，教授今天要我教兩個對數，它們很重要。

A: Yes, you will. The professor wants me to teach you two logarithms today, and they are important to know.

預備 校園 選課 新生說明 上課前 課堂上 課後交流 圖書館 體育館 餐廳 課外活動 申請獎助 當助教

預備 校園 選課 新生說明 上課前 課堂上 課後交流 圖書館 體育館 餐廳 課外活動 申請獎助 當助教

B: 好。

B: OK.

A: 那是個好問題，還有誰有問題嗎？沒有？那我要繼續了，今天講課時請自由提問，還有，等一下你們要小組練習今天的範圍，所以那時候也可以問。

A: That was a good question. Does anyone else have a question? No? I'll continue then. Feel free to ask any time during today's lecture. By the way, later you'll be working in small groups on today's material, so you can ask at that time too.

Word Bank 字庫

conference [ˈkɑnfərəns] n. 會議
logarithm [ˈlɔgəˌrɪðəm] n.（數學）對數

Useful Phrases 實用語句

1. 今天由我上課，因為教授不舒服。

   I'm leading the class today because the professor is ill.

2. 教授要出席研討會。

   The professor has to attend a conference.

3. 我們先複習上次教的。

   Let's go over what was taught last time.

4. 教授要我今天教兩個對數。

   The professor wants me to teach you two logarithms today.

5. 等一下你們會有小組練習。

   You'll be working in small groups later.

6. 我們今天要記筆記嗎？

   Will we need to take notes today?

7. 還有誰有問題嗎？

   Does anyone else have a question?

8. 請隨時自由提問。

   Feel free to ask any time.

9. 請在我們完成這一個重點時再提問。

   Please ask questions after we finish this point.

10. 請選一位組長報告小組結果。

    Please choose a group leader to report the group result.

 Tips 小祕訣

在教課方面，身為外籍助教因為語言及成長環境的文化差異，不僅需要運用適當的語言、組織表達能力及教學技巧來授課，也要注意肢體動作、表情、眼睛接觸、音調、音量各方面是否能輔助溝通，傳遞自己想要表達的訊息、情感及態度。

最好少用專用術語而以較口語的方式表達，對新生尤其該如此。學生必須了解的專有名詞應該清楚定義，講課的速度適中，重點的呈現可以用不同的方式表達重述，少用代名詞而是清楚說明，讓學生可以明確記下筆記。如果有學生提問，應該重複問題，一來讓大家聽清楚，二來確定問題再回答。

Does anyone else have a question?

預備
校園
選課
新生說明
上課前
課堂上
課後交流
圖書館
體育館
餐廳
課外活動
申請獎助
當助教

12.2 整學期授課
Leading a Course for a Whole Term

 Dialog 對話

A: 嗨,各位,我是安珀周,我是這門課的老師,我是戲劇藝術系的研二生,首先讓我先說我很榮幸你們選了這門課,儘管你們知道是由研究生教課。

A: Hi, everyone. I'm Amber Chou. I'm the teacher for this class. I'm a second year graduate student in the Theater Arts Department. First, let me start by saying I'm honored that you signed up for this class although you knew that it would be taught by a graduate student.

That's it for today.

A: 現在我來說明課程大綱，你們桌上都有一份，大綱有你們每週要讀的及準備的，還有解釋評分標準，必交作業以時間順序列在第3頁的底下，注意有兩份 4-5 頁的報告要交，學期有五次小考，每次在一週前先宣布，小考及考試的規則如下：小考時不能有書或筆記及其他可儲存資料的裝置；但考試時可以。目前為止有問題嗎？

A: Now I'll talk about the syllabus. You all have a copy of it on your desk. It lays out what you will need to read and prepare for each week, and also explains the grading criteria. Required assignments are listed chronologically at the bottom of the third page. Notice that two, four to five page papers are expected. There will be five short quizzes during the term. Each one will be announced a week ahead of time. The rules for exams and tests are as follow. There will be no use of books or notes or any other information storage devices while taking a quiz; on the other hand, while taking an exam such things can be used. Are there any questions so far?

B: 我有。

B: I have one.

A: 是的，請說。

A: Yes, please.

B: 考試那天你會自己監考這堂課嗎？

B: Will you be proctoring this class on exam days yourself?

A: 會，還有其他問題嗎？

A: Yes. Other questions?

預備　校園　選課　新生說明　上課前　課堂上　課後交流　圖書館　體育館　餐廳　課外活動　申請獎助　當助教

B: 我們上課可以吃東西嗎？

B: Can we eat in class?

A: 我沒關係，但是學校不喜歡，因為會造成髒亂。

A: It's OK with me, but the University frowns on it because of the mess it makes.

Word Bank 字庫

syllabus [`sɪləbəs] n. 課程大綱
lay out 列出
storage devices n. 儲存裝置
proctor [`prɑktə] v. 監考
criteria [kraɪ`tɪrɪə] n. 標準
frown [fraʊn] v. 皺眉表示不滿
mess [mɛs] n. 髒亂

Useful Phrases 實用語句

1. 這是課程大綱。
   Here is the syllabus.
2. 看課程大綱。
   Look at the syllabus.
3. 在第 2 頁。
   It's on the second page.
4. 我會為你們準備考試。
   I'll prepare you for the test.
5. 我們來複習小考 [考試]。
   Let's review for the test [exam].
6. 翻到 44 頁。
   Open your book to page 44.
7. 讀下面段落。
   Read the following passage.

8. 回答第 71 頁問題。

   Answer the questions on page 71.

9. 讓我把你們注意力移到這個效果來。

   Let me call your attention to this effect.

10. 我們開始吧。

    Let's get started.

11. 下週有一個小考。

    There is a quiz next week.

12. 請記得拿回你們的報告。

    Please remember to pick up your papers.

13. 今天到此為止。

    That's it for today.

14. 你們可以來辦公室找我。

    You can come to see me in my office.

 Tips 小祕訣

在任課前要先了解學生程度、背景及對課堂的期望，助教要掌握課堂氣氛，對學生的文化及次文化也要有一定程度的了解。教課需要準備才能引發學生的興趣，有系統的講解才能讓學生理解所教的內容，正面鼓勵 (但不必取悅) 學生，讓他們樂意主動參與課程的進行。

另外，為了上課時間及效率，學習了解如何有效利用黑板、做 PowerPoint 投影片或發講義等幫助自己上課的工具，並記住適時舉例也是相當重要的。

Language Power 字詞補給站

◆ 課堂大綱 Course Syllabus

assignment	作業
textbook	課本
reading assignment	閱讀作業
term paper	學期報告
research	研究

預備
校園
選課
新生說明
上課前
課堂上
課後交流
圖書館
體育館
餐廳
課外活動
申請獎助
當助教

exam	考試
quiz	小考
test	測驗
due date	到期日
deadline	截止期限
roll call	點名
lab	實驗
attendance (presence/absence)	出席 (出 / 缺)
office hours	辦公室時間
re-write	重做
lecture	講課
grading criteria	評分標準
class policies	課堂準則
take a leave	請假

◆ 教學常用語 Common Expressions for Teaching

1. 我們開始前，讓我先複習上次上了什麼。

   Before we start, let me review what we covered last time.

2. 我們今天從…開始。

   We'll start with…today.

3. 如果我們關於…沒有問題，我們就移到…

   If we do not have questions about…, we'll move on to…

4. 讓我重述…

   Let me repeat…

5. 簡單地說，…

   To put it simply, …

6. 換句話說，…

   In other words, …

7. 讓我重述重點…

   Let's recap…

8. 讓我概述…

   Let me summarize…

9. 總結…

   In conclusion, …

預備
校園
選課
新生說明
上課前
課堂上
課後交流
圖書館
體育館
餐廳
課外活動
申請獎助
當助教

12.3 回答學生問題
Answering Students' Questions

Dialog 1　對話1

A: 對不起，傑瑞，我可以問你幾個有關課程的問題嗎？

A: Excuse me, Jerry. May I ask a few questions about the course?

B: 當然可以，請問。

B: Sure. Go ahead.

A: 首先，我想知道關於出席，是強制的嗎？

A: First, I'd like to ask about attendance. Is it mandatory?

B: 不是，但是如果你不正常出席會很難通過這門課。

B: No, but it would be very difficult to pass the course if you did not attend regularly.

A: 但是哈夫門教授的課表上寫明會按照我們所寫的期末報告來打成績。

A: But Professor Hoffman's syllabus says we will be graded on the final paper we write and hand in.

B: 沒錯，但是如果你不上課，你無法了解要寫的性質是什麼。

B: That's true, but if you don't attend the lectures, you won't understand the nature of what you have to write about.

A: 我懂了。

A: I see.

Word Bank 字庫

mandatory [`mændə͵torɪ] adj. 強制的
attendance [ə`tɛndəns] n. 出席
hand in 交出
nature [`netʃə] n. 性質

Useful Phrases 實用語句

1. 如果你不正常出席會很難通過這門課。

   It would be very difficult to pass the course if you did not attend regularly.

2. 如果你不上課，你無法了解要寫的性質是什麼。

   If you don't attend the lectures, you won't understand the nature of what you have to write about.

Notes 小叮嚀

教課或思考問題如何回答時，少用嗯 (um)、啊 (ah) 之類的 non-words，而是用轉接詞 (如 in this way, for this reason, for that matter, in fact, for example [instance], on the other hand)，才不會讓講解或回答片片斷斷，既難以理解也顯得沒有說服力。另外也要小心自己的遣詞用字必須符合政治正確，避免不必要的誤會。

Dialog 2 對話 2

A: 我想了解我們要寫報告的長度。

A: I'd like to know about the length of the paper we must write.

B: 要介於 25 到 30 頁之間。

B: It needs to be between 25 and 30 pages long.

預備 校園 選課 新生說明 上課前 課堂上 課後交流 圖書館 體育館 餐廳 課外活動 申請獎助 當助教

A: 那行距呢？

A: What about the spacing?

B: 要雙行間距。

B: It should be double-spaced.

A: 要註腳嗎？

A: Should it have footnotes?

B: 要，而且要有目錄還有在最後列出所有參考資料的清單。

B: Yes. And it must have a table of contents plus a list of all references at the end of it.

A: 什麼時候要交？

A: When is it due?

B: 期末考週星期四晚上6點之前。

B: No later than 6 p.m. on Thursday of finals week.

A: 好，謝謝。

A: OK. Thank you.

B: 不客氣，再見。

B: No problem. See you later.

預備　校園　選課　新生說明　上課前　課堂上　課後交流　圖書館　體育館　餐廳　課外活動　申請獎助　當助教

Word Bank 字庫

spacing [ˋspesɪŋ] n. 行距

double-spaced [ˋdʌblˌspest] adj. 雙行的

footnote [ˋfʊtˌnot] n. 註腳

contents [ˋkɑntɛnts] n. 目錄

reference [ˋrɛfərəns] n. 參考資料

Useful Phrases 實用語句

○ 提問 To ask

1. 我想了解我們要寫報告的長度。

   I'd like to know about the length of the paper we must write.

2. 報告要多長？

   How long should the paper be?

3. 我們應該寫多少頁？

   How many pages are we supposed to write?

4. 我們的報告主題需要哈夫門教授的核可嗎？

   Do we need Professor Hoffman's approval on the topic?

5. 那行距呢？

   What about the spacing?

6. 要註腳嗎？

   Should the paper have footnotes?

7. 什麼時候要交？

   When is it due?

○ 回答 To respond

1. 長度要 25 到 30 頁。

   It needs to be between 25 and 30 pages long.

2. 要雙行間距。

   It should be double-spaced.

3. 要有目錄。

   It must have a table of contents.

4. 最後要列出所有參考資料的清單。

   It must have a list of all references at the end.

12.4 回答另一門課的問題
Answering Questions for Another Course

Dialog 對話

A: 哈囉，蘇，我可以問一個有關你幫忙當助教課程的問題嗎？

A: Hello, Sue. Can I ask a question about the course you're assisting with?

B: 當然可以。

B: Of course.

A: 我不確定那門課的規定。

A: I'm not sure about the requirements for the class.

B: 規定都列在課程大綱上，你哪個部分不了解？

B: They are listed in the syllabus. What is it you don't understand?

A: 課表說我們要來上至少 80% 的課。

A: The syllabus says that we must attend at least 80% of the classes.

B: 是的，沒錯。

B: Yes, that is correct.

A: 課表說 80% 的課是指 49 堂課，但這學期只有 36 堂課。

A: It also says that 80% would be 49 attended sessions, but there are only 36 classes in total this session.

預備
校園
選課
新生說明
上課前
課堂上
課後交流
圖書館
體育館
餐廳
課外活動
申請獎助
當助教

B: 我知道了，我應該說清楚點，每週也都有實驗課。

B: I see. I should have made it clearer. There is a lab class every week too.

A: 好，現在我了解了，我們也要算入實驗課。

A: OK. Now I understand. We have to count in the lab classes too.

B: 對。

B: That's right.

A: 現在我知道了，謝謝。

A: Now I see. Thanks.

Word Bank 字庫

attended sessions n. 要出席的課
lab classes n. 實驗課

Useful Phrases 實用語句

1. 你哪個部分不了解？

   What is it you don't understand?

2. 我應該說清楚點。

   I should have made it clearer.

12.5 點名
Roll Call

Dialog 1 對話1

A: 同學，我要告訴大家我不點名，但我會注意同學是否在這裡，出席不是強制的，但如果你不來，我不知道你們要怎麼通過。

A: Students. I want to tell you that I don't take roll, but I do notice if people are here or not. Attendance is not mandatory, but if you don't come to class, I don't see how you'll pass.

B: 顏先生，我可以問一個問題嗎？

B: Mr. Yen, may I ask something?

A: 可以。

A: Yes.

B: 萬一我們生病或某個程度受傷了而很長一段時間無法來上課呢？

B: What if we are sick, or get injured some way, and can't come to class for a long time?

A: 那就要聯絡我跟學校，告知我們情況。

A: Then it will be necessary to contact the school and me and inform us of the situation.

B: 在那些情形下還能通過嗎？

B: Is it possible to still pass the class under those circumstances?

A: 如果及早且負責地
處理，我想可以。

A: If dealt with early and responsibly, I'd say yes.

B: 謝謝。

B: Thank you.

Dialog 2 對話2

A: 我要所有修這門課的人知道，我不點名，但是我會確認出席（情形），如果你缺 3 堂課以上，我會從期末成績扣 20%。

A: I want everyone in this class to know that I don't call roll, but I do check attendance. If you miss more than three classes, I'll deduct 20% from your final grade.

B: 如果我們缺席有合理的原因，你會寬容嗎？

B: Excuse me. If we have a legitimate reason for being absent, will you be lenient?

A: 不，這門課任何人都沒有例外。

A: No. No exceptions for this course for anyone.

Word Bank 字庫

legitimate [lɪˋdʒɪtəmɪt] adj. 合理的
lenient [ˋlinɪənt] adj. 寬容的
exception [ɪkˋsɛpʃən] n. 例外

Useful Phrases 實用語句

1. 在那些情形下還能通過呢？

   Is it possible to still pass the class under those circumstances?

2. 你會寬容嗎？

   Will you be lenient?

3. 任何人都沒有例外。

   No exceptions for anyone.

 Tips 小祕訣

通常一個班級的人數並不會太多，助教記住學生的名字，顯示對他們的重視，所以記住學生姓名是很重要的一環，對課堂氣氛、上課效率也有很大的影響。

12.6 發還作業
Returning an Assignment

 Dialog 對話

A: 當你聽到你名字時，請過來拿報告。(一秒後) 山姆。

A: When you hear your name, please come up and get your essay. (one second later) Sam.

B: 有。

B: Yes.

A: 克莉絲汀。

A: Christine.

C: 有些人沒來，怎麼拿回報告？

C: Some people are not here. How can they get their papers back?

預備
校園
選課
新生說明
上課前
課堂上
課後交流
圖書館
體育館
餐廳
課外活動
申請獎助
當助教

A: 今天沒來的人可以在凱爾教授辦公室外面的信箱拿回報告。

A: Anyone not here today can pick up his or her essay from the box outside Professor Kyle's office.

C: 報告今天會在那裡嗎？

C: Will the papers be there today?

A: 是的，報告會放在那裡到這學期結束。

A: Yes. And they'll be there until the end of the session.

C: 謝謝。

C: Thank you.

Word Bank 字庫

essay [`ɛse] n. 短文，申論
session [`sɛʃən] n. 學期

Useful Phrases 實用語句

1. 他們怎麼拿回報告？

   How can they get their papers back?

2. 報告今天會在那裡嗎？

   Will the papers be there today?

3. 他們可以在凱爾教授辦公室外面的信箱拿回報告。

   They can pick up their essays from the box outside Professor Kyle's office.

4. 報告會放在那裡到這學期結束。

   The essays will be there until the end of the session.

12.7 考題說明
Explaining the Test Questions

 Dialog 對話

A: 大家注意，我現在要解釋考試。第一部分占 20%，是選擇題，第二部分是簡答題，占 40%，第三部分你會看到配合題，必須要找到每個公式的正確答案，第三部分占 20%，第四部分也占 20%，有兩個問題，只要選一個問題來寫。你只有一個小時作答，有任何問題嗎？

A: Your attention, everyone. I'm going to explain the test now. The first section is worth 20% and is multiple choice. The second part is short answer, and it's worth 40%. In the third section you'll see a matching section. You must find the correct answer for each formula written. The third section is worth 20%. The fourth section is also worth 20% and has two questions. Choose only one of the questions to write about. You'll have one hour to do this test. Are there any questions?

B: 桌上可以有空白的紙嗎？

B: Is it all right to have blank paper on our desk?

A: 可以，只要是全白的，有其他問題嗎？

A: Yes. As long as it is totally blank. Are there any other questions?

B: 我們何時會知道考試結果？

B: When will we know the results of the test?

A: 成績週一下午會公布在網路上。

A: Grades will be posted online by Monday afternoon.

預備　校園　選課　新生說明　上課前　課堂上　課後交流　圖書館　體育館　餐廳　課外活動　申請獎助　當助教

Word Bank 字庫

multiple choice **n.** 選擇題
short answer **n.** 簡答題
matching section **n.** 配合題
formula [`fɔrmjələ] **n.** 公式

Useful Phrases 實用語句

1. 桌上可以有空白的紙嗎？

   Is it all right to have blank paper on our desk?

2. 我們何時會知道考試結果？

   When will we know the results of the test?

3. 只要是全部空白就可以。

   As long as the paper is totally blank, it's all right.

4. 成績會公布在網路上。

   Grades will be posted online.

12.8 確認理解
Confirming Comprehension

Dialog 對話

A: 好，讓我再複習一次，你們都了解第四部分嗎？

A: OK. Let me go over this again. Do you all understand Part Four?

B: 我有個問題。

B: I have a question.

A: 是什麼？

A: What is it?

左側邊欄（由上而下）：預備 校園 選課 新生說明 上課前 課堂上 課後交流 圖書館 體育館 餐廳 課外活動 申請獎助 當助教

B: 如果第四部分我們兩個問題都回答，會有幫助嗎？

B: If we answer both questions in Part Four, will it help us?

A: 不會，如果你兩題都回答，我只會評你第一題的答案而忽略另一題，記住你只有 60 分鐘可以作答。

A: No. If you answer both, I'll simply grade the first one you answer and ignore the other. Also remember that you have only sixty minutes to do this test.

 Useful Phrases 實用語句

1. 何時考試？

   When is the exam [test]?

2. 我們可以用書嗎？

   Can we use our books?

3. 是帶回家的考試嗎？

   Is it a take home exam?

4. 這考試占總分多少百分比？

   What percentage of total grade is this exam worth?

5. 我們有多少時間？

   How much time do we have?

6. 能補考嗎？

   Will there be a make-up test?

 Language Power 字詞補給站

◆ 考試 Tests/Exams

percentage	百分比
fill in the blank	填空
blank space	空格
time limit	時間限制
choose	選擇

預備・校園・選課・新生說明・上課前・課堂上・課後交流・圖書館・體育館・餐廳・課外活動・申請獎助・當助教

預備
校園
選課
新生說明
上課前
課堂上
課後交流
圖書館
體育館
餐廳
課外活動
申請獎助
當助教

written answer	寫下的答案
results	結果
grade	分數
make-up/re-take	補考 / 重考
posted	登上（網）
worth	占（比例）
extra credit	加分

Notes 小叮嚀

　　助教要保持高度的敏感度，從學生的表情、提問、課後作業、報告、學生理解程度來了解學生的學習成效及其所可能隱含包括價值觀的部分，並修正自己的教學。

12.9 請人上臺
Inviting Someone to Go Up to the Stage

Dialog 對話

A: 好的，同學們，誰要先上臺報告？

A: All right, students. Who wants to come to the stage first and give his or her presentation?

B: 我來。

B: I'll do it.

A: 很好，安迪，謝謝，請上來。

A: Great, Andy. Thanks. Please come up.

B: 好。

B: OK.

A: 好,各位,請安靜聽安迪的報告。

A: OK, everyone. Please be quiet and listen to Andy's presentation.

12.10 複習
Review

 Dialog 對話

A: 我現在要叫一些人來複習,提姆,請回答這個問題。在哪方面第一個對數比第二個對數有用?

A: I'm going to call on a few people now for review. Tim. Please answer this question. In what way is the first logarithm more useful than the second?

B: 如果被測物是在極大壓力下,那第一個對數可能會更正確地測量最大負載。

B: If the test substance is under extreme pressure, then the first one is more likely to measure maximum loading more accurately.

A: 好,謝謝。珍妮,為何兩者對零重力測量都沒用?

A: Great. Thank you. Jenny. Why is neither of them useful for zero G measurements?

C: 因為兩者都不能對水平、無承載、分散的壓力分解因數。

C: Because neither are able to factor in horizontal, no load, spread stress.

預備 | 校園 | 選課 | 新生說明 | 上課前 | 課堂上 | 課後交流 | 圖書館 | 體育館 | 餐廳 | 課外活動 | 申請獎助 | 當助教

預備 校園 選課 新生說明 上課前 課堂上 課後交流 圖書館 體育館 餐廳 課外活動 申請獎助 當助教

A: 是的，但記住這不只是水平的，垂直的也是。

A: Yes, but remember that it is not only lateral, but vertical as well.

Word Bank 字庫

review [rɪ`vju] n., v. 複習
extreme [ɪk`strim] adj. 極大的
measure [`mɛʒɚ] v. 測量
horizontal [ˌhɔrə`zɑntl̩] adj. 水平的
factor [`fæktɚ] v. (數學) 分解因數
lateral [`lætərəl] adj. 水平的，側面的
vertical [`vɝtɪkl̩] adj. 垂直的

Useful Phrases 實用語句

○ **問學生問題 Asking Students Questions**

1. 我現在要叫一些人來複習。

   I'm going to call on a few people now for review.

2. 這題答案是什麼？

   What is the answer to this problem?

3. 請回答這個問題。

   Please answer this question.

4. 誰可以告訴我？

   Who can tell me?

5. 你認為呢？

   What do you think?

6. 哪個是對的？

   Which one is right?

7. 你會選哪一個？為什麼？

   Which would you choose and why?

8. 你會怎麼做？

   What would you do?

9. 你的意見如何？

What's your opinion?

10. 為什麼這個錯？

Why is this wrong?

11. 這個對還是錯？

Is this right or wrong?

◎ 回答問題 Answering Questions

1. 是的，正確。

Yes, that's correct.

2. 你是對的。

You are right.

3. 錯了，再試一次。

Wrong. Try again.

4. 好答案，但錯了，我告訴你正確答案。

Good answer, but wrong. Let me tell you the right answer.

5. 幾乎對了。

Almost correct.

6. 讓我再做一點不同的解釋。

Let me explain it a little differently.

7. 我了解你的論點，但是⋯

I see your point, but…

8. 我會再次解釋。

I'll explain again.

9. 抱歉，讓我試著再次解釋清楚點。

Sorry. Let me try to make it clearer.

10. 是的，很好。

Yes. Very good.

預備
校園
選課
新生說明
上課前
課堂上
課後交流
圖書館
體育館
餐廳
課外活動
申請獎助
當助教

Notes 小叮嚀

複習在教學上不可或缺，助教也藉此檢視自己的教學及學生的學習成果，如果學生不能理解某個部分，應該藉著複習機會加強理解及指定作業習作，而非一味按照進度。

課後的辦公室時段 (office hours)，不妨多鼓勵學生來問問題，如此較能對症下藥，明白個別學生的問題癥結，以便給予所需要的協助。

Appendixes

附錄

留學資訊站
More Information for Studying Abroad

1. 申請入學：條件、時間表及步驟
   Applying for School: Requirements, Time table, and Procedure

2. 獎助金消息網站
   Websites about Financial Aid

3. 關於在美國上學身分規定
   Status Regarding Attending School in America

4. 註冊 (包含網路註冊) 錯誤訊息說明
   Notes for Registration Errors, Including On-line Registration

5. 實用網站及政府單位聯絡資訊
   Useful Websites and Contact Information of Government Offices

1. 申請入學：條件、時間表及步驟

Applying for School: Requirements, Time Table, and Procedure

college 是學院，university 是大學，由不同學院組成，但這兩字經常交替使用。想要進入二年制學院至少要完成高二課程，四年制大學必須完成高中課程，申請研究所必須取得學士學位 (有些研究所規定必須取得本科學位)，雖然每個學校的申請要求不同，多數學校的入學許可至少是三要件審查的結果。

1. 標準測驗成績：大學部需要托福 TOEFL (Test of English as a Foreign Language) 及學業評量測驗 SAT I and II (Scholastic Assessment Tests)。研究所需要托福 TOEFL 及研究所入學測驗 GRE (Graduate Record Exam) 成績；商業研究所需要托福 TOEFL 及 GMAT(Graduate Management Admission Test) 成績。

2. 在校平均成績 GPA(Grade Point Average) 及工作經驗。

3. 個人自傳、研究領域自述及教授推薦信或雇主推薦信。

美國大學依照各學校所定的優先順序決定發給入學許可。申請人須在 12 到 24 個月之前就開始作業，除了準備考試之外，許多文件必須翻譯成英文或經過公證手續 (notarized)。通常學年是在秋季 (八月下旬或九月) 開始，但許多學校也發給春季 (一月) 開始就學的入學許可，申請人可以選擇要在何時就讀，但拿到入學許可至多延後報到入學一年。

September (倒數第24個月-24 months)

開始搜尋學校，拜訪最近的教育諮詢中心及圖書館，網路搜尋，與朋友、家人及曾經在海外就讀的朋友談話，向 10-15 所學校詢問資料。

October-November (23-22 months)

開始準備托福及其他入學考試 (如 GRE, GMAT, 或 SAT)。

December-May (21-16 months)

報名托福及其他測驗。

January (20 months)

選擇你要申請的學校，確定每一所要申請的學校資料都齊備，多數學校網路都有資料及申請表格可以下載。

March-June(18-15 months)

考托福或其他入學測驗，你必須在 11 月前考試，不然你會錯過

多數大學的截止期限。現在就考托福可以讓你再考一次增進成績。研究所入學考試 (如 GRE) 會連同以往考試紀錄寄給學校，因此要準備妥當再應試。

May (16 months)

與會替你寫推薦信的老師確認。

July (14 months)

閱讀大學入學申請文件及追蹤申請期限，讓自己有足夠時間完成。記得郵寄要一些時間，將選擇縮小到 10 間學校。

August (13 months)

寫讀書計畫及自傳的草稿，請朋友及英文老師修正。

September (12 months)

如果要再考一次托福及其他入學測驗，再次報名。

詢問你的推薦信老師，給他們需要的表格和一個已貼郵票及寫好地址的信封。

October (11 months)

完成你的文件及申請表格，包含獎助金申請表格。請學校寄出你的成績單到申請學校 (如果學校要你自己寄，成績單可連同文件一起寄出)。

如果必要，再考一次托福和其他入學測驗。

November (10 months)

與老師及學校確認你的推薦信和成績單皆已寄達。

December (9 months)

迅速回覆任何需要處理的後續。

April-May (5-4 months)

開始收到學校訊息，如果一直沒消息，聯絡入學辦公室。接受一所學校，將你的決定通知該校及其他學校。請該校寄來 I-20 入學許可 (或 IAP-66 form 公費留學)，安排校內或校外住宿，如果還沒有護照，要開始申請護照。

June (3 months)

申請簽證，參加國內即將出國留學生舉辦的說明會，安排出國事宜，至少在該校新生輔導日 15 天前到達 (如果需參加語言課程，要與學校確認提早到達)。

July-August (2-1 months)

留學新鮮人旅途愉快！ Have a nice trip!

如果你的調查及計畫妥當，在美國上大學可以簡單一些。除了透過連結網路社群外，有些留學生在暑期回國會為即將成行的新生舉辦

新生座談會，因此最好從學長姐那裡了解學校環境、當地的治安、天氣及地理狀況，知道該準備什麼衣物，什麼不可或缺以及到達當地可以從事什麼活動。當地對於學生有何支援系統，例如健康服務和任何對國際學生提供服務的特別機構，也需要了解，而加入該校的「台灣學生會」應能與台灣同學在國外彼此有所照應。

2. 獎助金消息網站 Websites about Financial Aid

國際教育財務支援資料庫 International Education Financial Aid (IEFA) ☑ http://www.iefa.com

美國大使館 (或駐台辦事處 AIT) ☑ http://www.ait.org.tw/zh

美國國際開發總署 (Agency for International Development, AID) ☑ http://www.usaid.gov

隸屬美國國務院 (the US Department of State) 之教育與文化事務局 (Bureau of Eucational and Cultural Affairs, ECA)
☑ http://exchanges.state.gov

美國教育諮詢 EducationUSA ☑ http://educationusa.state.gov

美國教育基金會 (AIEF) ☑ http://www.aief.org.tw

傅爾布萊特基金會 (學術交流基金會網站)
☑ http://www.fulbright.org.tw

學術交流基金會美國教育資訊中心 US Education Information Center ☑ http://www.educationusa.tw

教育部全球資訊網 ☑ http://www.edu.tw

　　教育部獎學金：1. 公費獎學金 2. 教育部與世界百大合作設置獎學金甄選 3. (一般生及弱勢生) 留學獎學金甄試 4. 教育部「學海」計畫：補助大學生出國研修或實習。

科技部 (科教發展及國際合作司) 菁英專案留學獎學金及國際交流方案補助 ☑ https://www.most.gov.tw

教育部補助留學生就學貸款—承貸銀行

　　1. 臺灣銀行

　　2. 合作金庫商業銀行

　　3. 臺灣土地銀行

　　4. 兆豐國際商業銀行

　　5. 玉山商業銀行

　　6. 中國信託商業銀行

　　7. 台北富邦商業銀行

　　8. 其他經教育部核可之銀行。

3. 關於在美國上學身分規定
Status Regarding Attending School in America

因為愛國法案及反恐規定，簽證申請規定經常被改變，在美國就學如果有家眷依附在自己學生身分下，務必要了解自己及家人的權利義務。

1. 到美國讀書需要 F1 簽證，配偶及子女可以申請 F2 簽證赴美同住，小孩可以在美就讀，但配偶不得在美就讀或工作。
2. 到美國讀書當交換學生需要 J1 簽證，配偶及子女可以申請 J2 簽證赴美同住，小孩可以在美就讀，但配偶不得在美就讀或工作。
3. 如果在美工作或訓練需要 H 簽證，配偶及子女可以申請 H4 簽證赴美同住，小孩可以就讀，但配偶不得工作。自 2015 年 5 月起，美國移民局開始接受持有 H 簽證並已開始申請綠卡者之配偶的工作申請。

以上所指子女必須是 21 歲以下。只要就讀或工作的簽證合法，且合法申請配偶及子女的簽證，他們的簽證及身分就受到合法保護，子女可以如當地居民的子女一樣免費就讀中小學。但有些美國公民才享有的權利，例如社會安全福利，並不包含在內。這是在成為美國公民 5 年後 (或更久，要看規定) 才有的福利，這些相關問題可以查詢美國公民移民法 (U. S. Citizenship and Immigration Services, USCIS) ☛ http://www.uscis.gov/portal/site/uscis

4. 註冊(包含網路註冊)錯誤訊息說明

Notes for Registration Errors, Including Online Registration

Course Closed 課程關閉

Why you got this message: You tried to register for a course that is already full.

為何有此訊息：你要註冊的課程已滿。

Solution: Use Search for Open Classes to see if there are other sections available and register for a different section. Or continue to occasionally check online to see if another student has dropped the course you want, and add if you find an opening. Or select a different course.

解決辦法：搜尋開放課程查看其他時段是否有名額並註冊或持續查看你要的課若有人退出就加入，或選擇其他課程。

If you want to discuss taking a course that is already filled and you have made a good attempt to add the course, check with the instructor and academic department that is offering the course. Only instructors/departments can override enrollment limits and many departments do not allow enrollment overrides. If you do obtain permission, the department will authorize you to register; it is then your responsibility to log back into and actually register for the course.

如果你很想修的課已額滿，與教授或系所洽談，許多科系並不允許超收，只有教授及系所可以決定超收限額。如果你確實獲准，系所會允許你註冊，然後你必須自己負責完成這門課的網路註冊。

Duplicate Course 課程重複

Why you got this message: You tried to add a course that is already on your schedule. You can only register for a course one time.

為何有此訊息：你加入你課表已有的課，你只能一次註冊一門課。

Solution: If you are trying to change sections of a course, first write down the Class Registration Number (CRN) of the course you are trying to add. Then exchange the classes with the Registration Menu. To exchange two sections, select the CRN you wish to drop from the list and enter the CRN you wish to add in the field provided. Press the Exchange Sections button to complete the transaction. You will not be dropped from your existing CRN unless you are successfully able to add the other new CRN.

解決辦法：如果你要更改課程時段，先寫下你要加選的課程編號，再交換註冊表單的課程。要交換兩種課程，選擇清單上你要退選的課程編號，再加入你要加選的課程編號，按下交換課程鍵完成交換。除非你成功加選，否則你不會退選原本課程。

If you think you should be able to register for a course twice, check with the department for assistance.

如果你認為可以註冊某一門課兩次，請系所幫忙。

Maximum Hours Exceeded 超出最高上限時數

Why you got this message: You tried to register for more credits than you are allowed to register for. Undergraduate, graduate, Law students, and community education students all have different credit limits and, for some students, different dates at which those limits are raised.

為何有此訊息：你註冊超過被允許的學分。大學部、研究所、法學生及社區大學學生都有不同的修課學分限制，某些學生的修課學分限制也有不同的起始日期。

Solution: Register for the maximum hours that you are able, then check the Registrar's website for specific information about the maximum enrollment limits/dates that apply to your situation.

解決辦法：修到你可能修課的上限，再查註冊網站對符合你情形的最高修課限制／日期之詳細說明。

Restriction Not Met 資格不符

Why you got this message: Many courses have restrictions that are checked during the registration process. You did not meet the restrictions for the course you attempted to register for. Most common restrictions are:

為何有此訊息：註冊過程中，許多課程有註冊限制，你並不符合想修課程的規定，多數規定為：

(1) Major/Minor (some courses are limited to students in a certain major/minor)

主／副修（有些課程僅限某主／副修學生）

   (2) Class (some courses are limited to students who are junior
      level or above)

      課程 (有些課程僅限高年級學生)

   (3) Level (graduate level courses are restricted to graduate
      students)

      程度 (研究生級課程僅限研究生)

Solution: Check the restrictions as listed in the online class schedule; "Search for Open Classes" (click on the CRN to view the detailed information about a course). If you do not meet the restriction, you will not be able to register for the class.

解決辦法：查看網路課程表列出的限制，「 找出開放課程 」(點選課程編號看某課程之詳細說明)，如果你不符資格，你將無法註冊。

If you want to discuss taking a course without meeting major or class restrictions, check with the academic department that is offering the course. Only that department can override major and class restrictions. If you obtain permission, the department will authorize you to register; it is then your responsibility to log back into online system and actually register for the course.

如果你要修不受主修或限制的課程，請教開課系所。只有他們可以逾越主修及課程規定。如果你獲得許可，他們會准許你註冊，那真正完成該課程網路註冊就是你的責任。

If you are an undergraduate who wants to enroll in a graduate-level course, please note the registration requirements for undergraduates enrolling in graduate courses at your university.

如果你是想修研究所課程的大學生，要注意大學生修研究生課程的註冊規定。

Pre-req or Test Score Error 先修或錯誤成績

Why you got this message: Many undergraduate courses have pre-requisites that are checked during the registration process. You did not meet the pre-requisite for the course you attempted to register for.

為何有此訊息：許多大學課程有先修規定在註冊時會查驗，你不符合欲註冊課程之先修規定。

Solution: Check the pre-requisites as listed in the online class schedule; "Search for Open Classes " (click on the CRN to view the detailed information about a course). If you do not meet the stated pre-requisites, you must complete the pre-requisites before taking the class.

解決辦法：查看網路課程表列出的先修規定，「找出開放課程」(點選課程編號看課程詳細說明)，如果你不符所述，你必須完成先修課再來選此門課。

If you want to discuss registering for a course without having the stated pre-reqs, check with the academic department that is offering the course. Only that department can override the pre-requisites. If you obtain permission, the department will authorize you to register; it is then your responsibility to log back into the system and actually register for the course.

如果你要討論不受先修限制的課程，請教開課系所。只有他們可以逾越先修課程規定。如果你獲得許可，他們會准許你註冊，那真正完成該課程網路註冊就是你的責任。

STOP: You cannot drop below full-time status
停：你不可退掉全職身分

Why you got this message: You are an international student who tried to drop below full-time status after the term has begun.

為何有此訊息：你是學期已開始卻想退掉全職身分的外籍學生。

Solution: International students should contact the Office of International Programs. Staff in the office will determine if you can drop below full-time credits and, if approved, send documentation to the Office of the Registrar for processing.

解決辦法：外籍學生應該聯繫外籍學生辦公室，教職員會決定你是否可以退掉全職學分數，如果可以的話，送文件到註冊組辦手續。

STOP: You cannot drop your last class 停：你不可退掉最後課程

Why you got this message: You are registered for a term and you tried to drop the last class from your schedule.

為何有此訊息：你註冊一學期，但你試著退掉最後一門課。

Solution: If you are trying to drop all your classes and withdraw from the University, you need to contact the Office of Academic

Advising.

解決辦法：如果你試著退掉所有課程並且從大學退學，你要聯絡學業諮詢室。

If you are trying to drop one class and add another in its place, use the Exchange Sections menu item in the Registration Menu. First write down the CRN of the course you are trying to add. To exchange two sections, select the CRN you wish to drop from the list and enter the CRN you wish to add in the field provided. Press the Exchange Sections button to complete the transaction. You will not be dropped from your existing CRN unless you are successfully able to add the other new CRN.

如果你試著退掉一門再加入一門課，請用課程表內交換區的課表項目。首先寫下你要加入的課程編號，要交換兩門課，選擇清單中你要退出的及加入你要的課程編號。按下交換鍵完成交換，除非你成功加選，不然你不會退選原本課程。

Time Conflict with CRN XXX 與課程編號 XXX 衝堂

Why you got this message: You tried to add a course that conflicts with another course already on your schedule.

為何有此訊息：你試著加入一門課，但與你課表已有的課程相衝突。

Solution: Select a different section of the course that you want (one at a different time), or try to rearrange your courses so there is no time conflict or choose a different course. Undergraduate students are not permitted to register for two courses that meet at the same time. Graduate students may request an exception to this rule (contact the Office of the Registrar for more information).

解決辦法：選擇一門不同時段的課程或試著重新安排課程化解時間衝突。大學生不許註冊衝堂的兩門課，研究生或許可以要求例外 (更多資訊請聯絡註冊組)。

Unable to Add Associated Course 無法加入相關課程

Why you got this message: This is a course that has both a lecture and an associated lab or discussion section; you tried to add only one part of the class.

為何有此訊息：這是有講課及搭配實驗或討論的課程，你僅試著加入一部分。

Solution: Choose both a lecture section and a discussion or lab section (choose one from the list directly below the lecture). If using the "Add/Drop Classes" method to register, enter both CRNs and press "submit changes."

解決辦法：選擇講課及搭配討論或實驗的課程 (直接選擇講課下方清單)。如果用加退選註冊，輸入這兩個課程編號並且按下「送出變更」。

5. 實用網站及政府單位聯絡資訊
Useful Websites and Contact Information of Government Offices

5-1 英文網站

美國移民局「外國學生交換學者資訊追蹤系統」(SEVIS)
- https://www.ice.gov/sevis/students

社會安全局 (Social Security Online)
- http://www.ssa.gov
- http://www.ssa.gov/ssnumber

外籍學生申請社會安全號碼 (Social Security Number) 資料網站
- https://www.ssa.gov/pubs/EN-05-10181.pdf

非公民之社會安全 Social Security for Noncitizens
- https://www.ssa.gov/pubs/EN-05-10096.pdf

美國公民移民法 U. S. Citizenship and Immigration Services
- https://www.uscis.gov

5-2 中文網站

學術交流基金會 http://www.fulbright.org.tw
教育部全球資訊網 http:///www.edu.tw

5-3 教育部駐境外機構轄區一覽表 (來源：教育部網頁)

☑ **駐美國代表處教育組**

Education Division, Taipei Economic and Cultural Representative Office in the United States

地址：4201 Wisconsin Ave. N.W., #20, Washington, D.C.20016-2137, U.S.A.

電話：+1-202-895 1918　　　　　　傳真：+1-202-895 1922

網址：http://www.moetwdc.org

電郵信箱：cul@tecro.us
　　　　　usa@mail.moe.gov.tw

緊急聯絡手機號碼：+1-202-297 9436

服務地區：阿拉巴馬州 (Alabama)、佛羅里達州 (Florida)、喬治亞州 (Georgia)、肯塔基州 (Kentucky)、北卡羅萊納州 (North Carolina)、南卡羅萊納州 (South Carolina)、田納西州 (Tennessee)、哥倫比亞特區 (Washington, D.C.)、馬里蘭州 (Maryland)、維吉尼亞州 (Virginia)、西維吉尼亞州 (West Virginia)、百慕達島 (Bermuda Island)、德拉瓦州 (Delaware)

說明：該組轄區涵蓋駐美代表處、駐亞特蘭大辦事處及駐邁阿密辦事處之業務轄區

☑ **駐波士頓辦事處教育組**

Education Division, Taipei Economic and Cultural Office in Boston

地址：99 Summer Street, Suite 801, Boston, MA 02110, U.S.A.

電話：+1-617-737 2055　　　　　　傳真：+1-617-951 1312

網址：http://www.moebos.org

電郵信箱：education@tecoboston.org
　　　　　boston@mail.moe.gov.tw

緊急聯絡手機號碼：+1-617-417 8273

服務地區：緬因州 (Maine)、麻色諸塞州 (Massachusetts)、新罕普什爾州 (New Hampshire)、羅德島州 (Rhode Island)、佛蒙特州 (Vermont)

說明：該組轄區與駐波士頓辦事處之業務轄區一致

☑ **駐紐約辦事處教育組**

Education Division,Taipei Economic and Cultural Office in New York

地址：1 East 42nd Street, 6th Floor, New York, NY 10017, U.S.A.

電話：+1-212-317 7388　　　　　　傳真：+1-212-317 7390

網址：http://www.edutwny.org/

電郵信箱：newyork@edutwny.org

　　　　　newyork@mail.moe.gov.tw

緊急聯絡手機號碼　：+1-646-369 6637

服務地區：康乃狄克州 (Connecticut)、新澤西洲 (New Jersey)、紐約
　　　　　州 (New York)、賓夕法尼亞州 (Pennsylvania)

說明：該組文教業務轄區與駐紐約辦事處轄區一致

☑ **駐芝加哥辦事處教育組**

Education Division,Taipei Economic and Cultural Office in Chicago

地址：180 N. Stetson Ave., Suite 5803, Chicago, IL 60601, U.S.A.

電話：+1-312-616 0805　　　　　　傳真：+1-312-616 1499

網址：http://www.edutw.org/

電郵信箱：info@edutw.org

　　　　　chicago@mail.moe.gov.tw

緊急聯絡手機號碼　：+1-312-330 8134

服務地區：伊利諾州 (Illinois)、 印第安納州 (Indiana)、愛
　　　　　荷華州 (Iowa)、密西根州 (Michigan)、明尼蘇達
　　　　　州 (Minnesota)、俄亥俄州 (Ohio)、威斯康辛州
　　　　　(Wisconsin)、內布拉斯加州 (Nebraska)、北達科他州
　　　　　(North Dakota)、南達科他州 (South Dakota)

說明：該組轄區涵蓋駐芝加哥辦事處及駐堪薩斯辦事處之部分轄區

☑ **駐休士頓辦事處教育組**

Education Division,Taipei Economic and Cultural Office in Houston

地址：11 Greenway Plaza, Suite 2012, Houston, TX 77046, U.S.A.

電話：+1-713-871 0851　　　　　傳真：+1-713-871 0854

網址：http://www.houstoncul.org/chinese.htm

電郵信箱：houcul@houstoncul.org

　　　　　houston@mail.moe.gov.tw

緊急聯絡手機號碼：+1-713-504 6060、+1-832-605-2888

服務地區：阿肯色州 (Arkansas)、路易斯安納州 (Louisiana)、密西
　　　　　西比州 (Mississippi)、奧克拉荷馬州 (Oklahoma)、德
　　　　　克薩斯州 (Texas)、科羅拉多州 (Colorado)、堪薩斯州
　　　　　(Kansas)、密蘇里州 (Missouri)

說明：該組轄區涵蓋駐休士頓辦事處及駐堪薩斯辦事處之部分轄區

☑ **駐洛杉磯辦事處教育組**

Education Division,Taipei Economic and Cultural Office in Los Angeles

地址：3731 Wilshire Blvd., Suite 770, Los Angeles, CA 90010, U.S.A.

電話：+1-213-385 0512　　　　　傳真：+1-213-385 2197

網址：http://www.tw.org

電郵信箱：info@tw.org

　　　　　losangeles@mail.moe.gov.tw

緊急聯絡手機號碼：+1-626-252 9957

服務地區：夏威夷州 (Hawaii)、加羅林群島 (Carolina Islands)、
　　　　　關島 (Guam)、馬紹爾群島 (Marshall Islands)、馬利
　　　　　安納群島 (Marianas Islands)、美屬薩摩亞 (American
　　　　　Samoa)、亞利桑那州 (Arizona)、加利福尼亞州[南部]
　　　　　(California[South])、新墨西哥州 (New Mexico)

說明：該組轄區涵蓋駐洛杉磯辦事處及駐火奴魯魯辦事處之業務轄
　　　區

☑ **駐舊金山辦事處教育組**

Education Division,Taipei Economic and Cultural Office in San Francisco

地址：555 Montgomery Street, Suite 503, San Francisco, CA 94111, U.S.A.

電話：+1-415-398 4979　　　　　傳真：+1-415-398 4992

網址：http://www.tweducation.org

電郵信箱：sfmoe@tweducation.org

　　　　　sanfrancisco@mail.moe.gov.tw

緊急聯絡手機號碼：+1-415-728 6525

服務地區：加利福尼亞州[北部] (California[North])、內華達州 (Nevada)、猶他州 (Utah)、阿拉斯加州 (Alaska)、愛達荷州 (Idaho)、蒙大拿州 (Montana)、奧勒岡州 (Oregon)、華盛頓州 (Washington)、懷俄明州 (Wyoming)

說明：該組轄區涵蓋駐舊金山辦事處及駐西雅圖辦事處之業務轄區

國家圖書館出版品預行編目資料

開口就會美國校園英語/黃靜悅, Danny Otus Neal 著.
——二版.——臺北市：五南, 2016.07
面；　公分

ISBN 978-957-11-8654-2（平裝附光碟）

1.英語　2.會話

805.188　　　　　　　　　　　　　　　　　105009873

1AC4

開口就會美國校園英語

作　　者	黃靜悅、Danny Otus Neal
發 行 人	楊榮川
總 編 輯	王翠華
企劃主編	鄧景元、溫小瑩、朱曉蘋
責任編輯	溫小瑩、吳雨潔
封面設計	吳佳臻
美術設計	吳佳臻

出 版 者　五南圖書出版股份有限公司
地　　址：台北市大安區 106 和平東路二段 339 號 4 樓
電　　話：(02)2705-5066　傳真：(02)2706-6100
網　　址：http://www.wunan.com.tw
電子郵件：wunan@wunan.com.tw
劃撥帳號：01068953
戶　　名：五南圖書出版股份有限公司

法律顧問　林勝安律師事務所 林勝安律師

出版日期　2010 年 5 月　初版一刷
　　　　　2016 年 7 月　二版一刷

定　　價　420 元整

TIME ZONES OF THE UNITED STATES

WA

OR

ID

MT

ND

SD

NE

WY

NV

UT

CO

KS

CA

AZ

NM

OK

TX

PACIFIC
（太平洋時區）

MOUNTAIN
（洛磯山時區）

CENTRA
（中央時區

HAWII-ALEUTIAN
（夏威夷-阿留申時區）

Honolulu

HI

ALASKA
（阿拉斯加時區）

AK

Juneau

開口就會系列

生活資訊、語言學習、社交禮儀、
經商技巧、疑難解決，全都帶著走

開口就會社交英語
✛
開口就會美國校園英語
✛
開口就會旅遊英語
✛
開口就會美國長住用語
✛
開口就會商貿英語

隨書附贈 MP3
讓你隨時聽、隨口說